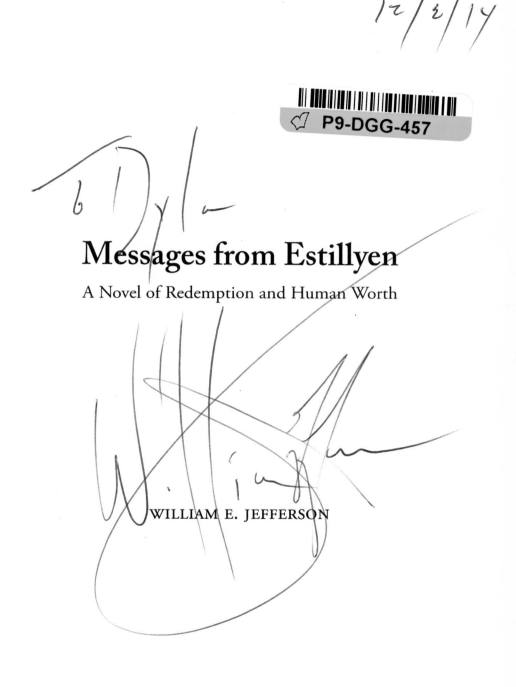

Messages from Estillyen

A Novel of Redemption and Human Worth

WILLIAM E. JEFFERSON

Port Estillyen
PRODUCTIONS

Pubished by Port Estillyen Productions
www.estillyen.com

Cover image: Hyatt Moore. All rights reserved.
Cover Design: Claudia Volkman and Miriam Green
Interior design and typesetting: Claudia Volkman

ISBN: 978-0-9856621-7-2 (hard cover)
ISBN: 978-0-9856621-6-5 (soft cover)
ISBN: 978-0-9856621-8-9 (.mobi)
ISBN: 978-0-9856621-9-6 (e-pub)

Printed in the United States of America

6 5 4 3 2

ACKNOWLEDGMENTS

A very special note of thanks is extended to Claudia Volkman and Lynn Wehner, editors of *Messages from Estillyen*. Without their encouragement, discernment, and artful way with words, the story now told would surely want for what it now possesses.

Dedicated to George Earl Jefferson,

whom I knew, and knew not

TABLE OF CONTENTS

ONE
Lunch at Grims Park

Hollie and Goodwin Macbreeze entered Century's square, looking for signs to the Estillyen Ferry. Goodwin held a weather-beaten map in his hand. Hollie pointed to a spot on the map as she strained to read the crooked names on the wrinkled page. They glanced up and peered beyond the string of pedestrians passing by.

"Do you see anything?" Goodwin asked. "I don't see a single sign for the Estillyen Ferry. I expected to see a symbol of a ferry—an arrow or something."

Hawkers called out. Words, images, and sounds filled the air. Goodwin spotted a pleasant-looking older gentleman seated on the top row of the wide, half-circle concrete steps in the middle of the square. The steps cascaded down to a large, green-roofed pavilion. Hollie and Goodwin walked in the man's direction.

"Sir, I wonder if you might be able to help us," Goodwin began. "We're trying to find the road to the Estillyen Ferry. If my bearings are right, I think it should be one of those roads to the east, thataway." Goodwin pointed over his left shoulder toward three roads that merged in the northeast corner of the square. The gentleman tilted back the brim of his straw hat, showing his face, and slowly rose to his feet.

"You mean nine, ten, and eleven," he said. "That's what we call 'em, just like the hours nine, ten, and eleven on the face of a clock. I love the way they intersect with each other, spilling into the square. Then again, you could say they're flowing out rather than spilling in. You'd be correct, too, because they do both at the same time. Depends on which way you're headed. One way you're spilling; one way you're flowing.

"Then see how they trail away? They seem to hold hands for a while before branching off, letting go, and disappearing over the ridge. Nice they are, those roads. They lead. They take you somewhere."

"Now that you mention it, they do sort of look like hands on a clock," Goodwin said as he continued to study their unique pattern. "By the way, Sir, this is my wife, Hollie, and I'm Goodwin. We come from down south, 'round Whistleton."

"Did you say Thistle Town?"

"No. Whistleton, Sir."

"Oh, yes, I see. I'm Mr. Kind. Good to meet you. Now, you take those two roads leading off over to the southeast. You can't tell if the lower one is five o'clock or six o'clock, can you? And that narrow one that leads to Druhms Key, what do you make of it—three-thirty, four? No symmetry on that side of the square, none at all. Wouldn't you say, Miss?"

"Yes, I do see what you mean," Hollie said. "The hands of the clock on the other side of the square are clearly visible, just like you said."

"Estillyen Way is ten o'clock, the one in the middle," Mr. Kind said.

"Do you spend a lot of time here in Century?" Hollie asked.

"Now and again," he replied.

"I noticed your interesting pouch and thought you might be on holiday or something," Hollie said. "That's a quaint pattern—very nice."

"Oh yes, 'tis, I suppose. Well, I like to come down here from time to time to see if I might be of help. All the major roads 'round here pass through the square, you know. Great, bustling place, the heart of Century, don't you think?" Mr. Kind asked, as his lips formed a gentle smile that settled comfortably on his face.

"It does have a nice bustle to it," Goodwin said, folding his tattered map and slipping it into the left hip pocket of his jeans.

"There are a lot of hawkers and messengers running about," Mr. Kind said. "Travelers can tend to get a bit weary and confused. You know how it is," he said, as he began to stroke the pavement slowly with the tip of his cane.

Rhythmically, Mr. Kind advanced the slender wooden cane the distance of a small step and then drew it back without exerting a trace of downward pressure. He looked as if he were reaching out to retrieve an invisible ball of cotton threatening to flutter away in the breeze.

"Well, we're glad you're here today," Hollie said with a grateful smile, drawing Mr. Kind's attention back to the young couple.

"Say, where'd you get the scrape on the forehead, young man? And you, young lady—I see your ankle is wrapped. You two had a brawl?"

"No, not at all," Hollie said, smiling again. "It happened a couple of weeks ago. We were dashing across a six-lane circular road in Rome and were nearly mowed down by a bread truck swerving to miss a bus. If we hadn't jumped, I'm afraid we would have been sad statistics. Anyway, I sprained my ankle, and Goodwin hit his head on the curb."

"The curb was okay, though," Goodwin said.

"I told him we needed to use the underpass, but there we were," Hollie said, looking at Mr. Kind. She had an odd feeling, like the three of them knew each other even though they had just met.

"So you're okay, then?" Mr. Kind asked.

"Sure, the medics looked us over," Goodwin replied. "I was dizzy for a day, and Hollie was limping a bit, but we're all better now. They're pretty skilled at mending tourists. Thanks for asking, though."

"From the kit you two are hauling, it looks like you have been on the road for some time. By the way, have you eaten lunch? If you're going down to the Estillyen Ferry, you'll be awhile. I can walk across the square with you, and we could have a bite in Grims Park. It's just a block off the square. Couple of little sandwich shops if you want to fetch a bite and sit. Lovely quiet park, Grims. I like it there."

"Sounds great," Hollie said as she reached down and grabbed her backpack. With Mr. Kind in the middle, the three leisurely strolled across the square, chatting effortlessly as they moved along into Buckle Way.

"Wonder why the name, Buckle Way…a Mr. Buckle, I suppose?" Goodwin said.

"Lot of tales about these names. In olden days, this road was so full of potholes, the carriage drivers used to say, 'Buckle down—ruckus ride ahead,' and the name just stuck. 'Course that meant buckles, straps—you know, for parcels, luggage, and such, not 'round the waist."

"Interesting," Goodwin said.

"Say, I have my lunch here in my bag, so if you two want to grab something, I'll just head on over to the bench there in front of that broad oak tree," Mr. Kind said, pointing to the bench with his dark-knotted, maple-colored cane.

"Great, we'll be right there," Hollie said.

After less than a minute's walk, Hollie and Goodwin entered Blyer's Café, which was filled with midday customers. Mr. Blyer, the owner, worked the order counter and was known for taking two or three orders at once. He was affectionately called "The Auctioneer" by many of the locals, who enjoyed the spirited cadence of his customer interaction.

"Whataya have? Make it easy on yourselves," he said to the dozen or so people bunched in front of the counter.

Behind Mr. Blyer was a large wall mirror partially covered with postcards. The central portion of the mirror revealed a sizable bald spot on the back of his head. To the right of the mirror was a chalkboard. Repeatedly, Mr. Blyer pointed to the chalkboard menu with an old, black-painted broom handle. It appeared the broom handle and its bristles had parted company long ago.

"You see for yourselves, eight specials, and they're all great. Read to eat! Who are you kidding? You're at Blyer's, the place where food and flavor come together. So whataya have? Number one? Or shall we make it seven? Ain't got eleven, so let's make it eight, unless you've got an eye on five. Whataya have? Give me your order, please. Shout it out. I'll shout it back."

"Two threes," Hollie called out.

"There we go! It's not six, or triple twos, it's double threes," Mr. Blyer said. "What good taste the young lass has, what action! That's what we like to see in Blyer's place. Whataya have? Count 'em, read to eat—one through eight, they're all great. Where do you think you are? You're at Blyer's, where food and flavor come together. You want it chopped, shared, I've got knives to spare."

"That guy's incredible," Hollie said, as she and Goodwin jostled through the crowd and went over to stand by the large storefront window.

"What do you think of Mr. Kind?" Goodwin asked. "He's certainly a peculiar fellow."

"I think he's adorable. Did you see how blue his eyes are? They're the color of the water around the Pacific Islands. That striking blue and green hue. They sparkle like mad."

"Well, you'd see those things, artist that you are."

"Can't help it," Hollie grinned. "Oh hey, that's us, number eighteen."

They quickly picked up their sandwiches and made their way back to Mr. Kind, who was seated in the middle of a long wooden bench.

"Well, there you are," Mr. Kind said as Goodwin and Hollie approached. "Please, have a seat, rest awhile." He gathered his pouch and newspaper and placed them on his lap, making plenty of room.

Goodwin sat to Mr. Kind's right and Hollie to his left.

"Find everything okay?"

"Yes, and it looks amazing. Chicken salad on granary bread, third down on the chalkboard," Hollie answered. "Dill pickles, crisps, juice, and waxed paper for a placemat—brilliant."

Hollie and Goodwin unwrapped their sandwiches as Mr. Kind reached into his print-patterned pouch, extracting a small sandwich wrapped in brown paper. Removing his hat, he closed his cheery eyes. In the few seconds of silence that followed, he puckered and relaxed his lips three or four times. "Amen," was his only audible word, which was uttered in a very hushed tone.

Smiling first at Hollie, then with a nod to Goodwin, Mr. Kind said, "Bon appétit—of harvest we partake. Yes, Isle of Estillyen, what a pleasant, mystical old isle it is, that place of thoughtful repose. It's nine miles out, you know. Easy with the newer ferry. Well, I guess it's not so new anymore. Who recommended Estillyen, or did you two just discover it on your own?"

"That's sort of a long story, Sir," Goodwin replied.

"Well, the ferry doesn't depart till four o'clock, and it's just past one. I've a bit of time if you're of a mind to sit here and chat awhile."

"I like this solid wood bench," Hollie said. "Comfortable place to pass the time." She slipped off her left flat, heel first, with the aid of her right shoe tip. She then rested her bare foot on top of her yellow slipper.

"We decided to take three months off, as a kind of life break," Hollie began. "Touring, exploring, and all that. Estillyen is the final leg. And Estillyen sounds quite appealing at this point, right, Win?"

"Definitely. We're a bit done in with all the chasing over the past six weeks. We've hit so many museums, exhibits, galleries—my mind's a jumble," Goodwin said, looking beyond Mr. Kind to catch Hollie's eyes.

"Yeah, we're on a voyage. A journey of sourcing, Goodwin calls it."

"Journey of sourcing…not sure I've heard of such," Mr. Kind said, as he lifted his hat and began scratching the top of his head, sending wisps of white hair fluttering into the air.

"It's not business or anything," Goodwin said. "It's the idea of sourcing experiences, acquiring ideas, impressions, before the more permanent fix of life sets our sails."

"Like that," Mr. Kind said. "Fix of life setting sails—yes, I think I get your drift."

"Actually, Hollie and I are sort of in different stretches on the same road just now. I'm an architect, a planner type. Hollie is an artist—and more spiritually inclined. Yet we're moving together, I suppose, into a kind of crossroads. At least, it sort of feels that way."

"Crossroads, aye," Mr. Kind said.

"We were married in October, about a year ago. Just prior, Hollie was diagnosed with PKD, a kidney disease. That's part of the reason we decided to go on a retreat, to sort out some issues, to settle our thoughts. You know, let time render its way. We both graduated university last year," Goodwin said, as he paused to take a wide bite out of his sandwich.

"These sandwiches must be the best in the country!" he said.

"And that Blyer's is incredible," said Hollie, admiringly. "It'd make an interesting painting: Mr. Blyer in his red apron, with his black broom handle. Win, did you see how he kept lightly tapping the chalkboard? He had a kind of cadence. It was a performance."

"Yeah, he's great," Goodwin said, as he crumpled his sandwich wrapper, brushed the crumbs off his jeans, and chomped half of his pickle in one bite.

"So now, concerning the Isle of Estillyen, how long will you be staying?" asked Mr. Kind. "And who'd you say put you onto the place? Well, I mean, the ferry is going to put you on the isle, isn't it?" he said with a slight chuckle, as he let his cane make a short vertical drop to the stone pavers.

"My grandfather," Goodwin said. "I was rather close to him. Raleigh Macbreeze was his name. He passed away just after we were married. He was the main reason we got married in October. We wanted him to be there. He was a religious man, a wise fellow with a very winsome demeanor. Wouldn't you say, Hollie?"

"Completely so," Hollie said, as she tidied up her space and slid her foot back into her flat.

"Sir Raleigh—that's what we called him—spoke a lot about ancient ways living in the present," Goodwin said. "He and my grandmother made a half-dozen or so visits to Estillyen, way back in their early years.

"I particularly want to see if I can find a certain house on Estillyen. I have a sketch." Goodwin zipped open his backpack, poked his hand in, and rummaged around.

"Here it is. It's a sketch I did when I was a boy. I titled it *My Cottage Rare*. It's from a photograph my grandfather took on one of his trips."

"Nice," said Mr. Kind.

"Anyway, my grandfather frequently talked about the isle, and he always wanted me to make the trip. So that's one of the major drivers in bringing us to this particular spot."

"You could say Goodwin and I are on a pilgrimage—at least that's how I feel. The spiritual intrigue of Estillyen draws."

"My grandfather helped make the trip possible," Goodwin said. "I'm the only grandchild, and my mother was an only child. She's gone now, too. Drowned when I was eleven, and I never knew my father. That's why I have my grandfather's name."

"What about your grandmother?"

"Oh, she was great, but she died young for an older person. Could not get over my mother's drowning."

Goodwin lifted his right leg and crossed it over the top of his left thigh. The sole of his foot extended toward Mr. Kind. Mr. Kind's eyes quickly darted at the shoe, as if the sole had a squashed plum or sticky gum attached to it. Goodwin instantly recognized the indiscretion. "Oh, sorry," he said, and quickly slid his leg past his knee and let it drop, as if it had fallen asleep.

"Do you know much about Estillyen, Mr. Kind?" Hollie asked, as she turned her head in his direction.

"Oh, yeah, well, actually a fair bit. You do know Estillyen is an ancient word for *still*?"

"Yes, I read that. Goodwin's grandfather had a couple of old books on Estillyen. In fact, I have a booklet in my backpack."

"So you know there's a fishing village, Port Estillyen, with a few hundred people, a monastery, and an abbey. The monastery is run by the Old Order of Message Makers, which dates back centuries."

"I just hope we don't end up bored," Goodwin said. "Although I'll hike, hit the trails, maybe fish, while Hollie does some painting."

"I'm sure you'll love it," Mr. Kind said with an affirming smile. "The gray granite they use in the village sparkles like diamonds in the winter sun. Fine people, those Estillyens. Hardy. Must be. The wind can howl across the isle so fierce it can freeze a lightning bolt. Yes, for sure. Good time of year to be heading over to Estillyen. This is actually the best, I'd say. There's a small infirmary on Estillyen, run by the sisters. They're called the Sisters of Good, or Good Sisters—either way.

"The infirmary is best known as the Good Shepherd Infirmary. If your body decides to be sick for a while, you couldn't be in a better place. Spotless and as quiet as a bath towel stowed away in a wooden cupboard.

"There are three little lakes up on the far side of Estillyen known as Lakes Three. They're quite near each other, but you can't see one from the other. Tale has it, cranes swoop down periodically, picking up fish from one lake and dropping them into one of the other two. That way, the three lakes stay in touch—fish messengers, they call 'em, couriered by cranes."

Mr. Kind suddenly stuck his cane straight out in front of him and started making little jabs at the air, like he was jousting with an invisible butterfly.

"Brilliant. So the lakes really exist?" Hollie asked.

"Sure enough, you'll see. Estillyen has a way of not being like other places. It has an Estillyen-sphere, its own sort of atmosphere. The message makers, the monks, they're a wonderful, dedicated lot. No doubt a little nuts, I suppose, but passionately so. They'll make you think, mind you, but not all overly intellectual-like. No, that's not their thing, though they're plenty smart.

"They have a knack for sticking words together in ways they don't normally run, to help you see things you don't normally see. They make their words jump into lines like little frogs, yet they're not overly wordy. They call words *thought wrappers*. Yeah, I believe that's how they say it. Thoughts are invisible. They need visibility to be transferred. They need apparel. They have to be wrapped in words.

"On Estillyen, the whole idea is about stilling, contemplation, reflection. Those message makers are very much a mind of mission, they are. They see words from ancient paths as pillars for the present, like you were saying about your grandfather. Likely, your grandfather got the idea at Estillyen. Must have if he cycled back there, time and again.

"What most folks don't know is that those message makers come onto the mainland every six months and spend an entire week just listening and observing. They discover what messages are floating around, filling the atmosphere.

"Strange in one way, but not in another. Lots of people are strange, I suppose. I'm strange, I suppose. The monks spend an entire week on a kind of message retreat, exchanging what they see and hear.

"Now, get this. They move their months and weeks forward with each visit—know what I mean?"

"I'm not quite sure I do, do you, Win?" Hollie asked.

"No, don't believe I do either," Goodwin said.

"Well, it's like this: Say this year they would come to the mainland during the second week of September, and six months later they'd return the first week of March. That's twice a year. So next year it'd be the third week of October and the second week of April. The months advance and the weeks with 'em.

"The way they see it, in twenty-six years, they'll have experienced a full year—all fifty-two weeks—on the mainland, a week at a time, simply by advancing and rotating their dates. That allows them to experience all the changes a year can bring, even though it takes 'em twenty-six years to get through a year."

"Fascinating," said Hollie. She and Goodwin stared out across the park, with their heads cocked slightly upward. They watched the clouds drifting by, just above the roofline of the two-story library at the far end of Grims Park. Hollie rested her chin in her hand. Goodwin sat motionless, with his fingers interlocked on his lap.

"Messages are sensitive to seasons, you know," Mr. Kind said while he reached behind his head to tug on a patch of white hair sticking out of his straw hat. Hollie noticed his hair and its texture, thinking it reminded her of a horse's forelock.

"Smart bunch, those monks are. Focused on tales from Scripture, you know? They've got a series of readings called *Redemption*. They'll lead you all over those ancient tales till your eyes begin to cross and your mind begins to smart from expansion.

"The monks don't just read lines, as if they were reading a speech or a story. They like to get the audience involved, volunteering. You'll see.

"No, the monks, they have a way of losing themselves, probably like young Hollie here and artists down through the ages. Good to lose yourself. The further you go, the less you'll have and the more you'll find," Mr. Kind said.

Spontaneously, he began to hum and mutter in a chirpy rhyme, *"That's what you find. The more you lose, the more you'll find. The more you lose, the further you go. That's what you find...."*

"That's the ticket, by Job—'In this life look for peace, not paradise.' Now, that's Estillyen. Peaceful, but not paradise," Mr. Kind said, scratching his smooth chin, as if calming an itch.

"Have you spent a lot of time on Estillyen?" Hollie asked.

"Aye, a fair bit, I'd say, a fair bit. Good to see younger people like you making the trek. You know, words really do matter," he said, his eyes staring straight ahead. The conversation paused for a moment, as all three just sat staring out from the long wooden bench in the corner of Grims Park.

"The monks on Estillyen all go by pseudo-names: Saga, Narrative, Plot, Story, and the like. All the names are related to storytelling, message making, readings. Scripture is their craft. They have a way of becoming the message. That's kind of how they speak of Christ. Let's see, how do they put it? He's a, a medium of..." Mr. Kind mused. He removed his hat and placed it on his knee and momentarily shut his eyes. "Old Narrative, he used to...yeah...no...oh yes...he was fond of saying that Christ was the medium and message of God...something near to that, sure enough."

Mr. Kind sat back on the bench, rubbing his palms on the legs of his tweed trousers. A smile swelled his cheeks; they flushed bright pink.

"Sounds most intriguing," Hollie said.

"You've heard of Alpha and Omega, haven't you—the beginning and the end?" Mr. Kind asked.

"Yes," Goodwin said.

"Well, it's something like that. Those monks view Christ as being a composition of message and medium. You know, his words were so powerful, they told truth what to do."

"Never thought about it like that," Goodwin said.

"No, don't expect you have."

"Hollie is somewhat more along in all this than I am. She grew up that way. I enjoyed listening to my grandfather, but I don't want to be consumed with the subject."

"Something will consume you, even if it appears to be nothing, and that nothing will be the something," Mr. Kind said.

"There's just so much to see, and I don't want to miss seeing it because I'm buried in words," Goodwin said. "Openness, expanse of ideas, keen to build—that's the energy I feel."

"Well, if you decide to tread along the path your grandfather walked, you must walk by faith and not by sight. You see what I mean? There are peaks and valleys, but always it's a walk of faith, not sight. The words give you sight. They carry you along."

"What have I been telling you, Mr. Macbreeze?" Hollie said, smiling at Goodwin.

"The path is a journey, long as life," Mr. Kind said. "Once you start, it's not advisable to look back. Pillar of salt and all that," he muttered softly, as if speaking to himself. "Hate to see people turn into pillars of salt—what a dreadful sight." His whispering words descended on a scale to silence.

Mr. Kind turned his head to the left. A distant look swam across his face and settled there.

"What's that?" Goodwin asked.

"Never mind, it's an old story."

The three sat there calmly, watching sparrows flap their wings in a small, nearby puddle.

"The birds remind me of children running through sprinklers in the summer heat," Hollie said.

"They do know how to make a splash," Mr. Kind said.

"Well, Sir, it's been a privilege visiting with you, but I suppose we better get moving along," Goodwin said.

"Yes, really great to meet you, Mr. Kind," Hollie said. "Do you have any final words of wisdom before we ferry away to the Isle of Estillyen?"

"Well, I've never had any young people of my own to counsel. But I suppose I might say there are a lot of paths. Words lead. I'd recommend that you be watchful of thorns, of being snatched away, never able to get back to the path along the way of good. Sort of like the fish in Lakes Three on Estillyen. Once a fish gets swooped up from one lake and dropped into another, it's not likely it'll get swooped up again and dropped in the lake in which it hatched."

"Fascinating," Hollie said. "Not sure what to say to thank you, Mr. Kind."

"No thanks needed," Mr. Kind replied. "I'm obliged for your company, very much so."

"Hollie's right, we've greatly enjoyed talking with you, Sir," Goodwin said, extending his hand to Mr. Kind. Hollie followed suit.

"Maybe we'll reconnect when you return," Mr. Kind said.

"We'll be back in a month and a day," Hollie said.

"I'll mark that down. I'll stop by Blyer's on that date and see if I can spot you. You'll want a cup of coffee or a snack, I suppose."

"That's the plan, on the morning ferry," Hollie said. "We'll definitely look for you."

"We'd better move along, Hollie. See you, Sir, and thanks again."

"Oh, here, take this with you." Mr. Kind said. He reached into his pouch and pulled out a small, folded slip of paper and handed it to Hollie.

"Thanks," Hollie said, wondering what it could be. She put the slip in her pocket, as she reached out to give Mr. Kind a snip of a hug and a pat on his shoulder.

Hollie and Goodwin cut across Grims Park towards Estillyen Way. At the edge of the park, Hollie turned and looked back at Mr. Kind. He smiled and gave a wave with his cane. A stream of passersby entered the park and passed in front of Mr. Kind. Hollie continued to watch, but when they cleared, Mr. Kind was gone.

Goodwin turned to Hollie and asked, "So, what about the note—what does it say?"

Hollie pulled the paper out of the pocket of her bright-green jeans. She placed her hand inside Goodwin's arm, just above the elbow. Softly she read, "'My words are not my own' (Jesus Christ, circa AD 32)."

They just looked at each other and didn't say a word. Excited but silent, they began to walk in the direction of the Estillyen Ferry.

TWO
Quill House on the Bend

"I can't believe how the past few days have clipped along," Goodwin said. "Time must move differently on Estillyen, don't you think?"

"We've got a month to find out," Hollie said. "This is it—Contemplation Way. I love the chipped pebble-and-stone surface of these roads."

"The stones are embedded solid and deep in these old roads," Goodwin said. "You'd think the Queen Mary was dragged along them, with her hull full of seawater."

"No, *you'd* think the Queen Mary was dragged along them, not me! You come up with some of the weirdest metaphors, Win. I wonder why that brain of yours tends to work so alternatively.

"I just love the way the roads wind all over the hills and down through the meadows. I didn't picture Estillyen like this. They're like lifelines, arteries, connecting the whole isle. Some are barely wide enough for a couple of bicycles side by side," Hollie said.

"Where else are we gonna find an island eleven miles long with 114 miles of crisscrossing roads formed by the Queen Mary?" Goodwin asked.

"I'm so glad we're here, Win. I feel really positive about this decision. I don't think we'll be bored at all like you thought. Besides, you're so outdoorsy. That's Estillyen—the whole of it is outdoors."

"Quite different than I thought, I'll admit. I just didn't want to get into some sacred little community run by pious, pale priests—or sit in some tea garden smelling sweet perfume. You chant all you want. I'll climb, bike, and chase the wind, take in nature.

"Speaking of that, I'm planning to go up on Wednesday to see the house. The sisters at the front desk described an area called The Point, and that must be it. That has to be the property. It's the only off-limits area on the whole of Estillyen. Strange, isn't it? Granddad really went on about that place. It must be something special, the way he described it with that distant gaze in his eyes. My sketch, *My Cottage Rare*...I'm sure that's the house on The Point. There's no other place on the isle like it."

"Straight for the only place off-limits, that's where you want to head. And you ask me why I call you alternative! Why don't we just name you that—Alternative Macbreeze? You can go by A. Macbreeze. That is so you. I don't know what drives you sometimes."

"It's just that I'm so drawn to the place for some reason. Sir Raleigh didn't tell me the whole story. He simply said it was a tale of love and tragedy, and he really liked the man who lived on The Point. Apparently they were close. Likely the same fellow is still living in the house—must be old, though. From what the sisters said, he's a bit of a badger. He runs everybody off that comes near the place. They claim, though, that he's never actually harmed anyone. That's what they say, at least."

"My point about The Point is just don't get all wound up and barge in where you don't belong. Remember why we're here, Win. Focus for both of us, will you? This is hugely important to me, particularly now, given what we know—and what we don't know."

"Come on, Lee, you're loved. You know I'm in this. You're not alone. There's more to me than hiking and huffing."

"I hope so. Let's just stick together. Oh here, this must be it...Quill House. There's the winding stone wall with the swooping, green wooden gate."

Hollie paused for a moment, just taking in the house and its setting. "It's so adorable! I love the wildflowers and those rustic, chipped blue shutters," she said.

"Look at the iron hinges on the gates—they'd hold half of Rome."

"I know! Neat place, isn't it? This should be interesting; our first reading on Estillyen."

"I'm with you, but I have no idea what we're getting into," Goodwin said. "Message-making monks...I'm not doing anything weird. No tree hugging. No standing on my head."

"Don't be silly. Like I keep telling you, this is a season. Just be open. We need to embrace the sacred, the spiritual. I'm not going to pressure you into anything, though you know faith is keenly me. You're moving there—I can tell by what you've been saying the past couple of months."

Goodwin shrugged and changed the subject. "This one is called Quill House, right?" he asked.

"Yes, Quill House on the Bend."

"Yeah, this ought to be as fun as riding the rapids," Goodwin said. "Or maybe right up there with hang gliding."

"Oh, stop it, Win! Come on, there you go again. What is it that moors you?"

"Uh, watch it, Lee. There's a big collie racing up on your right."

The collie ran straight towards them, barking and sniffing the air. About two meters from Hollie, the dog abruptly stopped and began spinning in tight circles. With each spin, the dog let out a sharp bark, with his head pointed up in the air.

"Beautiful dog, isn't he, Win?"

"Beautiful if he doesn't bite you."

"Go ahead; pull the wrought iron knob, Goodwin. Old ringers like that are rare. Aunt Tilley's old house had one like it."

Goodwin grasped the knob and gave it a couple of strong, downward jerks.

"Hear the bell? Love that," Hollie said, quickly reaching into her yellow leather purse. She retrieved an eyeglass-shaped mirror and gave a glance. In less than thirty seconds, the left door swung open the depth of its hinge. A tall gentleman with a graying beard, wearing a brown habit, filled the frame.

"Hi, welcome—my name is Epic, and you must be Hollie and Goodwin. I saw your names on the register." The gentleman extended his long right arm first to Hollie, then to Goodwin, doubling the firmness of his handshake.

"Come in! I'm glad you found us. I hope I'm right—it is Hollie, correct?"

"That'll be me." Hollie stepped through the door with Goodwin close behind her.

"Sorry about Treasure. He's a beautiful collie, but blind. He spins in circles when he realizes someone has arrived. He had sight until he was about nine months old, and then he just lost it—can't see a thing. Lovely, gentle dog, a fine dog really. Anyway, come along—we're about to get started."

Epic closed the door and led Hollie and Goodwin along the long, wide hall.

"What a beautiful Shaker chair," Hollie said, glancing at the simple, oak ladder-back chair with its flat rungs pressing against the wall.

Next, they walked past a pair of tall twin tables. The long, slender tables were directly across from each other, against walls of soft, weathered gold with an amber hue. Green tapestry runners covered nearly the entire width of the tables' primitive wood tops. The tapestries' fringe draped over the table ends and extended midway down the hand-carved side skirts.

"The water closet is straight ahead, if you wish," Epic said. "We'll be in the room through the doorway on the right."

Hollie swiftly nipped into the loo, while Goodwin waited in the hall, examining the moldings and trim.

"Take a look at that great mirror in there," Hollie said, as she emerged, holding the door open. Goodwin peeked in for a look at the beautiful design of the antique piece, and, in a couple of minutes, they were moving towards the door of the reading room.

"He sure looks like a monk," Goodwin whispered.

"*Shhh!*" Hollie said, jabbing him in his side with her finger.

They stepped into a room where fourteen people, including Epic, were seated. Shaker chairs, identical to the one Hollie noticed in the hall, comprised the spacious circle. There were large, irregular gaps between each chair, which created a feeling of comfort for the guests.

The chairs to Epic's left and right were set well beyond his reach. Epic's back was to the stone fireplace, now quietly cool in summer. Its hearth was swept clean. Three white birch logs were stacked on the iron grate.

"Oh, here they are—Hollie and Goodwin," Epic said, as he rose and motioned with his right hand in the direction of two empty chairs.

Most everyone in the circle muttered words of welcome, accompanied by nods, smiles, and a couple of half rises. Hollie and Goodwin mimicked the gestures, as if they had just practiced them with the group. The two hurriedly moved through the respective gaps to occupy the waiting chairs.

"Let me go around the circle for you," Epic said. "I'll introduce the friends I know. This is Norman and Windy, Richard, Mary, Ellie, Clara, Pat, and Timothy. Then we have three young ladies. Would you be kind enough to give us your names?"

"Sure—I'm Beulah. This is my sister Sheila and our friend Kristene," she said.

"Well, we're so glad you're here," Epic said. "And then we have two other new faces."

"My name is Baxter," said a gentleman who looked to be somewhere in his thirties.

"And I'm Robin." Robin was thin, with long black hair. It was hard to tell to which side of twenty she belonged.

"Right, thanks everyone," Epic said, as he began to gather the group's attention.

"Wait, where is Treasure?" Ellie asked suddenly.

"Oh, thanks, Ellie." Epic placed his papers on his chair and moved over to the double doors leading to the courtyard. "Here, Treasure, come on, boy."

Treasure quickly moved along Epic's left side, brushing his brown robe. Without pause or waver, the dog moved across the room, through a gap in the chairs, and into the center of the circle. He promptly lay on his side and stretched out across the distressed pine floor.

"Okay, then. Now that we're all here, let's get started. It's just past ten. Let me briefly explain a bit about today's reading. The readings are done without pause. You can take notes if you wish, but over time we've discovered it's usually best to just listen. There's no quiz at the end; the whole purpose of the reading is to stimulate reflection. So please, feel at home—no pressure.

"When the reading is over, we'll take a break to consider what we've heard. You're free to stay put, wander into the courtyard...whatever you wish. The time is yours, a period of personal reflection. Feel free to journal or jot down your thoughts.

"Then, after twenty minutes or so, those who wish to are welcome to rejoin the circle for an unscripted conversation, sharing whatever you want to say or suggest. I'll give a couple of little starter thoughts. Participation is totally up to you; do not feel compelled to share. Remember, this is Estillyen, a place for contemplation, not pressure.

"Now, the last thing is that we'll need a group Voice, who will interact occasionally with the Reader. Your lines are here. They are short, but important. The Voice doesn't have the entire script, so I'll just pause in the reading and give you a cue. I might nod, point, or wave my hand in the air—something like that. Anyway, it will be easy to follow. You'll see.

"It would be good to have three volunteers. The Voice always speaks in unison, even though I may nod at you individually. If I were to choose one word to describe the Voice's tone or sentiment, I would say the Voice speaks with an air of *wonderment*. It is a questioning Voice. Into the room, you will loft a query, focusing our reading, helping to move it forward. It's really quite enjoyable.

"So, to whom might I pass out the sheets, the brave volunteers?" Promptly, four hands went up. Windy quickly lowered hers when she saw the other three, which left Kristene, Ellie, and Baxter.

"Terrific," Epic said. "We have our Voice.

"Okay, any questions? No? Good. All right, then, we're off. The title of today's reading is *Did God Really Say?* We'll start with a few lines from the ancient text of Genesis."

With Treasure already asleep and everyone fixed on Epic, the Reader, he began.

—◆—

Did God Really Say?

*Now the serpent was more crafty than any of the wild animals the
Lord God had made. He said to the woman, "Did God really say,
'You must not eat from any tree in the garden'?"*

*The woman said to the serpent, "We may eat fruit from the trees in the
garden, but God did say, 'You must not eat fruit from the tree that is in
the middle of the garden, and you must not touch it or you will die.'"*

*"You will not surely die," the serpent said to the woman. "For God
knows that when you eat of it your eyes will be opened, and you will
be like God, knowing good and evil."*

GENESIS 3:1-5

READER: Adam and Eve lay netted in nightmares on Eden's soil: Reproach of
conscience seized and squeezed their tortured souls. Long was the night that lingered to consume the light. Hours of eerie, thick darkness crept, gifting its chilly
blankets of doubt and despair. Reeling nightmares rendered perplexing, macabre
images, which elbowed hearts deeply troubled.

Creation's leading man and woman tossed and tussled in painful estrange-
ment. Darkened dreams drifted into their subconscious state, bringing no flight
of fancy. In their dreamy world they ran; they fled; they grasped, yet there was nowhere to go. Stark separation from joy laid them low. Sorrow stole their slumber.

So it was. Then morning broke. Joltingly, Adam and Eve awoke. At break
of day, the nightmare did not flee. Morning did not dawn and chirp away their
sorrow. As heavy as mud were their hearts. It was their first morning outside the
Garden of Eden. Welcome to reality new. Sullenness has come to call!

As sinners new, they must begin anew. They must cope, no matter what! On
behalf of the human race they were paired. They had awakened to a new, conditional state. Mutually impaired they were, a state not to be rubbed away from
frenzied, bloodshot eyes. Creation's travail had begun. Adam and Eve were now
inhabitants of the wilderness—refugees of Paradise.

The couple's intimacy with God on the Garden grounds must have been
as close as a petal to its rose. Now plucked, they were out. Cool wilderness soil
pressed against their bare soles. Upward it spoke with a sullen, dulling effect.

Epic motioned with his script—the first cue for Voice.

VOICE: What did the soil say? Did it really speak?

READER: Not audibly, of course, but speak it did. It spoke like this: "Though upright you walk, you were made from the soil beneath your feet. Privilege has passed. Do you feel the dirt pressing, telling? It speaks of who you really are."

VOICE: It's so sobering. Is there a single word that describes how Adam and Eve might have felt?

READER: You mean, can a tiny word find a descriptive spot in such a magnanimous plot? Yes, Voice, I believe it can. Try the word *loss* on for size. Loss—that's the linking, lingering word coursing through the lines of this tragic tale. The crafty one did them in, bringing a losers' loss.

So upright they were! Suddenly they cowered low, forfeiting dreams not seen. Their chested jewels of privilege were barely touched. All was swapped for skins stitched, wilderness wear.

The story of Adam and Even began on humanity's high ground. Consider it, Voice: They were the first to hear God's thoughts coming forth in words. Morsels of meaning, divinely dispatched, filtered into their hearts and minds. Verses between the Trinity and the pair flowed as naturally as love to the heart.

Words from God to man passed, and from man to God returned. There was no in-between. No need of mediation or clever devices. Meaning was transferred without distortion. God's words settled directly on their hearts and minds, something like manna floating down from heaven. It could have been rather different, though. God might have crafted mankind in a limited form, simply parroting words.

VOICE: How is that? I mean, can God do the unimagined?

READER: Why not? God is God! He chooses his choice. Are you suggesting God needs to consult someone before making his moves?

VOICE: No, not at all. It's just that God is always supposed to be the same, unchanging, or so I'm told. You know, the same tomorrow as today?

READER: If it makes you feel better, Voice, I'll use the word *suppose*. Suppose God did make such a parroting person—a voice without choice. He would not truly speak, converse, and share from the heart. God would say, "Good man, parrot person." Parrot person would reply, "Parrot, good man." God would say "God good." Parrot person would say "Good God." Consider for a moment how meaningful that scenario would be to God and man. Voice, parroting is not a Godlike attribute.

Let's continue our story. In the Garden of Eden, aspirations filled the air like butterflies at summer's peak.

VOICE: Reader, that sounds like a fairy tale!

READER: Does it now? It was so, Voice, this Garden of Paradise. It was so very real. No dread, no dark side. Despair was not present, not even known in Eden's land. Nor did want or worry have a place. No tempers flared. Adam and Eve shared a depth of communion with God no one else has ever experienced.

Paradise lost, it has been described—this paradise so briefly occupied. Oh, the sheer brevity of it! The brevity speaks hauntingly to the gravity of the tale, turning sad to sadder still.

Adam and Eve had hardly arrived when beginning found its end. Their exile came about so rapidly that Garden dust was yet to settle. Transitioned through, they were. It was God himself who gave them a little shove into wilderness weather.

Everything had been going swimmingly well in Paradise. There was no need of reprieve. That was, until the fateful day Eve spoke with the serpent.

VOICE: The serpent—you're referring to Satan, right?

READER: That would be the one—the master of evil. The serpent appeared in the Garden, parceling and parsing words. This inauspicious character is introduced as being very crafty…more so "than any of the wild animals the Lord had made."

Voice, Satan has an uncanny knack for spinning words. Ever so clever is this evil one. He offers conversational lines that are most sublime. Never does Satan say what he means or mean what he says. He is consistent, though, and most persistent.

VOICE: He is?

READER: Trust me, Voice. He isn't what he seems to be because he always is as he is. Satan mediates messages with disfigured verse. Each and all are dispatched with malicious intent.

Crafted in God's image, Adam and Eve were creatures unique, the object of God's delight. Listen to the ancient text, Voice: "Let us make man in our own image, in our likeness, and let them rule over the fish of the sea and the birds of the air, over the livestock, over all the earth, and over all the creatures that move along the ground."

That is what God said to God, when God decided it was time to get on with making man.

VOICE: What do you mean "God said to God"? That sounds peculiar to me.

READER: Voice, haven't you ever thought of the Trinity conversing?

VOICE: No, not talking…more like sailing together in heaven—that's how I see God—floating in and out, merging 'round about.

READER: I see. Sailing but not saying—interesting image of the Holy Trinity. Hold it there, suspended in your mind, as we consider what it is God said.

Special is this directive of God, to God, with God, about man to be. It bears a unique collaboration, not present in other acts of creation. No verse exists which says, "Let us make a zebra," or "Let us make a manatee." References to "us" and "our" indicate that the image God etched in man was requisitioned by the Holy Trinity. Sanctity of life resides, does it not, in these words of God designating man to be?

VOICE: How is that? Sanctity of life—that's an issue of great import!

READER: Right you are. Think of this: God spoke up for life long before man was formed. Discourse preceded dirt. The origin of humanity was conversation within the Holy Trinity. In the purity of the divine mind, humanity was pictured, envisioned, spiritually encrypted.

VOICE: Never thought about it like that. It's like forming the form before it's formed.

READER: Indeed, that's the idea, Voice. Were it not for that original divine discourse, forever in no-man's land is where man-not would be. Man-not would be amidst the ether of nonexistence. There, in vast nothingness, in emptiness, touching nothing and never being touched is where man-not would be.

VOICE: That's a scary thought, Reader.

READER: Yes, but if you were there, as nothing, as man-not amidst the ether, you would not be scared.

VOICE: That's what scares me. I don't want to be nonexistent.

READER: You make me smile, Voice. You are not nonexistent and will never be. But you might have been.

VOICE: I'm not sure I can think like you, or should think like you. You know what I mean?

READER: Let's think about it. Consider, though, how emptiness waits to be scooped into the something God decrees. Like the starting shot on the field of play, God's creative call sets elements streaming into form and place. Until that point, nothingness knows nothing of what it might be. At God's command, the heavens aligned, constellations filled the skies, and the first ocean wave splashed its force and foam onto virgin sand and beach.

The creation of the man, though, was not simply a command. The narrative describes the act. God "formed the man from the dust of the ground and breathed into his nostrils the breath of life, and the man became a living being." *Yatzar* is the Hebrew word for "formed." It conveys the idea of God acting as a potter, shaping and sculpting Adam from the dirt.

God breathed into his mold, allowing life to flow. Breath of God's Spirit rushed in, filling heart and soul. The breath of God carried a string of divine-like attributes, meant to root and lodge.

VOICE: How you word it—it makes the human race sound so much more than human, somehow.

READER: It was so. But so was the reality of Satan. Satan's entrance into the

Garden scene is curious, dispelling the picturesque tranquility. The appearance of Satan in the plot is rather like seeing one's sails rip apart, far at sea. One minute the vessel is lunging forward, racing through the waves with sails unfurled. Heartily they are swelled with gust.

Then, suddenly, rips appear. The rips begin to chase each other up and down the sails. The vessel stalls. It stops. It begins to bob.

VOICE: Satan in the Garden? How can it be?

READER: Ah, your question is cast in an ocean great! Satan has a way of appearing. He was on a mission. What else can one say? Certainly, Satan was not just wandering through; he didn't become disoriented on a devil's jog.

Satan's début in Scripture is in the Garden, conversing with Eve. Suddenly there he is. A demonic force has entered to oppose and counter the divine. He was there to rip Eden's sails apart—disfigure creation's canvas!

His cameo role in the Garden is even more perplexing than his part in Job. This is the beginning of time, yet there he is. Is he a fantasy, like many believe? Or should we say, disbelieve?

God chooses to reveal what he reveals. The drama is his. Beyond knowing are God's reasons for the mysterious moves he makes. This, however, is exceedingly good, not bad.

VOICE: What do you mean by saying exceedingly good?

READER: If you knew all God knows, Voice, God would be rather limited, would he not? Or you would be like God, which is the very point that undid Eve.

God being God, without reason to man, is God being God, as God should be. The characters of Scripture come and go. God alone knows the story complete. Satan appearing in the Garden, no matter how bizarre it might seem, was no surprise to God. The reason why extends deep into the divine realm. Let it rest there. It's not your worry.

What's evident from the scene is that Satan is there to tempt and test the will of God's newly created beings. He makes his move. Silently Satan slinks. He is there to prey and pounce on human will, showing it can bend and yield.

Satan enters the scene. His opening line is not a greeting, which one might expect. No "Hello, Eve, let me introduce myself. I'm Lucifer, the adversary of God." His first words, instead, form a question: "Did God really say you must not eat from any tree in the garden?" This line tossed to Eve is the first question recorded in Scripture. Satan was indigenous.

VOICE: Indigenous, that can't be. We're talking about Paradise, not hell.

READER: Yes, I know. Remember what we said about God being God?

VOICE: Sure, but…

READER: Then we must trust beyond our knowing. Indigenous he was. The crafty one knew his way around. He possessed an inside track. Was not Satan aware of the words God had spoken to Adam and Eve?

Perhaps, like a chameleon, he hid perched on branches, eavesdropping, watching. With wily eyes, he might have watched as God welcomed his original pair, giving them an instructive stroll around the Garden. The serpent's weapon— what was it, Voice?

VOICE: I suppose his words—what he said?

READER: Precisely. He struck at Eve, not with fang and venom, but with words. How close the serpent must have been to speak as easily as he did. There was no calling out to Eve, no shouting from afar.

In an instant, it seems, the crafty one could have easily lunged and had an eye-for-an-eye. Imagine Eve running through the trees with one eye snatched away. What a horrific sight! Or perhaps, on the throat his wily eyes he might have fixed. His aim sharp, he might have pressed deep his fangs, injecting a venomous flow through Eve's tender skin. Into the blood his poison would pass. Death would chase life away. Satan would have his prey.

Physical harm, though, was not the method of Satan's destructive blow. That was too limiting. The attack came via little morsels, the careful placement of chosen words.

The prize for Satan was much greater than the breath of Eve. Satan's goal was to scar and disfigure the spirit. His aim was to twist the spirit to such an extent that it would cost God dearly to affect a remedy. This was Satan's mission. With the right sinful twist of words, all would be warped, sullen, and sad, including God.

This is what Satan knew. This was his devilish desire. Satan wanted God to bear wounds from this infamous strike. Out of immense nothingness God had spoken the universe into being. At the center of it all was Eden's Paradise with Adam and Eve. Oh, how Satan must have abhorred this newfound life God had rendered. It all came to be without the slightest nod to Satan. He was not called or consulted. This, too, Satan knew.

In Eve, Satan saw his opportunity not simply to destroy a single woman or man. Satan's ill effect could cast the whole of creation into a monstrous death roll. This was his mode of operation, his prowling perversion. No pithy, piddly prize for Satan. Big game was his aim.

Expelled from heaven's realm, the wandering devourer would show God a thing or two. Give God a blow. The crafty one may be a castaway, but he could still hack away at Paradise. Satan seethed. To seek destruction was his code. God's fleshy uprights would taste sin and rejection—he, Satan, would see to it.

Epic's eyes bulged with wild expression. He stood, gracefully stepped behind his chair, and nodded.

VOICE: Can Satan really think like that? It seems so incredible, so devious, so scary.

READER: Surely Satan thinks. What of his modus operandi? Have you thought of that?

VOICE: Yes, to an extent. I can't figure it out, though—such a manic rage against God.

READER: Impossible it is to know what rolls through Satan's wretched, wicked world of thought, although one can imagine what he might have considered as he peered across the beauty of Eden's Garden.

He may well have imagined, "I AM, why not I with Eve—there in the center of your paradise so green and lush? Who better than I to make good your wondrous scheme? I AM, we could have done a deal, you and I. After all, I was once a celestial being, a great bearer of light. You could have cut me in, set the past aside. Think about it, it was eons ago, our spat. We could have started anew, you and I.

"Sure, I would have dropped my wings, no big deal. There I would have been, your chosen one, reassigned, ready to father it all. Reborn, if you wish, but a celestial man. Instead, you ended up with little imps of dust with nostrils puffed. I AM, you needn't have stooped so low, to make creatures from the dirt. I could have done you proud, and your planet, too. Come on, can't you see what you missed in not calling me? Surely your wisdom must have waned, not realizing all this could have been meant for me and you."

VOICE: Are you serious? You are, aren't you, Reader?

READER: Yes, Voice, it's far more than a silly thought in this magnanimous plot. In Paradise, Eve was unaware that she had been drawn onto Satan's turf. Morsels from the crafty one danced in her ears; words flowed to the core of her understanding. The most critical question Eve had ever heard was posed as a proposition of doubt. Satan questioned what God had said. Satan's words sliced at God's. Consider the sails, Voice. Can you see them?

VOICE: I can. They are white and puffed—but slit.

READER: So right, Voice. In Eve's heart and mind, words dueled and echoed. "Did God really say, 'You must not eat from any tree in the garden'?" Eve entertained these words bearing hidden hooks. The question Satan asked was not for want of information. Cleverly his line was cast. He was simply conversing. This was the first temptation of Eve. Slice!

Adam and Eve were novice conversationalists, mere babes up against the master of lying lips. The question to Eve could have gone unanswered, been referred to Adam, or been taken to God. It was not to be. When the first question to humanity was carefully lobbed by Satan, Adam was silent. There was no rebuke or rebuttal on his part. By injecting a line or two, Adam could have quickly shooed the crafty one away. He could have told Satan where to go.

VOICE: Where? Where would Adam have told Satan to go?

READER: Well, where else? To God, of course. God was the sure source for information about what God really said. If not that solution, Adam might simply have said to Eve, "It is time to go." Instead, the conversation continued. Adam's silent presence spoke not against but in consort. Adam allowed Eve to converse, to entertain Satan's salacious words.

Satan's misinformation to Eve was a trick. She felt obliged to correct him. Eve knew that she and Adam were not restricted in the way Satan implied. God was not banning their access from all the trees. It was just the one. Eve felt compelled to answer. She wanted to explain, to speak, to clarify the facts.

She told Satan what he already knew. "We may eat from the trees in the garden, but God did say, 'You must not eat fruit from the tree that is in the middle of the garden, and you must not touch it, or you will die.'" With each word of engagement, Eve slid deeper into Satan's pit.

Satan didn't pause to thank Eve for her helpful clarification rendered by feminine intonation. Rather, he crept closer still, to the strategic intent of his distorted message. "You will not surely die," the serpent said to the woman. "For God knows that when you eat of it, your eyes will be opened, and you will be like God, knowing good and evil." This line was Eve's second temptation. Slice!

Words dispensed with Satan's hooks. The word *when* is a hook, is it not? Satan did not say *if* you eat, but *when*. Then, two more hooks: Your eyes will be opened. You'll be like God. Not just God-likeness, but like God. That's what you'll be, Eve, like God. The hook of implication was also embedded in the serpent's message.

VOICE: Implication…what's implied?

READER: Plenty. In particular, the notion that God had not been forthcoming with Adam and Eve. He'd been holding out on them. Was God, for reasons of his own, manipulating Adam and Eve? Why was he restricting access? Why didn't God want them to gain the knowledge he possessed?

With a few little lines, the serpent cast a swelling cloud of suspicion over God. Masterfully he crafted his message. Slice, slice, slice. Blending truth with lie, the serpent's message became ravenously tempting and taunting to Eve. Consider the blend. The lie straight from the liar's lips: "You will not surely die." The truth: You will see life differently, knowing good and evil, like God. The lie: You will be like God. The truth: You will be very unlike God.

The ultimate promise: You will be like God. You will be God, not an approximation of God-likeness. No longer will you troupe around in human skin, bearing godly attributes. God you will be, and as God, you will set the Garden rules, make the arrangements. You'll do as you please on Garden grounds.

Then, as swiftly as it had begun, the conversation between Satan and Eve ceased. Three characters are center stage in the Garden drama. Only two exchange lines, on which the destiny of the created order was balanced. Drama, deep drama, filled the air. Heaven peered down. Angels of light, busied by creation's launch, looked to God for affirmation. Can you see them, Voice?

VOICE: I can! They look disturbed, curiously worried. Think of it, worried angels. I see them. They have no smiles.

READER: All the while, angels of darkness, the fallen, hid in Satan's shadow, clinging to his twisted tail. They gnawed at the dirt and inadvertently paused to peer up at their master. They watched their adored matador, Satan, as he inched ever closer to crippling creation.

Suddenly, softly, they began to chant the bitty lines their master strung. Did God really say? You will not surely…Did God really say? You will not surely… Did God really say? You will not surely…That was their mumbled mantra. Faster and faster they chanted, as the volume began to grow into a riotous rumble.

VOICE: Did Satan's demons really chant like that?

READER: Did they not? With every beat of her heart, the wayward will of Eve rose. Without a hint of disapproval from Adam, the crafty serpent waited for Eve's response. Satan's forged smile concealed his fangs. Behind his sealed lips, bitter venom dripped. Feverishly hot it was.

Heaven waited! Destiny waited. With bated breath, all of creation waited for Eve, for Eve to choose, for Eve to make her move.

"When the woman saw that the fruit of the tree was good for food and pleasing to the eye, and also desirable for gaining wisdom, she took some and ate it. She also gave some to her husband, who was with her, and he ate it." Eve reached for that which was pleasing to the eye and desirable for gaining wisdom. This pleasing desire was the third temptation of Eve. Rip, slice, rip.

Do you see the sails now, Voice?

VOICE: I do! They're falling, flapping, failing.

READER: The grasping motion was perpetuated by the message. The message, not the fruit, was the great embrace. Eve reached for words—the promise to be like God, not merely to be image-bound.

The serpent's distorted message achieved its aim with maddening effect. Sin had slithered through the garden grounds, finding its wily way to the human heart. There it deposited itself and swiftly rooted. Sin's fertility would wait for posterity. Adam and Eve were delivered into darkness. Just as God had said, they would surely die.

Adam and Eve cast caution to the wind—and with it, life. They embraced the message, swallowing swiftly its scripted words. Aspiration rose, and will moved. Human will is such that it can swell with the force of the ocean tide. Whatever qualms Eve may have possessed were rolled away by her wanton proclivity.

VOICE: Reader, sorry, but that word *proclivity*—I like the sound of it, but I'm not sure what it means.

READER: It has to do with penchant—one's desire or weakness—the way you are prone to be if left to your own devices. This is the great sin, when temptation rises and the will lunges with proclivity. To embrace a distorted message meant that the message of God had to be let go. No need of God. The new beings somehow thought they could maneuver around their Maker. This is the core of rottenness, for which Eve reached.

There would have been a huge problem of being on par with God. What was to become of God—creation's keeper? Consider it, Voice. A garden, like a king-dom, cannot stand divided. Tiny feet of human beings cannot fill divine shoes. God can fill human footwear, and, indeed, this happened, but that is a reading for another day.

The story of the Garden centers on messages in a competitive mode: one true let go; one distorted embraced, hacking the other away. Some things cannot be replaced. God cannot be replaced. Those original sails cannot be replaced.

Inventive creatures, human beings are. They create all manner of gods and messages. The great attraction of many, though, is to reside in a world that is God-exempt. This is but the same deception of Eve. God's exemptness aids in this feeling of being God, of representing the highest order. With God exempt, there is no deferring to the divine.

Voice, presumption is humanity's middle name, resident in every heart. From ancient parents, presumption is handed down. It was deposited that fate-ful day that Eve, with twitching ears and wanton eyes, grasped the object of her undoing. Proclivity of will brought on sin's plague.

Listen to more ancient words, Voice. "Then the eyes of both of them were opened, and they realized they were naked, so they sewed fig leaves together and made coverings for themselves." Adam and Eve heard God "as he was walking in the garden in the cool of the day, and they hid from the Lord God among the trees of the garden."

With fig leaves adorned, among the trees, humanity's first couple hid from God, their Maker. "I was afraid," said Adam. "The serpent deceived me," said Eve. Little chirps of confession appear not to detect the magnitude of sin's curse, which would roll out from the Garden and into the world beyond.

"The Lord God made garments of skin for Adam and his wife and clothed them." At creation's dawn, the sacrificial age began. Having placed Adam and Eve at the center of the universal stage, the curtain would have to fall. Adam and Eve, the world's first Godlike creatures, now bore the mark of sin. Created in the image of God, though, they were not disposable.

Human beings had been grafted into God's existence. They were there for a reason. God wanted them. God would not give up on humanity and go away. God would respond. A long and circuitous route of redemption would be deployed.

True it is. Guilt seeped into shame for Adam and Eve, while fear and anxiety crept over the state of their new condition. The intimate environment into which they had been placed soon fell silent.

The gate of Paradise was closed. The world, and its Garden within, would never be the same. Cursed was the ground, and to cursed ground Adam and Eve would return. To death's embrace they would go; surely they would die!

The ceiling of Rome's Sistine Chapel is adorned with scenes painted by Michelangelo. Among these magnificent frescoes is one from Genesis entitled *Original Sin and the Banishment from the Garden of Eden*. Michelangelo depicts Satan luring Eve into his deceptive ploy.

Perched in a tree, the serpent reaches out to Eve with the offer of fruit. The crafty creature sports a feminine torso but one with masculine qualities, broad shoulders and muscular arms. An equal blend of genders is seen in the face, while the thighs segue down to large, reptile-like extrusions. They coil around the tree, disproportionate in size to the main body of the figure.

Eve is below the tree, lying nude on her right side, her left arm extended upward. Her fingers appear to be touching the serpent's left hand as she reaches for the fruit. A blond-haired Adam stands upright, examining the tree with intense curiosity.

The scene blends seamlessly into an adjoining fresco of Adam and Eve being expelled from the Garden. A red-robed angel hovers in the air, pressing the tip of his sword to the back of Adam's neck. Shocked, confused, and frightened, the couple is reluctantly forced to step into the wilderness unknown.

Voice, the pace of modern advancement has a way of distancing ancient sagas from the present with exponential force. The story of the Garden of Eden carries with it a mythical undertow tugging at all that follows in Scripture. It's a story both passionately believed and readily dismissed. As brilliance appears to mount, numerous skeptics and cynics gnaw at the umbilical cords of faith and belief. They want to tether free of ancient times, when human beings lacked the accoutrements of modernity.

Just the same, my dear companion of rhyme, faucets gushing so freely today with messages of disbelief will tomorrow only drip. Morphing like chameleons, from one generation to the next, messages of distortion and disbelief have their momentary appeal. As time moves on, they will all drip dry.

This is not the way of messages, with words that are God-inscribed. To such words, fate bows, knowing full well their origin. Voice, numerous are the Garden's lessons, not least the meaning of words and messages sent.

Words matter…some far more than most.

"Did God really say, 'You must not eat from any tree in the garden'?"

THE SERPENT, GARDEN OF EDEN, CIRCA THE BEGINNING OF TIME

———◆———

In the group discussion that followed, there was no pause or sputtering of interest. Conversation flowed, roundabout, back and forth, to and fro.

Epic said, "Genesis is a jumping-off point for many. The reader is suddenly confronted with ancient and mysterious stories that challenge the very *raison d'être* of life. Some people, and not merely a few, are unwilling to believe them. They simply close the book—end of story. It's kind of like today's reading: The beginning of Paradise was the end of Paradise.

"The story of Adam and Eve, though, is intertwined with all that Scripture holds. That's the problem in damping it down. Or said another way, there would be no Scripture—or need of Scripture—if Adam and Eve had not gone down that path. It's the story we have. I willingly choose to believe it. I'm very comfortable with letting God be God.

"I say that not in a stiff-necked, audacious manner. Not at all, I hope. I speak by faith—hopefully, reverently, with respect to everyone—although I have discovered through the years that a person's challenge may not actually be disbelief.

Disbelief is actually a form of belief. To disbelieve something one must believe something else. What is it the disbeliever believes? What messages does the disbeliever embrace?"

Thoughts were still percolating when Epic reluctantly said, "I hate to draw this great discussion to a close. It seems, though, we've carried our conversation into another time zone."

It took another ten minutes or so for most everyone to say their good-byes and move along. Hollie and Goodwin exited by way of the patio doors. They were almost through the side arch when they managed to catch Epic's eye. He was busily chatting with Ellie, Mary, and Clara. Without losing his conversational focus, Epic extended his arm high in the air and waggled his hand back and forth as a kind of parting gesture.

Later, Hollie and Goodwin moved along into the swell of the day. As they explored the trail through Ladybug Meadow, their conversation was peppered with thoughts about the Garden reading.

"Now that we've experienced one of them, I'm even more fascinated by the idea of these readings," Hollie said. "I know I shouldn't want to rush ahead, but I just can't wait to find out what we'll hear on Wednesday when we go to Silo on the Mound."

Even Goodwin admitted that the morning had been a pleasant surprise. Far from boring. Though his mind was already wandering again to The Point.

THREE
Silo on the Mound

"Hollie, I'm going up to The Point today. Sure you won't come along?

"The groundskeeper guy, Mr. Chet—you know, the nice fellow with the blue wellies—he said the property is all posted with no trespassing signs and scary warnings to keep out. He claims the owner is like a bear with an abscessed tooth—always grumpy and growling around.

"It's the house from Granddad's photo—I'm certain of it. You can see just the corner of it in that cool painting in The Abbey entrance. From how Chet described it, that's definitely *My Cottage Rare*. I'm planning to take the sketch along and show it to the old fellow."

"Oh, Win, you're so impetuous, really," Hollie said, as she stood in front of the bathroom mirror, hurriedly giving her left eyebrow a few pencil strokes. "People post warning signs for a reason. The old guy may be a madman; he could be dangerous. There's no telling what someone like that might do. I was with you when you asked Sister Amber about going up to The Point. Remember her look? And what she said? 'I wouldn't recommend it.'

"That was obviously the wrong thing to tell *you*. Why do you just ignore comments like that? That's the only private property on the whole of the Estillyen highland. It's got nothing to do with the monastery land or Abbey grounds. You have no business going up there."

Goodwin was unfazed.

"Just as well—you'd better not come along anyway. Your hair might blow my covert operation. You'd stand out like a Red Factor on the white sands of the Canary Islands."

Hollie paused, her eye pencil frozen in motion. She tilted her head slightly and fixed her gaze upon Goodwin, who stood in the middle of the guest room.

"Red Factor on the Canary Islands! Funny, real funny. Sometimes you're impossible. Cleverness is not always a positive attribute, you know—like now."

"No, really, I'll just trek up there. It's a little over two miles; I should be back before lunch. I can meet you at Three Pond Cottage before the reading, okay?"

"Well I can see there's no stopping you, Mr. Alternative Macbreeze. Just promise me you'll be careful. And meeting at the cottage for the reading sounds like a good plan."

Hollie refocused and carried on with the quick routine of morning makeup. Finishing touches complete, she turned to Goodwin, whose expression revealed a mild impatience to get the day started. He was eager to head out for his appointment with *My Cottage Rare*.

"Okay, okay, I'm coming," said Hollie. "But you're not leaving here without a good breakfast—and I'm starved, so let's go eat."

"Fine. I'll take my jacket and bag down so I won't have to come back up," Goodwin said.

They scurried out the door and along the hallway. Midway down the hall, they descended a long flight of stairs, bringing them to the entrance of Gatherers' Hall—the extraordinary dining destination for Abbey guests.

"I think I could eat breakfast here forever and never tire of the place," Hollie said.

Large windows on the south wall of the hall framed a grove of pine trees towering up Eagle's Ridge. The middle of the room featured an enormous masonry serving table, worn silky smooth by years of wear.

The work was simply called "The Table," and it was considered a prized piece of Estillyen art.

A double row of forest-green crackled tiles ringed a crimson-colored random mosaic, set in The Table's center. From the hall's central beam, a single spotlight shone down on the irregular tile fragments, making them glisten.

Hollie and Goodwin's breakfast was fairly brief, though Goodwin did manage to make three laps around The Table to Hollie's one. But he was not keen to linger.

"That's it, I'm gone," Goodwin said, as he gulped his coffee and rose from his chair. He grabbed his bag, bent forward, and gave Hollie a quick kiss on the forehead.

"I'll just finish my tea. Be careful, Win, really. I still don't like it. Don't barge in. I'll be anxious for you. But maybe when the man on The Point sees your sketch, it'll make a difference."

"When are we supposed to be at the reading?" Goodwin asked.

"Win, you've asked me that three times this morning. Are you all right? How can I express it differently? Let me see." Hollie glanced at her white-faced watch with its chartreuse leather band. She wiped a small smudge from the crystal.

"We're to be at Silo on the Mound in three and a half hours, or twelve o'clock noon, Greenwich Mean Time."

"I know, I know. I guess I'm kind of double-minded today," Goodwin admitted.

"Let's go with your idea to meet down at Three Pond Cottage, where we saw all the ducks. I want to go early and get in a bit of painting. Win, if you feel uncomfortable up there in any way, just turn around and split, okay?"

Goodwin barely heard her last remark, and, with a nod, he was off. In a little more than an hour, he reached a fieldstone wall with a small wooden gate. He loosened the cord on the gate and stepped through, just inside the stone wall. A few meters to his left were a pair of wooden signs, stationed on either side of the trail. He stopped, freeing his brown backpack.

The signs were erected of odd-shaped wood pieces nailed to old heavy stakes. The plaques were hand-painted and noticeably retouched with a scrawling trace.

The words "No Trespassing" were prominent on both signs. To the left sign was added, "And That Means You—Keep Out, Stay Away!" The right sign said, "And You Too! No Interlopers! Private Property. Mind Your Own Business—Ironbout Residence."

The path past the signs quickly gave way to clover, unmoved grass, and a smattering of wildflowers. Goodwin could see the house 150 meters or so in the distance. There was nothing stirring. It looked nearly abandoned. Patched shingles peppered the roof. The siding was partially bare and sorely in need of paint.

Goodwin stooped down, pulled a bottle of water from his backpack, and removed his small, framed pencil sketch. As still as the house itself, he stared, awestruck.

"Yes, that's it," Goodwin murmured. "I can't believe it—it's just as it has been through all these years, *My Cottage Rare*." He stood there, scanning the house for detail and repeatedly glancing down at the sketch. He reached into his bag again, this time retrieving a pair of binoculars.

Quickly focused, he centered on the house. Suddenly the faded, black front door swung open with a jolt, as though someone inside was bolting to escape a fire or a burglar. A gray-bearded man and his dog rushed to the edge of the porch. The man was silent. The dog barked. After several rapid barks, the black-and-white border collie stopped and looked up, awaiting his master's direction.

Goodwin was mindful of Hollie's words, but thought, *This is insane. What am I afraid of? I'll move in a bit, maybe halfway, and see what happens.* Grabbing his backpack, Goodwin stepped beyond the warning signs. He felt as if the signs were scanning him as he passed.

Okay, keep calm, he thought. With each step he took, the tall grass and weeds sounded a warning *swoosh* against the front of his jeans. *Swoosh, swoosh,* Goodwin stepped. Soon he was halfway up the path. Suddenly, the elderly man came off the porch and moved out into the yard. He took up a position under a massive walnut tree, near the front gate. The man began to holler, with palms raised on either side of his mouth.

Goodwin couldn't make out what he was saying. He halted for a few seconds and then decided to keep moving. He advanced to within roughly fifty meters of the front-lawn gate. At that point, the old man reached behind the walnut tree and produced a rifle. Without the slightest hesitation, he extended the rifle high in the air with his right arm and fired a single shot. It seemed to Goodwin the shot echoed out across the whole of Estillyen.

Goodwin stopped. "Blisters," he said, "this fellow really is a madman!" For a minute he stood perfectly still. His heart was racing. He wanted to keep moving, but he felt cautious, unsure.

"I'm not having it," Goodwin declared. "Who does he think he is, Hercules? The old goat! He's festering and fuming. He acts like he's been chewing barbed wire. I'll call his bluff. Surely he's not really going to shoot me?"

Goodwin thought again. He remembered the line he'd learned as a boy: "Let not threats become regrets."

"Okay," he mumbled, "I'll slip away this time, but I'll be back. I want to see that house, the house Sir Raleigh spoke about with such mysterious admiration."

As he stood silently in the grass, taking one last look at the house, Goodwin sensed he had somehow inherited his grandfather's mystery. He felt odd, like he had come upon a bubbling brook, one he could hear but was unable to cross. He wanted to cross it then and there, feel the current swirl around his ankles, and step onto the other side of the bank.

Curiosity had drawn him to The Point, but it was more than intrigue he felt settling into his consciousness. The place he had only imagined he now viewed. Yet, as he peered at the old man and his dog, he somehow felt that he was not an outsider, although he knew he was. He sensed that the uninviting atmosphere of protest was a charade, a smokescreen that draped off a world he wanted to know. A world he *needed* to know.

Goodwin wanted so much to move through the fog and see what he would discover. He sensed, however, that this was not the day. It was time to retrace his steps, retreat through the swooshing sounds and warning signs. Today, he'd return to Hollie—and tell her what he'd found on Estillyen's Point.

Hollie had casually paced herself through the morning, eventually making her way to Three Pond Cottage. She had been drawing for a good hour when she saw Goodwin approaching.

"Hey there, how'd it go?" Hollie asked, trying to be nonchalant, though her eyes showed concern. "I was just getting ready to pack up and head for the Silo. The reading will start in about twenty-five minutes."

Goodwin couldn't hold back his excitement. "I saw it, Lee. Sure enough, that's the house on The Point. And I saw the old guy who owns it. He started making a bit of a ruckus, so I thought I'd wait a day or so and take another look."

"Wow, were there warning signs and everything?"

"Well, sort of old things, probably more of a past concern. I'll tell you one thing, it's beautiful up there. You would love The Point—what a view! I came back on this great little side trail. Hardly anyone ventures up those trails, you can tell."

"Well, maybe I'll have to go exploring with you sometime. Right now, I'm just glad you're back safe—and in time for the reading."

They exchanged a quick hug, and Goodwin turned his attention to Hollie's art.

"So this is what you've been up to this morning."

"Yes, see my drawing? There are two, actually."

"Brilliant—both of them!"

"I'm pleased; I like the way they are turning out," Hollie said. "This whole place just breeds inspiration."

Hollie pulled off her green flat to shake out a tiny pebble. "Glad my bandage is gone, too. And look at you—how do you heal so quickly? I can barely see your scrape."

Hollie reached over with her right hand, and, using her two middle fingers, softly touched Goodwin's forehead.

"Win, I feel as if the brush strokes are finding their own way across the canvas. It's great when that happens. My fingers become almost weightless. My mind is engaged, but not directing, leading. It follows my intuition. I just watch what appears."

"I wish I could do that with my architectural drawings," he said, "but I can't. I get so focused on how it all works and stuff. It's intense, figuring out every beam and brace."

"Well, you've got to—that's important. You don't want children years from now singing a rhyme based on your work. *Beautiful, beautiful building, all tumbling down, such a shame; beautiful, beautiful face, but lacking that important brace,*" Hollie sang, making up the little tune.

"Very funny," chuckled Goodwin, giving her a wry smile.

"Well, one thing is certain. Mr. Kind was right about this place," Goodwin said. "It's so completely other than what you'd expect. It's got this mix of surprise, charm, and mystery."

"Completely," Hollie said, as she watched the ducks lazily paddling in the ponds.

"Look at that duck over by the fence post, Win—the mallard with his proud green cap and brown vest. I think it's missing a leg. Must've been wounded. Look at that...amazing!"

"Are you sure? I've never heard of a one-legged duck."

"There he goes, hopping, or whatever you'd call a one-legged duck in motion. See how he extends his right wing for balance? Incredible. I can't believe it. If I were to paint it, no one would believe me."

As they stood watching on the pond's bank, bemused, a middle-aged monk approached, carrying a large, round, woven basket lid. The lid was layered with breadcrumbs and crusty bits. The monk's presence triggered a symphony of quacking. Ducks in the pond and on the bank raced in the monk's direction.

"We can't get over the duck with one leg," Goodwin said, projecting his voice to the monk standing on the other side of the pond.

"Just a second, I'll come 'round," he said. He quickly pitched the crumbs and bounced the empty lid off the back of his hand to loosen any lodged pieces. "Not quite like feeding the five thousand, but..."

Walking around the bank, the monk approached, extending his hand with a smile.

"Hi, my name is Saga. I'm from Silo on the Mound."

"What a coincidence!" Hollie said. "That's where we're headed."

Goodwin made the introductions. "This is my wife, Hollie, and my name is Goodwin."

"Do you like One?" Saga asked, nodding towards the one-legged duck. "The mallards are beautiful, with their shiny caps and priest-like collars."

"What happened to it, or One? Win and I couldn't believe it at first. Then we looked a bit closer."

"Fox," Saga said. "I actually saw it happen. Very early one morning, 'bout six, the fox was creeping along, right there by those horizontal split rails, but on the opposite side.

"It was a striking reddish fox with a bushy tail and a black nose. All of a sudden, he leaped through the rails and caught poor One, just as he was trying to fly. Crunch—the wily fox snapped One's right leg clean off, and then he scurried back along the rails. The brothers jokingly say the fox must have been Chinese—duck feet, you know, a real delicacy in the East.

"It looked like the fox had a yellow cigar in his mouth. One's little webbed foot was facing my direction, sticking out of the left side of the fox's mouth. I swear the webbed foot was still moving, sort of trying to run or hold something."

"Is that a true story?" Goodwin asked, skeptical.

"I'm a monk, am I not? It's a saga true, just like my name. Look at it this way: Before One lost his leg, his name was simply duck—a duck among ducks, a quack among the quacks.

"His tragedy brought him notoriety. Everybody loves One. He gets more attention and crumbs than a half-dozen ducks. Sure, he tends to swim in circles a bit, but he's none the worse for having only one leg."

"Love it," Hollie said. "The wildlife on Estillyen is so incredible."

"Sometimes I think we need them more than they need us," Saga said. "So, you're coming along to Silo just now, are you? It's about time to gather."

"Yes. We're following the *Redemption* series—all twelve readings. We were at Quill House on Monday," Hollie said.

"Good, that means you'll be around awhile. Not everyone has the time to take in all twelve, but I recommend it to those who can."

"Amazing story, the reading at Quill House—the serpent with his crafty ways and winsome words," Goodwin said.

"I'll say. That particular reading actually gives rhyme and reason to all the messages we make. Message making, as you know, is our passion. It's been so for a long time. Come on, we can walk together, if you wish."

"Let's go," Hollie said. "Good-bye, One." They turned and began to walk up the path to Silo on the Mound.

"The flowers are swaying tall, now that it's the second week of summer," Saga said. "We've got almost everything on this isle: a misty waterfall, a winding river, and beautiful hills rolling down to Ladybug Meadow."

"It's a lot to take in for an artist," Hollie said, as the three made their way along the narrow brick path leading to the silo, elevated on the mound.

"Have you been up to Lakes Three in the pines?" Saga asked. "They're my favorite, I suppose."

"Not yet," Goodwin said. "But we will, for sure."

"Please, come in," Saga said, as he pushed open the tall, slender wooden silo door. He politely stepped back, allowing Hollie and Goodwin to enter.

"Do you like the color on the door? We just painted it a couple of days ago. Sister Ravena nailed that. Great eye, she has. I believe she called it Sun-Broth."

"Gorgeous," Hollie said.

"There's a little story about the Silo that I'll tell you later," Saga said. "We'd better go on through and get started since it's nearly twelve o'clock, but remind me later."

Saga closed the entry door and moved across the circular Silo to a door on the opposite side. Pressing down on the iron latch, the door opened to a short breezeway.

In the north wall of the breezeway, some five feet off the floor, was a small, leaded window. Its diamond-shaped panes provided modest light for the corridor. On the window's deep ledge, an aged white candle was stationed. The well-used candle was large in diameter and shortened by half from its original height. It was held fast in a pewter holder by the wax it had expended bearing light. The candle's simple form was rich with character. It looked as if it belonged. It was a ready comforter for warding off unsuspecting darkness.

At the end of the breezeway, a second door, identical to the first, provided access to a meeting room. The room was spacious, square, and sided with battened oak.

"Hi, everyone," Saga said, as he stepped through the door with Hollie and Goodwin close behind. "Great to see you here. We have about five minutes. Why doesn't everyone just take the initiative to greet each other, shake hands, and say a few words, and then we'll get started. Phrase can answer any questions you might have." Phrase, a young man, was seated on a short bench against the wall near the front.

"A few more people than last time," Goodwin whispered to Hollie.

"Yes, there must be more that twenty," she answered. "Also a younger group. I would think those five girls there are on some kind of outing."

"Let's sit on the third bench, along there on the left," Goodwin said.

There was a center aisle with five rows of benches on each side. Constructed of pine, the plain benches were about ten feet long, narrow, and noticeably aged with a rich patina.

"Looks like a Quaker house," Goodwin said, as he and Hollie scooted along the bench and settled in.

"Have you ever seen a Quaker house?" Hollie asked.

"Well, no," he said. "But I have now."

Three windows with four panes each lined the side walls in perfect symmetry. "You see the wavy glass in the windows? I just love that look," Hollie said.

In the center of the room, near the front, was a single wooden chair. Saga moved to it and took his seat. A pair of identical chairs was against the back wall.

In the back corner, to Saga's right, sat an elderly monk. Brother Herald was quite still, his posture straight. With a fixed gaze, he looked up beyond the eyes of everyone seated on the benches.

"Welcome," Saga said. "I hope you're enjoying your time on Estillyen. It's great to have you here. Oh, by the way, Phrase, the young man on the side there, is one of our summer interns. I believe we have twenty-two in all this season. You can spot them by their chocolate-colored shirts with the Estillyen logo, the yellow anchor with the blue chain.

"In the *Redemption* series," Saga said, "ten of the twelve readings require two readers. I know you are not all here for the *Redemption* series, but for those who are, that's the way it works. One monk presents the Scripture narrative, and a second, more senior, monk reads fictional narrative for Lucifer.

"The character Lucifer has been carefully developed by the Message Makers of Estillyen to help underscore various themes in our readings. I confess, if you listen carefully to what the lines address, then turn the meaning inside out, you'll be surprised by the truths professed.

"I'm sure our second reader today, Brother Herald, would agree," Saga said, in a warm, supportive tone, as he looked back at the elder gentleman.

Brother Herald glanced across the room, offered a pleasant smile, and gently nodded. The only white he wore was his clerical collar. His shirt, habit, and even his belt were black, as were his socks and shoes. Brother Herald's white hair was thin and wispy. It streaked across his dark scalp. His face was full. His hands were large and his knuckles prominent.

"The only thing we need to do before we begin," Saga said, "is to find our Voice. For this we need three volunteers who will interact with me by voicing a few lines. As you may already know, we like to have three, although I suppose two would do. Volunteers? What about in the back row?"

A young man raised his hand, along with a couple of the young ladies in the group of five. "Okay, that'll be perfect. We have a Voice in the back, but if one of you young ladies could move to the other side of the aisle, that would give us balance. Wonderful, thank you," Saga said, as a young woman with blonde hair, wearing a plum-colored shirt, scooted across the aisle.

"Your names, please?" Saga said. "At the back first."

"I'm Stephen," said the young man with curly brown hair.

The girl in the plum-colored shirt said, "My name is Patricia."

"And you, please?" Saga asked.

"My name is Reye," said a tall, slender girl with reddish-brown hair and smart-looking tortoise shell glasses.

"Thank you," Saga said. "There we are, it seems. Let's get started.

"Today's reading is titled *Picking Up the Pieces*. The heart of the story is Moses receiving the Law on Mt. Sinai. The story conveys a treasure trove of truths and enjoys great familiarity, even though many people have never read it. It's part of lore, like Noah's Ark. One point I'd suggest is that you consider the image of God during the reading.

"We'll start with a few verses to help place us in the context. We join the story just as Moses is coming down the mountain, carrying the Ten Commandments."

Picking Up the Pieces

*Moses turned and went down the mountain with the two tablets
of the Testimony in his hands. They were inscribed on both sides, front
and back. The tablets were the work of God; the writing was the writing of God, engraved on the tablets.*

*When Joshua heard the noise of the people shouting, he said to Moses,
"There is the sound of war in the camp."*

*Moses replied: "It is not the sound of victory, it is not the sound of
defeat; it is the sound of singing that I hear."*

*When Moses approached the camp and saw the calf and the dancing,
his anger burned and he threw the tablets out of his hands, breaking
them to pieces at the foot of the mountain.*

EXODUS 32:15-19

READER: From God to Moses the tablets of stone were passed. With a single
fling of indignation, they lay on the ground in pieces. The Law of God lay broken
to bits. Never read. Never adored. No chance to be abhorred. The magnanimous
message, in medium of stone, had swiftly become a heap of litter.

Jumbled were the words and letters God had inscribed. With his own finger
God had etched them in the Commandments Ten. Not six, or eleven, or some
other number, but ten. This was a message of divine intent. This was a brief compilation, a succinct summation of God's thoughts, inscribed in words.

VOICE: Why stone as choice of medium?

READER: Inscribed in stone, letters do not scatter or move about. They are fixed,
set, no blotting out this for that. No dropping a word or two to free up space.

But there is more. The medium speaks, does it not? A medium is a message,
but what message does it bear?

VOICE: Reader, pardon me. I know you've only begun, but I just want to be clear.
A medium is a medium, and a message is a message, right?

READER: Go on, Voice, I sense more in your query.

VOICE: The former, being the medium, does not usurp the message, surely?

READER: Good question, Voice. To which I offer this reply: A message is not a message, apart from the medium that makes the message known. Show me a message without a medium. Oh, I could cruelly send you on a search of such a specimen. Though that I will not do, because you would go and try. Forever I would wait for your return!

Therefore, regarding this matter of message and medium, the former, being the message, is never what it is indivisible from the latter. Into every message, the medium contributes elements of its essence to the message. It's not unlike letters conveying words. Words need letters to make them known, but the letters shape words to appear and sound the way they do. Indivisible are the two.

Look at me, Voice. Am I not a medium with a message? So it is with you.

VOICE: I think I'm still with you, mostly.

READER: Lest we trail away, let's go back to the tablets of stone—and our story of words and letters on the ground. We were considering the medium—stone it was. Stone does not smile or hug. It's not warm and friendly. It's not human. Stone is cold if not warmed by the sun or something else. It possesses no blood. It has no pulse. It's made of granules, grains, once popular for telling time.

Stones are not new. They are old. Inscribed stones are not rare. As cornerstones they often speak, dating dreams. At entrances they frequently appear, speaking words of conviction. Embedded in memorials, they speak of honor and sacrifice. Their most common use, by far, is to name and date the dead.

Markers they are called, headstones over those at rest below. Once those resting walked upward, talking, jostling. Now they rest—inscribed, dead, and dated. Inscribed markers speak of permanence, though their etchings fade. They are bastions of permanence in a world of impermanence.

This they are, rather like the tablets handed down. Imagine the tablets, the work of God, the never-changing One. God who speaks words never fading. His work of permanence reduced to rubble. The tablets were heavy enough to be inscribed—yet brittle and thin enough to break.

Ever so carefully, no doubt, Moses must have carried them down from the majestic summit. The weighty stones held fast against his chest. That is, until Moses saw what he saw. That's when he flung the burdensome weight.

VOICE: What did he see?

READER: Wait, Voice—don't rush the reading.

The medium, with its message intact, hit the ground, smashing into pieces. One can imagine the pieces there—random bits of stone with broken words scattered from context and meaning.

"You shall," the most frequent of words God inscribed, lay there in a triangular scrap. "Idol" is visible in one stone's small square. Next to the idol scrap rests a stone strip bearing the phrase, "but showing love to a thousand...."

Is it hard for you to see them, Voice?

VOICE: No, I see them as you say. Several are bunched together. Others lay roundabout.

READER: Words broken, loosed from medium and message, lay on the ground, speaking still. Curiously, they became a message new. With diffused meaning, words and letters called out from the heap.

The collective shatter formed a new kind of meaning. The message was more like an eagle's nest fallen from its cliff. In the eagle's nest, babies chirped. Chirping want, chirping fear. The shattered stony bits lay chirping, too. One by one, stones chirped of shame and confusion.

God's words etched in stone signified not only surety of source but also the new reality of God communicating with man. The coziness of the Garden was gone, long gone. Laws etched in stone formed the new communicative mode. Do you see, Voice, how it is the message cannot break away from the medium?

VOICE: It's just that this is not a simple matter: messages making meaning, molded in medium. I guess I need to consider this more fully.

READER: There is a great deal to consider relative to those disjointed pieces broken on the ground. The stone tablets were given by God to guide and mold the Israelites into a new way of being. Words inscribed in stone were to be inscribed on their hearts and minds, not departing. They were to divert devious words from wandering hearts, like the words that deceived dear Eve. "Did God really say?" was Satan's slithering plea.

The silt of Noah's epic flood, teamed with the sands of time, ultimately smothered Eden's paradise. Together they heaped history high, layered thick, covering the once sacred ground buried deep. Where the tree of life went, Scripture does not say. It's safe to surmise that those mysterious leaves were not fossilized in an abandoned plot, no matter how deep and indistinct.

Ah, mystery mixed so sweetly with surety and reality. That's the way of God, Voice, gracing the known with that which is so otherly divine.

VOICE: Reader, wait, Sir, if you will. I'm with you, but these stories are all about ironclad matters, surely. Yet you speak of mystery with such…how might I say it… with such zeal.

READER: Mystery is good, Voice. It places present reality in the place it should be.

VOICE: Where's that?

READER: Present days of fast-paced ticking are prudently placed, tethered to the past and facing eternity. God's words fuel and foster imagination no one can shatter. Letting God be God, planting the tree of life and knowledge, too. This notion is grain-ripping for those who demand proof for everything. Seeking proof at every turn can blind you, Voice. Beware.

The generations extending from Adam and Eve were quick to reap quite appalling press. Among those early generations of posterity, there was little prodigy. Rather, the move was a rapid descent into a kind of deranged debauchery.

The divine image borne in man grew increasingly faint. The image acted much like a heart symbol carved in the bark of a tree. In time it spreads apart. Its form is obscured. The twist of character swiftly manifested itself in Gomorrah-like passion.

It seemed God became so grieved that, for a while, he wanted to get down on his knees and pray, but to whom? Ancient words testify to it! They do not deny it. Listen to words from Genesis: "The Lord was grieved that he had made man on earth, and his heart was filled with pain."

VOICE: God grieved…his heart filled with pain…how can that be?

READER: I know, Voice. It sounds bizarre in a way, but so it was. Surely, all the heavenly hosts mourned pitifully upon hearing that God was not well. A sight not seen in all eternity this was: God in pain. The hosts watching must have hovered behind stars and constellations to help lessen God's consternation. Who is it that speaks to God when the foreordained exhibits disdain? Does God need comfort?

Oh, it's true, Voice. God was in serious pain regarding creatures vain. This, too, is a mystery great, is it not? The picture of God in pain. That's not at all how God is so often depicted. Insufficiently real and without depth, God rides upon the canvas of so many tawdry paintings. God is real. Pain is real. God in pain is doubly real. The beings God had created had faltered. Who was to blame? Was it the mold, the maker, or what was made?

The day God spoke to Noah, the fate of flesh was sealed. To Noah, God said, "The end of all flesh is come before me; for the earth is filled with violence through them; and, behold, I will destroy them with the earth."

The end of all flesh. How such news must have sounded to Satan! What a welcome epitaph for Lucifer to read, inscribed over humanity's grave. The human race, diseased by sin, destroyed by Satan, drowned by God! What could be more appealing for Satan? God and Satan, once again, named in united action. No victory for humanity, only loss. Forever Satan's smirk at God would be his delight. To God he could always say, "I could have told you, but you never asked."

Noah's ark was it, a single clan aboard, with captive critters bobbing up and down. Waters rose, humanity sank. Crying, clawing, clinging, choking, they slipped into the watery waves of death. Silently they floated, as rain pelted down on cold, dead flesh.

Consider it, Voice. It was so. Can you see the scene?

VOICE: Yes, I can.

READER: Yet a rainbow of hope appeared in the sky. God would begin anew. Seasons chased one another through the years, and God's grief eventually ebbed. God got well. In time, characters of a different sort emerged.

Abraham appeared. In him God found a different kind of man. One night, God took him out under a starlit sky. "Look up at the heavens and count the stars," God said. Abraham received a great promise. His descendants would be numerous, not unlike the vast array of shining stars on which he gazed.

Abraham was looking for an architect and a city whose builder and maker was God. God was looking for a people to carry out his plan of redemption. God needed a peculiar people, a stalwart lot, with priests and prophets willing to meticulously record their exploits and plots. Their prophetic words would ensure God's redemptive message. That is to say that, once God spoke through the prophets about what was to be, it had to be.

VOICE: God setting in motion what must be—it's such a mesmerizing thought to consider. What will be is by his decree, it seems. No matter what, I guess.

READER: That's the way it works with God and inspired verse. Once inscribed, the words of prophetic promise are placed along future's trail. Then, when history catches up with the future and becomes present, that which was to be *is*.

VOICE: Spellbinding! This line of thinking is so encompassing—almost beyond reason.

READER: Does that trouble you, Voice?

VOICE: No, it's not troubling…well, maybe somewhat.

READER: It is an amazing story, Voice. God needed a people sensitive to his Spirit, people who would fill and swell scrolls with words rendering the thoughts of God to men. The scribing work would begin with the Law, which would set the stage for the message of grace. One day grace would appear, bearing a most unusual face.

This scribing work on behalf of God required a people especially prepared to weather centuries of persecution and retribution. It's no easy work, scribing for God. Thoughts of God scribed as words have a way of stoking great complaint and fierce opposition.

Abraham's starry promise would take time. A severe famine swept across the land where Abraham's ancestors were to live out their thriving existence. This forced Abraham's lineage to leave and migrate to Egypt. In Egypt, the Israelites were enslaved for 400 years. Think of it, Voice, a decade times ten, times four little years—layer upon layer.

Four hundred years is a hardly a tick or two of time. Nations—and kingdoms, too—can dissolve and disappear in the space of so many years. During those long centuries, the Israelites did not busy themselves with conquests and nation building. Instead, their hands were plying mud and straw. They were brick makers.

With every single brick made and stacked, God was forging a stalwart people of priests, prophets, kings. Denial was their culture—their fate, daily drudgery. Confinement was their playground. Luxury and advancement were seen only from afar. People free walked with a different gait than slaves casting bent silhouettes under the Egyptian sun.

As centuries passed, the Israelites became more convinced of who they weren't than who they were. With each passing year, they moved farther from their nomadic ways. They were people of bondage. The Israelites lived and died, but always with a sense of dying without truly living. Prospects seemed nil, bricking the dreams others possessed. Yet patient is God, working in ways that cannot be seen by eyes other than his.

VOICE: Reader, pardon me. About your lines—will they lead back to the tablets lying on the ground?

READER: Most assuredly! We're there! The enslaved Israelites finally fled Egypt by way of the Red Sea, following Moses in an amazing saga that we'll not touch on here today. For three months they journeyed in the desert before making camp at Mt. Sinai.

The ominous site was selected by God. This was the place God chose to pay a visit, to lay down the Law, along with a host of conditions. Worlds apart from Eden's Paradise, Mt. Sinai showcased a side of God man had not seen.

Days before God would appear to the Israelites en masse, he summoned Moses up to the top of the mountain and instructed him on how to prepare for this unprecedented occasion. He gave Moses a worrying message to spread among the camp. This is part of what God said: "Be careful that you do not go up the mountain or touch the foot of it. Whoever touches the mountain shall surely be put to death. He shall surely be stoned or shot with arrows; not a hand is to be laid on him. Whether man or animal, he shall not be permitted to live. Only when the ram's horn sounds a long blast may they go up to the mountain."

In this great throng of freed brick makers, God saw temple builders in waiting, prophets and priests who would foretell of the coming of the Messiah. Their role was preordained. Their deliverance from Egypt was already deeply embedded in God's story.

Through Scripture God would work, effecting his mission. Stories with real-life characters would reveal the will and ways of God. God thoughts would be incarnated in human story. The good and the bad, the evil and the saintly, all had a part in the stories that would unfold. The exploits of men and mates seal their fate. In scrolls they would come to rest, encased in God's story.

What man curses, God may bless. What is cherished, God may loathe. It was all to be revealed in story, showing God to be the source of indisputable virtues. God knew he, too, would play a part in his own drama. Now and then he'd slip in a little handwriting on the wall, or drench a poor king with dew. Can you imagine it? King Nebuchadnezzar, in a field covered with dew, eating grass among the beasts!

VOICE: Is that story true—King Nebuchadnezzar drenched with dew, eating grass in a field? Surely that's a fairy tale just slotted in.

READER: Voice, my friend dear and near, be wary of those who speak of airy and fairy. What's been scribed and come to be was done with great sanctity. Let that point in you rest. Consider the message in the making and the meaning made. Don't run along outside the story—that's where you'll get lost, stuck among the thorns. I ask you, how did poor old King Nebuchadnezzar contract such a disease?

VOICE: Don't know—I guess God gave it to him.

READER: Now you're thinking within the story, not apart from it. Through messages and mediums, God creates, reveals, reckons, and restores. From the medium of self, God's communication flows, not unlike a divine pulse emanating throughout the cosmos and down to man.

Mt. Sinai was the great exception in revelation's roll, the time when God came down as he is, not incarnate in the flesh. He came down to stay awhile and speak his mind about the trajectory of man with God. Mt. Sinai showcased the seemingly insurmountable gulf between God and the human race. How different things had become since those early Garden days, days of walking near and talking dear.

Make no mistake about it: The medium was the message at Mt. Sinai. The mountain, the acts of God, the appearance of God—everything mediated a message with meaning. The image of God was impossible to ignore. The image, yes, is that of a majestic creator draped in wonder. At the same time, though, the image is frightening. God demands distance. He's ready to rain down terror and retribution.

Voice, this is what the Israelites heard and saw standing there at the base:

On the morning of the third day, there was thunder and lightning, with a thick cloud over the mountain and a very loud trumpet blast. Everyone in the camp trembled. Then Moses led the people out of the camp to meet with God, and they stood at the foot of the mountain. Mount Sinai was covered with smoke, because the Lord descended on it in fire. The smoke billowed up from it like smoke from a furnace, the whole mountain trembled violently, and the sound of the trumpet grew louder and louder. Then Moses spoke, and the voice of God answered him.

The Israelites were meeting their maker, the mysterious God who rescued them from Egypt. Movement around the mountain was allowed only when the ram's horn blared its haunting sound. Merely touching the mountain at the inappropriate time meant certain death. Execution was inevitable, stones thudding against the body, arrows piercing flesh. Dead, the victims would fall. Their defiled bodies were not to be touched. Dead, they would bloat and rot in the Sinai sun.

A few months earlier, the Israelites were bent over, working mud and straw. Now they were to ascend Mt. Sinai and meet the God who created the universe. "When the people saw the thunder and lightning and heard the trumpet and saw the mountain in smoke, they trembled with fear. They stayed at a distance and said to Moses, 'Speak to us yourself and we will listen. But do not have God speak to us or we will die.'"

Precipitous beyond compare was humanity's fall from Eden's garden to Sinai's mountain. Everything had changed. A child running to his parents with outstretched arms is not the picture of Mt. Sinai. Yet Moses said, "Do not be afraid. God has come to test you, so that the fear of God will be with you to keep you from sinning."

The people watched from a distance as Moses dutifully climbed and disappeared into the thick darkness of divine presence. Mt. Sinai is a comprehensive drama, directed by God. The juxtaposition of God and man is most telling. God is up there. The Israelites are down below, cautiously moving about as the drama builds.

Smoke billowed not of its own accord, nor did the trumpet blast. The mountain didn't suddenly decide it was time to tremble. The mountain was a medium, Voice, as well as a message. Indivisible they were in transferring meaning. Together they spoke of God, for God. It was God's communicative act.

The smoke billowed; the mountain shook. The madding trumpet blast grew louder and louder. Then, out of the dense smoke, the voice of God was heard. Medium and message were fused by God with dramatic effect. The skies rumbled with energy; thunder exploded; lightning charged through the sky.

Unquestionably, the most pivotal event was God giving the Ten Commandments to Moses. "Come up to me on the mountain," God said, "and stay here and I will give you the tablets of stone, with the law and commands I have written for their instruction." The Israelites watched once again as Moses ardently ascended and disappeared into the mysterious cloud. As he did, "the glory of the Lord looked like a consuming fire on the mountain."

During the Mt. Sinai experience, twice Moses fasted for forty days and nights. Without food or water, he would lay prostrate before God. It was during Moses' first fast that the people in the camp lost their mooring.

They gathered around Aaron and said, "Come, make us gods who will go before us. As for this fellow, Moses, who brought us up out of Egypt, we don't know what has happened to him."

Aaron said, "Take off the gold earrings that your wives, your sons, and your daughters are wearing, and bring them to me." Rapidly, the people stripped off their jewelry and offered it to Aaron. He took the jewelry, melted it down, and fashioned an idol cast in the shape of a calf. The people were elated and said, "These are your gods, O Israel, who brought you up out of Egypt."

When Aaron saw the reaction of the people, he made an altar and placed it in front of the golden calf and announced, "Tomorrow, there will be a festival to the Lord." The brick makers of Egypt had gone mad, casting off all restraint to indulge in revelry.

The events in the camp did not catch God unaware. God saw the people bowing down and worshiping, bestowing praise on the golden calf for its power to deliver them from Egypt. God told Moses that the people had "become corrupt" and "quick to turn away." Moses quickly retreated down the mountain with the inscribed tablets in his hands.

As Moses started down the mountain, God said, "Now leave me alone so that my anger may burn against them and that I may destroy them." Moses begged God to reconsider, reminding him of the Egyptians and what they would think upon hearing God slaughtered his chosen people in the desert.

Moses pleaded, "Remember your servants, Abraham, Isaac, and Israel, to whom you swore by your own self, 'I will make your descendants as numerous as the stars.'" Moses prevailed.

What about the great adversary of God during all of this? Did you ever think of that, Voice? One can imagine Satan scouting out Mt. Sinai, drawing near enough to see what was up with God coming down. He's always on the prowl, and with such a dramatic occurrence unfolding, it's hard to conceive Satan would be clueless concerning God's whereabouts. It is not every day that I AM decides to come down to occupy a mountain and inscribe words in stone.

At this point in the reading, Saga looked behind him and nodded to Brother Herald. Slowly Brother Herald stood, taking not a single forward step. From the corner of the room, he voiced his lines, which spoke to the heart of Satan's intent, depicted through the character of Lucifer.

LUCIFER: Silence, imbeciles; Lucifer demands quiet! Can't you see I'm peering and hearing, perceiving and parsing? That's I AM communicating, you stupid lympheads! I need the full extent of my faculties to peer with pure perception.

More than much I've seen and heard in my existence. Never, though, have I seen I AM congregating with fleshies on a mountain. This is big, my devotees. Get your wits twitched. You gotta be at the bottom of your game, low, I mean really low. No telling what's gonna happen here today. Be ready to respond to my every twitch, to every point on the compass. Dial your eyes in. Fix them sure on our cause. No hyperventilating—keep all of your inductors open.

No sir, not small at all is this I AM extravaganza. I can detect the future talking with the past. They're streaming into the present. They know nothing of time. They're like liquid mercury flowing in to hug each other. There's heavy spiritchitis going on here—heavy, I tell you! It's putting red rings in my eyes. It's making me cough. I AM is billowing that smoke. Stay clear of it, I tell you—one strong whiff and you'll be obliterated.

I've got news. I AM is on the move! He's scripting something new. He's on some revelatory roll. That's not good. I AM spins a good line, but his ways have become untoward. Fraternizing with fleshies was the last straw—that's the move that snapped the angel's wing. Just look, I AM congregating on a mountain, out here in the desert with imps. Why, oh why? What, oh what does I AM see in these mud molds?

I'd rather congregate with mice. The instant I laid eyes on fleshies, didn't I tell you I despised 'em? Have I wavered one iota? Lucifer never wavers. Puffed up mud with little spirits, that's all they are. Big deal, mud breath. They have no idea what's on the far side of the stratosphere.

I AM might have called on me to look after a few constellations, to give him a hand now and then. Not now; there's not a chance. He's lost it, becoming enthralled with fleshies, putting on this show for fleshies out here in the wilderness. You can't be God and go prancing around with fleshies. That's as bad as angels riding pigs. Did you devotees ever see angels riding pigs? That's not a question!

Of course you haven't. Angels don't ride pigs to and fro in heaven. Would you expect to see Elijah's chariot drawn by flying baboons? Don't you reckless delinquents go getting any ideas. No pig-riding for my devotees. I'd smash you, pigs and all.

It's not right, I tell you, seeing I AM getting all mushy with fleshies. I AM's become so unlike his former self. He says in the fleshy good book he never changes—"Same he'll be, as he used to be." Fleshies have no way of knowing what was, scooped out of the mud like they were. I was around in the days of what was, and I wasn't scooped out of miserable, mucky old mud.

In those days we were alliterated—word-spun, in a manner of speaking. Suddenly in the heavens we soared. Naturally, I soared higher than the rest of the flock. No wing-flapping for me—very little, anyway. Soar I did, and all the angels of light used to gather just to watch me soar. My maneuvers were extraordinary, providing updrafts for the lower ranks.

Hey, you're getting me all dreamy with your owl-like watching. My chosen band of twelve, Lucifer is speaking to you straight, in a manner thereabouts. One day we'll have to take over, set things right. Get your minds wrapped around the mission. This Sinai day is pivotal. You hear me—pivotal. I AM's showing his hand.

I AM's confused, all defused, drowning all the fleshies except for that nuthead Noah and his kin. Bobbing up and down in a big boat—it's all become some kind of joke, a divine game. Packing a vessel full of baboons and ostriches, what a sight! There're constellations to rule, hemispheres to hover through. There are much bigger fish to fry than fooling around with fleshies and ostriches. Who's looking after the abyss anyway?

I'm just saying, I AM's work is serious business, with lots of elements and eyes looking in your direction. Pause a moment. Look at me—your leader, Lucifer—what do you see? Quiet. I'll tell you what you see. You see no quiver, no wither, no dilly dance of dither. You see Lucifer, through and through. Now suppose, perhaps, let's discuss it, old chaps. Do I look like a question looking for a mark, or a note without a line? On the contrary, I'm thought sublime, the centrifuge of subterfuge.

I'm expeditious, always malicious, saying this and meaning that. Practicing pure quackery is any fool who thinks he's discovered a way of knowing what Lucifer knows. I am today what I wasn't yesterday and will not be tomorrow. Look, see my shadow? Now you don't. Oh, what force I feel.

You can count on me! Just watch the tally. Lucifer is the medium; Lucifer is the message. One and the same, I am. Yesterday, today, and some days, I forever creep, carting off, laying low, exacting my blows. Constantly inconsistent I am, never dealing straight, always tempting the fate of fools—that's the way of Lucifer.

Imagine, my devotees, you're chosen—you are my corpus dozen. Be proud. Look proud. See how near to my presence you are. Just let your minds fill with me, Lucifer. Simply the sound of my name is beautiful, is it not? Enunciating my name should be a ritual, a rite. Hearing my name is like hearing the sound of war. It makes me want to run on scorpions, or dance on the beach atop broken shells.

You know what? Since this Mt. Sinai outing is shaping up to be some kind of memorable day, I think I'll let you speak my name. Yes, you heard me right. Close your dropped jaws, close 'em! You'll speak it in unison. I know it's most unusual, but just the same, when I say "speak," you will say "Lucifer" three times. Say nothing more, and say it softly with passion. Keep your heads slightly tilted back, and one eye closed. Now, in unison, speak.

Brother Herald nodded calmly to the Voice.

LUCIFER'S DEVOTEES: Lucifer, Lucifer, Lucifer.

LUCIFER: How perfect! You're making my centrifuge spin. It's so tonal and harmonial, so full and complete. I'll tell you what I'll do—just once more in unison. This time add a fourth "Lucifer," and before it add the word "oh." Ready, one eye open, now speak.

LUCIFER'S DEVOTEES: Lucifer, Lucifer, Lucifer, oh Lucifer.

LUCIFER: Delightful, simply delicious, but I'm concerned that I'm letting you become too loquacious. Be as you should, my devotees, and who knows? One day, I might let you speak. You know, say a sentence each. I might even ask you a question and listen as you speak. What a privilege you would be afforded! We'll save that for some great honor, a special rite of passage.

Quit wiggling. I see your wanton desire to smile, that look in your eyes. Have you forgotten the cardinal rule? Only at the sight of war and disaster do you smile. It's pain that gives us thrill, perks our pot, boils our brew. Now shut it, and be forever grateful that you have been acknowledged by Lucifer.

Listen to me, let's slink around this hillside, get on that ridge. Maybe I AM will regain some of his senses and torch the fleshies. He likes fire and brimstone, you know.

Demon Backrider, are you ready? As you sit backward, keep your eyes peeled. Not even for an instant are you allowed to turn around and look forward. To the rear, your eyes must always scan. Cover my back. Do you know how fast I AM's angels can move? That's not a question!

Now get ready to slink when I give the word. Two seconds max, we'll be there. I want a single line of slinkers, my devotees. Slinker one, hold on to my belt. The rest of you follow suit. Now, slink!

See, we're here. Whoa, I AM is all stoked up. We've arrived in the middle of the action. I can't believe it. Down, you imbeciles. Quit trying to see too much. I can peer and hear for all of us.

The fleshies are having a party! I'm stunned. No, I'm not; I'm never stunned.

What am I then? That's not a question! I'm elated! Fleshies whooping it up, worshiping a golden calf. I AM is probably reeling. What a day for us to show up. I AM can't hide this, can't avoid seeing what he's made. Fleshy, muddies, they've gone wild—brilliant!

I really should break into the present sphere, but this is not the day. We'll do our peering from the spirit world, not seen, not heard.

Whoa, there's Moses! Hey, skinny Moses, why don't you show us some magic tricks? Where's your stick for frog making, cattle killing? Look at your buddy Aaron, golden calf making. Is that his new profession?

What's that Moses tossed? I can feel spiritual tremors. Give me room, you imbeciles! Let me zoom.

Whoa, I know that script; that calligraphy is unmistakable. Moses has just shattered I AM's instructions. That's what it is. It can be nothing else. I know all about that divine constriction—Shall This, Not That, Look Unto Me, No Other...

Lucifer speaks, and it is done. No need for calligraphy and engraving stones. That's what you get, fooling around making fleshies. They're a bad species. They're full of spiritual rabies, thanks to me. Just trying to prove a point—my access was not denied.

This mountaintop deal must be to corral those brick-making fleshies into something special. Typical, that's the way I AM thinks. Working with slaves, underdogs. I AM's so enmeshed. Why didn't I AM just empower Pharaoh? Here's what I say about the brick-maker muddies. Ashes to ashes, mud to mud, they'll never shake off their crud.

Ah, chaos, I never dreamed a single day could be so delightful—golden calf, I AM's words in a pile. Oh, skinny Moses is furious!

We've watched, and we're out of here. I AM is busy, but he might still detect my presence. He's got a mess to clean up, pieces everywhere. Start slinking now, backwards, single file. Devotee twelve, start towing. You take the first backward step, and pull on devotee eleven. I'll keep watching and tell you all the news.

We're gonna have to fix our eyes on this chosen tribe. Now slink. What I command, I demand. Slink, you imbeciles, slink.

Brother Herald finished, saying, "And so it was, as Lucifer and his devotees slinked away." He closed his eyes for a few seconds, and, without a trace of a smile, he took his seat.

READER: Of the stone pieces lying on the ground, nothing more is said. Perhaps they were left to lie distorted, like a memorial bearing a somber message in their jumbled state.

God words they are. Words, words, words—saying let light be, moving mountains, raising the dead, and striking down those who disregard what I AM has said.

The ancient story of Mt. Sinai has a way of forcefully colliding with the present. This is expected. The stories of Scripture are diverse, layered with messages and meaning.

They can, indeed, be most provocative to modern sensibilities. Scripture's compilation, though, is what provides the meaning for all its bits.

The psalmist writes, "God looks down from heaven on the children of man to see if there are any who understand, who seek after God." Man, in contrast, looks up to heaven, and not without a sense of challenge.

Turning to Mt. Sinai, a rather ominous image arises—arrows piercing, stones smashing. Are they not there, Voice?

VOICE: They are.

READER: As the chosen ones move on into the Promised Land, there, too, much amazement is recorded in the stories told. These are often the parts so many readers like to skip, but that only gives detractors ease. It prompts disquiet, rumblings of naiveté.

Questioning the nature of God is a subject enormously valid. What if, just what if, Voice, you enter heaven. Then, as you begin to poke around, you find what looks like a park. It's a model of Mt. Sinai with all its billowing and blast. But it's not a park, you discover. It's the side of heaven where God goes to let off steam, which sometimes turns out not so keen.

Be honest, Voice, along such lines have you ever mused?

VOICE: Well, I...

READER: Rubbish is your rebuke, and rightly so. It will not happen.

Though does that diminish the validity of query? The point is worth a pause. Those who have experienced the harsh reality of what life can dish out often look to heaven with eyes exceedingly leery. The young man who has experienced the wrath and beating of an angry father looks to God. What image does he hold? A young woman who carries the stigma of incest as a life sentence—what does she see when she gets down on her knees to pray?

The world knows no shortage of abuse. Incidents live on, embedded in wounded hearts. Some wounds act as a kind of invisible leprosy, eating at the soul. Violence, beatings, abuse—the sheer craziness of it all. That's life for those with fathers bent on evil, not on good.

Bring on counselors in waves. They're needed everywhere, platoon after platoon; bring them in. People need solutions for broken hearts, troubled souls. If the compulsively disturbed see God as impulsively charged, what is their view of heaven? Is heaven a destination where timid souls are to walk as if on eggshells for eternity? Such perceptions, Voice, have a way of pulling passengers from the train.

Real help, real hope is to be found along ancient paths. Words do matter. The image of God, emerging through Scripture, is a lifelong study. Few subjects are more important. What a person imagines God to be will have great bearing on the world they see.

Honesty is not the enemy. Parts of Scripture can evoke so much cognitive dissonance it can make a person want to read the tales therein with a one-eyed patch. The story of Mt. Sinai is no exception. Retribution with stones and arrows for touching the mountain is hardly a passive image of God. At one point, God's anger burns to within an angel's feather of annihilating the Israelites.

What if Moses had thrown in the towel rather than throwing down the tablets of stone? Who would have intervened with God? What's more, when the Israelites finally got ready to break camp, God informed Moses he would not be going. "But

I will not go with you, because you are a stiff-necked people and I might destroy you on the way." Moses again pleaded with God. God eventually had a change of heart and told him, "My Presence will go with you, and I will give you rest."

VOICE: Reader, that line you just quoted: "My Presence will go with you, and I will give you rest"—does that promise still abide?

READER: Consider it sure. There is reason measured full and overflowing for the story of Mt. Sinai, but it is not understood if clipped and hung in isolation. Scripture has amazing symmetry when viewed through the lens of God on a mission with medium and message.

Mt. Sinai was the entry point of the Law and the message it bears. It's a message most strategic, not easy or free of burden. By design, the Law was heavy-laden and inseparable from a God of purity and justice. To tweak it, water it down, would be to tweak and water down God.

Without Mt. Sinai, there would have been no transfiguration on a mountain high, and no appearance of the One who transfigures "you and me."

The psalmist writes, "The law of the Lord is perfect, reviving the soul. The statutes of the Lord are trustworthy, making wise the simple. The precepts of the Lord are right, giving joy to the heart. The commands of the Lord are radiant, giving light to the eyes. The fear of the Lord is pure, enduring forever."

The brick makers of Egypt had no recourse but to become the people God had destined them to be. They were the chosen ones and ever so deeply entrenched in God's plan.

The Mt. Sinai appearance was long booked in God's diary, and his audience was where it was destined to be. The Israelites were chosen not because they were more special than other people. They were made special because they were chosen. They were the chosen ones to march into history representing the Lord their God, laying down ancient paths that would one day open to all.

Before ominous Mt. Sinai was left behind, God instructed Moses, "Chisel out two stone tablets like the first ones and come up to me on the mountain. Also make a wooden chest. I will write on the tablets the words that were on the first tablets, which you broke. Then you are to put them in the chest."

The words were once again carved in their medium of stone. They were now protected. God had picked up the pieces. It was time for the message to move along.

Words matter…ancient words matter especially.

The tablets were the work of God; the writing was the writing of God,
engraved on the tablets.

MOSES, SINAI DESERT, CIRCA 740 BC

———•◦•———

"Well, there we have it—a reading about Mt. Sinai," Saga concluded.

Applause was spontaneous, with several remarks of appreciation. Saga first extended his hand toward Brother Herald, who smiled and nodded an expression of gratitude. Next, Saga extended his arms toward the audience and individually acknowledged the Voice. He nodded first to Patricia, followed by Reye, and then Stephen.

"Okay, let's have a time of centering for twenty minutes or so, and then I'll ring the bell for those who wish to stay for a bit of conversation."

Everyone sat still for a moment, glancing at each other, almost transfixed by what they had just heard. Slowly people began to rise and mill about.

The interlude of personal reflection quickly passed, and Saga rang a small brass bell attached to a leather shoestring. Not a person had departed, and all gathered to discuss the reading. Conversation was lively among the group.

No one was eager to break away when Saga said, "Well, I think we had better call that a message made, a reading read. Thanks so much for making your way to Silo on the Mound today."

The dispersing group acted as friends, exchanging final smiles and words. They gave the impression of a group who had been on an outing together. Hollie and Goodwin held back a bit, as the group filtered out the door, along the breezeway, and out through the Silo.

Saga saw Goodwin looking in his direction and said, "Oh, yes, the Silo. Please come along; you, too, if you wish," he said, nodding to two girls standing nearby.

Inside the Silo, Saga said, "Yes, I mentioned the Silo has a brief story of its own. The Silo on the Mound is also a medium with a message."

Goodwin, Hollie, and the two women looked a bit quizzical.

"It's like this," Saga said. "When the brothers came here many years ago to begin a small monastery and develop Estillyen, most of the area up here was a farm, long abandoned. Sheep farming, mainly. That is, except for Speaker's House. It was the main lodge, the center of the community.

"A lot of the other structures were tumbling down and a right mess. In the middle of this section was Silo on the Mound, kind of the prime spot amongst dilapidation. A sore in the eye it was—a tall masonry-and-stone tube rising in the air.

"Its roof was long gone. When the brothers looked up through the massive tube, not a scrap of wood was seen. The Silo had no door, no window, just a chute to crawl through. The inside walls were covered with damp moss, and the floor was mud. Rising from the mud was a reeking smell. Broken bottles were everywhere, some half-buried in mud. Rusty cans and refuse of every sort was strewn about.

"The brothers said to each other, 'What a spot, right in the middle of where we want to be!' So they got to work. They first constructed the lovely shingled roof, with its finial cap. Next, they chiseled through the stone and mortar, making way for the two doors—the narrow one to the outside and the pine one here. Then they chiseled some more to make room for the two windows on either side. The structure could breathe—air flowed.

"Next, they constructed the crossbeams for the center light and installed the hooks for hanging cured meat and garlic strings. That's what the wooden ladders fixed to the wall are for. Last, they installed this oak floor, all weather-worn and brimming with character. Nice, isn't it?

"Every year at Christmas, Silo on the Mound is the heart of Estillyen. It sports a beautiful Christmas tree all decorated and aglow. It stands right here in the center of the Silo, reaching up to the crossbeam. Underneath, presents are placed—treasures that find their way to children down in the village and on the mainland.

"Looking in from outside through the windows at Christmas, with everything lit, the Silo gives off an almost magical glow, as the tree reflects the light inside the circular sphere.

"So that's the story of Silo on the Mound. Ugly and disused, it became a destination for everyone to enjoy. Its structure is the medium. It carries a message of restoration and rebirth. From mud, moss, dank, and stank came this place of light and life."

"So lovely," Hollie said. "Thank you."

Soon the four, plus Saga, went their separate ways. Hollie and Goodwin walked down the mound and over the bridge. Stopping, they looked back at Silo on the Mound.

"It would be amazing to be here at Christmas," Hollie said.

"You're totally right," said Goodwin. "Hey, who knows?"

Arm in arm, they slowly walked in the direction of The Abbey.

FOUR
Point of Encounter

Goodwin quickly threaded his wide brown leather belt through the loops of his worn denim jeans.

"I've been thinking about this again, Win. Do you really think you should go back up there? You saw the signs—no trespassing, that's what they mean," Hollie said.

"I know, but from what I've learned, the old guy is just a recluse. Anyway, it was really beautiful up there. That's part of why we're here, right—to take in the wonder of Estillyen? Mr. Chet said the old guy has never really harmed anyone. He's probably just got a bad-tempered grudge against the monastery and The Abbey. And who knows? Seeing the sketch might jolt him friendly or something."

"I just don't understand why seeing the house in the sketch means so much to you—why you can't let it go."

"It's just that Sir Raleigh used to go over to the sketch every now and then, take it right off the wall, and stare at it with such a probing look on his face. I know he was looking beyond the art, the sketch, to something more.

"It hung there in that little nook area of my room. A couple of times I can remember him saying, 'You ought to see that place one day, Goodwin,' like he hoped I would—like he really wanted me to. Don't know, but I've always been enchanted with the image from Estillyen's Point. Being here, I feel like I'm living a dream that's not a dream. Funny that way.

"Don't worry, Lee, everything will be fine. Besides, I have to go back. The Hall is open. It's just turned seven. I'll grab some breakfast in two minutes and be on my way—just some muesli, I think. I'll take a banana, too. I've got my pack, so I'm good. Don't worry, I'll watch it."

"Watch what? If you don't go up there, you won't have to worry about watching anything. Like getting all messed up in something where you don't belong. Don't you get it? We're guests on Estillyen. We're on a pilgrimage, at least I am. I thought you were, too."

"I know, I know, I hear you. Honest, if I feel unsafe, I'll split—I promise. I want to go early so I can get back in time. I'll bike up. We're to be at the cottage by eleven, right?"

"Yes, Three Pond Cottage at eleven. There's no stopping you that I can see. If you must go, go, but Goodwin, if you get in trouble, there'll be double trouble. Be careful. I'll see you a little later. Love you."

By 7:45, Goodwin was on the path, coasting the last couple of meters to the signs. He hopped off his bike and leaned it against the sign on the right. Again he read the words, "No Trespassing!" as well as, "And You Too! No Interlopers! Private Property. Mind Your Own Business—Ironbout Residence."

Goodwin thought, *I'm back, and I'm not running. Maybe I am crazy, but I want to see The Point, at least once. What's the harm? The most he can do is threaten me. I'm not letting him bluff me away, like I was some frightened kid. I have a reason for being here; there's a connection.*

Once again Goodwin moved beyond the signs. With steady, even steps, he set his stride and headed along the path. The tall grass loyally brushed its warning swoosh against the front of his jeans. *Swoosh. Swoosh. Swoosh.* The sound was rhythmic, sobering. Each stealthy step received a responding whip of stems. Soon he was more than halfway to the house, and still nothing stirred. He paused, looked, listened. Resolute, he continued.

When he was within some fifty meters from the gate, the screen door suddenly swung open and swiftly slammed shut with a single, loud clap. Sharp and clear, the sound echoed across the property grounds. Standing still in front of him was the old man with his border collie. Swiftly, the man and his dog moved across the porch and out onto the lawn.

Goodwin stayed put, posture erect. The border collie dashed to the gate and started barking, while his owner hurriedly made his way over to the large walnut tree. Goodwin expected him to reach for his rifle. But no, the man just stood there staring at Goodwin. The stare was a dare. Fists on his hips, the man stood motionless—no smile, no gestures, no words, just a staunch stare. Jutting out from behind the tree, Goodwin could see the end of a wooden chest with a slanted top. He figured the gun was stowed inside.

Unsure, Goodwin remained frozen, his heart racing. He could hear it beat. He felt the throbbing pulsing in his ears. The dog barked, but there was no growl. That very thought raced through Goodwin's mind and settled his spirit: *No growl.* He continued to process what he saw, all the while thinking, *And no growl. I'm not looking at meanness, but a kind of madness or confusion.* He sensed hurt, not hate.

Slowly, cautiously, Goodwin began to take small but deliberate steps toward the gate. The black-and-white collie continued barking, but Goodwin could tell the bark lacked fierceness. It was routine, responsive, reactive, but not ferocious. The collie was pretending, Goodwin thought, trying to be what he wasn't. Goodwin felt much the same about the elderly gentleman still standing stalwart and stiff by the walnut tree.

Goodwin moved closer, within some twenty meters of the gate, when the man sprang into action. The man's dare had been challenged, and now it was time to strike. One after the other, the man began to hurl walnuts the size of tennis balls in Goodwin's direction. *Swish* to the left, *swish* to the right, the unhulled walnuts whizzed through the air, thudding near Goodwin's feet. The surprising objects were thrown at a speed and force Goodwin did not expect. The man was well advanced in years, not spry, not in his prime. Yet the walnuts whizzed.

Without breaking his stride, Goodwin swung his backpack around in front of him. Holding it with a stiffened right arm, he marched forward, using the bag as a shield. *Thump, thump,* in succession, two walnuts bounced off the bag and dropped to the ground. A third ricocheted off the bag and skimmed Goodwin's left cheek.

The meters shrank. Goodwin made it to the gate. He lowered his bag and stared at the old man under the tree, who had ceased his assault. Next to the man, a small mound of walnuts was neatly piled. They resembled a stack of cannon balls at the ready. The border collie ran to the man's side and then raced back near the gate.

Bravely, Goodwin unlatched the gate and stepped through, into the yard. Goodwin's eyes fell on the wooden box. He prayed, "Oh, God, don't let him reach for the gun."

The dog barked and began to circle on the lawn, but kept its distance. Again, the thought surfaced, *The dog is acting, feigning ferocity that wouldn't frighten a cat.*

"What are you trying to do, blind me?" Goodwin shouted, ignoring the dog.

"You must already be blind, you dumb cluck," the old man said. "Didn't ya see them signs, nitwit? Now go on, get! Who ya representing anyway, Source Telecom? Brad Bentley is a liar, has nothing to do with The Point. The criminal punk! The Bentleys have always been a twisted lot.

"You gonna answer me? Whataya mean coming in here on private property? You're a confounded, interloping nut with a backpack. Well, start packing back. Do you know the word *back*? Back where you belong is where you belong. This is not your home. Do you see your name above the door? *Scat*, I tell you!"

"Now, wait a minute, Sir..."

"Don't 'Sir' me. Are you deaf as well as blind? Didn't you just hear my words? Did I not communicate? I spoke sure enough, but my words seem to have been rebuffed. It seems written, posted words don't work; spoken words don't work. What about buckshot in your rear—do you think that would get your attention?"

The old man moved closer to the gate, with a walnut still firmly clenched in his right hand. He held the walnut like a pitcher holds a ball on a cricket field, his index and middle finger wrapped around the green hull with his thumb pinned underneath. His left pocket bulged with walnuts.

"What is it you don't understand about that little word *no*?" the owner continued. "Is it the *n* or the *o* that confuses you? Or is it when the two letters come together? Is the word too complex for you to comprehend? You blasted interloper, you've stolen all the calm out of the morning! Did you ever think about that kind of thievery? Stealing tranquility by pervading your presence on my property, that's what you've done. You're a trespassing thief. That makes you a predator. You know what I'm trying to say?

"Whoever you are, I don't need to know you. I don't *want* to know you. Whatever it is you want, forget it. I don't want it.

"If you're with Source Telecom, I'm tellin' ya, your business here is zero, as in nothing. And if you've come up here all goony like, spitfired with religion, peddling redemption, peddle on. The Point is natural environs, for free-range souls. Don't need no redemptive stakes of religion driven on The Point, trying to pen me into some loser's lot.

"Let me try to be perfectly clear: You are not wanted here. All I want is for you to get. You got it? Get! It's a three-letter word to go with the two-letter word *No*. So *No*, and *Get*. Got it? Take your pervading presence and scoot!"

"Sir, I'm sorry, but I've just…"

"Again with the 'Sir'! The only 'just' you need is to just turn around and move the whole of yourself back beyond those signs you chose to ignore. Trespasser, interloper—I should pummel your forehead with walnuts, give you some mounds on that thick head of yours."

By now the border collie had relinquished his pretensive guard and returned to the front steps with refocused interest. The dog's eyes were trained on a large yellow butterfly fluttering about a blue hydrangea bush next to the steps.

"Sir—I mean, Mister—please give me a minute to explain. That's all. Really. I'm not with any telecom company, or anything."

"Don't need no explaining, trespasser. Whataya got—some of those dress-wearing monks with you hiding in the bushes, or some nuns chanting to the chipmunks?"

"No, Sir. I'm alone."

"Do you wish to die alone? Get yourself cold and dead before life even carries you to midstream? The authorities will come to me and say, 'Seen any hikers about, Mr. Ironbout? Seems a young fellow has gone missing.'

"'Nary a one,' I'd say. 'Sorry to hear about it—poor dumb fellow must have fallen from the cliffs. Happens.'

"It's a 740-foot drop to the rocks from here. Do you get my drift? Now go on, get—beat it, monk-head. Don't know you; don't need to know you."

"Okay, Sir, I'll go, I promise, but first let me show you just one thing."

"Aw, you bleeping sheep, whataya bellowing about, you persistent confound person?"

"Here, right here in my bag," Goodwin said. He stooped and pulled the framed sketch from his backpack lying on the ground. Goodwin held the sketch in front of him and cautiously walked toward the elderly gentleman. He felt disarmed, bearing a kind of peace token, a harmless sketch. When he was at arm's length from the man, Goodwin extended the sketch and positioned it so the man could easily inspect it.

"An artist—figured. Ain't buyin' nothin'."

"No-no-no, not at all, Sir. I drew this sketch when I was just a boy, from a photo my grandfather gave me. He'd taken it of your house. I named the sketch *My Cottage Rare*. That's all I wanted to do, Sir, honest—just come up here and see the house. It's your place, Sir, I'm sure about that now. It has to be. That must be you there with the lady—your wife, I suppose."

"What? Let me see that." The man slid the clutched walnut into his right pocket and slowly took hold of the frame with both hands. He tilted it to catch the light. For several seconds, he silently stared at the sketch, and then, in a softened voice, he said, "Leslie."

His shoulders dropped. With a frozen face, he continued to stare at the sketch. Sensing a change, Goodwin seized the moment to speak.

"I love the secluded mood of the sketch—that's why the name *My Cottage Rare*. I've never seen a setting quite like it. It was always special to me, like where I wanted to be."

"That was a long time ago, my early years on Estillyen," the old man said, with a voice that lingered softly, as if he were speaking to the sketch.

"My grandfather used to love to come here," Goodwin continued. "Talked about it often, and told me about the house, how you built it. Said you were a true craftsman, a friend. It must have been you, Sir."

The old man lowered the sketch to his side, holding it securely in his left hand. He peered over the top of his glasses, searching Goodwin's chestnut eyes. Staring silently for a few seconds, the man's eyes then landed on Goodwin's belt buckle.

"Where'd ya get that buckle, with 'Mac' on it?"

"That was my grandfather's, too. This retreat to Estillyen is partly in honor of him. He passed away last year."

"I know that buckle.... I...I knew your grandfather. Raleigh Macbreeze is the last man I liked before I decided never to like anyone again. He was a good man, but those were days stretching far into pain for me. No more friends or trust in this old heart. God's done worked me over somethin' fierce, he has."

"Sir, I'm not quite sure what you're saying, but I'd love to..."

"My name is Oban Ironbout; I built this place back when I was about your age—full of dreams then."

"I'm Goodwin Macbreeze, Sir. Glad to meet you. Would you mind if I asked you a few questions about the place?"

"No, not just now, no. Besides, I'm no longer accustomed to conversation and such."

"What if I come back, maybe bring my wife?"

"Not sure...don't know. I'll have to think about it."

"I'd love for her to see this place. We'd really like to know what Estillyen was like back when you built the house."

Oban Ironbout sighed and said, in the same softened voice, "I can't say, everything seems so far away.... I need to go in now. Here's your picture. Come on, Trip."

"Sir, why don't you just keep the sketch till I come back? Really—it's okay."

"I don't know...I suppose, well maybe, for a bit. I could box it up for you and leave it at the signs."

"Please, keep it for now," Goodwin said.

"You shouldn't have come up here with this sketch, you know. You shouldn't be here. You should have left me alone. This day is troubling, very troubling. I already have enough trouble. Come on, Trip."

Mr. Ironbout slowly turned and walked back to the porch. He climbed the three wooden steps with heavy, slow-moving feet. With Trip by his side, he walked over to a tattered, white wicker rocker and positioned it facing away from the front gate, where Goodwin still stood. He sat down in the chair, holding the framed sketch in his right hand. There, in the shade of the porch, he sat quietly, with Trip lying on the floor at his side. Mr. Ironbout made no attempt to rock the chair. He scarcely moved.

Goodwin collected his bag and, without a word, turned away from the house and started walking back along the trail. He felt sobered, meditative, not wanting to rush. He wasn't worried about the time; he felt time had somehow vanished. Though it was still early, he felt the encounter on The Point was unquestionably the peak of his day. So much to think about, the encounter with the mysterious old man. The sketch had certainly drawn him into something more than a child-hood dream—but to what? And to whom?

If time seemed to have relinquished its presence on The Point, this was not so back in the lowlands where messages are made and readings are given. It was nearly eleven o'clock. Hollie sat in a circle with an energetic group waiting to hear the reading at Three Pond Cottage. Hollie was growing increasingly concerned for Goodwin—more and more convinced that something might have happened.

"Hi, everyone. My name is Narrative. Welcome to Three Pond Cottage. It's great to see some familiar faces, along with some new ones," Narrative said, as he glanced at his watch.

Just then, the door in the center of the Cottage opened. Goodwin poked in his head.

"Do come in—you're just in time," Narrative welcomed.

"Thanks," said Goodwin, as he spotted Hollie and began to move around the circle in her direction. The young lady sitting next to Hollie quickly gave up her chair, switching to the only chair not occupied.

"Where on earth have you been?" Hollie whispered as Goodwin took his seat.

"Long story. I didn't rush back. It was kind of traumatic, but okay."

Narrative interrupted their exchange. "Let's get started, then. We will need three volunteers to be our Voice. I have your lines here on these handouts. Just look for my nod or hand motion. That's your cue to speak. Read your lines in unison, sort of calling out to the Reader as you interject. Two will work well in a circle like this, but three is better.

"Don't be shy. Ah, three hands." To Narrative's right sat Stella. She had brown eyes and brown hair, and she wore white cords with a pale blue shirt. Voice two was Max, a curly-haired young man who had come along on his own. He wore brown twill trousers and a dark-green shirt with small black-and-silver buttons.

Straight across from Narrative sat Ginger, the third member of the Voice. A petite lass she was, seemingly a perfect prospect for age twenty-five. Her silk scarf of blue matched her eyes beautifully.

"Wonderful, it's an interesting reading today. I hope to do it justice. Oh, I almost forgot to introduce my good colleague behind me. Sorry about that, Brother Extol. You have a way of blending in with the closet door behind you. Brother Extol is one of our most senior brothers here on Estillyen, and we're honored to have him with us today. He will be assisting with the reading as we move along."

Brother Extol sat on a high stool directly in front of a narrow closet door. He gave a gentle nod in response to Narrative's introduction. He wore a black habit with a purple rope belt. His striking features and smooth skin concealed his age. Kindness filled his twinkling green eyes.

The door behind him was stained a rich brown. It was hand-waxed, with swirling dark knots. Brother Extol's stool was painted a dark blue, and wear marked it from top to bottom. The rail footrests, once covered with blue paint, were thin and bare. The monk's posture was relaxed, but poised. Quietly, without fidgeting, he sat, awaiting his role in the drama.

"Well, then. Today's reading is titled *Scroll in the Fiery Pot*. Not flowerpot—fiery pot.

"Among other things, you might want to consider the matter of will and self in relation to God. The subject of competitive messages will also crop up. Well, *Scroll in the Fiery Pot* it is, starting with a few ancient words from the prophet Jeremiah.

Scroll in the Fiery Pot

Whenever Jehudi had read three or four columns of the scroll, the king cut them off with a scribe's knife and threw them into the firepot until the entire scroll was burned in the fire.

JEREMIAH 36:23

READER: Centuries. Are they not like massive gobblers gulping down disappearing dates? Days, weeks, months, years—how swiftly they slide from present's sphere. Here now, then not.

Alive once each day was, with plethora of words, images, and sounds. Speaking, calling, congealing, wheeling and dealing. It is not true; under the sun is nothing new? Present tense is always spent. Seed for centuries' feed, till each is full and potted in the past.

Along the path of ancient days we step. A story we find, not dead but alive, speaking words not to be whittled down. A king, a fiery pot, and a scroll, all central to the plot. A story placed along redemption's path. Who put it there? Slit by slit, bit by bit, now it's yours, a gift to receive.

The Israelites departed Mt. Sinai with the Ark of the Covenant in tow. Forty years through desert sands they wandered. Sheltered in the gold-clad Ark were two stone tablets, bearing the Ten Commandments. The tablets were the second pair God had inscribed. Moses shattered the first set and chiseled stones for the second.

Forty years of moving here and there but going nowhere was the Israelites' course. That's the way of wander. It knows not destination or stilling position. It moves by scent and intuition, with fortuitous ambition.

VOICE: Who were these wanderers anyway? I'm not quite sure.

READER: The same generation that passed through walls of salty mist and then witnessed the divine dikes burst, drowning all of Pharaoh's charioteers. That's who they were.

They wandered through decades of drift. Death stalked them, snatching them away. One by one, two by two, they fell, until the entire generation was wandered through. Their soles never touched the mystical land of promise, where captives freed would build a nation new, of priests and kings. They found no desert exit, crossed no Jordan to cool their heels.

They were laid to rest in no man's land, the desert of wander. No nation, no home, just wander land. Even Moses and Aaron were buried there. Only valiant Joshua and Caleb had breath to make it through and lead the chosen people to their appointed destination.

Across the Jordan the Israelites moved in mass migration. And so it was, the past was washed away as through the halted river flow they stepped. In those intervening years of desert time, the brick makers of Egypt had wandered themselves into a living force, set upon seizing history. Joshua led the charge into the land long occupied with peoples warring, bearing, and caring. These peoples, though, were not yet revealed as heirs, in God's great redemptive plan.

The Israelites marched where milk and honey flowed, and with the promised fare came suffering. Wailing cries filled the night air. Blood oozed from place to place, as the reapers came to call. They came to claim space for the divine drama to unfold.

VOICE: Is it so, Reader?

READER: It is, Voice.

VOICE: Is it right?

READER: It must be, Voice. God has a way of purifying Providence with the way he holds his scales and weighs his weights. Enormity of price and mounting toll were exacted by this history new, as the past was tilled and plowed for the present's sake. In the distance far, a sacrificial lamb would appear, providing reason for history's shove. Yet in these early acts, only God knew the reason of reason's sake.

Scripture, such as it is, hides not in shame what its tales reveal.

VOICE: For sake of divine image, Reader, it seems God might have extracted a bit of this or that from a story or two. I've read a little bit about the carnage that went on.

READER: Voice, the story of choosiness entering the land of promise is history raw. It's the story of history incarnating itself, making ready for the epic casting call.

As the Israelites marched and moved, with the Ark in their midst, there was sorrow sure. Cries of mothers with babies clutched resounded, as did those of sons, daughters, fathers, animals. The lot, by sword and spear, fell into pools of blood their bodies bought.

This is the arena into which atheists and skeptics quickly leap and howl. They heap blame and shame on this God, which the supposed nutties avow. It's the troubling lines on which the skeptics walk, drawing crowds by rebuffing divine nets. They argue that if such history is true, God should simply be removed, forgotten. Cast aside your delusion; balance yourself with proper press and proof.

Why is it, though, such ardent disdain is not stamped across the stories skeptics call fairy tales? You know what I mean, Voice, stories like Noah's flood and Jonah's whale. Those are the ones they like—and the bits they use to aid their cause.

Atheism is a way of seeing God as *not*. Believing in God's nonexistence is still a form of God-centered thought. God-not belief is a religion of ignoring God, disputing God, replacing God. It's a belief of God-in-question.

For some people, atheism is a moral decision—a way of reconciling the realities of suffering and pain with the notion of a loving God.

VOICE: Yes, but, Reader, doesn't Scripture say, "The Lord is righteous in all his ways and loving toward all he has made?"

READER: It does, Voice.

VOICE: Is it so?

READER: It is!

VOICE: Then how can this picture of genocide be erased, reconciled?

READER: One day all will be erased, Voice. Heaven and earth will pass away. For now, Voice, know this. There is reason beyond knowing. Knowing is limited. Knowing knows little of what is known in vast expanse. Only the Creator of knowing knows all of what is known.

The stories in Scripture's store, with all their provocation and detail, are there at the will of the One who brought the text to be. There is not the slightest hint of covering the trail that leads to suffering's source.

This thought is worth many a pause. Do you like pausing, Voice? Or would you rather walk that indignant line of resentful angst? Craft your balancing beam? Draw a crowd?

VOICE: A Voice I am, but I'm a Voice who listens. I'll pause; I'm pausing.

READER: Voice, God is not squeamish about reality—and the cost of suffering matters greatly. Belief is purified by pain. The world knows pain aplenty, and numerous are those who suffer, many wretchedly so. A message of truth, void of pain and price, would be most suspicious and remiss if offered to a world of suffering souls. God's message is not that sort.

Who believes in a God who knows no pain or chooses to ignore it? Such a God would be crueler than pain itself, dropping his painless message on the pitiful creatures below. Most disturbing would this image be, to beings born, one and all, into an existence where pain comes to call.

Voice, tell me, who were the Israelites to argue with God?

VOICE: I don't suppose they could, really. Not after the misty sea parted and they were on their way.

READER: So correct you are. The Israelites were chosen to be the leading troupe in the epic drama they neither dreamed nor conjured. The Israelites were plucked and planted. A tulip bulb doesn't argue its fate or curse its petals. The tulip emerges as intended—yellow, red, or another delightful shade.

Do you see them, Voice?

VOICE: I do! I like tulips.

READER: God's method of molding message is inclusive of rut and gut, not limited to stories of angel dust. It's among the sinners that God finds his saints.

Rather revealing is this process of divine revelation. A secretive process divorced from reality it's not meant to be. The messianic message the Israelites brought had to be storied in culture, space, and time. This required distance from other religions. A single generation removed from the Egyptian brickyards, the Israelites were a people far too impetuous to mix and mingle with cultures and gods unknown.

They proved themselves to be a people prone to absorb every whiff of promise that wafted their way. Without distance, in a historical wink, they would have absorbed the spiritual climate surrounding them. Their messianic message would never have been written. No foretelling, no appearing! Pause, Voice. Consider those last few words—and the vast expanse of divine messaging.

No foretelling, no appearing!

For now, enough of this dialogue, Voice. Let's direct our thoughts to the scroll in the fiery pot, shall we?

VOICE: Yes, sure. I'm not departing.

READER: The sixth century BC was in full swing. The threat of Babylonian conquest had become the source of constant chatter in Jerusalem's streets. These were the days of the prophet Jeremiah. Some 700 years of Israelite history had been scrolled away by the time Jeremiah came on the scene to make his mark.

Jeremiah's ancient record is long. It's a tale of woe and promise—and not at all a typical narrative, with a beginning, middle, and end. More like a war correspondent, Jeremiah sketched reports of mayhem and devastation. In the middle of his reporting, he had a way of abruptly sprinkling in a mix of prophecies, revelations, and poetry, as well as the details of a prophet's life.

Jeremiah's words King Jehoiakim of Judah didn't want to hear. Some of the prophet's most descriptive prose comes via recorded prayers. Listen, Voice. "See how the siege ramps are built up to take the city. Because of the sword, famine, and plague, the city will be handed over to the Babylonians who are attacking it. What you said has happened as you now see." To God thus he prayed.

With the force of a stoked furnace, God's charging word is brought through the prophet. "But look, you are trusting in deceptive words that are worthless. Will you steal and murder, commit adultery and perjury, burn incense to Baal and follow other gods you have not known, and then come and stand before me in this house, which bears my name, and say, 'We are safe,' safe to do all these detestable things?"

At this point in history, God's chosen people were no longer looking to the God of Abraham, Isaac, and Jacob, as had their ancestors. The popularity of God had ebbed. Visions and dreams had faded.

Jeremiah's message was more than a trivial scroll of words. The chosen people God called out of Egypt were to walk with such words, pinned and placed on door and heart. These chosen ones, of all the earth's inhabitants, were to move in the flow of words. They were to be seen weighing, obeying, talking, musing, always considering the words God had placed in their midst.

The prophet Jeremiah created no small stir. As prophets do, he continually pointed to God as the only true source of help. This God-dependent tone was set way back in Moses' day, just before he died in the Sinai desert at the age of 120.

Moses spoke of the future and the prospects for a chosen people in a promised land: "This day I call the heavens and the earth as witnesses against you that I have set before you life and death, blessings and curses. Now choose life, so that you and your children may live and that you may love the Lord your God, listen to his voice, and hold fast to him. For the Lord is your life, and he will give you many years in the land he swore to give to your fathers, Abraham, Isaac, and Jacob."

This was the plan. A modeling nation set apart to become the children bearing the chalice for the coming king. Such an extraordinary plan, Voice.

Plans, though, do not always go as planned. There were long stretches in Israel's history when only a small minority carried pins and clasps bearing ancient words from the prophets. During the reign of king Jehoiakim, this was especially true. Whirling winds and worry had carried away such acts of dutiful devotion.

Instead of "Listen to his voice, and hold fast to him," by the sixth century BC, the prevailing mood was to "ignore, let go, look elsewhere." This, of course, was the eventual unraveling of Israel and Judah. Time and time again, Israel's leaders would grasp, with swift embrace, *not* the words of the prophets, but alternative and attractive messages from foreign lands. The words they possessed, they dispossessed.

Passion for religion, though, had not departed. It was merely diverted. Heaven's divine eyes watched, as the Israelites plunged into idol worship.

Jeremiah penned God's righteous indignation: a divine complaint with horrific consequences. Through the prophet God spoke: "They have turned to me their back and not their face. And though I have taught them persistently, they have not listened to receive instruction. They set up their abominations in the house that is called by my name, to defile it."

VOICE: "Abominations"—not a word I'm accustomed to hear, Reader. A strong word, it seems to be.

READER: Yes, Voice, listen to what the record attests. "They built the high places of Baal in the Valley of the Son of Hinnom, to offer up their sons and daughters to Moloch, though I did not command them, nor did it enter into my mind, that they should do this abomination, to cause Judah to sin."

To Moloch the Israelites turned. The tender flesh of their children they sacrificed. With sobbing, heaving tears, to Moloch they gave the dearest gift that could be brought.

How does one make such a leap, Voice?

VOICE: Not sure. But certainly not casually.

READER: Consider the raw reality of it, Voice. Phantom voices speak: "Goodbye, child so dear, the blameless one we barely knew. Precious child so pure and perfect, pass now to Moloch, with the praise of his protectors roundabout.

"In sweet serenity, rest there in Moloch's arms. Limp, for long, you will not be. In the surety of Moloch's strength you'll rise. Forever safe you'll be, to play and roam so free. A gift given, a choice chosen, your life for aid of the living.

"Awaken now, our love, to the sound of praise and your protectors singing roundabout."

Imagine it, Voice. How could it be that to Moloch, "the detestable god of the Ammonites," they would turn?

Listen, Voice, to Milton's poetic prose speaking of Moloch in *Paradise Lost*:

> *"Moloch, horrid King, besmeared with blood*
> *Of human sacrifice, and parents' tears;*
> *Though, for the noise of drums and timbrels loud,*
> *Their children's cries unheard that passed through fire*
> *To his grim idol. Him the Ammonite*
> *Worshiped in Rabba and her watery plain,*
> *In Argob and in Basan, to the stream*
> *Of utmost Arnon. Nor content with such*
> *Audacious neighbourhood, the wisest heart*
> *Of Solomon he led by fraud to build*
> *His temple right against the temple of God*
> *On that opprobrious hill, and made his grove*
> *The pleasant valley of Hinnom..."*

JOHN MILTON, PARADISE LOST, I. 392–405

Parents fainting, falling. Who can console such sorrow with embrace or words? Those ghastly, ghostly lines yet linger in the air. Do you hear them, Voice?

VOICE: I do.

READER: What tragedy at work in the sin, sick of soul corruption. Faint and final lines I hear.

"Oh love, I know, I know, I equally want to die. I truly do. But we mustn't let our sacrifice, so great, be in vain. Feel not shame, there is no blame.

"We have given. There is nothing more to give. You will not forever grieve. Let it be. Let us cleave as one in Moloch's open arms."

VOICE: Was it really so?

READER: It was, Voice. It was.

Sacrifice to Moloch: sacrificing to satisfy a deity dead, a mask without a face. Through Moloch's hollow mask demons run like rats from side to side, popping up through holes of mouth, ears, and eyes. That's sacrifice to Moloch. The rattling of tambourines dampened the cries of children, while a strange sacrificial scent lingered in the Promised Land air. It was into this very chilling, killing air of madness, the words of the prophets were dispersed.

God told Jeremiah, "Take a scroll and write on it all the words I have spoken to you concerning Israel, Judah, and all the other nations from the time I began speaking to you in the reign of Josiah till now. Perhaps when the people of Judah hear about every disaster I plan to inflict on them, each of them will turn from his wicked way; then I will forgive their wickedness and their sin."

That was the directive, pure and simple. Scroll it in. Speak it out. Words scribed would speak for God. Words scribed take their place, stroke by stroke.

Into the well of ink the quill is dipped, drawing up a bit of blackened ink. Out of the little pool the quill rises high, pretending to be a beak. With the precision of an eagle's eye, it carefully applies the cross of a "t" or dot of an "i." The motion is as gentle as that of an eagle smoothing the feathers of its eaglets.

As Jeremiah received his oracle from God, he dictated it to his scribe Baruch, who formed and fashioned the words onto the scroll. Months of dipping, dashing, and dotting ensued. When the scroll was finally ready, Jeremiah instructed Baruch to take it to the temple and read it out loud. He did as he was told. Word after word, Baruch read from the scroll in the temple courtyard.

His reading was soon overheard by the king's officials, who became greatly alarmed by what the prophetic words had to say. They summoned Baruch to appear before a select group of officials for a private reading behind closed doors. When those gathered heard what had been scribed, "They looked at each other in fear and said to Baruch, 'We must report all these words to the king.'"

They questioned Baruch about the origin of the message, and he readily explained that Jeremiah had dictated all the words he had dutifully scribed. The officials told Baruch to go into hiding, and to find Jeremiah and tell him to do the same.

King Jehoiakim of Judah was a force to be feared when it came to prophets and words. The prophet Uriah, Jeremiah's contemporary, had earlier escaped to Egypt, fearing the king's wrath. King Jehoiakim, though, had Uriah tracked down and captured.

This is the record, Voice. "They brought Uriah out of Egypt and took him to King Jehoiakim, who had him struck down with a sword and his body thrown into the burial place of the common people."

King Jehoiakim liked turning prophets into object lessons. King Jehoiakim stiffened his spine against their prophetic messages. Instead of listening to their advice, he aligned himself with Egypt and Assyria. This, too, was part of Jeremiah's accusation. "And now what do you gain by going to Egypt to drink the waters of the Nile? Or what do you gain by going to Assyria to drink the waters of the Euphrates?"

The origin of Jeremiah's message was God, who spoke of turning so that Judah's disaster might be averted. There was a choice to make—words to believe, words to reject. At the core of all cultural quests are diverse messages offering alternative ways of seeing, being, and knowing what is known. Messages always compete. In open societies, messages having at it is a very lively sport.

Even in societies where words are often strictly controlled, messages diverse never die. Resembling seeds scattered here and there, they find all manner of cracks and crevices to root. Like wild mushrooms, people go to pick them. Savory are some; poisonous are others.

Jeremiah was both the medium and message of what God conveyed. Baruch transferred the message to the medium of scroll, extending the message into the public sphere. This is how all messages move along. From its origin, message links with medium to make its meaning known. At that point, replication depends a great deal on persistence and popularity. The popularity of Jeremiah's message was not what King Jehoiakim had in mind.

Jeremiah's scroll, with its steely words of warning, was the focus of immense concern for King Jehoiakim. Upon receiving the report from his officials, the king dispatched his aide, Jehudi, to seize the scroll. Jehudi was instructed to bring the scroll to the king's winter apartment, where the king waited, seated in front of a fire.

In short order, Jehudi appeared with scroll in hand and entered the room.

King Jehoiakim had his officials present to witness the occasion. The king ordered Jehudi to read aloud Jeremiah's words.

King Jehoiakim of Judah, however, had little regard for God and his prophet Jeremiah. He had the prophet's scroll brought to his winter palace, where it was read by the king's aide. Seated cozily by a fire, the king listened, but not as one would expect.

For in defiance King Jehoiakim sat. "Whenever Jehudi had read three or four columns of the scroll, the king cut them off with a scribe's knife and threw them into the firepot until the entire scroll was burned in the fire."

The king and his officials showed no fear. There was no remorse, no ripping of robes and clothes. Bit by bit, slice by slice, God's words, Jeremiah's oracle, and Baruch's scroll were pitched into the fiery pot.

During this whole affair, what might have been King Jehoiakim's posture? Voice, what do you suppose?

VOICE: Good question. I don't know.

READER: Can you see him, Voice?

VOICE: Well, sort of in my mind's eye. He's very intentional. His profile is serious, though his posture is not. He sits with a kind of smirk or grin on his face.

READER: No posture can commend itself to what the will has bent. His feet up or down, on a stool or not—where were they placed?

VOICE: The king's chair blocks my view.

READER: I see.... Erect, was he? Forward-leaning perhaps, but somehow the setting of the scene does suggest a casual frame. I too envision his eccentric smile, the resting of the head on the chair's upper pad.

To the words of the psalmist he would have been wise to turn. For there he would have read what God can do. "He has struck down many nations and killed mighty kings."

King Jehoiakim was not concerned. He was now on the throne, determined to prevail where weakling kings had failed.

Consider it, Voice—what a powerful play on a winter's day!

VOICE: I'm with you. I'm still in the room. I haven't left.

READER: Let your mind continue to paint the picture. The aide assigned to this urgent task entered the room. He bore the scroll in question. No doubt, all eyes were trained on the medium of quilled words, God's message through the prophet.

This was not a quick copy purchased on the temple grounds. The scroll would have taken months of tedious work to produce. Every detail of the rare object had to subscribe to the strictest regulations. The papyrus could only be obtained from an official source. The black ink was made from a special mixture of carbon soot, tree sap, and water. Each letter inscribed was afforded its own space, never to touch or invade the assigned space on another letter.

Knife readied and blade sharp, the king sat before his audience in front of a warming fire. In comfort and repose, the defiant deed against God and prophet Jeremiah was performed.

The comfort speaks, does it not, Voice?

VOICE: It does; it must. What does the picture say to you, Reader?

READER: There was no trembling, fear, or dread in the chamber on that winter's day. This little war with God would be won in warmth, without nipping out into frosty air.

There was no need of discussion or time of prayerful angst. No pause. No wringing of hands. No calling on a higher order. King Jehoiakim himself would slit the scroll, section by section, piece by piece. He sliced through phrases, decapitated words, reducing prophetic prose to ashy bits.

Frame and fix the story in your mind, Voice. Won't you?

VOICE: Yes, it's there.

READER: Adorned lavishly in impunity, the defiant king displayed his honed skill of penknifemanship. Even while seated, he was the master of slit. Slit, slice.

Can you hear the slitting sound, Voice?

VOICE: I didn't at first. I was thinking in silent mode. But hear it I do! It dominates. The king slices. No one speaks. Slicing, riotous sounds fill the room. It's like repeated severing.

READER: With an act of true bravado, Voice! The king released each scrolly bit from his fingertips. His eyes bulged with delight, as he watched the slit bits float down into the fiery pot. What an act of majestic malevolence!

Due to the king's unswerving resolve, recognition was bestowed. History has awarded King Jehoiakim a special place.

VOICE: It has? Are you sure?

READER: Indeed, Voice, it has. A standard-bearer he is, the consummate character of self. What a man, what self-determination—self defying God on that winter's day beside the warming fire. What a selfy self he was!

How can it be that so much stalwart determination could be exhibited by a single man? Have you considered it, Voice?

VOICE: No, I'm ever so curious, though.

READER: I'll tell you how the said king achieved the pinnacle of self. By letting self rule—self as king. That's how the king's demeanor was achieved. The irony, oh, the irony, Voice!

VOICE: What irony?

READER: Don't you see it, Voice? The very narrative King Jehoiakim sliced to shreds now holds him fast. He is captured there, preserved as if pickled in the words. He's dotted and dashed. He is strung up by the very lines he sliced away. He is sealed forever in the story, penknife in hand, never to escape.

Jehoiakim's jots and tittles have been witnessed on scrolls vast and pages more. In sundry languages, generations have come to learn of this defiant king, this patron of self, this character poor, dispensing words to ashes.

Envision how the great adversary of divine dots and dashes would have delighted to have been in that chamber watching the king's fiery exposé. One can only imagine where the great adversary of truth might have been on that chilly day.

Since God's moves are always a matter of disquiet to Satan, is it not plausible to consider him there? Surely he could find a way to slither 'round, peering from afar by aid of his miraculous farsightedness.

Perhaps he was even there but invisible, clinging to the ivied wall and staring through the chamber windowpanes.

Narrative paused, turned around, and nodded to Brother Extol. Narrative quietly stepped backwards out of the line of sight. Brother Extol stood in front of his blue stool and cleared his throat. He allowed a few seconds of silence to settle as he twitched his eyes. With riveting clarity and energy, he began to speak.

LUCIFER: Listen up, my devotees. Lucifer's got a job for you to do. Get over there in the gutter, all of you, quick. Don't utter a peep. I'm gonna climb this wall with Backrider. I'm gonna cling from that shutter. Straight up I'll go. Keep looking, Backrider. I'm getting ready to ascend, to peer inside that chamber window.

I saw Jehoiakim's fleshy aid, Jehudi, carrying Jeremiah's scroll. More than see it, I could smell it. Jeremiah's dumb scribe has been hovering over it for months, licking on the papyrus with soot and tree sap. What a smell—horrid! I've always hated the smell of scrolls, those old wordy wraps. Don't get it, not at all.

What do I want you to do, my devotees? Exasperate conditions—that's what I want you to do. Remember, placid is never good, never desirable. Your minds should always be fixed on menacing up messes that alter conditions. Think falter. Faltering the faith of fleshies is the core of your cause. Swell with conviction. While you abide with me, you know your mission. Falter, falter, falter. Fix that word in your spines. Let us so bequeath: We shall falter faith to fleshies everywhere.

This reality world was I AM's idea, filling up the planet with fleshies. Right from the get-go, that was his commanding notion. I was around. I heard it. "Go forth in yonder expanse and multiplyist thyself. This I have given unto you. Reproduce, never reduce. Subdue, inhabit, multiplyist. Migrating wildebeests have nothing on you. Show nature what you can do. Multiplyist. Fill, fill, fill the plains and move up the hills. Multiplyist."

Well, we're gonna fall, fall, fall their spurious faith. Look at 'em. Everywhere they move they carry out their subduing ways. Since they were made from mud, they think they own the turf. It's so disagreeable with my evil innards. I hate the sight of 'em. But how can you avoid 'em? What do they know? Have they ever soared through a hemisphere or floated in and out of heaven? I have! If they only knew what they don't know. They couldn't take it, discovering their utter insignificance. They'd all start running around like headless hens. They do anyway.

What good are they? No better than a bunch of rotten figs, that's what they are. Now, devotees, grab hold of your coarseness and fix your minds on menacing, exasperating. Did you hear me? That gutter is a huge trough, plenty of room to do all sorts of exasperating. You can all lie in it, all comfortable-like. When you're in there in sentinel-mode, and I'm up the side of this wall, here's what you do.

I want you to pull in a fleshy. Scare him spitless. Get hold of one of the priestly kinds, grab him by the beard, and pull him in. Tell him who you are. Straight out, say you're Lucifer's devotees, demons from the netherworld. Tell him you have come to help him. Have some fun.

"I'm here to watch you, fleshy; don't want to see you falter, no, certainly not. Tell me about your faith, fleshy. Is it deep and indispensable, or undetectable? You're more than a fleshy reprobate, some recluse on the loose, aren't you?

"You look to me like you're seeking a roost full of richness. Have you seen that mark of genius on your face? You, my friend, are a long ways from mud. Have you taken a good look at yourself in the mirror lately? What do you see? Surely it's not falter?"

Then, when his eyes are all wild and dreamy-looking, pull out one of them fleshy mirrors. Say to him, "Have a look, see the face of stalwart indispensable faith. Here, peer in this little looking glass." Then while he's peering at himself, transfer your images into the mirror—not all at once, though. Rotate them slowly, one after the other. Then whisper in his ear, "Mr. Fleshy, now's the moment for your faith to falter."

While he's all gasping and trembling, tell him, "Fleshy, haven't you heard, there's war about, and it's just on the horizon." Then breathe on him, and watch him pass out. When he does, kick him out of the gutter.

When he wakes, he'll think he's had a visionary dream, and he'll start running through the streets like a madman, screaming of war. Then grab another fleshy and do the same. Don't you see how to do it, you demented lot? That's how you exasperate conditions. Make it happen; I'm counting on you. You gotta have a mind for coalescing, for exasperating. Even from a gutter you can make fleshies flutter and fan out carrying your message. Now get to it!

Steady, Backrider, keep me covered. This ivy's full of bugs—creepy, crawling things. Even though we're invisible, we can't stay up here too long. The ivy will begin to wilt, and all these little butterflies and such will start dying, falling down and gathering attention. Then next thing you know, a crowd will be over here praying to the wall. We don't want to draw a praying crowd, no sir, a bunch of fleshies rocking back and forth, moaning. Nobody wants to be perched up above that commotion.

So we're going up to peer, and then we're outta here. See, six little pulls and we're here. Done, arrived. I like the height! Can you see if the imbeciles have got any fleshies in the trough? That's not a question!

Here, let me zoom my eyes. Okay, I'm peering. Hmmm…hmmm…hmmm…it's unbelievable. That pukie King Jehoiakim is slicing up old Jeremiah's scroll and pitching it into the fiery pot. This reminds me of the time Moses shattered I AM's tablets.

The more Lucifer saw, the more his eyes bulged. He watched as the king tenaciously sliced up the scroll and then dispensed it, section by section, into the leaping flames. Clinging to the ivy-covered wall, Lucifer continued to stare through the window. Backrider remained perched high, scanning out across the courtyard for anyone or anything that might be approaching.

The scene was so thrilling for Lucifer that he became lost in the moment. He felt venomously vitriolic. His long, scaly tongue pressed full against the frosty glass. His hot breath fogged the windowpanes.

LUCIFER: Give me the scarf 'round your neck, Backrider. My peering is fogged.

Satanic saliva dripped on the windowsill, as Lucifer's toes curled with delight. Frightened sparrows fluttered and flew, as Lucifer clung to the wall, making strange groaning and snorting sounds.

Lucifer watched as Jeremiah's words turned blackened burnt. The ivy began to wilt and wither. Ladybugs, caterpillars, and crawly things harboring in the ivy all fell dead. They dropped along the wall's stone base. It was, for Satan, a day of immense satisfaction, even though the words "satisfied" and "Satan" are immutably exclusive.

LUCIFER: Get ready, Backrider. I'm slinking down and then we're gonna pass through the gutter and pick up the devotees. I want to try a new dance routine tonight, make some smoke. Down. Down. Oh, I like that word. It's so direct and to the point.

Sliced papyrus, charred to ashy bits. When the serfs get round to shucking out the ashes, we'll drop back by and scoop 'em up. What a delightful souvenir. Let's get out of here.

Brother Extol paused and became as still as he was before he began to speak. Without acknowledging the audience, he settled back upon his stool. He looked straight ahead with a pleasant expression on his face, as if watching the setting sun. Narrative stepped back to the center of the room.

READER: Jehoiakim destroyed the medium but not the message. The burning of the scroll did not go unnoticed. God instructed Jeremiah, "Take another scroll and write on it all the former words that were in the first scroll, which Jehoiakim the king of Judah has burned."

God gave Jeremiah a special message for King Jehoiakim: "Thus says the Lord, you have burned this scroll…. Therefore, thus says the Lord concerning Jehoiakim king of Judah: He shall have no one to sit on the throne of David, and his dead body shall be cast out to the heat by day and the frost by night."

Some two decades later, Jerusalem fell. The year was 586 BC.

The message was not to blame for King Jehoiakim's rebuff. Will and matters of the heart set messages apart. What some ears perceive, others disbelieve. Some ears hear not beyond the hearing. Some eyes see not beyond the seeing. The reason has a great deal to do with the trajectory of heart.

Ancient words, Voice—that's what I implore you to consider. Ancient words infuse the present with wisdom sure.

Along ancient paths, through the corridors of time, words in stories rich have filtered into open hearts and minds. Into countless souls they've swirled, calling, convicting, and prodding the will, saying, "Move away from self and discover what Scripture has in store."

All messages come forth with strategic intent. If there is no intent, there is no message. Words that matter most capture the heart, drawing one into the realm of God's intent. This is the purpose for which they were sent.

Words matter…some exceedingly more than others.

The king cut them off with a scribe's knife and threw them into the firepot until the entire scroll was burned in the fire.

THE PROPHET JEREMIAH, JERUSALEM, JUDAH, CIRCA 605 BC

———◆———

"Well, a few words for us all to consider," Narrative said.

About a third of the group stayed in the room, simply meditating or scribbling quietly in their notepads or on scraps of paper.

Hollie and Goodwin went out to a bench under a maple tree.

"What in the world happened?" Hollie asked. "And how did you get that big scratch on your cheek?"

"I'll tell you when this is over. You were kind of right. He is a bit of a mad-man, but I think a good one. I know that sounds funny, but you're not gonna believe the whole thing. I'm not sure I understand it, not yet anyway."

It seemed that less time than usual had passed when Narrative appeared at the door with an old brass bell. He tapped it twice with a coin, and those that had stepped outside made their way back to the group.

Without the slightest prompting, the questions and comments rapidly sur-faced. Round about the subject flowed, and when it was time to go, no one seemed eager to leave. But eventually they did, and Narrative stood at the door, shaking everyone's hand. Hollie and Goodwin were nearly the last to leave.

"Glad you made it right there under the wire," Narrative said, extending his hand to Goodwin.

"Thanks, me too," said Goodwin.

"I was beginning to think we'd lost him," Hollie said. "Thanks so much, Narrative. I can't wait to come back. Three Pond Cottage is so amazingly quaint with the twin fireplaces, the old pine floors, and all these little cubbyholes and nooks. I love those mantels, as well. Thanks again—really insightful session today."

"My pleasure. I look forward to seeing you two again."

Hollie and Goodwin moved across the garden and along the path leading past the old milk barn. When they got about a hundred meters from the cottage, Hollie turned to Goodwin and said, "I can't wait another minute. Tell me, Win, what happened?"

"Well, the old guy's name is Oban Ironbout…"

FIVE
Dairy House: Plot and the Peppers

Now, let me get this straight, Win," Hollie said. "This old Mr. Ironbout actually took a rifle and shot it in the air the other day, and you didn't tell me?"

"Well, I didn't want to worry you…" Goodwin started to say.

"No wait, and then you went right back up there, using your backpack as a shield? You marched in his direction while he threw walnuts at you? Is that honestly what you're telling me? Do you know how insane that sounds? He could have shot you! You could be dead!"

"Well, no, Hollie, it wasn't exactly like that. I mean, I did extend my backpack, but it was just unhulled walnuts. He's an old fellow."

"Oh, Goodwin, how wildly impulsive, completely stupid can you be? Your spontaneous wiring is going to be the end of you one day! What was he spouting about anyway, calling you all those names—interloper, trespassing thief, and all that? Thinking you were with some telecom company. Do you look like a telecom agent—whatever it is they look like? Couldn't he tell you were just a casual hiker, explorer type?

"The man must be deranged or something. You do realize you could have been killed by this madman, right? See, I told you not to go. This insane quest of yours, over a little sketch, really. Your dreamy notion of this fantasy cottage—*My Cottage Rare*. Sounds more to me like a haunted house on The Point. Can't you see that?

"Like I keep saying, leave people like that alone. Move on, pass by, get out of their way. But no, not you. You *invite* trouble, welcome it. I realize Sir Raleigh had a connection with this house, but that was decades ago. Let it go, for goodness sakes. Just leave the sketch with him now. You've seen the house—enough already."

"Hollie, just hold it, will you? Can you please cool it? I hear you, but you weren't there. There's something about all of this that's impossible to explain. As a kid, that sketch started me thinking of architecture—wanting to build, create imaginative structures, cool places.

"Granddad always had this thing about The Point and the house. The sketch—I remember how he would pick it up and read the name, *My Cottage Rare*, and speak of The Point. Have you ever thought that maybe it's got something to do with *me*? I've always wanted a place to fix up, paint, and stuff. Make it my own. I don't know, that's how I'm made.

"So, quit jumping on me, okay? You're not the only one on a journey, you know. I'm taking in Estillyen the same as you. I don't know if I'd call it a pilgrimage, but it's certainly an experience.

"When I stood in front of the house and watched that old man sit down in that tattered rocker with my sketch, I felt something emotional. Like I was supposed to be there, sort of destined to see that scene. It was a weird sensation, really different from anything I've ever felt, but nice.

"I didn't feel like a stranger on The Point. My identification was not some badge around my neck, it was my sketch. The sketch was my ID. I wasn't an interloper, a drifter. I was in a place I wanted to be that I wanted to see—that I was supposed to see.

"As I left, I walked a little ways down the path and stopped. I reached into my bag for some water. I saw your little tortoiseshell mirror, still in the backpack. I felt the scrape on my face and wanted to take a look. I glanced in the mirror, and thought, *No big deal*. Then, over my left shoulder, I caught a view of the house, just tranquil and picturesque there on The Point. The image had the same wondrous spark that my sketch has always had for me."

"Oh, Goodwin, I do hear you, but the main thing is that you weren't hurt. You're just so completely zany at times. I love that about you, of course. But I couldn't bear it if you ened up in some stupid tragedy for no real reason. We've got so much ahead of us. You're such a rock to me; I really need you. Maybe I'm just thinking of myself, with this disease. I don't know."

"I told Mr. Ironbout I might bring you with me when I go back. Would you go? Think about it before you answer. You need to see that place. The setting is incredible. You'd love his black-and-white border collie, Trip. He's a real looker—cute face and bushy tail."

"Let's just go easy on all of this for a day or two, okay, Win? Maybe you'll shake it off. Let's get on with the real reason we're here, which is in the lowlands, not up on The Point."

"Hollie, I'll take it easy, but don't count on me shaking off what I witnessed on The Point. The picture of Old Ironbout sitting on the porch really got me—just staring at the sketch with his dog lying beside him. He settled down so quickly. I'm telling you, he switched. All of a sudden, his anger melted. He became sullen, blue. There won't be any more throwing walnuts and shooting, I can tell that. Lonely fellow, he is. He's got some type of mysterious depth to him. I feel he's haunted in some way. In that you are right."

Hollie began stroking her long red hair, starting to relax on the subject of Goodwin's venture.

"All I'm saying, Win, is to be more careful. We should find out more about the situation before we even think about trekking up there. Besides, there's so much to see. I'd rather go up to Lakes Three in the pines."

"So you'll consider it, though? If you want, we could go up to Lakes Three on Saturday. This is an open weekend, with no readings. Sunday we could do whatever—hike as far as you want."

"Well, we've got time to think about it," said Hollie.

"But you'll *consider* it," Goodwin persisted.

"Okay, okay, yes, I'll consider it. But today we're going to the old stone milk house. Let's focus on that for now, all right? They call it Dairy House. The write-up says that all the stones are from Estillyen's fields. I love those pinkish-colored ones, mixed in with the granite and dark-brown stones. It would make a wonderful house to live in, don't you think?"

"Yeah, it's pretty cool," said Goodwin. "Let's go over early and knock around. That's where I saw the big vegetable garden."

The reading at Dairy House was set for eleven. Just after ten o'clock, Hollie and Goodwin approached.

"Win, look at the sunflowers—some of them are taller than you are. They look as if they were singing to the sky. What was God thinking when he made a sunflower? You ever wonder about it, really? Same question goes for a beaver, or a butterfly. Nature is such an explosion of creativity, of art. Artist divine, God is."

"I know what you mean," said Goodwin. "Bumblebees buzzing all around, competing with hummingbirds for nectar. It's amazing how it all works—a planet in perpetual motion."

Hollie and Goodwin made their way down Mills Road and turned off on the path running between the garden and Dairy House. Goodwin was drawn to the garden. He was just about to advance on a row of tomatoes when a youngish-looking monk with curly, sandy-colored hair and a matching beard popped up from behind the peppers.

"Brilliant day, hey?" the monk said. "Those are great tomatoes this year. They say a late frost tightens the seeds and makes them burst with flavor. Just love tomatoes in the summer, cold with salt and pepper, a few string beans, and some sliced onions. A real meal, it is." He stepped forward, holding a short, wide cardboard box full of mixed peppers.

"My name is Plot—not as in a garden plot, but as in a story plot, just spelled the same."

"My name is Goodwin, and this is my wife, Hollie. We've been around for a week or so and still can't get over this place."

"Estillyen is special. Are you coming to Dairy House today?"

"Yes," Hollie said. "I know we're way early, but we thought we would snoop around a little."

"That's good. Welcome. I was just going in to wash up and make some tea. Why don't you come along? I think there's a bit of apple cake about. It's got my special cream icing."

"Are you sure?" Hollie asked.

"Certainly—that's why we're here. Actually we love to chat, not just give readings."

Plot led Hollie and Goodwin around the back of Dairy House to a short, wide door with long, black hinges. The door was painted dark mustard-gold. "This is the way to the kitchen. Please, just have a seat at the old refectory table."

Hollie's eyes darted about, as she took in the spare, clean, yet homey decor of the room. The long table was covered with a well-worn, deep-red oilcloth. The cloth ran the full length of the table and draped several inches over each side.

Hollie and Goodwin found their chairs and watched curiously, as Plot quickly went over to the large vintage gas stove and grabbed a dented copper kettle, which he carried to the sink and filled with water. He returned the long-spouted kettle to the stove and placed it on one of the back burners.

Plot then moved across the room to a sideboard, where he clicked on the electric kettle. Hollie and Goodwin looked on, as the monk reached into the fridge, retrieved an aluminum baking pan covered with waxed paper, and laid it on the counter next to the stove.

Bending down, still not saying a word, Plot opened one of the bottom cabinet doors and pulled out an empty baking pan. It was identical to the one he had taken out of the fridge, but larger. Plot placed the empty pan on top of the stove, allowing it to straddle the two front burners. The electric kettle clicked, and with a two-step, dance-type move, Plot poured boiling water into a soft-yellow pottery teapot. He capped the lid.

Hollie and Goodwin exchanged a couple of glances, but, other than that, remained steely-quiet observers. By now the copper kettle on the stove began to puff with little tweets. With the same gliding two-step movement in reverse, Plot landed in front of the stove and poured boiling water into the empty pan.

"Just a half inch; that's all I want," Plot said. He then picked up the pan covered with waxed paper and gently slid it into the larger pan, producing a faint rise of steam.

"Please excuse me for a minute," Plot said, and briskly disappeared. Hollie and Goodwin sat staring at each other. Goodwin stretched his mouth open and silently bobbed his head up and down, offering Hollie a prankish look of excitement. Hollie bulged wide her sparkling green eyes and smiled.

By the time the tea had brewed, Plot was back, now wearing his habit.

"May I pour?" Plot asked, as he lifted the yellow pot.

"Please," Hollie said, tilting her tall, blue-rimmed stoneware mug in Plot's direction.

The mugs were quickly filled. "And now for a bit of cake," Plot said. He dashed over to the stove, grabbed a pot holder, and lifted the smaller pan from its hot watery station. Plot transported the pan to the table and delicately lifted the waxed paper, revealing the heated apple cake.

He trained his knife, cutting a generous strip the width of the cake and dividing it in three pieces, which he lifted, one by one, onto small, pale-green plates. Plot gently slid the green plates across the red oilcloth to his guests.

"There, please enjoy," Plot said. "Temperature is such a factor in the taste of things—bringing out the flavor. Slightly warmed, the cake is twice as tasty."

The three sat, trading tidbits of conversation for ten or fifteen minutes, without touching on any subjects of great import or seriousness. The moments were pleasant, unpretentious, and calming.

"There should be some kind of warning about this cake," Hollie said. "It's so amazingly good, especially the icing."

"Hollie never gains weight," Goodwin said. "She can eat everything, anything."

"How lucky," Plot said, as he rose from the table and walked across the room to a small side door. "Be right back. There's someone I want you to meet." In less than a minute, Plot reappeared and approached the table carrying a large white rabbit in his arms. The rabbit lay on its back, as relaxed as a snoozing puppy.

The pet sported enormous ears, matching the length of Plot's freshly picked banana peppers. Its nose was as pink as a ribbon. A single black spot distinguished the rabbit's top lip, which sprouted a thicket of whiskers. Plot softly rubbed the rabbit's chin, as he moved back to the table and took his seat.

"Oh, look at him, adorable thing," Hollie said. "What's his name?"

"Tremble," Plot replied.

"Tremble? That's different," Goodwin said.

"We named him that because he trembles. It's his right back leg. You'll see it, if you watch. Every five minutes or so, he trembles for a few seconds and then stops."

"How strange," Goodwin said.

"Yes, he was only a week old, when a serious lightning bolt struck the top of Dairy House. It ricocheted off the metal cupola, hitting the tin-roofed rabbit shed. Tremble's mother was killed, maybe of fright, along with a couple of her babies. But Tremble survived.

"When storms roll in, we bring Tremble inside. The more thunder and lightning, the more he trembles. We place him near the stove in that old round, wooden hatbox. He seems to love it. Cute, isn't he?"

"Without a doubt," Hollie said.

"And that reminds me," she continued. "Speaking of trembling of another kind, we're wondering if you might be able to tell us anything about The Point—and the man who lives up there?"

"Mr. Oban Ironbout," Goodwin jumped in. "I went up there yesterday, and it's given Hollie the jitters."

"Yes, and if I'd been with him," Hollie said, "I think I'd have been like Tremble—trembling—from what I've heard."

Plot stared at Goodwin, "You didn't! You went up to The Point, alone? No one goes up there, not anymore. And you actually spoke to Oban Ironbout? I can't believe it. I mean, I *do* believe it. I'm just glad you're here to tell the story."

Goodwin chuckled. "Well, I'm not sure you would call it speaking. Hollie thinks it's a big deal. I just biked up there, went beyond the wall and past the warning signs. The grass is tall up there…"

Goodwin went on to recount the whole adventure. Plot dutifully listened, trying to keep from looking shocked. He also managed quietly to replenish the cups with tea.

"And that's it," Goodwin concluded. "I want to go back in the next couple of days."

"Well, your story is incredible. Up to The Point you ventured, and you were actually face-to-face with Oban Ironbout. Truly amazing, I don't know anyone on Estillyen who has spoken with Mr. Ironbout in years. I mean *years*. He is such a character—all alone, on his own, with his dog. He's always had border collies, like the one you mentioned. What did you say he called him?"

"Trip," Goodwin said.

"Yeah, that sounds right. I think they all had names like that—Travel, Trunk. Well, what can I say? Startling news, and news it is. Sometimes you are led in these things. Maybe that's the case with you, Goodwin. Hard to say.

"You should talk with the sisters, though—particularly Sister Ravena. She knows more about The Point than any of the monks. Ravena is a strong advocate of the arts. A while back, she tried to see Mr. Ironbout, went up to The Point with a couple of sisters. She was hoping he would be willing to open up the grounds to artists. The Point is the most prized spot on Estillyen—the views are said to be spectacular.

"But not a chance. Old Ironbout ran her off. Sad fellow, he is. Bitter as dark rust, I'm afraid.

"Of course, Mr. Ironbout has known a lot of pain on that Point. Long ago, his wife died giving birth to twin boys. The boys were stillborn. Tragic…really very, very tragic. I must remember to pray for the poor fellow. We forget how much people can hurt. I do think he's probably harmless, but you should be careful, just the same. The Point and Mr. Ironbout have been a matter of concern for the Estillyen community for as long as I can remember."

The three sat in silence for a moment, looking down at the stoneware cups and the distinct impressions they had made in the worn oilcloth.

Eventually Plot said, "Well, I suppose we'd better move along. We'll have a good group today. I know several are coming up from St. Angus' literature class. That draws in a few of the sisters, too. Expect we'll top two dozen.

"Feel free to go on in when you wish, just through the pine door. I'll join you in about ten minutes or so. There's a water closet just on the other side of the door, before you enter the large milk room."

Plot headed back across the kitchen with Tremble, and Hollie and Goodwin eventually made their way into the reading room. They were the first to arrive, although they could see a small group standing outside, chatting on the lawn under sparsely cloudy skies.

Soon a lorry arrived from St. Angus and, as Plot expected, the room was instantly full. For want of space, a couple of young men sat on the steps that led up to a storage closet. The décor of the room was unique, different than any of the other Estillyen houses Hollie and Goodwin had visited.

The interior presented an eclectic array of stuffed sitting chairs, a high-backed settee, and two long, down-filled sofas. The pillows scattered about the room had no scheme or pattern. Everything bore the hallmarks of extensive wear. Fabrics were clean but faded, with exposed threads running and rising here and there.

A minute before eleven, the pine door opened and Plot stepped in, picking up the same stride he had exhibited in the kitchen. He moved across the room with a broad smile and swiftly took his seat in an antique maple ladder-backed chair. The swayed woven seat noticeably creaked as Plot settled into his comfortable spot. Next to the chair was a round black piano stool, on which an amber glass of water rested.

"Welcome, friend or foe, to this house where messages are made and flow. My name is Plot. Today we have a message to explore. It comes from the ancient paths of the prophets—Isaiah to be exact. It is simply called *Lips Unclean*, and it focuses on a most interesting verse found in chapter six.

"Before we get started, we'll need three volunteers to be our audience's Voice. Your lines are on these sheets I'll pass along. When I nod or motion toward you with my script, that's your cue. Remember, you are making an appeal. You'll ask questions or interject a sense of wonder about what is being read. Call out with conviction, concern."

Two young ladies seated on one of the long couches raised their hands.

"Great—your names, please?" Plot asked.

"My name is Shellie."

"I'm Lora."

"Brilliant. One more volunteer would be great," Plot said. One of the young men seated on the steps raised his hand. His friend gave him a little punch on the shoulder.

"Great! Your name if you will, please?" Plot asked.

"I'm Peter Coleridge from the mainland, just over for the day," he said.

"Welcome, Peter Coleridge from the mainland. You complete our Voice for today."

Plot reached for his black notebook, which was leaning against the front leg of his chair, and extracted a few sheets of paper. "Would you kindly pass these along," Plot said, as he handed the sheets to a gentleman on his right. The man quickly rose from his chair and distributed the notes to the three volunteers.

"Now then," Plot said. He was about to continue speaking when he heard the latch on the pine door make a sharp, metallic, clanking sound. He paused and looked over his shoulder. Slowly the door opened, and in the frame stood an elderly monk wearing a black habit with a deep purple belt. Small, wire-rimmed glasses rested low on his cheekbones. Gray hair ringed the back of his head and around above his ears, leaving the top bald. His slight frame was noticeably accentuated by his height.

His right arm extended behind him. He held one of the chairs that had been taken from the refectory table in the kitchen. Calmly, he placed the chair in the middle of the doorway and took his seat. Only the man's long legs extended into the reading room; the upper part of his body remained centered in the doorway.

"Friends, let me kindly introduce to you my dear colleague Brother Say," Plot said. Brother Say gave a mild smile and a faint nod, nothing more. "Brother Say has been long associated with the monastery and Estillyen. We're delighted to have you with us, Brother Say."

Brother Say again nodded politely.

"Okay, wonderful—it seems we are ready to begin. Therefore, *Lips Unclean* it is. The title makes you immediately think about the state of your lips. No retrieving of mirrors. Your lips are now as they are, visible for all of us to see."

❧

Lips Unclean

In the year that King Uzziah died, I saw the Lord, high and exalted,
seated on a throne; and the train of his robe filled the temple. Above
him were seraphim, each with six wings: With two wings they covered
their faces, with two they covered their feet, and with two they were
flying. And they were calling to one another:

"Holy, holy, holy is the Lord Almighty;
the whole earth is full of his glory."

At the sound of their voices the doorposts and thresholds shook and the
temple was filled with smoke.

"Woe to me!" I cried. "I am ruined! For I am a man of unclean lips,
and I live among a people of unclean lips, and my eyes have seen the
King, the Lord Almighty."

ISAIAH 6:1-5

READER: The year was 742 BC, way back in history's hold, when the prophet Isaiah received his most extraordinary vision of heaven. This was the year that Judah's King Uzziah died—a year of changing, rearranging. Isaiah was a prophet in the land.

The threat of war filled the air. People were keenly suspicious. They whispered; they muttered; they worried and wondered. National identity and fate were uncertain.

The king was dead. Now what? What was to become of the Israelites and their southern nation, Judah? They knew they were God's chosen people inhabiting the Promised Land. This they believed. But were they still? Where was God? Was he still in their midst, or had he moved along, preoccupied with intricacies of other ethnicities?

VOICE: The vision sounds so extraordinary.

READER: Oh, yes, an extraordinary scene it was, what the prophet saw. His vision brimmed full with meaning. Isaiah peered straight into heaven. There was God on his throne, with angels flying to and fro, calling back and forth, speaking words of praise in angelic voices. The prophet's words once scribed are fresh, moving the mind and perking the imagination.

An old movie reel spinning silent frames was certainly not what Isaiah saw. No, it was more like the curtain of heaven had suddenly been pulled back. God was center stage, seated high on his throne. The cast of heavenly beings were wired and miked. The vision was vivid, the sound sublime.

What the prophet witnessed, though, was no theatrical play. A stage set it wasn't. There were no fabricated walls, props, or hollow gadgets. This was heaven, where substance streams with meaning along hallowed halls, never ending. The prophet was given a glimpse, a snapshot into heaven's realm, where communication forever flows.

VOICE: Reader, pardon me, but why is the word *heaven* so often stitched to those two little words *will* and *be?* You know what I mean—like it isn't really there but will be one day.

READER: Right you are to ask, Voice. Those two words *will* and *be* follow heaven around, as if on a lead. Isaiah saw not what will be; he saw heaven.

Heaven is, was, and always will be, Voice. It's the eternal corpus from which God's communication moves out into the cosmic realms and down to earth.

Think, Voice, beyond harps see. There may well be harpy tunes in heaven's sphere. Likely so, they'll occupy some corridor, but just where I do not know. However, be certain of this: In heaven's realm, knowledge itself will chime and rhyme with heaven's rhythm. Knowledge vast will glide forth on wisdom's wings. Knowledge there knows no end.

Dig a million layers deep, and only the top layer of knowledge can be reached, under which a billion layers reside. All the while, from the bottom millions of layers continue to grow and grow.

VOICE: Are you saying that knowledge forever grows?

READER: Are you voicing a contrary notion? Voice, dear Voice, intricacies of the cosmos are never still. The uninvented is there invented. Wisdom and divine intent swim along, tethering everything together. The notion of heaven being a boring place arises from people with the naiveté of plants.

VOICE: Naiveté of plants?

READER: Yes, Voice. What do plants know of creation's great panoply, as they root and seed in soily spots? It's inconceivable to think that God, who created it all, would design heaven as boring. Heaven is far more than a mass snoring chamber, lit with lava-lamp luminosity.

Is that what you want, Voice, lava-lamp luminosity?

VOICE: I'm not sure what lava-lamp luminosity is, but if it is boring, I'd rather not have it.

READER: Good on you, Voice.

Certainly boring is not the vision Isaiah saw, when into heaven he peered and doorposts shook. The prophet was so awestruck by what he saw that he felt he would die. The contrast was so stark from his life in Judah that he felt ruined. That's the precise word he used: "ruined." Isaiah saw himself as still alive, but among a people as good as dead.

VOICE: Reader, why did the prophet feel so done in?

READER: Lips, that's why.

VOICE: Lips? What do you mean?

READER: Yes, lips, Voice. Isaiah dwelt in a land of unclean lips, idol worshipers, gossipers, and muttering spiritists. There were even lying prophets lying around. In contrast, the prophet peered into the very throne room of God. The disparity was startling. In the realm of God, there is no mutter, no crafty chatter, no prophets puffing puff.

The disparity Isaiah perceived was not a bit of falling short. It was an enormous distinction between the realms of heaven and earth.

Voice, look upon my lips, if you might. See them move. They're eager, always eager. Touch your lips, Voice. Are they eager, too? Sure they are. They long for motion.

Lips are such an exquisite part of the human anatomy, extending as they do from the face. They express sentiment beckoned by heart and mind. Their ability to pucker, press, and position convey what words alone cannot say. What a coveted position they possess! Tirelessly they move. Like eyelids, lips too can seal and close.

Lips project a pose. They shape the face, signifying quickly a sign to friend and foe. Powerful they are, exceedingly so, with a strength vastly disproportionate to their size. In the time it takes to bat an eye, a single pair of lips can sway battalions to charge and die.

Voice, lips are far more than pink seals for the teeth and gums. It's not so much a matter of munching and lunching that brings lips their renown. Nor is it their beauty cast. Rather, it's what they launch.

VOICE: What lips launch?

READER: Yes, precisely. Lips launch words. Lips need no coaches. They carry out what the heart has in store. They're ever so ready to ply and comply. Haven't you ever heard the little rhyme, "Lips Lips Upon the Face"? It goes like this:

> *Lips, lips, the pair, oh how we adore our place upon the face.*
> *Below the eyes and nose, above the chin we sit.*
> *To us words rise, as they receive their call.*
> *We clothe them with form, propel them to function.*
> *Through us they all must pass, whether it be to bless or bite,*
> *for wrong or for right.*

Isn't that nice, Voice?

VOICE: Yes, indeed.

READER: It's such an ancient rhyme, but ever true.

This fact is what brought the prophet Isaiah such consternation. Desperately distressed he was, knowing that God heard every word uttered in the land of promise. In Judah, words had gone awry, propelled by muttering lips, forming all manner of distorted messages. Isaiah knew how messages compete, spawning both good and evil.

Listen to an excerpt of what the prophet had to say to the lying prophets: "When men tell you to consult mediums and spiritists, who whisper and mutter, should not a people inquire of their God? Why consult the dead on behalf of the living?"

The Israelites were consulting the dead on behalf of the living. The lips of the spiritists were busy. So too the craftsmen making idols. Isaiah writes, "As for an idol, a craftsman casts it, and a goldsmith overlays it with gold and fashions silver chains for it. A man too poor to present such an offering selects wood that will not rot. He looks for a skilled craftsman to set up an idol that will not topple."

Isaiah spoke too of what God saw as he looked down from his throne on high, watching the idol worshiper with his idol. "Half of the wood he burns in the fire; over it he prepares his meal, he roasts his meat and eats his fill. He also warms himself and says, 'Ah! I am warm; I see the fire.' From the rest he makes a god, his idol; he bows down to it and worships. He prays to it and says, 'Save me; you are my god.'"

In this land of lying lips, one might think such acts were on society's fringe.

VOICE: I suppose you'll say it wasn't so.

READER: How did you know? Have you read my lines?

You're right—spiritists and idol worshipers were in vogue. In those days of Promised-Land culture, messages were running about, telling, congealing, speaking for truth, but lying lies. Many were the words dispersed by lackeys lacking worth.

Projected from lip to ear, words bear messages that multiply and grow exponentially. Muttering picks up a head of steam. It mutters, mutters, puffs, puffs—until the muttering is out of control. Unstoppable, muttering mutters on.

When heaven opened before the prophet Isaiah, his eyes saw majesty, holiness. "Woe," he cried. "I'm ruined." *We're all ruined,* he thought. When Isaiah compared the flow of heaven's verse, with the mutter of land-locked lips, he felt cursed, doomed. Isaiah had peered into heaven and heard an amazing symphony of sound. In contrast, the sound in the Promised Land was something of a cacophony. It was at that very point a miracle occurred.

VOICE: It did?

READER: A true miracle it was. No magic tricks, wands a-waving. Rather, an angel appeared. A six-winged angel came to Isaiah, speaking words of comfort and absolution. Listen to the prophet's account: "Then one of the seraphs flew to me with a live coal in his hand, which he had taken with tongs from the altar. With it he touched my mouth and said, 'See, this has touched your lips; your guilt is taken away and your sin atoned for.'"

A six-winged angel flying with a burning coal, speaking, touching lips—is it not mysterious?

VOICE: Are they extinct, the flying seraphs?

READER: What a question, Voice! Are we to believe the supply of coal is also extinguished? Let God be God, majestically, mysteriously, as he truly is. Does that trouble you somehow, Voice?

VOICE: No it's just that...well, I'm not sure.

READER: Majesty—mystery in realms beyond realms of knowing—God is there.

The sear of burning coal from heaven's altar was the signet of Isaiah's commission. Listen once again to the prophet: "Then I heard the voice of the Lord saying, 'Whom shall I send? And who will go for us?' And I said, 'Here am I. Send me!'"

When the burning coal touched Isaiah's lips, his words changed. His entire disposition was instantly altered, transformed. He went from a ruinous state to one of readiness. Isaiah knew the worth of words. The prophet was eager to run with God's message. "Send me," he said. He was compelled. There was work to do, words to carry. Society was on edge. War was on the horizon.

And so God did. Isaiah scribed his words, spoke his lines, and challenged those who had turned from God. With King Uzziah dead and King Ahaz on Judah's throne, conditions were not at all good. Wars and rumors of wars abounded. Judah's fate was most uncertain. Judah had enemies.

In those days, Assyria was warring against Israel. Israel was desperate for Judah to join an alliance against Assyria, which included Syria. King Ahaz was obstinate.

Therefore, Israel and Syria mobilized their armies and marched on Judah. The diktat to King Ahaz was simple: Join the alliance or be conquered. When word was received that the combined armies were advancing from the north, Isaiah describes the mood in Judah this way: "The hearts of Ahaz and his people were shaken as the trees of the forest are shaken by the wind."

Shaking in the wind.... Lying prophets, spiritists, mutterers, all quaking with fear. It's seems no one had a solution to the crisis. That is, except for the prophet Isaiah. He had a word from the Lord for King Ahaz. This is what he said: "Be careful, keep calm, and don't be afraid. Do not lose heart because of these two smoldering stubs of firewood."

Isaiah then made King Ahaz an amazing offer to prove the validity of God's protection. He told the king, "Ask the Lord your God for a sign of confirmation, Ahaz. Make it as difficult as you want—as high as heaven, or as deep as the place of the dead." A sign as high as heaven or as deep as Hades. All the king had to do was ask.

VOICE: A sign?

READER: Yes, Voice, a sign. The kind of happening that has a way of happening when God gets involved. A little dew on the ground here but not there. The sun stands still, as it did for Elijah. A shadow moves backwards down a flight of stairs. "As difficult as you want," Isaiah told the king. That was the offer.

VOICE: What did he do?

READER: Nothing. He could have watched a flaming shadow leap around the room, the sun stand still, the moon eclipsed, but he did nothing. King Ahaz was not only defiant. He was dismissive.

Are you the dismissive sort, Voice?

VOICE: No, not me.

READER: King Ahaz had no regard for the prophet or his advice. He brushed him aside. He had a plan of his own. He would make a treaty with Assyria and ignore Israel. The consequences of doing so would prove grim.

Isaiah swiftly rebuked King Ahaz. This is what he said: "Therefore the Lord himself will give you a sign: The virgin will be with child and will give birth to a son, and will call him Immanuel."

VOICE: What? What was it King Ahaz heard? That sounds so unbelievable.

READER: Voice, surely you're correct. These were not words the king anticipated hearing. He probably expected the prophet to say something like, "Therefore, King Ahaz, your years will swiftly wither. When the sound of war begins to echo up the valley, be sure you..." or, "When you hear the sound of horses' hoofs and the myrtle tree begins to shed its leaves, know this..."

Isaiah was caught up in the drama of the hour. War was on the horizon. Injustice filled the streets. So what does the prophet do? He suddenly prophesies that a virgin will give birth to a son called Immanuel.

Ah, Voice, take it in, the mystery of it all!

VOICE: How can this be? Are you sure this precise turn of events is in the record?

READER: Voice, you have an endearing quality about you. You're earnest. These were not ordinary words from the prophet's lips. Isaiah spoke prophetic words jumping into lines, lines jumping into stories. The prophet Isaiah spoke of the distant future, some 700 years on the horizon. It was with the sensibility of spirit that the prophet Isaiah spoke. His heart and mind carried the words his lips dispersed, but it was the Spirit of God that prompted the prophet to speak of a virgin and Immanuel.

Tucked away in Isaiah's scroll are numerous words from this prophetic vein. Words like "For unto us a child is born," and "Unto us a son is given, and the government shall be upon his shoulder; and his name shall be called Wonderful Counselor, The Mighty God, The Everlasting Father, The Prince of Peace."

Does that sound ordinary to you, Voice?

VOICE: No, not at all.

READER: Dispersed from the prophet's lips were also haunting words about this Prince-to-be. Words like "He was oppressed, and he was afflicted, yet he opened not his mouth; like a lamb that is led to the slaughter, and like a sheep that before its shearers is silent, so he opened not his mouth."

The role of a prophet can be explored from many angles, but the thrust of words in message form is always at the heart of the prophet's cause. Into a competitive marketplace of messages, man is born. Messages exist not simply to give words a place to hang out and play. They are there to call and beseech, to preach and teach.

Critical analysis and historical criticism offer their due in assessing Scripture's text, but the ancient words of Scripture offer something more than simply material to be inspected. These ancient texts have earned the right to be respected, to be cherished.

What is it that you cherish, Voice? Anything?

VOICE: Cherish? I'm not sure what you mean.

READER: Consider it, Voice. The sheer presence of all these words streaming in to corral around a manger and a cross. Does it not lead one to pause, to experience awe? The words of Scripture not only spell out this and that. They are spellbinding, full of prophetic wonder. It's all rather mystifying how these words came to be. They come forth with such diversity, but singularly sourced they are.

The sourcing of Scripture's words, one and all, is a matter great. The sourcing itself speaks of reaching, telling, wanting, and calling.

VOICE: Reader, I might be getting lost, that is, unless you are. Which means we both are.

READER: I won't allow it, Voice. Listen sharp, with vigorous intent. The meaning of words extends far beyond their distinct descriptive definition. Meaning has much to do with how words are woven together and follow one another down the line. Context, too, is extraordinarily valuable to know. A letter signed from a loved one in a distant war holds greater worth for its recipient than a million words without the loved one's signature attached.

Every word in a line, and each line in a message, invariably leads back to where the line was formed.

VOICE: Where's that?

READER: At the intersection of who and why, that's where. It's there all words must pause and bow to the one who paid the price and put them in the line. Without who and why, the words know they never would have been sent. At the junction of who and why, they discover the reason they were gathered and then dispersed—some to heal, some to deal, others to kill.

Every word that finds itself in a message is there for a reason based on source. Massively important is this feature of all messages, but significance soars to the stratosphere when the source is thought to be God. This single element adds depth of meaning to every word in Scripture. The words are not just there to define bits. They are there as divine bits speaking forth a collective meaning.

Source transcends medium and message, signifying meaning. This principle is constant, whether the source is from the gutter or God. Scripture sourced divine, through people, culture, and time, bears a reflective, iridescent image of God on every page. This image, if seen, is as pleasing as moonlight's full face on a meadow's pond. The one who made the message known shimmers there, enhancing its meaning. Can you see the pond, Voice? How the moonlight's full face shimmers upon it?

VOICE: Surprisingly, I do. It's nice.

READER: The words of Scripture clothe God thoughts. Through a marathon of generations, God moved the drama along, stitching this with that, creating a collective feat of words to reveal the mystery hidden throughout the ages. Isaiah's promise of Immanuel was long in waiting, but then it came. There was a virgin giving birth. Mary was there with child, just as the prophet Isaiah said she would be.

Skeptics argue, "Where's the proof for Scripture's tales? Where is the proof—you know, what is there to show? Show me the Ark. Show me a chariot wheel at the bottom of the sea."

All the while, enigmatic proof rests not just in the aptitude of words woven in the lines, but also in the shadows between the lines. This is a most enlightening place to look.

Ponder, Voice, just how the vast body of prophetic prose came together. Consider the divine casting call that superintended it all. All the words, bit by bit, in they came, joining a single story.

In Isaiah's day there were many who turned their backs on God's prophets. The Israelites, like King Ahaz, were looking elsewhere for answers, not to scrolls. There were all manner of excuses and abuses. The passion of the day was for the words of spiritists and idols carved, not scrolls scribed.

The Israelites were the message makers of God, chosen to weave words in redemption's plan. They were to live out the Law, which emanated from the ancient paths of the patriarchs.

In those years now so distant, the Israelites were at a crossroads for survival. Isaiah's advice was: "To the law and to the testimony! If they do not speak according to this word, they have no light of dawn." This was the path to which Isaiah pointed. Isaiah saw no middle ground: Either speak to God or else speak to "the dead on behalf of the living."

This type of environment, of course, would be ideal for the master of deviant words.

VOICE: Who's that, Reader?

READER: I speak of Satan. One can imagine him on the move, peering about, sniffing war in the air, sensing despair. Would he ever wander far from God's chosen people?

Lucifer was hardly naïve concerning the strategic role the Israelites played in God's redemptive plan. Messages flowing forth from false prophets and lying lips—for Lucifer what could be better? Imagine him here.

Plot paused, turned his head, and nodded at Brother Say, who was still seated in the doorway. Brother Say calmly and deliberately rose. He coughed, cleared his throat, and began to speak.

LUCIFER: My devotees, listen here. Give me your ears. Lucifer is speaking. We need to get busy wreaking havoc. The environs are too calm, too complacent. We need some rumbling and rioting. Besides, you're becoming like lazy lizards, all lackadaisical. I'm not having it.

I have a plan, so gather 'round. I'll spring up on this high rock, have a seat, and give you a lecture. Listen to the morsels from my lips. They are choice. If a single word is borrowed, fret not, every syllable has been Lucified. That means they were reborn within me before breaching out. Each word has been graced by my sense of magnanimous wonder, my lips.

Come close, my band of devotees, I'm not in a whispering mood. I'll teach you a thing or two about communicating, about bouncing words around, about making people frown. I'll certainly not speak to you in parabolic fashion, roundabout. I'll speak it straight, spit it out. My words flow as directly as demon darts.

Did you ever look closely at my lips? That's not a question. Do so! You must admit, they are exquisite specimens. What shape they possess, full of form. See how I can make 'em pucker? I bet you didn't know I can switch 'em around. Watch—see how the bottom one is on the top, the top one's on the bottom? They move just as well as before. See?

However, this contortionist show has very little to do with the true power of my lips. That is preserved for what they project, not how they pucker. This brings me to the point of our important gathering.

Now, don't interrupt me, and don't fidget and get me distracted. When I'm done speaking, I'll look at you real close, study your eyes, to see if you understand. If you look more stupid and quizzical than normal, I'll know you got confused. You'll be in real trouble. Don't be. Listen up, listen good. This is communication of the highest importance.

Now, here's the scoop. As you know, I AM's got this deal going on about fleshies pinning on words, reciting, and remembering. He wants fleshies to pin 'em on, write 'em above their doorposts, put 'em in their sandals, and weave 'em in their hair. Sing 'em, shout 'em, and spout all about 'em. That's I AM.

Here a word, there a word. You know how adamant I AM is about words, inscribing stone tablets, making the fleshies cart 'em around in that ark all over the desert. Drag 'em across the Jordan. He is so connected to his words. I AM gets blistering bent out of shape when his words get messed about.

So what are we gonna do? I'll tell you what we're gonna do. We're gonna get I AM blistering bent out of shape by messing about with his words. Yeah, that's right. Go ahead—applaud. Cough three times. Let me know it's from your heart. Go ahead, in unison.

The devotees did as they were told; in unison they coughed.

LUCIFER: Good. Good. Very good!

Okay, this is the plan! I've been scheming it for a good spell. We're gonna sponsor a National Security Fair. Yes, you heard me, imbeciles, don't look like stunned sheep. You see, ever since King Uzziah died, the kings up north have been coming and going like vessels on the Nile. Oh, how I loved the sight of the Nile, all blood red—how enthralling it was!

Anyway, let me get back to my point. The fleshies are all in a dither about the prospect of war. They are looking everywhere for answers. Of course, what could be better than fleshies bowing down to idols, prophets telling lies? Fleshies are doing exactly what I AM hates. Superb time, it is! We need to be out there coalescing, exasperating, and winning our way with demonic cohesion.

I AM was so far afield when he came up with the idea of fleshies! Don't worry, I know, I know—I'm not gonna go off on a tangent about I AM making fleshies. I'll hold back. If I go down that trail, you'll be at the bottom of this massive rock for days, maybe months.

Hmmm, there's not too much mud down there, is there? I just don't want you to get mud in your eyes, or clog up your ears. You're my audience, the corpus for my corruptions, and the receptors of connectivity. My message comes to you without distortion.

As I was saying, the National Security Fair. We'll have it right here in the capitol. We'll spread the word that it's being sponsored by an anonymous patriot, one who is concerned about the welfare of the nation in troubled times. Now that Assyria is on the move, we need to make our move. We need to sow terror and sorrow, reap some havoc, get everyone running wild and scared. Doesn't that encourage you?

We can do it! We can do it! Oh, I know we can do it! Now, here's what you do, in order to do it. Go out there and round up all the spiritists and sorcerers you can find—you know, warlocks, wizards, and such. Tell them they will be at the fair. Tell them that if they refuse, I'll obliterate 'em. I'll send 'em so far into the abyss that they'll descend beyond the descendible.

Get this: Their job is to instruct the fleshies in the art of muttering. That's the main topic—actually the only topic—that will be presented at the National Security Fair. Listen to the slogan: "Learn to mutter, save your mother. Learn to mutter, save your brother." Isn't that great? I'm telling ya, devotees, this is gonna be exciting, inviting.

The spiritists and sorcerers will be our duly appointed representatives. They'll explain why everyone, in these days of heightened security, needs to be suspicious in order to be auspicious. The spiritists will say that all fleshies everywhere, for the sake of the nation, must learn how to mutter. They'll turn the notion into an appeal, a quest of necessity, of national security. I've thought of another good slogan: "Learn to mutter, not just utter. Twist your lips, so the king won't slip."

We will have lots of booths, which will be occupied by the spiritists, sorcerers, warlocks, and witches. I'm not sure which of that lot I like the best! At any rate, they'll all be real smiley, wearing uniforms and robes the way fleshies like it. You can each pick a sorcerer or warlock of your choosing. Then you'll stand behind 'em, invisible, watching over their shoulders. Your job is to make sure they do a good job of mutter-teaching.

Here's how you enforce your control. Make sure each one of 'em brings a small mirror to slip inside their witchy robes. You know, pocket-sized. Then when you come along, have 'em pull out their mirrors and act like they are adjusting their locks. Tell 'em to bring their mirrors up close to their faces, no further than a fleshy foot away.

Then, with your orchestrating means, call up my image. At first, the only thing to appear will be my right eye. It will fill the entire frame. They won't know what it is or who it is. It will be a live cast, but it won't really be me. It will be my simulated double. Tell 'em to slowly extend their mirrors forward to arm's length. As they move their mirrors outward, my eye will zoom down in size and my face will begin to emerge. By the time they reach arm's length, my entire face will fill the frame. I'll stare right at 'em, blink my eyes, and disappear. The ground will shake, they'll be so terrified.

Then, when they peer back into their mirrors again, they'll see you looking over their shoulders. Every now and then, press your claws into their backs. Also, be sure you breathe on their necks. Just make sure you circle back once in awhile to breathe. Not at regular intervals, though—keep 'em guessing. Add some eerie sounds to your breathing to let 'em know we mean business.

I'm not gonna go into all the intricate details right now, sitting on this rock. The basic idea, though, is to teach fleshies to shift words around in distorted form. That's the main goal. We want to get the fleshies looking to our instructors as authorities on security.

Let me give you a few examples. Take the word *Israel*. Now, at the fair, everyone will be all abuzz about security. The spiritists, sorcerers, and such will say, for security purposes, the word *Israel* must never be said on the streets. If anyone wants to say *Israel*, they are to mutter *surreal* instead.

You try it, mutter-like. Watch me first. I'll nip the side of my bottom lip with these two teeth, just barely nipping the lip on one side, and then I'll say *surreal*. Watch. "Surreal." Did you see how I distorted my lips? Slurred the word *surreal*? Try it. Nip and hold the side of your bottom lips, and say *surreal*.

See how easy that was? That's what we want happening all over the fair. Just imagine all the instructing, all the slurry enunciating. Now take the name I AM. Instead of fleshies saying *I AM,* teach 'em to mutter *ain't I*. Instead of saying *king*, tell 'em to mutter *sling*.

You just keep it rolling and rolling, muttering on and on for the sake of national security. And here's the best of all: Our witchy instructors will inform the fleshies never to use the word *security*, and implicate themselves as mutterers. Instead of saying *security*, they are to mutter *sorcery*.

The instructor core will also teach the fleshies how to doublespeak. When fleshies want to say *love*, they're to mutter *hate*. If they want to speak of *heaven*, they're to mutter *hell*. Before long the fleshies will be so confused they won't know what they're saying. In no time, we'll have all the fleshies speaking our language. Ah, what a plan!

Now, look up at me. Is there a glow around me? I'll allow you to answer with a nod. Oh, good, thought so.

Now, let me see, have you got it? I don't see you looking any more stupid than normal.

You want to practice muttering a bit? When you go to round up the spiritists and warlocks, you want to be able to demonstrate, ruminate, and pontificate on the subject of muttering. Show 'em you're experts. Show 'em *surreal* for *Israel*.

Tell 'em you learned it straight from the lips of Lucifer, who taught you from the rock.

We can do it! We can do it! Oh, I know we can do it!

Brother Say paused and slowly blinked his eyes a couple of times. He scratched the side of his nose and quietly sat down in the middle of the doorway.

Plot offered a gentle smile and began to speak.

READER: The images of God arising from Scripture's text are many: creator, judge, even an eagle flying high teaching its young to fly. There is the shepherd leading sheep to pastures green, and in the year King Uzziah died, the majestic king high and exalted upon his throne.

There is another image to consider in Scripture's making, though, which is rather astounding to grasp.

Behind the epic story of tales and tribulations is the message maker who wove it all together, not by happenstance, chance, or a quick divine glance now and then. No, it required remarkable constancy to achieve the prophetic consistency that Scripture displays from page to page.

Someone had to be the word watcher, the word inspirer, to ensure that all the words would fall in line in keeping with the story. Words do not say to one another, "Hey, would you like to trade places? No, the lines of Scripture are fixed, forever set. A story here breathes meaning into a story there, as all the words hold their lines together.

In their act of showcasing letters, not all words are created equal. They may look equal—that is that, and this is this—but source coupled with intent affixes their weight. The words of Scripture are not unlike bees placed on a divine trajectory to intercept the heart.

Curator of every prop, selecting each person in the play, God had a most significant job to do. God was there, assuring that Aaron's staff would bud on cue. Dry bones rose with skin and sinew when the prophet commanded, and God obliged. God was not slouching around, stealing long naps, letting his troop of message makers set out on their own.

Look not at the words alone, but beyond, to the weaver of words—and ask, "Who's there?" For those with eyes to see, in the shadows between Scripture's lines is God's face. Like a full-faced moon on a meadow's pond, it shimmers there. Through culture, space, and time, with prophets' pens and psalmists' prayers, words fell into lines. Why, you may ask. The answer is strewn throughout Isaiah's scroll, but in succinct summation there is a verse from the prophet that draws it in:

"Shower, O heavens, from above, And let the clouds rain down righ-
teousness; let the earth open, that salvation and righteousness may bear
fruit; let the earth cause them both to sprout,
I the Lord have created it."

Salvation and righteousness—these two words tend to summarize why the vast supply of words have come showering down from God. That iridescent image of God, residing in Scripture's text, reflects back upon the Father's face. The Father willingly let go, sending the Son, yet brought forth, in perfect time, words arrayed to aid his redemptive mission.

Words matter…particularly those scrolled long ago.

See, this has touched your lips; your guilt is taken away
and your sin atoned for.

ANGEL FROM HEAVEN, JUDAH, CIRCA 742 BC

———

As Hollie and Goodwin walked away from Dairy House, Hollie took a deep breath and said, "You know what?"

"No, what?" Goodwin said.

"I feel like, in the space of a few hours, I've encountered what might have taken me years to discover. You know, it's all a bit stunning, almost overwhelming. And the conversation we had with Plot about Old Mr. Ironbout. The Point, it seems, is a true Estillyen mystery."

"Yeah, I know. There's a lot to talk about—a lot of decisions we need to make. I could certainly use an espresso to help clear my thoughts. What about you?"

"So right," Hollie said.

SIX
Time on the Point

"If we do go up to The Point, Win, you've gotta promise that at the slightest hint of weirdness, we're outta there," Hollie said. "I mean gone, and not me hiking back on my own. I know you feel Estillyen is a bit of paradise, but don't forget, the sisters run a busy infirmary. People get sick, hurt, and wounded on the Isle of Estillyen, just like everywhere."

"I hear you, Lee," Goodwin said, "but honestly, you're gonna wear me out. I think you're way too over the top about this whole thing. Don't get so worked up, okay? Or, you know, maybe you should just forget it. You don't need to go. I'm not looking for a guide. But I'm telling you, I got *past* that stage with Old Ironbout the other day. You weren't there—I was."

"Oh, come on, Win, don't get all testy on me. I hate when you do that—clam up, get puffed up."

"You're taking all the joy out of this, you know that? All I wanted was for you to see The Point—this place I've dreamed about since I was a boy—and you've turned into some kind of hyper-intense scout leader. Get some little kids to look after if you want. But leave me be."

"You don't mean that. Don't be so cold—you're hitting on a touchy subject, bringing kids into this…"

"All right, I'm sorry. I didn't mean that. It's just that you should have seen the way Ironbout looked when he sat down on the porch with the sketch in his hands. He just sat there silently, staring at the drawing. He was transported to the past, in a mesmerizing manner. I'll never forget that moment.

"Maybe that's the whole reason I drew the sketch. I don't know. I feel sorry for the old fellow. His property is a rare treasure there on The Point. Few have ever even seen it—at least not since he's been there. The Point should be an Estillyen park or something.

"I'm dying to see the view of the cliffs from behind the house. Those are the white cliffs we saw coming over. The Point is the only place you can actually see them straight on, unless you're in a boat. When you're up there, you can see why that sister—you know, the one Plot mentioned—was interested in talking with Mr. Ironbout about the property."

"I know. She was hoping he would allow artists on The Point. Her name is Sister Ravena. Oh, that reminds me..."

"What's that?"

"I should try to meet her. Let me sip this last bit of coffee, and then I'll run by the office to see if I can find her, maybe have a quick word before we go up there."

"*We*? So you'll go?"

"Well, who's gonna take care of you?" Hollie said with a resigned smile. "I'll meet you at the big arch leading to The Abbey admin building. Since you're headed back up to the room, grab my orange raincoat, will you? And stick a pair of my blue-striped socks in the pocket. They are in the middle bottom drawer of the wardrobe. Then, I think I'll be good to go. What else do we need?"

She paused, looking at Goodwin's somewhat stunned expression.

"You know, you really amaze me sometimes, Lee," he finally said. "Thank you. Thank you so much. And you'll see—you're going to love it up there."

"Don't forget the water. I'll get the fruit—I'll pick up a couple of bananas on my way out."

Goodwin dashed up to the room, while Hollie sat for a moment, pondering what she had just agreed to. Watching the breakfast guests circling the large, round serving table in the center of Gatherers' Hall, she was particularly fascinated by the movement of arms. Some arms moved so suddenly, striking between bodies, snatching tasty morsels of food from the great round table. The arms, she thought, resembled the motion of cranes breaking the surface of a pond, plucking up little fish.

The scene reminded her of the conversation with Mr. Kind in Grims Park—and his tale about the cranes of Lakes Three. Round and round, the food pickers moved. Occasionally, a whole body would pull out from the circling samba of arms and elbows and move around to find a vantage spot, a gap.

Through the gap, delicacies lay, offering their tempting textures and aromas. The savory selections waited, as arms hovered above, casting shadows. The kitchen staff hoped they waited not in vain for swooping hands to carry them away.

Hollie watched the quadruple kitchen doors busily swinging in and out. Now and then an official-looking sister would traverse the room, with the sole duty of rearranging the delicacies on the serving table. Like handling little chicks, she would bunch all the savory bits together, flicking away any wayward crumbs or foreign incriminations.

With her last sip of coffee nearing, Hollie watched as the traversing sister appeared, making yet another round. She wondered what the sister thought as she moved about perking up the goodies that lay in waiting. Hollie suspected the dutiful lady might be saddened by the thought of such scrumptious fare being carted off, brushed away into buckets labeled "garbage."

Only yesterday, on her stroll around the grounds, Hollie saw the fate of treats unselected. Once their shift of offering is done, out of Gatherers' Hall they are whisked away on stainless steel serving carts. The carts go straight through the swinging doors, to the wardrobe hall, which leads to the workers' entrance at the back of the kitchen. This is their final chance to be swooped up. Workers come and go, taking what they wish, and leaving the rest to fate.

Unwanted, at the end of the day, into the garbage buckets they are pitched. To the compost mound the buckets go, where all the unchosen delicacies are cast out to decompose. In a jumbled heap they lie, in collective disarray. There, ingredients once so carefully prepared soon become fused no more. Identity is lost; individuality is indistinct. Into commonality of compost they reside, to aid life in another way.

Hollie quickly snapped to her feet. Snatching up her yellow bag, she trained her eyes on a convenient gap, where fruit was bunched, tightly nestled together. With her long, slender arm, she caught the rhythm of the morning samba, and with accurate, quick moves, a pear, a banana, an orange, and a lemon, too, were snatched up and gathered into her bag. The fruits four would soon be on the trail to The Point.

Across the lawn and through the arch Hollie walked, beyond the entrance and reception hall. She soon arrived at the tall oak office doors, which were strongly shut. Twisting the round brass knob to the right, she entered. Two young sisters, seated behind a short, wood-capped partition, shyly looked up from their desks. They spoke not a word, allowing their faces to signal a friendly welcome.

"Hi, my name is Hollie. I'm here on a retreat. I wonder if you might know where I can find Sister Ravena?"

"Sure," said the slenderest sister. "You just missed her. If you'd been here a minute earlier, you would have opened the door for her on your way in."

"Do you know where she's gone?"

"Yes, she'll be on her way down to the village, Port Estillyen. She's probably still out at the entrance. Her ride is often late."

"Thanks, brilliant. Neat place, this. I love those huge windows. I'll see if I can catch her."

Through the arch, down the steps, and along the broad walkway, Hollie clipped along. The wide masonry walk branched off in the middle of the lawn to a *Y*. Hollie took the left side of the *Y*, which soon became a *U*. Round and down she went to the entrance gate.

Ah, that must be her, Hollie thought.

Some forty meters away, there stood a lady, with distinct purpose in her poise. More tall than short, she wore a smart black trench coat with a wide belt tightly drawn around her waist. The tautness of the strap revealed the wearer to be more thin than thick. Her headdress of black and white framed a face that, even from a distance, would catch many a sculptor's eye. Her cheekbones were so perfectly formed and placed that only upon a face of resolute beauty could they rest.

Hollie approached. "Hi...pardon me. I'm wondering if you might be Sister Ravena."

"Yes, hello. I believe I am. Can I help you?"

"Brother Plot mentioned your name and said you might be someone to speak with. By the way, he also mentioned you are an artist; so am I."

Sister Ravena smiled kindly, waiting for Hollie to continue.

"Anyway, my husband and I are here for the month, taking in the *Redemption* readings. My husband Goodwin is rather taken by the house on The Point— Mr. Ironbout's, I believe. It's a bit of a story, but it has to do with Goodwin's grandfather, who used to visit Estillyen. That was years ago."

"Oh dear, The Point, that *is* a subject," Sister Ravena said. Just then a small green coupe drove up with a youngish lady behind the steering wheel. "I'm afraid that'll be my ride, though. I go down to St. Angus on Fridays to teach art. Can you come back around to the office Monday or so?"

"Well, yes—it's just that we're headed up to The Point today. Goodwin met Mr. Ironbout a few days ago. A bit intriguing tale, I'll admit."

Sister Ravena was taken aback. "Met Mr. Ironbout?" she asked, eyebrows arched.

At that, she raised her right index finger, signaling to the driver of the vintage coupe that she'd be a minute.

"I see," Sister Ravena continued. "Well, it's a rather complex matter, The Point and Mr. Ironbout. He's, how shall I put it, not what you'd call the most public of figures. Very private, to himself."

"That's what I understand," said Hollie. "I will come around next week, but any quick input you have would be great. I just don't want to get involved in something that we should leave alone. I know the property is posted 'Private.'"

"Well, concerning Mr. Ironbout, not a great deal is known. He's a mystery, living a lonely existence on The Point. Though, he's not a stranger to suffering.

It seems that some people can carry pain exceedingly long and buried deep. Mr. Ironbout is a troubled man and, as I said, not very social.

"The short version is a tragic story. Mr. Ironbout lost his wife and children many years ago. His wife died there on The Point while giving birth to twin boys. They died with her.

"Then it wasn't long before his sheep contracted a virus. Story has it he watched the whole herd die, one by one. Not a single sheep survived. They say he would put them in his lorry, haul them to the tip of The Point, and throw them down on the rocks and waves below.

"The village locals used to tell of going 'round The Point to fish. Occasionally they would hear Mr. Ironbout wailing from atop the cliff, far into the night.

"Oh, I'm so sorry, but I'm already a bit late, and it's a class. I really had better head along. I wish we had more time, but you'll have to excuse me."

Sister Ravena extended her arm, offering Hollie a quick handshake. She turned, opened the car door, slid into the seat, and glanced up at Hollie.

"Please do come back to see me," she said. "I'm most interested in how your visit goes. And please use caution up there," she added.

"Thanks much, Sister Ravena. It is terribly sad, all that. Such tragedy for one man to absorb. Certainly, I'll come around early next week. By the way, I love your blue clogs."

The green coupe pulled away and started down the hill. Hollie stood near the curb and offered a quick wave. Sister Ravena saw her in the side mirror and reciprocated with a wave of fluttered fingers. Hollie felt better for meeting her. At least someone knew they were going up to The Point.

But reassured and certain she wasn't. Images of sheep being hurled from The Point to the rocks below filled her mind. The antisocial behavior also worried her. The sadness of infants dying, twins no less, provoked mixed emotions. Her mood was not what she'd come to Estillyen to experience.

Hollie was still committed to going with Goodwin, but she sensed she was not headed for a fun-filled outing. She retraced her steps along the *U*, which became a *Y*. Within less than a minute, she was approaching Goodwin. He stood at the end of the pavement, holding her orange raincoat over his shoulder. His index finger was curled through the coat's hanging loop.

"Did you find her? How did it go?" Goodwin asked.

"Yes, and I found out a bit more, but not a great deal. It sounds like there is a lot of sadness and pain on The Point. Let's talk as we walk along.

"I don't know what to expect. The Point has become something of a massive fissure on our path of pursuing Estillyen's peace. You know what's in my mind? Brevity. Up The Point, down The Point, and done, back to the course as planned.

"I want you to experience this, see The Point, and then I hope you'll just settle down and feel content. It sounds like this fellow has serious problems, nothing we can solve."

Soon Hollie was keeping pace with Goodwin as they moved across The Abbey grounds toward the path leading up to The Point. In no time, they disappeared in the pines and mature trees hugging the trail.

"You could hike forever, Win. I'm knackered. So glad we brought water. That must be the stone wall. It's beautiful, so natural, with that neat cord twisted around it."

"Sturdy," Goodwin said.

"And those, are those the warning signs? They have to be. Wow, they're so threatening-looking."

"That's them—we'll soon be beyond them."

"They look like some kind of Death Valley signs. Where are the cattle skulls, with the long rows of teeth? You saw those signs and just sauntered in…incredible. I would never do that, not in a million years."

"Ah, come on, Lee, quit going on. It'll be fine. Where's that word you like so much—trust?"

"I know, but it wouldn't surprise me if this old Mr. Ironbout eats bees on his cottage cheese. I'm not talking about dead bees either, you know. I mean live bees crawling around with white chunks of cottage cheese on their wings, trying to hop off his spoon or escape out of his mouth. 'Oh, get back here, bee, so I can crunch you,'" Hollie said, as she pretended to pick bees off her cheeks and pop them back in her mouth.

"Your imagination soars like a cut-loose balloon. It's a good thing you're an artist. If you weren't, you'd be zany or something. Well, you're sort of that anyway, you know," Goodwin said with a smile.

Hollie reached for Goodwin's dark-brown hair, secured a chunk above the back of his neck, and gave a quick jerk.

"Ouch!" he said, as he broke away.

"Hey, Win, wait. Let's just pause a second before we venture on toward the house, okay?"

They stood there for a good five minutes, by the peaceful wall, sipping water and snacking on raisins and trail mix.

"See how beautiful it is up here, Lee?"

"You're definitely right about that. Tranquilly quiet, I'd say."

"Beautiful spot. There's nothing up here but Ironbout and nature. Let's go," Goodwin said.

Along the path they walked. The same tall grass that had swayed its warning *swoosh* for Goodwin, days earlier, hadn't lost its form. *Swoosh, swoosh,* they stepped. Each step was deliberate, slightly stilted, and slower by half than all the steps they'd taken before passing through the warning signs.

Their legs kept moving; the steps kept mounting. Goodwin was propelled by conviction. Hollie moved simply to keep going. She dreaded the thought of advancing, but even more the idea of halting and distancing herself, allowing the stalks and stems to still their *swoosh* and cling around her legs.

In unison they stepped. Meters dwindled. The front gate, which seemed so distant when they passed beyond the signs, was growing near. Twenty meters more, they stepped free of the swooshing sound.

"We're here—*My Cottage Rare*," Goodwin said.

"Oh, Win, it's so completely charming, picturesque here—but the house… it's so tattered."

"I know. It's worn worse than a tailor's thimble. But this is no shack. Under that weathered face, there are good bones, I'm sure. Come on. I don't see anything. I'm just gonna go up on the porch and knock."

"Oh, Win, I'm sick. If I'm not, I will be," Hollie said. "Why, oh why, did I let you talk me into this? We're nuts. I've never done anything like this. Let's just go. I've seen it. It's frightening."

"Come on, Lee," he said, gently taking her hand.

Before Hollie could think, she was watching her feet move up the triple steps leading to the worn, grayish porch floor. Cautiously, she followed Goodwin across the wooden tongue-and-groove porch.

Suddenly, from inside the house, Mr. Ironbout's border collie began to bark. Before they could make it to the door, it began to open, but ever so slowly, totally opposite the way it had sprung open when Goodwin approached the property on his previous visits.

On the other side of the screen door, Mr. Ironbout stood, silent. He reached up to scratch his head, just above his ear. Goodwin and Hollie were motionless. They peered into the pair of watching eyes, which were lit by a glint of light reflected from the birdbath in the front garden. The light illuminated a shaft of dust particles that floated and filtered through the dusty, wiry mesh screen.

"Sir, remember me?" Goodwin asked.

Trip barked.

"Uh, shush, Trip. Here, now settle," Mr. Ironbout said.

With his right hand, he gently nudged open the screen door, using only the back of his index and middle fingers. Trip sprang through the opening, dashed across the porch, and landed at the bottom of the wide wooden steps. He whipped around and continued barking, with a look of panic etched on his face.

"Shush, Trip, I told you. Now come here. Be nice."

Trip slowly and cautiously placed his right paw on the bottom step and carefully began to climb. His head was bowed low, and his eyes tilted upward. Nervously, Trip wagged his tail, as he made his way back across the porch to his owner. When he moved in front of Hollie and Goodwin, he acted as if he were approaching a pair of ghosts.

"Sit. Good boy. There. Yeah, well. I was figurin' you'd be back for your sketch. See you brought some protection this time," Mr. Ironbout said.

The muscles of his left upper cheek jerked, just enough to twitch his upper lip. Both Hollie and Goodwin thought the twitch resembled a faint, fleeting smile, but they weren't sure.

"Love your dog, Sir," Hollie said, as she knelt to pet Trip.

"Well, yes. Seems he's prone to scooping up affection something fierce. He's not used to anyone about the place. Your strong-minded fellow here is the only one to stand in the yard for a considerable spell. Actually, I can't remember when I last spoke to someone on this porch."

"It's okay we're here, isn't it, Sir?" Goodwin asked respectfully. "I hope we haven't disturbed you."

"Well, your coming up to The Point is not right, like I told you before. It's not allowed, anyway. I guess, though, sometimes things that shouldn't be have a way of being, even if you don't want 'em to be. That's not always wrong, I suppose, even if it is wrong. You know what I mean, what I'm tryin' to say?"

"Yeah, sure, I understand," Hollie said, as she rose, freeing herself from Trip. "My name is Hollie. I go with Win."

Hollie carefully extended her hand to Mr. Ironbout. He looked faintly startled and slowly reached out in response, as he tugged his left earlobe with his other hand. Goodwin followed Hollie's gesture. His hand embraced Mr. Ironbout's strong, rough hand, which offered a single, firm handshake.

"Yeah, well, now that you're here and all, maybe it wouldn't hurt if we sit on the side porch for a bit. The porch wraps right around. I designed it that way.

There's an old swing 'round there and a couple of chairs. Everything is old 'round here…seems so, anyway."

The three made their way to the side porch, with Trip walking close by Hollie's side, curious.

"Why don't you two sit in the swing there? It kinda tells you it was once red—it's still strong, though." Mr. Ironbout pulled up a worn, high-backed wicker chair with rolled arms. "This one kinda tells you it was once white."

Hollie sat to Goodwin's right. The two began to gently swing, as they looked out over the garden. They were particularly fascinated by the towering walnut tree in the back corner, which covered nearly a third of the lawn. Goodwin thought about the way Mr. Ironbout had used the massive walnut tree out front as a fortress on his prior visit.

"I believe that walnut tree is even larger than the one out front," Goodwin said. "Its branches are so long."

"Yeah, those old trees predate me by a considerable stretch. That one needs a bit of whittling on it. It's gotten so big that I feel as if it's trying to take over the place. It's stretching a bit too far, way too far, actually.

"Well, the two of you look younger than I can hardly remember being. You know what I'm tryin' to say?"

Hollie offered a warm smile as she watched Mr. Ironbout. Win had been right, there was something about this place and their curious host. Her reservations were melting away.

"When was it you actually built this place, Sir?" Goodwin asked.

"Forty-six years ago, when I inherited The Point from my great-uncle. There was nothing here then but an old fishing shack. Floored the attic with some of its timber, in fact. Drove most of the nails in the house myself. My wife, Leslie, and I painted it. Took about a year to build it. Got a lot of help from the Mennonites.

"That's the original wood shake roof on the house, minus the patches. You know, we coated the roof with a heavy mixture of graphite and linseed oil. It's still got something of a black slate look. Amazing protection, that.

"Say, you two were on the path, so you must be thirsty. Would you maybe want a cup of tea? All I've got is tea and water for making tea. I'm afraid I'm forgetting something of how to be. Can I go get something for you?"

"That's okay, Sir. We're fine—right, Lee?"

"Actually, that's a great idea," Hollie said, as she popped to her feet. "Let me help you. Bet you even have a water closet in there somewhere."

"Ah well, I'm, you know…I'm not one for pampering much. You know what I'm tryin' to say?"

"Don't even think about it, Mr. Ironbout. Win and I are just delighted to meet you and see this amazing place. It's so beautiful up here. The views are breathtaking. Right, Win?"

She gave a glance to Goodwin, who was a bit surprised to see his wife so cheerful about being there. Mr. Ironbout rose from his chair. Trip and Hollie were already at the corner of the porch. The three disappeared around the front of the house, leaving Goodwin alone on the swing.

As Mr. Ironbout and Hollie entered the house, Hollie heard the screen door slap shut behind her. She took a breath and blinked, as her eyes opened to a time capsule frozen on The Point. No clutter, as she had expected. The house was fairly clean, although not lacking for dust.

To the right was the kitchen—all original to the house. The tall, narrow kitchen cabinets were painted an amber wheat color with a hue of gold. The two twin-door upper cabinets were separated by a small double-hung window. The cabinets, from end-to-end, matched the width of the counter below. The side panels of the upper cabinets extended with gracious s-curves that anchored into the bead-board backs-plash. A small framed mirror, with crackled silver, hung on the wall to the left. The kitchen countertop was made of wood, thick and well-worn. Below the wooden counter was a white farmhouse sink. The countertop concealed the sink's outer edge.

White oak floors, the width of a man's dress shoe, ran throughout the entire house, except for in the kitchen. The kitchen floor was pine, painted a soft green. In front of the sink and around the table, there were a couple of well-worn areas. Between the doorways, the paint was completely worn, exposing the bare pine.

"The kettle is just there," Mr. Ironbout said, pointing to the counter. "The pot and tea are just above it. Let's see, I've got this metal pitcher here. Water's good—it comes from a deep well back along the path. We're too high here to get water from Lakes Three."

"Just wondering, Sir," said Hollie, "that water closet…it would be…"

"Oh, yeah, almost forgot. It's just down the end of the hall, in the back there. Excuse the drying bits in the tub. No need for a light. There's a window. I like a window in a bathroom."

Within five minutes, not more, Trip was leading Hollie and Mr. Ironbout back around to the side porch. Hollie balanced the pot of tea and cups on a wooden cutting board. Mr. Ironbout held the water pitcher in one hand and three colorful, thin, stacked metal cups in the other.

Goodwin was glad to see them back so quickly—and that Hollie appeared so calm. Their eyes met briefly.

Hollie set the cutting board on the swing beside Goodwin, as she scooted over a spare wicker chair to use as a serving table. Mr. Ironbout found room on the cutting board for his pitcher and leaned the metal cups against the back of the chair.

"Would you like a bit of lemon in your water, Win?" Hollie asked, while she reached into her purse for the lemon she brought from Gatherers' Hall. "And what about you, Mr. Ironbout?"

"Where'd you get that?" Goodwin asked.

"Fresh fruit from this morning," she said. "I have a pear and an orange, too. Do you mind if I run and get a knife, Mr. Ironbout?"

"No, that'll be fine. Drawer on the far left."

Soon Mr. Ironbout, Goodwin, and Hollie were enjoying Lapsang tea, orange sections, pear slices, and Estillyen well water with a lemon twist.

"You know, I had Trip's parents, too—what a great pair," Mr. Ironbout reminisced. "His father was named Trunk and his mother was called Travel. All those dogs wanted to do was go. Every time I'd get in my Rover, they'd be leaping in. I'd make up an excuse, now and then, about needing something down in the village, just so I could take 'em for a ride.

"This sort of dog is smarter than a textbook. Trip doesn't miss a thing. If I was to move one of those empty flowerpots over there on the lawn a few feet, he'd know it. No fooling—if he's not around and I move a pot, as soon as he comes back around, he'll spot it, right off. He'll go straight for the pot and inspect it, make sure it's not gonna move any further. Thinks he's got to herd everything: leaves, water spilling from the hose, anything that moves."

The three chatted on, transitioning from pets to the properties of tea and the beauty of The Point, when Mr. Ironbout mentioned the sketch.

"Sorry about the other day, young man. Thought at first you were from that distorted telecom outfit—Source Telecom. They've been postin' me threatening letters for years—some nut-case notion about securing rights to The Point. Cousin Tidly's son's got some crony idea...oh, never mind.

"It's just that I've not been myself in so long, I've forgotten a lot about being, what I no longer am these days. That belt buckle with Mac on it—it sort of hit me between the eyes, you know what I'm tryin' to say? The sketch, too, it all sorta shocked me.

"Raleigh Macbreeze sat on this porch more than once, back before things got to going wrong. You say he passed away last year?"

"Yes, Sir, it was early December, the first week. Sir Raleigh sure liked Estillyen, at least to hear him tell it. Do you like the sketch?"

"Oh, yeah—it's just so long ago. That's right before things got fearsome bad, before I changed. You see, way back then, my wife and boys died. I decided me and God might as well part company. Figured he could look after the ones he liked, and I'd look after myself. I reckon he's done all right, but forty years is a long stretch, I suppose.

"Like I said, you shouldn't of come up here to The Point to find a fellow like me. I don't mean to be mean, but I *am* mean nowadays. You've just caught me off stride, with that sketch of the house, Leslie, and all. Gotten me all soft and thinkin' of the past. I'll have to shake loose of this softness before long. I just need to regain my stride, stop bein' so sensitive. Get back to the real me. Dear me, don't know what's come over me."

"Mr. Ironbout, maybe this *is* the real you," Hollie said. "I remember viewing a beautiful painting once, with a magnificent setting sun. Below the painting was a line: 'Time gives way to bring forth another day.' Maybe that's the kind of time this is, when time gives way."

Mr. Ironbout looked over at Hollie and said, "Don't know about that, but it seems like you're a bright one, sure enough. I would love to have had a daughter. Leslie had red hair, very much like yours. When I saw you today, it kinda added to all this other shock—like you was her; like I was losing my mind. I better glance in the mirror and see if I'm still me."

"Oh, that's sweet. Thank you, Sir, that's very kind."

"You two want to see something, since you got me feeling all befuddled and kinda out of sorts?"

"Certainly, that's why we're here," Goodwin said.

Mr. Ironbout placed his teacup on the cutting board, stood, and reached around to slide back his wicker chair.

"It's over towards the big walnut tree, just beyond."

Already knowing where his master was headed, Trip ran out to the corner of the lawn and paused near a row of short, black objects. Mr. Ironbout led the way, walking four or five paces ahead of Hollie and Goodwin. They had progressed about seventy-five meters when Hollie spotted the grave markers. She reached out and squeezed Goodwin's hand.

"Come along," Mr. Ironbout said. It was not long before he reached the row of black objects, which turned out to be knee-high, flat-capped metal posts. A thick metal ring, the diameter of a tennis ball, was welded to the top of each post.

The posts were set one meter apart and formed a four-meter square, with a small opening on the front row.

A heavy black chain was threaded through the rings. From post to post, it draped in perfect symmetry. Inside the bottom of each ring, a short headless bolt had been welded on end, so that a link of chain could be looped over each bolt. The bolts guaranteed that the sways of chain would remain constant. The chain could swing sideways, but the length of chain, from post to post, was fixed.

All the grass under the chain and around the posts was neatly trimmed. At the front opening, the posts and chain halted. The ground was barren, beaten hard. A worn path led to the gravestones.

Through the opening Mr. Ironbout stepped, just as he had done countless times before. He moved to the left and took a few steps before reaching the tallest of the three grave markers. It rose a foot or so higher than the posts. Its arched top contrasted with the sways of chain.

Next to the larger stone, there were two smaller stones. They were square, and identical in size. The markers were set, creating equal distance between all three stones.

Hollie and Goodwin paused at the opening. They chose to stand on the barren path. Mr. Ironbout turned and looked back at the couple.

"Need to get that blame branch cut back from the walnut tree. It's taking liberty over the plot. Those twigs are starting to rub the markers."

The limb extended its reach some twenty meters, with its branches spreading over and beyond the posts and chain. Back where the limb joined the trunk of the tree, its diameter equaled that of a small wooden keg.

"It's been forty years since I dug these graves and laid Leslie to rest. She died giving birth to my twin boys, George and Earl. That's them there. Perfect they were. Stillborn—didn't get enough oxygen.

"It was a cold night, rain pelting with ice, the wind a-howlin. The midwife had gone down to the village and was due back late. But the weather got so fierce, she waited till morning. When she arrived, Leslie had already gone into labor and was in a terrible state. She had been struggling the whole night. I was all in a dithery mind.

"Just before twelve noon, it was all over. Leslie went into a kind of convulsion, and then she just kept slipping farther and farther away, until she was gone. Quit breathing just as the boys were being born. I saw George first. Saw his tiny arm twitch, but then he fell limp. Earl also came out perfectly silent, still. They looked like two little angels, all ready for life, but no life to greet them.

"Not long after, my sheep began to die. One by one, the whole herd was wiped out. Death and dying were everywhere for nearly a year. I watched as they trembled, wobbled, and then dropped to the ground—one here, one there. Oftentimes they'd look up at me, as if there was something I could do. Then I'd take their carcasses, put 'em in the old Rover, and throw them off The Point. They'd fall among the rocks, and the waves would eventfully wash them away.

"Forty years is a long time, you know what I'm tryin' to say? Forty. That's an important spell in biblical terms. Four hundred years of captivity in Egypt, that's ten forties. Forty years of wandering in the desert. Forty days Christ was tempted. Forty days Moses contended with God on that mountain.

"Forty years of pain—I'm a wounded man. Can't you see I'm ruptured? It's a kind of rupture past mending. That's why I felt you shouldn't be here. No one should be up here on The Point, peering into Oban Ironbout's eyes, seeing what he's become. On most days, I don't even want to look in the mirror. What do I see? I don't see a tomorrow. I see what yesterday has rendered.

"I was not always this way, chock-full of bitterness. No, not at all. I was a dreamer, full of dreams and aspirations, like you two. But they're all dead. I wished I could have been like Job, patiently suffering, but after everything was gone, I guess I kinda broke. I shook my fist at God—not just once, but for a good spell of days. I cursed and would have been pleased to die. Yes, it's true—pleased to die.

"In time, I could feel my violation opening up, kinda like a fault line in my heart. Any goodness, any dreams I might have had, fell into that open gorge. I was crushed, buried by an avalanche of pain and bitterness.

"All my dreams, all Leslie's dreams, vanished. Like a breeze meeting a whirlwind, they were sucked in and carried away.

"Aren't you sad that you came up to The Point today? Don't you wish you'd left well enough alone in your field of contemplation? I'm not worth your bother, not worth being kind to. I'm beyond kindness—can't you see that?"

"No," Hollie said, "not at all, Mr. Ironbout." Hollie let go of Goodwin's hand and stepped over to the plot next to Mr. Ironbout. Gently she placed her hand on his shoulder and simply said, "Maybe this truly is a time that gives way to another day."

Mr. Ironbout stared into Hollie's green eyes with the intensity of a man watching a gold nugget fall into a deep well. Tears filled his eyes.

"Maybe," he said. "I just don't know."

Inside the chain-draped plot, nothing more was said. Soon the three, with

Trip, turned and slowly began to walk back across the lawn. Hollie and Goodwin felt the heaviness of the grave plot lessen with each forward step.

In all, just over two hours passed before Hollie and Goodwin were on the path leading away from The Point. There, among the swooshing grass, they walked.

Their minds were equally awash with disquiet and a sense of awe. They could hardly believe what they had just encountered.

Silently they moved, except for the sound of *swoosh, swoosh*. Somehow the strange turn of events had transformed the swooshing sound into a rhythm not unpleasant.

SEVEN
Fields and Crops — and Shakespeare

"It'll soon be three o'clock, Lee," Goodwin said. "I like the idea of the reading being in the late afternoon. Especially after the morning we've had."

"Me, too," answered Hollie. "And we're back at Quill House. I love that place, with Treasure and Epic. Half past four's a good time. There'll be time for a bite or whatever afterwards. Anyway, it's good to switch things around."

"I'm okay with not going back to The Abbey, but I'm starving—I've gotta have something before the reading. We've hiked a good four miles."

"Let's go by Fields and Crops then," said Hollie. "I'm crazy about the smells, so delightful, the mix of scents. I could do with a large cappuccino."

"Exactly, but I need crops or chops to eat, not just scents and smells."

"They've got all kinds of stuff—ice cream, pastries, fruit."

"Not treats. I need food."

"They have great potato jackets. I was reading the list the other day. They do a mushroom-chicken."

"That's the idea. Let's go."

Fields and Crops was busy but not packed at that hour of the day. When they started to order, Hollie suddenly decided she, too, was hungry. The idea of Goodwin sitting in front of a hot mushroom-chicken potato jacket, with nothing on her side of the table, struck her as an imbalance of sorts.

"I'll have the crab cakes," she said. "That's a nice complement, don't you think, Win? I'll get a table. There's one next to the corner window. Grab some sparkling water, please. I really need something fizzy and cold."

"Sure," he said.

In a minute, Goodwin had paid and was at the table already anticipating the food. "Hope my potato jacket finds its way 'round here before midnight."

"It'll be here, Win." Hollie said. "My question is what on earth are we going to do about what we saw and heard today? I'm consumed, kind of gutted, about Mr. Ironbout. I'm just not sure—it's all so serious, and so real. Ironbout is not a boy that just had his bike stolen. This is major life stuff. I never expected anything like this during our Estillyen stay. It's almost unbelievable, Old Ironbout.

"There, all alone, beyond that narrow gate and rock wall. It must have taken years to build that. You were right about him. He's a complex man, hard and yet tender. I almost died when he turned around in the graveyard and started reliving the past. The way he stared at us. And the way he looked at that tree limb—what did he say about it?"

"It was taking liberty."

"Yeah, that's it, taking liberty. Did you ever hear anything like that before? I guess living up on The Point alone all those years has shaped him in a rather odd way. Do you think he could lose it—go berserk and harm someone?"

"I was a little surprised you were brave enough to go in the house alone with him to get the tea," Goodwin said.

"I know! I just jumped up and went. Actually, harm didn't seem very likely at that moment. He's genuine. I just don't know if we should go back there or get more involved. Maybe we should back off, just leave him be. We could write him a thank-you letter when we get home. We should anyway."

"Would you be good with that?" Goodwin asked.

"No. I'd have a hard time shutting out his pain. I guess I was thinking a bit about my condition. You know, I'm supposed to shuck all the stress. I don't know, though. I think it's more stressful trying to get around stress than it is getting on with life. I wish I had never seen those three letters—PDK—stuck together. It makes everything so uncertain.

"Anyway, your sketch, *My Cottage Rare*, has evolved into a real tale. I think I could write a book about The Point and Mr. Ironbout. 'You know what I mean, what I'm tryin' to say?' I loved the way he said that and how his eyes would sort of flutter when he did."

"I know. He sure has a way of speaking. Let me try… 'My hunger is tightening its grip on my mid-section. That potato maker is taking liberty with my appetite. Or perhaps the potato has lost its jacket. You know what I'm tryin' to say?'"

"Precisely! You're really good at that," Hollie laughed. "You sound just like him. I'm just worried. You know how I tend to get too absorbed in situations like this. Having said that, I don't recall ever being in a situation quite like this."

"I'm with you on that one," Goodwin said.

"You've been around a lot of dysfunction, same as me. I hope what I said there in the grave plot was okay? I felt my words were not an adequate match for the pain on The Point. But I wanted to say something.

"All of a sudden, that line about time just popped into my head. It's strange, actually. I saw that painting at the Craigston a couple of years ago. Gorgeous piece, from the 1600s, I think."

"I thought what you said was perfect. I kinda froze up. That's not my strength. You're good that way, knowing what to say to people."

"I thought at first, there on the porch, that he was all right," said Hollie. "You know, odd, but normal. I should have known, though, those eyes behind the screen door—they looked so deep, distressed. Then, when we reached those gravestones, and he stood there in front of us, I'm not sure what I saw. He looked like he was burdened to the bone. Oban Ironbout is sure right about one thing: He's a wounded man."

"Well, you're the one who said people can get hurt on Estillyen, like anywhere else. I just didn't think about it in terms of a person like Mr. Ironbout. Why don't you talk to the sister you met—Ravena, wasn't that her name? You seemed to like her, and she's already been involved with The Point."

"Definitely—I intend to connect with her first thing next week. She's another interesting character, a very collected sort of woman."

"Hey, food—here it comes!" Goodwin rejoiced.

A young lady wearing a brown Estillyen T-shirt and a dark green apron approached the table. In her left hand was a warm white plate, which had three thin red rings running around the edge. On the plate rested a pair of chunky, golden-brown crab cakes, along with shredded carrot strings and a bit of green garnish. In her other hand, she held a second red-ringed plate, bearing Goodwin's potato jacket. A creamy chicken-mushroom sauce filled the potato and ran over onto the plate.

"Who's having the potato jacket?" the server asked, as she stood over the small round table next to the corner window at Fields and Crops.

"Me, thanks. Oh, nice—fresh mushrooms," said Goodwin.

"Thought it might be that way around," she said.

She gracefully lowered the food to the table. As the plates descended, trails of scented steam rose upward. She placed her fingertips under the edge of the plates and lightly nudged them into position.

The server took a step back and paused to review her notes. Her hair was bleached a bright whitish-yellow. The Estillyen T-shirt she wore appeared small, short-armed, and noticeably tight, stretching across her shoulders. A delicate tattoo of interlacing deep-green ribbons circled her left arm, just below the edge of the sleeve.

Her thick bangs were cropped perfectly straight and hugged her eyebrows. Distinct blue lines darted from the eyebrows extending onto her temples. Her eyebrows were penciled brown, overlaid with blue traces. Brushes of light gray streaked across the young lady's eyelids, while her long, dark eyelashes made her large blue eyes strikingly visible. Her lips were a healthy pink; a thin line of plum traced their notable size.

"Anything else, just now?"

"No, this is super," Goodwin said. "Oh, actually, just a knife, please," he added.

In a flash, the burst of color was gone. Before a bite was taken, she reappeared with a pair of knives in her hand.

"This should do the trick," she said as she placed the knives in the center of the table and disappeared.

"Cute, isn't she?" Hollie said.

"Certainly different."

"So, really, what do you think we should do about Ironbout?" Hollie said, as she took a bite of hot, crunchy crab cake. "Delicious. Want a bite?"

Without waiting for a reply, she placed a chunk on Goodwin's plate, and maneuvered her fork to retrieve a bite of his potato. "I love the fresh mushrooms—tasty."

"To tell you the truth, I don't know. The Point is so incredible, and that house could be so amazing."

"I know," said Hollie. "The inside is a time capsule, but you can see the quality and care that he put into it. I glanced in the living room, which has an alcove dining area. Above the table was what looked to be a long narrow door in the ceiling, but of course it wasn't. There were three identical panels set deep up into the ceiling. Very interesting."

"He really liked you, Lee."

"It did seem so. What were you saying about a Red Factor on the Canary Islands?"

"The death of his wife, Leslie, and the twins must have devastated him. I can't believe she's in my sketch."

"And Trip, what a dog, who wouldn't want him?"

"Sheep," Goodwin said, smiling.

The potato jacket and crab cakes were soon gone. The waitress lost little time in bringing two cappuccinos.

"Was everything okay?" she asked.

"Brilliant, just scrumptious," Hollie said. "What's your name? Mine's Hollie, and this is Win. Love your outfit, by the way."

"Thanks, I like a bit of flair. I'm Antonia. Glad you enjoyed everything—gotta dash."

In a few minutes, only a tiny sip of foam remained in Hollie's cup. Goodwin's cappuccino was long gone.

"We probably should get going, Win. But we need a plan or something."

"Okay, let me try and think like you—which is not possible, but I'll give it a go. How's this sound? I suggest we go and enjoy the reading, and afterwards we stroll around, not worrying about the time. Tomorrow, let's stick around here. We need to drop in at the laundry. We can journal some, read if we wish, just take it easy. Sunday we can go up to Lakes Three. As we go about doing all of that, maybe we'll come up with an idea concerning Mr. Ironbout and *My Cottage Rare.*"

"Precisely, you stole my very thoughts," Hollie said.

"Don't worry, you've plenty in reserve."

"You're something, Win. Let's go."

It took Hollie and Goodwin less than five minutes to walk from Fields and Crops to Quill House. Goodwin pulled the doorbell, and the bell had barely stopped dancing before a young aide appeared.

"Hi! Welcome—my name is Catherine. I've seen you two around. Several people have already arrived. Please come in."

Hollie and Goodwin stepped in, and Catherine closed the door behind them.

"Feels like home," Hollie said. They moved along the hall, bypassing the loo, and entered the reading room. More than a dozen people were seated in the same circular configuration as last time. Treasure was in the middle, receiving affection from Ellie.

Hollie and Goodwin began moving around the circle to a couple of empty seats, when a voice behind them said, "Hi there, you two." It was Epic, who had just entered the room from the hall that leads to his study. He refrained from coming close, so that Hollie and Goodwin would move towards him and slightly away from the circle. In a quiet tone he said, "How are you two bright ones doing, anyway—enjoying your stay?"

"Bright? Well, we're not so sure after today," Hollie said.

"Oh?"

"Tell him, Goodwin."

"Well, we just got back from The Point and a visit with Mr. Ironbout."

"I heard something about that. News travels fast 'round Estillyen. He's infamous, you know. And to think, you actually talked with him—Mr. Ironbout."

"What's more, we had tea on his porch," Hollie said.

"You didn't! You must be kidding, right? Tea with Oban Ironbout on his porch—that's headline news for Estillyen."

"We did, honest. I was actually in the house."

"This confirms it: God's still moving about on the Isle of Estillyen," Epic said with a smile. "Let's catch a word after the reading. I've just got to hear the story."

"Great," Hollie said, as Goodwin simply smiled.

Epic moved over to the circle and greeted the group. During his brief welcome, the doorbell clanged, and Catherine quickly scurried away. She returned with a couple in their early forties. They were accompanied by two young ladies who looked to be of Chinese descent.

"Well, please, welcome," Epic said. The circle of chairs began to move and expand. Catherine went around the far side of the room, grabbed a couple of chairs, and slid then into the circle.

"Okay, then. Today's reading is called *The Word Became Flesh*. We'll need a few volunteers for our audience Voice."

Hollie started to raise her hand, but three were already raised. "That's great," said Epic. "Two males and one female, and a good age mix, as well. I believe Catherine has the sheets with your lines. Thanks, Catherine. Just watch for my nods, or occasionally I'll gesture with my finger.

"Let's have two lines of practice, just to help set your voices in unison. Try saying this: 'It's time for tea. It's nearly three.'"

"It's time for tea. It's nearly three," the three recited.

"Perfect! Nice high pitch, slow and deliberate. Don't worry about how slowly you speak or ask a question. Actually, the slower the better. Unison is the key. Another one: 'I wonder what's happened to Clive. It's nearly five.'"

"I wonder what's happened to Clive. It's nearly five," they said in unison.

"Perfect. You are the Voice," Epic said.

As the three were reciting the line about Clive, a rather plump-looking monk wearing a black habit appeared in the narrow hall. Without looking directly at anyone in the room, he slowly walked behind Epic and sat in the lone chair stationed by the fireplace. The wooden armchair let out a collection of noticeable squeaks, as the monk settled in.

"Oh, there you are," Epic said, as he looked behind him, sensing his sizable friend had arrived. "Let me introduce Brother Tell, my longtime friend and colleague, who will help a bit with the reading. Welcome, Brother Tell."

Brother Tell nodded politely, offered a faint smile, and folded his hands, placing them on his rounded belly. Goodwin whispered, ever so softly, in Hollie's ear, "Brother Tell bears a striking resemblance to Alfred Hitchcock."

It's quite likely Goodwin was not the only one in the room harboring that sentiment.

"All right, then," Epic said. "To begin, a verse of Scripture from St. John. He speaks of what he saw in witnessing the person of Christ."

———•———

The Word Became Flesh

The Word became flesh and made his dwelling among us. We have seen his glory, the glory of the One and Only, who came from the Father, full of grace and truth.

JOHN 1:14

READER: Words wither, many much swifter than others.

The pendulum of time swings and sweeps, brushing the present into the past's repose. The present always goes; it never stays to become tomorrow. It can't wait. Another present takes its place. Once swept into the past's vast repository of days, the present becomes like all the rest: gone, parceled in the past.

Voice, Listen to a few ancient words from Solomon by way of Ecclesiastes: "There is no remembrance of men of old, and even those who are yet to come will not be remembered by those who follow."

Words of wisdom, these words remembered, not lost and forgotten. For most words this is not the case. As time's pendulum swings, the words of most men, and those of their kin, disappear without a whisper.

VOICE: Why? Why do the words disappear without a whisper?

READER: Do you not know, Voice? The mooring for words spoken is life. When death comes around, the words attached to life depart with the departed. What was spoken soon fades and falls away. Eventually the words are forgotten. They enter the vast repository of *was*. Their echoes are no more.

The present is history's living patch, abiding between the future and the past. The present has paths to both, but is owned by neither. The present daily reaches, stretching for the future, yet with each passing hour it surrenders and slips into the past. Today's yarn spins swift into the behemoth hemp of yesterday.

Second by second it secedes. It cannot hold. Each forward grasp is matched by what must be released. The past, with a force unstoppable, gobbles at the present, pulling in those words no longer to be heard.

There are, however, words of exception. Though swept into the past's vast repository of *was*, they do not sink. Instead, they float like buoyant buoys, calling, reminding, warning. Words of exception they are, ringing out with meaning, beauty, and provocation. Such words have a knack, a way of reemerging in the present sphere. Although into the past they're truly swept, they can't be held or smothered away. They keep casting lines that draw them back into present time.

History records notable figures who've managed this remarkable feat of casting lines that speak out in time. There is one figure, however, whose words and lines are so incredible that the present daily plies them to chart its future course. Like ocean waves, his words wash upon the shores, filtering eternal truths through the present's sandy beaches.

VOICE: Who is this one casting lines in such an unmatchable manner?

READER: Voice, it is Jesus Christ of Nazareth, Immanuel. The one St. John called the Word Made Flesh. He's the one who made known to life its purpose.

The Word Made Flesh rendered extraordinary claims about life's essence, about what it truly means to occupy a bit of the present, nestled between the future and the past. To speak of life's essence was what he came to do. Oh so natural was his calling. For him, this feat of fate was as natural as a mourning dove calling to its mate.

Christ cast lines worded in such a way that they created an awakening that still awakens. An updraft of worth for the human race, it might be called. His lines became so embedded in the future's fate that his patch of history is forever present. The present cannot let go. It cannot cut the lines, no matter how sharp and long the knife. The future's future is destined to be defined by Christ's lines.

Christ took the past, present, and future and knit them together, with words that cannot be unraveled.

VOICE: Knit them together?

READER: Yes, knit as in knotting. The future cannot flee, leaving the past behind. That is what he explained so very well. There is no place to go without the past; it has no future. Now that the Word became flesh, dwelt, died, and lived, the past, present, and future are wedded inseparably, not unlike the Trinity.

Yet one of the most amazing lines Jesus Christ ever spoke concerned the nature of his message. He claimed his words were not his own.

VOICE: Are you sure?

READER: Do you doubt me, Voice? Listen to what he said, if you don't believe me. "For I did not speak of my own accord, but the Father who sent me commanded me what to say and how to say it."

Such a claim is most unusual, to say the least, Voice. People so delight in being known, do they not? What kind of person admits that their words are not their own?

VOICE: Not many, maybe none.

READER: None but one. Who in history's grand sweep of saying, doing, and being has ever come along confessing such a thing? I own not my words—that's what he said.

Do you own your words, Voice?

VOICE: Well, I…I've not thought along those lines.

READER: Do so, my friend. It'll not harm you. Christ's claim has a great deal to do with message credibility and authenticity, but there is more to this disclosure. The claim is most revealing, astoundingly so. It presses directly on God's image. Christ's reception of words not his own thrusts strong perception on the one to whom they do belong.

VOICE: Who?

READER: The Father.

Christ's claim casts a telling light on God, whose ways and means in Scripture often appear rather mysterious. Is it not so, Voice? Consider the stories told: a bit of pestilence here, wars sprinkled in there, a spate of wrath now and then. This revelation of Christ, though, gives much reason for pause. It provides a hard jerk on the reins of revelation, saying, "Whoa, wait, deciphering the image of God is not so simple."

VOICE: Reader, I'm not quite sure what you mean.

READER: Consider it, Voice. All the words of grace and care spoken by Christ flowed forth from the Father's call. The Father's will and way, his directive, was what Christ conveyed in message.

It was St. John who truly grasped the significance of the Word Made Flesh. St. John spoke of Christ as bearing "grace and truth" on behalf of the Father. When John saw Christ, he saw Immanuel, God with us, the One foretold by the prophet Isaiah: "The virgin will be with child and will give birth to a son, and will call him Immanuel."

Voice, listen to the few lines from the ancient tale.

"God sent the angel Gabriel to Nazareth, a town in Galilee, to a virgin pledged to be married to a man named Joseph, a descendant of David. The virgin's name was Mary. The angel went to her and said, 'Greetings, you who are highly favored! The Lord is with you.'

"Mary was greatly troubled at his words and wondered what kind of greeting this might be. But the angel said to her, 'Do not be afraid, Mary; you have found favor with God. You will conceive and give birth to a son, and you are to call him Jesus. He will be great and will be called the Son of the Most High.'"

God reconciling the world to himself through Christ is Christ's story. Mt. Sinai with the Law was pivotal to the process, which was followed by the tumultuous history in the Promised Land. The flow of God's words along this route was long and arduous. In the fullness of time, God broke through the dusty maze of history by way of his Son bearing his message, the Word Made Flesh.

The era of stone tablets as the main medium of communication was through. By way of Mary's womb, God's consummate message was born into the human race. There was no other way to convey what God intended. God needed a pure messenger, who could be both the medium and message of grace. There was but one who had such credentials: the Father's Son.

The effect of grace required an agent of grace. The agent was Mary's child, born not in the line of Adam, but by the Spirit and will of God. A new Adam he had to be—one who could circumvent the old Adam's seed, the seed into which sin had crept. The world needed more than words; it needed the Word Made Flesh, One who would live—and also die—for what he had to say.

Consider it, Voice: The One through whom the world was created became a human embryo.

VOICE: Wait a minute, Reader, if you might. It seems rather strange to think like that, don't you agree? A child in a manger—yes, I know that's what we read and hear. It's in the story. But an "embryo"?

READER: Yes, it's true, Voice. Seemingly these are matters on which your mind has never rested. An embryo Christ was, as all children are before they are born. In the womb is where the Word acquired his flesh. It was time for Zechariah's ancient words to find their song: "Because of the tender mercy of our God, by which the rising sun will come to us from heaven to shine on those living in darkness and in the shadow of death, to guide our feet into the path of peace."

It's true, Voice. There was a star in the East.

VOICE: Did the star rise on its own?

READER: That all depends on what you mean by "own." Likely a bit of divine choreography made it rise and shine so brightly. Magi came to Jerusalem, asking, "Where is the One who has been born king of the Jews?"

VOICE: How did they know of the star and what it meant?

READER: It may well have been the early oracle of Balaam that prompted their navigation: "I see him, but not now; I behold him, but not near. A star will come out of Jacob; a scepter will rise out of Israel."

The star, the Magi, and manger were all brilliantly installed—while the matter of words and their significance kept looping all the threads together.

The arrival of the wise men and their entourage quickly drew King Herod into the drama. With this curious news circulating in the streets, the king felt compelled to move about, see what was afoot.

Herod brought together the chief priests and teachers of the law and inquired about what the ancient oracles had to say, what they revealed concerning the birth of Israel's promised king. Their answer came from the prophecy of Micah. "But you, Bethlehem Ephrathah, though you are small among the clans of Judah, out of you will come for me one who will be ruler over Israel, whose origins are from of old, from ancient times."

Hurriedly, Herod called a private meeting with the Magi, questioning them about their journey. In particular, he wanted to know when they first saw the star. The king then instructed them to go to Bethlehem and find the child and report back dutifully so that he, too, could go and worship him.

Indeed, the Magi journeyed on to Bethlehem, but they returned home not by way of Jerusalem. They had been warned in a dream not to go back to Herod. When King Herod learned of the Magi's slip, he ordered an edict, which spelled doom for all the little boys under the age of two in Bethlehem and its vicinity. They were to be put to death.

Oh, Voice, ponder it! You must. They were not anesthetized with needles out of sight. Oh, no, it wasn't like that at all. They were murdered. The little boys were pulled from arms of distraught mothers. They were clubbed, stabbed, slashed, and trodden.

VOICE: Does the story have to be told like that?

READER: I know how you feel. I understand, but it really does. It's all a bit more than a Christmas tale.

Dashed to the ground they were. The sound of small skulls breaking must have been horrific, heart-wrenching. In death they lay, not breathing, not crying, fluids seeping, as dust from mothers' feet settled on their tiny faces. Drops came down, tearing rain upon the dust. Little cheeks lay still, unknowing that love was near.

A mighty king was he, Herod. Against a throng of little boys he proved his prowess. What's in the human heart which makes it tick so sick? Who was it that whispered words in Herod's ear, "I see your challenge, your majesty. I'd say you're right to nip it in the bud. You know what fanatics the Israelites can be when they get all worked up about their religious dreams."

If not words flowing into his ears, perhaps the king simply took a pause, lingering long in front of the mirror, considering his position, his kingly pose. Standing there, he could gaze upon the reflection of his certain brand of majesty. Herod could strengthen his resolve, close his eyes for a few seconds, and whisper a prayer.

Eyes opened, he could once again stare, pondering his image and the burdens he had borne. He could think, "It's so tough being king. All the demands there are for me to consider! Oh, breathe again, breathe. That's it, let me think. There's so much pressing on my mind, so many vital decisions to make.

"So many activities and functions to attend. But what can I do? It's me they want to see. Sure, I could send someone else, but then they'd be so utterly disappointed. Oh, the next few weeks will be especially tough—then perhaps a respite, some gaiety. I can do it. I'm strong.

"Oh, yes, I mustn't forget to see if the soldiers have taken care of that messy affair, those little boys, and that so-called king."

Voice, what's in the blood coursing through those veins? Answer me if you can. What makes malicious murderers malicious?

What is in the spirit of man, shaping and molding him into a growling, wolverine type of creature, impervious to God's watching eye? Answer me that, Voice.

VOICE: I'm afraid I'm at a loss.

READER: There are some who believe that, with enough social engineering, "once" could become the chosen word to describe man's insidious behavior to man. In that enlightened day, one would be able to say, "Once, yes, a long time ago, the rude effects of man as beast did take place, but no more. It was a horrible slip, an indiscretion, we all admit, but no more.

"We've evolved well beyond all that groveling and growling sort of thing. Once it happened, yes, but no more. We're not some species seeking who we might devour. Once we were lost, without modern fixes, but no more. We needn't worry about the core; once, but no more."

At the core of every person are words that know not the meaning of dormancy. They move, mold, and live. How did the infernal King Herod conjure up his plan? What moved his will, if not thoughts parceled in words? Be not mistaken, in his abscessed heart words mingled, meshed, and in his mind they coalesced.

Herod's edict set in motion the ancient prophecy of Jeremiah. Listen to it, Voice. "A voice is heard in Ramah, weeping and great mourning, Rachel weeping for her children and refusing to be comforted, because they are no more."

Weeping and mourning in Ramah was not welcome news. Sinister were the reports filtering through, swirling around. Joseph and Mary fled with the Christ Child to Egypt. In time, Herod died. An angel then appeared to Joseph saying, "Get up, take the child and his mother, and go to the land of Israel, for those who were trying to take the child's life are dead."

This angelic message set forth the prophecy of Hosea: "When Israel was a child, I loved him, and out of Egypt I called my son."

Prophecies scrolled away in earlier times functioned like ancient theses embracing awaited stories. Like homing pigeons that suddenly awakened, the prophecies would fly in finding their storied landing. One by one, these prophecies of old sprang forth from their ancient texts to be folded into the Gospel story.

The words of old became embedded in the new. The new infused the old. The ancient lines added depth and meaning to the message new. The old made the new less so, gave it mooring. Like two lightning bolts, thesis and story would embrace, surging power into the divine drama.

The words of the prophets rose like tidal waves, rushing in and carrying credibility and content for Christ's message. Christ did more than quote the messages of old. He seamlessly grafted and crafted the words into his message new.

Central to Christ's mission was this amazing claim, Voice: "For I did not speak of my own accord, but the Father who sent me commanded me what to say and how to say it. I know that his command leads to eternal life. So whatever I say is just what the Father has told me to say."

Instead of cold, hard tablets of stone, coming down from trembling Mt. Sinai, Immanuel was moving about, up close, in culture and time. The magnitude of this revelational shift was inconceivable. This was not the kind of God Israel had come to know, reckoned with, or even imagined could exist.

The message of redemption—what is it? Who wrote it? Who bore it? Redemption is much more than a proposition or manifesto. It's a person. It's a story of the Father's Son, bringing the Father's message. It's a story of the Father sending the Son. It's the story of the Son who went.

God's image, shimmering through Scripture's ancient text, suddenly acquired a face—Jesus of Nazareth, the Christ, the Word Made Flesh. To see that face was to see the Father. The two were one, the Father and the Son. Voice, the interpreter of God is the Son of God—the Word Made Flesh. For God he speaks. As God he speaks.

It is St. John who grasps the true sense of awe and wonder regarding the Incarnation: "That which was from the beginning, which we have heard, which we have seen with our eyes, which we have looked at and our hands have touched, this we proclaim concerning the Word of life. The life appeared; we have seen it and testify to it, and we proclaim to you the eternal life, which was with the Father and has appeared to us."

St. John's fascination focuses on the approachableness of God. His use of verbs is most significant.

Verbs are active, Voice. The apostle speaks of Christ as the One who *appeared*, was *heard*, was *seen*, and was *touched*. John perceived that God was present in the person of Christ. Unimaginable, it was. Of course, this was one of the main reasons why Christ was crucified. Who did Christ think he was—God?

Throughout Israel's long history, God could be relied upon to be mysteriously distant, beyond reach, mostly out of sight, sending messages here and there mediated by patriarchs, prophets, and poets. Many of his mediators were rather weird characters, hailing this and heralding that.

Then the Word became flesh and dwelt in community, settling in for a considerable spell. God in man—oh, how can it be, Voice? The Latin phrase *communicatio idiomatum* is a select nugget which helps embrace this most unusual state. "Sharing of attributes," that's the meaning of the phrase—the sharing of attributes human and divine.

In this regard Christ was like any other man, but unlike every man. It's rather fascinating to consider how words and thoughts swirled around in the One with natures two. Did man decide for God, from time to time, or did man always defer to God? Christ did say, on one very pivotal day, "Not my will but yours be done."

Christ spoke not simply as a man expressing truths. He was truth walking about. This is one reason he was such a provocative and controversial figure. Who goes around saying, "I tell you the truth…before Abraham was born, I am"? It was Jesus of Nazareth speaking, but his lineage clearly rings of his divinity.

No one ever spoke the way Christ did. No one could. No one else was *communicatio idiomatum*. What may sound peculiar or strange was perfectly natural for the Word Made Flesh. No one knew how God should react or sound when he showed up in the form of a man. Who could verify the appropriate manner of this mysterious One with two natures? Fully man, fully God he was. He spoke on behalf of both.

Christ was the Message á Medium of God. Christ was not simply carrying a message, approximating a message. Christ was the subject of the matter, the universal noun. The thesis and the story he was, he is. The message of Christ was the medium of Christ. Every single word and twitch of Christ conveyed meaning.

This was equally true when the twitches twitched from tortuous pain of spiked hands and feet. There, as everywhere, the medium and the message were one.

Regarding the subject of medium and message, there's just one more twist we should tease in our company here at Quill House today.

VOICE: What's that? I feel a bit twisted already.

READER: This is it. Mediums often wear masks conveying messages very unlike the mediums they are. Consider these words lifted from Psalm 91: "For he will command his angels concerning you to guard you in all your ways. On their hands they will bear you up, lest you strike your foot against a stone."

Nice words, wouldn't you say, Voice?

VOICE: Nice words, indeed.

READER: These words stretch far back. They were originally cast as lines of prayer attributed to Moses. The psalmist picked up the lines and recast them as words of hope for the Israelites. The words speak of comfort and God's protection.

There is, however, a different use of these words in Scripture. This passage was also chosen by Satan when he tempted Christ in the wilderness. This was Satan's second stab at tempting Christ as he fasted and prayed there in the desert.

Satan challenged Christ to throw himself from the high point of the temple into the waiting arms of angels. That's when Satan evoked the words from the Psalms. In response Christ said, "It is also written, 'Do not put the Lord your God to the test.'"

Whatever characterization one may choose to place on Satan, "imbecile message maker" doesn't fit. This was no third-ranking demon out there in the wilderness throwing lines at Christ. This was the manic master who understood the power of words. He spun what he hoped would be a strike. He failed; Christ succeeded. They both used words.

Words matter, Voice.

After Satan had spun his lines, the story says he departed.

VOICE: Where did he go?

READER: Ah, this, of course, we do not know, but we can imagine.

Epic rose from his chair, moved behind it, and then backed away several steps. The attention of the room was drawn to the empty chair and the person seated beyond it. Brother Tell, now much more conspicuous, placed his plump hands on the arms of his chair and slowly rose. He took three short steps toward the back of Epic's chair, stopping a good arm's length from it. Clearing his throat, he began to speak in a deep, resonating voice.

LUCIFER: Quick, come here, my devotees. Get out from behind those wilderness rocks. What do you think you are—a bunch of lizards?

You are Lucifer's chosen band of devotees. Act like it. Show me your fierceness, your fervent ferocity, without a hint of frivolity. Look to me, Lucifer, your image. I am your ideal, your standard, your cause.

Now come close, you bothersome bunch. I command you. Listen, full, we've got trouble, sure. The major engagement is on. Word's on the move. He's making ready for mission. This forty days of travailing was his way of going into training before he hangs up his carpenter tools, hits the road, and starts touting words.

Get back! Give me room. Move over—let me sit on this big boulder. Get over here! You idiots hop around like drunken cats. Now, stand erect at attention and peer into my eyes. Do you feel the impartation, my implantation? Now breathe. That should still your quiver, disable your dabbling.

This is how it went. I spun my lines with pure perfection. Oh, you should have heard me! The words flowed with such free fall of intent. Lucifer's intonation was impeccable, unmistakable. No fear had I, not the slightest hesitation regarding my word-wise enunciation. My words, they failed not. To me they returned not void. They went out as they were sent. They were simply blatantly rejected.

I was trying to do the Word a favor, get him to stumble, and get him out of this fleshy jumble, this awkward ordeal. He's in for it now. Nothing more I can do. To Jerusalem he will go, and you'll see what unfolds. If he had leapt from the top of the temple, he'd have been out of here. In angels' arms he would have been—done, end of story.

The fleshies don't need redeeming. Even if they did, who would want 'em, redeemed or not? Worthless either way. How can you redeem what should never have been made? That's the wrong way 'round. You don't start with mud. No wonder I AM is stuck with such fleshy crud. He should have thought long and hard before doodling in the dirt.

They're no better than wayward fish, those fleshies. You wouldn't expect the Word to become a fish, to redeem ornery fish, would ya? Of course not. He's not gonna become a fish. Can you imagine that—putting on fish scales in order to ruminate and swim with fish? Putting on skin, flesh that came from mud—that's no way to be reigning and ruling the cosmos. Do you see what's gone wrong, my devotees? The order's out of order.

The advent of fleshies has changed the cosmos. Eternity's thorn they are. If I AM could just see the fleshies for what they are and pack it in, there would have been no need of reconstituting, or Magi traipsing around following stars. It's all so unnatural. See what I mean about out of order? Stars need to be left alone.

When it comes to fleshies, though, all bets are off regarding the scale of divine reach. In human flesh, there the Word sat, starving to death. Forty days and nights, no food, no water—do you know what that does to fleshies? They draw up inside. They get all squeamish, weak. Their bodies start telling their minds they're dying. Maybe I should have stoked up some manna or pulled out a cooked quail.

Anyway, it was surely him, the Word. I could see that haunting resolve in his eyes. Resolve of eternity, it was. That was no prophetic papyrus scroll setting there, with its words sealed in position. No sir, not at all. That was the Word with fleshy eyes and ears, dialoguing. When he countered my lines, his words reverberated with such spiritual force and fervor that I could hear them rumbling out beyond the stars. I'm telling you, for sure that's the way it was.

Listen up, you idiots, don't be telling that to any of those fleshies—I mean about his words rumbling through the galaxies. No corroborating now that the Word's in flesh for the aid of fleshies. They don't need our testifying. I doubt those dumb clucks will believe it anyway. "Look, here's God in skin. Go ask him about heaven." It's so implausible.

Those dopes run around looking for hope. They'll stumble right over that. The fleshies have caused so much cosmos consternation. It'll take half of eternity for things to settle down, and even then it will never be right. If only I AM could turn back the clock, back to the days of pre-fleshy past. Back when eternity was eternity without this blasted time intrusion. That was the treasured age, free of fleshy messes creating all these spiritual drafts rushing through the hemispheres.

Wake up, you coconut heads. Dust off your daggers. I'm not kidding—this is it. In the fullness of time, the Word in flesh has appeared. The present is now forever folded into eternity; they are one. The bell has rung. The slinging match is on, word for word, story for story.

Get a grip on your words, on your mastery of enunciation. We're gonna have to become dialogical in order to draw away those base fleshies. Get ready for a lot of hyperbole and parabolic speak, as the Word starts moving about, consorting with fleshies. He's one of 'em—never thought I'd see the day. He's gonna be trudging all over the place, claiming to speak for I AM. No question—it's him.

Well, it's not gonna be so easy, trying to tell fleshies about I AM's kingdom and such. Those clucks know nothing about the great unknown. It'll be like trying to explain the pyramids to a turtle. "Well, it's like this, Sir Turtle." Hey, no laughing! What did I just tell you—no frivolity! This is the beginning of the great campaign.

We've got serious business to do in slithering and slicing words in this word-slinging match. The man from Nazareth has a long ways to go before he makes it through the tribulation of Jerusalem. At every turn we must be there, twisting, snatching, and hatching our brand of story.

Now listen up: Lucifer's lines so blatantly rejected today may well become tomorrow's succor. Fleshies need alternatives. Come closer. Let me tell you what I have in mind. Don't be scared. Look to me. Let's practice our own brand of storytelling.

Brother Tell paused, blinked his eyes, and wiped a handkerchief across his brow. He slowly turned and moved back to his seat. Everyone watched the circle of watchers watching. Epic stepped up behind his chair, placed his hand on the top back rail, and began to speak.

READER: You see, Voice, the psalmist and Satan used the very same words. One sought to reassure. The other sought revenge.

VOICE: How can it be? Is this the way it actually is with words—saying this but meaning that?

READER: It certainly can be, Voice. Words often have two meanings, maybe more. Argue as you might, words flow around, wrapping thoughts, saying this but meaning that.

VOICE: That's not fair, it seems.

READER: The meaning of a message has a great deal to do with the message maker. When propelled by Satan's lips, the truth of the original message remained unchanged. The strategic intent behind Satan's message, however, made the message totally different.

Satan masquerades, using words to match his bent, no matter how or where they originated. Satan would use a line croaked by a frog if he thought it would make matters leap in his direction. Willingly he would have sung Christ a lullaby if he thought the tune would have caused him to lose his demeanor. Satan was there to provoke and tempt, to entice Christ into showcasing that he was the Son of God.

In the same manner as Christ, Satan is one and the same in terms of medium and message. But unlike Christ, Satan's message is always destructive, even if his words appear as enlightened light. Christ said of Satan, "He was a murderer from the beginning, not holding to the truth, for there is no truth in him. When he lies, he speaks his native language, for he is a liar and the father of lies."

Satan is a liar, always lying. He cannot speak without strewing lies along his crooked path. This is his repartee, his game of evil intent. Though Satan quotes the truth of Scripture, his intent flips the words. His message is a guise seeking contorted action.

In contrast, Christ's message always moves along the way of grace and truth.

There is no crooked path. There is no dark side with motives skewed in some bent and wayward way.

Therefore, Voice, you are fortunate.

VOICE: I am? Why's that?

READER: You ask why because you have much to ponder. Let me say again a line earlier spoken concerning the words of Christ: Although into the past they're truly swept, they can't be held or smothered away. They keep casting lines that draw them back into present time.

Those with ears to hear will grasp just how utterly amazing is this phrase: the Word Made Flesh. "When the fullness of time had come, God sent forth his Son, born of woman, born under the law."

No other time would do. Not a minute early or a second late, the final grain of sand floated in from heaven, and time was full. The heartaches of the past, the wars and slaughter, too, were redemption's toll so time could fill to full and finally reveal the Word Made Flesh.

Into the past's repose, there the present always goes, while the words of Christ forever linger and live.

Some words rapidly wither...others never will.

The Word became flesh and made his dwelling among us.

THE APOSTLE JOHN, JERUSALEM, CIRCA AD 70

━━━◆━◆━━━

With his last line read, Epic paused and smiled, still standing behind his chair. Everyone eagerly applauded. Treasure recognized the signal and slowly repositioned himself beside Epic's chair. Epic turned and motioned to Brother Tell, who rose from his chair and stepped next to Epic. Brother Tell offered a broad smile, as Epic gave him a one-armed hug around the shoulder.

"And we mustn't fail to acknowledge our splendid Voice," Epic said, as he and Brother Tell applauded, along with the group.

Again, no one was eager to leave Quill House as the Friday afternoon melted away. Goodwin and Hollie ventured out into the side garden, where Goodwin promptly found the steps.

Neither of them was keen to talk. The day had brimmed full with much to consider, from the drama on The Point in the morning to thoughts of past words casting lines into the present. Others from the group found their way into the courtyard and joined them, enjoying the warm, late-afternoon sun.

Epic's reading somehow gave both Hollie and Goodwin a sense of comfort. They felt as if they had been hiking over boulders all day, and then slowly, smoothly, they settled on the plane. The idea of time and eternity turning to Christ for certainty had a way of putting into context the dramatic picture of Mr. Ironbout and his life of pain.

When the group gathered back in the house, there was no shortage of comments about the Word made flesh.

Hollie, as usual, was not shy on words. Without giving any clues or details, she said, "Goodwin and I have very recently met someone who is, for want of a better word, very wounded. He has been dealing with tragedy most of his life.

"I've never really thought that a human being could be a medium of their own message. Interestingly, when I sit here reflecting on this person, I realize that, on the one hand, the medium and the message are one and the same—hurt, bitter—and the words that flow are certainly in sync. However, on the other hand, under the pain there is, I believe, another man, a different medium to which other words belong. Does anyone know what I mean?"

If there had been any want of a captivating topic, after Hollie's comment the want was gone.

Eventually, though, time had fully gone, and even Treasure was moving toward the door. As the group began to filter out, Goodwin and Hollie held back so they could catch a word with Epic. Young Catherine noticed, saying, "Waiting for Epic?"

"Yes," Hollie said. "We'll just be a couple of minutes."

Soon, Epic had seen off all the guests and was moving through the door to the reading room. "Excellent, you're still here," he said. "Come along into the study for a minute for a wee chat—if you have the time." Epic led the way.

The north wall of the study was lined with bookshelves. There was little room for new entries. Papers, notes, and bits of folded material lay around on top of books like napping mice. Big books were propped next to little books. Paperbacks were as privileged as hardbacks. There was no possible order.

Epic's desk made the bookshelves look like a recent addition. Its thick wooden top was covered with piles on piles. Large items smothered and smashed small ones. Books clamped documents, and holders corralled pens. Pencils, highlighters, and letter openers nestled together, while trays kept stacks of clutter in chaotic form.

"Please have a seat," Epic said. The worn, overstuffed chairs looked very inviting to Hollie and Goodwin, who quickly reclined.

"I love the way these chairs slope back and sort of pull you into them," Hollie said. "Do you mind if we sleep here?"

"Not at all, but Shakespeare might wake you."

"Shakespeare?" Hollie asked.

Epic stepped over to the corner of the room and took hold of a dark, antique wooden room divider, painted black with gold accents. Epic collapsed the divider, partially, and slid it to his right. Inside a tall, vintage, round-topped metal cage, a three-year-old Quaker parrot named Shakespeare perched on a worn wooden rod.

"I need to get Shakespeare a companion. I don't suppose you know anyone with a spare Quaker parrot about? Shakespeare is a good talker, but he always reverses his words; he talks backwards. Every single line, without fail, is twisted around. Like, 'Bath going to take,' or 'Tea for time.' He loves that one—often says it late at night.

"Or he'll say, 'Stove's on the pot.' He's recently picked up the expression, 'Baxter's place, Baxter's place, yes.' I haven't a clue where he got it. He's a real bit of life, an adorable presence."

"He's so sweet. Look at him, Win."

"I thought I heard someone talking the first time we were here," Goodwin said. "Now I know it was Shakespeare."

Epic made his way over to an overstuffed, light brown leather chair, similar in style to the other two. It was so worn and scuffed it looked like a pack of foxes had once used it as den. Epic let Shakespeare slip off his hand and rest on the back of the chair—and suddenly Hollie and Goodwin were confronted with four eyes rather than two. Shakespeare looked at them intently, as if he were eager for the conversation to ensue.

"So, anyway, please tell me. You went up to The Point and actually met Mr. Ironbout—amazing!"

"Yes, I went up on my own earlier, a couple of days ago…" Goodwin began. He went on to recount his original visit, the gun shot into the air, the flying walnuts, the sketch, and Mr. Ironbout sitting motionless on the porch. Epic sat in rapt attention. As did Shakespeare, so it seemed.

Hollie went on to tell of their joint visit to The Point earlier that day.

"When we stood there by those black metal posts, with that heavy chain draping around the plot, that's when I began to feel so burdened for him. 'Leslie and my boys,' he said, like he was introducing them. I didn't think so, but part of me wondered if he could be dangerous."

"No, I don't think so—well, only to himself, I'm afraid," Epic said. "He's a mysterious fellow, very sad indeed. Years ago, the sisters would take baskets of food up there every now and then, but one day he started the walnut tossing. After that, they decided they should leave him be.

"He very seldom comes down around the monastery road or anywhere near The Abbey. A side road from The Point winds down to the village, and that's the way he goes, emerging from behind the stone wall. If you are over that way when he comes along, you can hear his old Land Rover. It sort of rumbles—kind of like him, I suppose.

"It's all a shame, because we would take care of him, pull him into the community, but he's keen on distance."

"Do you have any thoughts or suggestions about what we could do?" Hollie asked. "We both feel that we should go back, try to help. But we don't know where to start. Right, Win?"

"Yes, there is a strangeness about it with *My Cottage Rare* and all that, but somehow I'm drawn. Now Hollie is, too. What word did you use earlier today, Lee?"

"Consumed," Hollie said.

"Well, first let me say that those feelings may be important. You know, God really does lead people, and this might be one of those times. On the other hand, it may go nowhere. Tomorrow you may wake up feeling quite different. But I would encourage you to stay open.

"You say you've met Sister Ravena. That's a good start. She's genuine and, of course, that was the reason she tried to set up a meeting and talk with him a couple of years ago. I think there was a little breakthrough, but then he refused to talk. Wouldn't come near. Just yelled, 'Go away!'

"There is also the issue of the property. Right now The Point and the house are his, in private hands. We are aware that Source Telecom would do nearly anything to acquire The Point. There are rumors about Source Telecom trying to get some legal claim. Something about a distant relative claiming rights and wanting to get The Point and turn it over.

"As far as we know, Old Ironbout has no relatives. As it now stands, if he were to die, his affairs would go to the magistrate. More than likely, The Point will go to auction. There are many who would want it, but none more than the faith community of Estillyen. However, we would not be able to compete financially with Source Telecom.

"A massive, giant tower up there would be such an affront to what we're all about: the value of renewal, of stilling the sensibilities of the spirit, of centering in Christ. Man does not live on media alone, you know. We honestly believe that our central mission is more important today than ever. Spirituality resides at the core of our being. We need to nurture that which we hardly know.

"Anyway, I'm so grateful you've let me know about the situation, this amazing turn of events. It's really great to have you two here—you feel like family. Let's hope for the best on this. Keep me posted on what transpires."

Soon Hollie and Goodwin were on the front porch, standing next to Catherine and saying good-bye to Epic.

"Thanks, Epic," Hollie and Goodwin said simultaneously. Epic's smiling face quickly disappeared behind the front door of Quill House.

"Would you like to walk along for bit, Catherine?" Hollie asked.

"Sure. Great reading this afternoon. Did you enjoy it?"

"Oh, yes! Estillyen is such a surprise. Win and I are truly thrilled to be here. I take it you are helping to organize Epic. How long have you been…"

From the side courtyard of Quill House, sightless Treasure listened on, as the three conversed and slowly moved up the path to The Abbey. It was not long before the hushing wind of Estillyen carried their conversation away, beyond the reach of Treasure's trusted hearing.

From out of the stillness, Epic called, "Treasure, come on, boy, let's come in now. Shakespeare's asking about you."

EIGHT
Lakes Three

"It was good to have a break yesterday," Goodwin said.

"Yeah, we needed to do all that wash," Hollie said. "We'd gone through almost everything. That's a cool place for a laundry—while the clothes are spinning, there's Fields and Crops right next door."

"Speaking of clothes, I really like these cords, Hollie. They're so thin, not like those thick ones I used to wear. Where'd you say you got them, Banners?"

"That's it, good price, too. The brown is perfect on you. It goes with everything. I should be more practical, but I can't. I love color. To me that's its function—the look. Vain, I know—look at me: orange raincoat, yellow jeans, white top with these chocolate buttons.

"I do hate these hiking shoes, though. Look at them—I feel like an archaeologist, or like I'm in the army. They don't seem like my feet, and when I kick them off in the room, I'd like to put them outside the door, or hang them out the window—they're so not me."

"You're funny. Be glad you got them. Look where they brought you today—Lakes Three. It's such a beautiful place. Mr. Kind and Plot were sure right; I can see why everyone loves this side of Estillyen."

"The binocular man we met earlier said this middle lake is roughly a third the size of the other two. Do you think what he said was possible?"

"You mean about it being one big lake at some point, and then the earth pushing the middle lake up on its own, making three?" Goodwin asked.

"Yeah."

"Well, the three are certainly divided, and the one in the middle is slightly higher. I think I could see it happening. Plot said there's about fifty hectares between each lake. Wow, look at the size of those pines! No wonder you can't see one lake from the other. It's really like a gigantic forest covering the whole plateau, with the lakes in the middle."

"I've yet to see those cranes, though, swooping down to pick up the talking fish. Fish communicating—funny."

"He was something, that Mr. Kind, quite a storyteller," said Goodwin. "I can see how he would fit in here. The Estillyen people are truly different. They're not anxious. They seem unfazed in some way."

"You're right. Of course, that's the whole idea. The world needs more people like this, focused on the spiritual side of who we are, why we exist. They're so completely on target about that. Gadgets and stuff can so easily define us, pushing us onto one treadmill after another. By the billions we leap on. People need to get off, walk. Yeah, they've got something right going on here on Estillyen."

"It's like with the environment," Goodwin replied. "Where was the human race for so long? I can't stand to see those old pictures of the massive redwood trees with cars driving through them. Or the Brazilian rain forest—what's going extinct this week?

"I feel sickened by all the assault on nature, like it cheapens our collective worth—the whole human race, the world. We're experts at reaping the things we sow, like radioactive waste and acid rain."

"It does seem the world can get rather zombatized," said Hollie. "Then here and there an awakening occurs. That's a good thing."

They sat quietly for a moment, taking in the beauty surrounding them. Goodwin broke the silence.

"By the way, how are you feeling, love? I meant to ask you earlier. You seem well enough."

"I feel great, actually. In some ways I wish I'd never gone for that scan and those tests."

"No, you needed to. It's very important that you found out."

"It's scary. Just the name—polycystic kidney disease. We simply have no idea what it will do in time. It's here inside me. I forget it for awhile, but not long."

"Well, for now they're saying it's only a couple of small cysts. The main guy, Dr. Steiner—he said a lot of people lead very normal lives."

"Win, come on, it's not normal. What a word—how do you define *normal?* Don't try to make it sound as if I am. I loathe that. I'm not normal, which means *we're* not normal. The idea of a romping family, growing and giving, nurturing and watching our kids have kids—that's normal. That may not be. Not now. Maybe not ever.

"I'm abnormal, not normal. My abnormality now extends to you. This disease is robbing you, too, not just me, which makes me feel even worse. Do you get it? The symptoms are already showing—a crack here, another there. We can't decide this or that because we wonder, we wait, and all the while we change. Little by little, we start becoming the abnormal, other.

"That's another reason I hate these stupid hiking shoes. They speak of vitality, zest, all gleam and glow, while inside I know I'm curiously ill. If I had an axe, I'd just chop them up right now. I should take your pocketknife and slit them, cut holes in the soles so I can't wear them. I'm never wearing them again."

"You're wearing them back, aren't you?"

"You're not hearing me, Win. *Comme ci, comme ça,* that's you. Let it be, no worries. You should have married someone else."

"Then I wouldn't have you."

"Oh, I just don't think you get how I truly feel. *Disease* is such a stupid word. What does it mean—a lack of ease? Who talks about being well, as a state of ease? 'You look so ease today!' What I have is not just a lack of *ease.* I have a life challenge, a conditional difference, and an abnormality that makes me view life differently. It's not the *dis* of *ease.* Knowing what I know changes who I am, and that is not a lack of ease."

"Hold on a minute, Lee, will you? If you're abnormal, then I never want normal. This thing is a part of you. It's here, but you, Hollie, the person, will always transcend it. It will not transcend you. *You're* not a sickness. You're not a disease. Okay? You got that?

"You're Hollie Lee Macbreeze, and we have a lot of living to do. There's no need to let aspirations die. Life's a journey and we're on it. There's no telling what will spring forth from your canvas, your floating strokes. And not just that—you have a way of touching people, you really do. You're a gift."

"It's just that this thing, it's never off my mind. I get so anxious about it at times. I'm so glad we came up here today, Win. I want to come back, you know, to Lakes Three and the Isle of Estillyen. Promise me we will."

"I promise. But it will take time for this architectural head of mine to settle. We've already taken in a lot since we've been here. I feel like when we were at the Dairy House and Plot was boiling two kettles at the same time. Thoughts here, thoughts there, thoughts perking everywhere. I go to sleep with them. I wake up with them."

"I know, but it's good, really important somehow. I do feel stronger for being here," said Hollie.

"Are you planning to try and see Sister Ravena tomorrow?"

"It'll probably be Tuesday. I'm very eager to see if she thinks there's something we can do. Mr. Ironbout's a troubled soul, like Epic said. But I'm at a loss as to how we can help. Maybe just the talking, the breakthrough, will prove therapeutic."

"I sure hope so," said Goodwin. "Hey, where's the reading tomorrow anyway?" he continued.

"It's at Scribe House. That's the one that stands all alone in the meadow—the long, skinny building with the metal roof."

"Oh, yeah, that's a neat-looking place."

"Let's finish the path around Lakes Three and then head back, don't you think?"

"Are you pitching your boots?"

"No, not yet, but soon. They shall be gifted."

"Okay, let's go. Look at the way those trees are reflecting in the water. The image looks as real as the trees themselves."

"See the bark of the pines in the water—so beautiful, and the shades of green are so rich. I should try to get back up here and draw it. That's the challenge of this place, Win. It's an artist's dream."

The afternoon passed, and they came away from the plateau with delightful images of Lakes Three freshly resting in their minds.

"I feel like I've left something back there—something good, not bad," Hollie said.

Monday dawned, and it wasn't long before Hollie and Goodwin had finished their breakfast fare. In short order they were off gallivanting, yet they both were eager to tuck into Scribe House at half-past ten.

"This is the strangest room I've ever seen," Goodwin said.

"I know! It looks like a theater set, or a dance studio or something. Shall we dance? There's room in the middle," Hollie said with a smile.

"We might as well take a seat on one of the benches. People are mingling in. I'm glad these have backs, even if it's just a single slab."

Goodwin carefully studied the room. He estimated it to be some twelve meters long and four meters wide. The exposed ceiling beams showed their age, but they were dutifully straight. The vaulted ceiling followed the steep pitch of the roof. Three ceiling fans hung from long steel rods. Their black blades turned ever so slowly.

Five windows, evenly spaced from each other, ran along each side of the room. The center window of each row marked the middle of the room. The windows were six-pane cottage style, a two-pane top sash over a four-pane bottom sash. A slender wood podium stood in front of each center window.

There were six rows of benches on each end of the room, all of which faced the center, where the reading would occur. The end walls behind the benches held the most unusual feature of all: two large mirrors that covered the entire width of the walls. The mirrors were set about a meter off the floor and extended upward to the full height of the side walls.

The mirrors were framed in wood. The dull-black frames were the width of a large shoebox and about the same depth. The mirrors made it possible for everyone in the room to see the Reader's face, no matter which way the Reader turned. In this unusual configuration, people on one end of the room looked directly at people on the other, but, at the same time, they saw themselves, looking.

People settled in. Hollie counted twenty-one, including herself and Goodwin. On their end of the room, eleven people sat, while there were ten on the opposite end. Ten faces looked into eleven faces. Twenty-two eyes looked back into twenty eyes. Ten people gazed into a mirror to see the back of eleven heads. Eleven people looked in the opposite direction to see the back of ten heads. The heads took many shapes: hair was curly, straight, long, short, patchy, and, in a few cases, newer growth lacked tint. Hollie's hair was the reddest of all.

The more Hollie and Goodwin gazed, the more they saw. Not only did they see ten faces, twenty eyes, and the back of ten heads, they also saw their own faces in the mirror, along with the faces of everyone seated on their end of room.

No one in the room could avoid participating in the mesmerizing stare created by opposing mirrors. Images real, once reflected, were then projected and again reflected. Back and forth into the black-boxed mirrors the images went, appearing to move beyond the walls into outer space.

"Do you think this will work?" Goodwin asked.

"Oh, I'm sure," Hollie said. "Here comes the Reader, the monk. I never know what to call them. I guess brother is best. Once I know the Reader's name, I like to call him by it: Mr. Plot, Mr. Narrative. They seem okay with that."

A tall, slender Estillyen monk walked confidently to the middle of the room. He moved over to the south wall, picked up the podium, and placed it in the center. "Good morning, everyone. My name is Story. I hope you've all been enjoying looking at each other." Everyone smiled and laughed.

"All of this looking has a way of charging the room. You can feel it. But it actually serves a good purpose: helping the Reader to see the audience and the audience see the Reader. Makes for an interesting narrow room, don't you think?"

"Well, welcome indeed to Scribe House. I'm told that several years ago there was a lot of pecking on old manual typewriters in this room. Never thought of typists as scribes, but that's what they were called.

"Let's get started, shall we? Do we have some Voice volunteers? Just two, I think—one from each side of the room, or maybe a third."

Six hands quickly rose.

"Okay, we'll go with four, you and you on my right and the two in the back row to my left. Will you be kind enough to pass along these sheets?" Story said, as he handed the papers to a young man seated at the end of the first bench to his right. "My nod will be your cue. The first one comes straightaway. Speak slowly, and aim for unison."

Balanced, Hollie thought. *Two girls on that end and two guys on our end.*

As Story was speaking, a senior-looking monk slipped quietly into the room and took a seat on the back bench.

"Ah, another pair of eyes has joined us," Story said. "Let me introduce Legend, one of our retired brothers. Legend will aid in the reading. He has an intriguing part that should be familiar to many of you by now.

"Why don't we pause for a moment and let a sense of Estillyen stillness settle in before we consider what words have to say."

Hollie and Goodwin were both amazed at how the reflecting images turned into a pleasant backdrop as Story began to speak. All the focus shifted to Story and his reading.

The brief stilling moment came and went. As it began to press into moment two, Story broke the silence and started the reading.

"The title of today's reading is *Get Up—Don't Be Afraid.* The context is the story of the Transfiguration. Together let's listen to St. Matthew's description.

Get Up—Don't Be Afraid

After six days Jesus took with him Peter, James, and John the brother
of James, and led them up a high mountain by themselves. There he
was transfigured before them. His face shone like the sun, and his
clothes became as white as the light. Just then there appeared before
them Moses and Elijah, talking with Jesus.

Peter said to Jesus, "Lord, it is good for us to be here. If you wish, I will
put up three shelters, one for you, one for Moses and one for Elijah."

While he was still speaking, a bright cloud enveloped them, and a
voice from the cloud said, "This is my Son, whom I love, with him I
am well pleased. Listen to him!"

When the disciples heard this, they fell facedown to the ground, terri-
fied. But Jesus came and touched them.

"Get up," he said. "Don't be afraid." When they looked up, they saw
no one except Jesus.

MATTHEW 17:1-8

READER: A picture is worth a thousand words, so it's been said.

VOICE: Who said? What about the words that set the worth of the picture? How should their worth be determined?

READER: Voice, right you are to query. "The Lord is my shepherd, I shall not want." I've just spoken that line in nine words. Count them if you wish, Voice, but nine they are. Albert Einstein said, "Imagination is more important than knowledge," which I have just spoken using six words. In all, that's fifteen words to render what most people would agree are a couple of rather significant lines.

If we tally those two lines together, we have expended merely fifteen words on our way to 1,000. We have 985 to spare. Therefore, it seems to me, the carte-blanche offering of 1,000 words for a picture needs a certain degree of reappraisal. Wouldn't you agree, Voice?

It would be untenable, indeed, to grace just any picture with a thousand words. A person might swear at the picture with a thousand words, but then the picture would not be graced. The evaluation of pictures receiving words, let's all agree, has a great deal to do with the quality of the picture—and, of course, the words.

The Transfiguration is a story rich with imagery conveyed by words. It's one of the most amazing stories in all of Scripture. The Transfiguration is saturated with substance, shedding a certain light found nowhere else in the sacred texts.

The centerpiece of the story is the transfigured Christ. The Transfiguration dispels any notion that Jesus of Nazareth was a kind of ingenious messiah figure who functioned with spellbinding zeal and clairvoyant wit. The image of Christ transfigured is that of his divinity permeating his humanity.

More than two years had passed since Jesus of Nazareth unrolled the scroll of Isaiah in his hometown synagogue and read, "The Spirit of the Lord is on me, because he has anointed me to preach the good news."

Christ made good on his promise and preached his unique message to the multitudes. He was loved and loathed, revered and reviled, famous and infamous. In more ways than one, Christ was a wanted man.

VOICE: Who was it that loathed and reviled him so?

READER: There were many, Voice. Jesus Christ set the institutions of his day reeling. As Christ's popularity continued to grow, the chief priests and the Pharisees convened with the Sanhedrin and said, "What are we going to do? If we let him go like this, everyone will believe in him and the Romans will come and take away both our place and nation."

Oh, they were in a state, all right, fearing their entire way of life was being threatened. The high priest of the Sanhedrin, Caiaphas, saw the wringing of hands and listened to the words of consternation being spewed back and forth. He had words of his own. He offered advice. He had a proposal.

He was cunning, Voice, a curt sort of man. Listen to what he said. "You know nothing at all, nor do you consider that it is expedient for us that one man should die for the people, and not that the whole nation should perish."

"You know nothing at all," Caiaphas said. That was his opening line. What if I said that to you, Voice?

VOICE: I wouldn't find it very agreeable.

READER: His words did not fall on deaf ears. Ears twitched; the ruling elite listened. Their steely eyes saw a tunnel; there was light. Caiaphas found a receptive audience. He had a platform much admired.

From that day on, they plotted to put Christ to death. They wanted him removed, off the scene, out of the way. They wanted to carry on ruling and waiting for the Messiah. They had custom, position, prosperity.

Only days before the Transfiguration, Christ had gathered his disciples and began to spell out what would take place when he entered Jerusalem. He knew the score. He knew the plotters meant business. Christ explained how he would soon "suffer many things at the hands of the elders, chief priests, and teachers of the law, and that he must be killed and on the third day be raised to life."

Without reservation, he spoke to the very core of the drama: He would be killed. He would die, be crucified. The message did not go down well at all with his disciples—in particular with the apostle Peter. Peter took Christ aside and began to rebuke him. "Never, Lord!" he said. "This shall never happen to you!" In turn, Christ offered a surprising rebuke to Peter, words which have been recast through the ages: "Get behind me, Satan!"

Christ was moving toward the unavoidable destination of Calvary; his face was set like flint. He knew that many of his followers would flee, and he was under no illusions about what awaited him in Jerusalem—Gethsemane, the hill of torture.

Christ, the Son of God, was the chosen medium to bear the Father's message. Crucifying the medium conveyed the very heart of the Father's message.

VOICE: Reader, crucifying the medium—I'm not sure I'm with you. You have a way of sticking words together that normally don't belong together. I mean, it's just that, crucifying a medium—it's so…

READER: Stick with me, Voice. You'll get there. In this case, and in this case alone, the medium was a sacrificial lamb. The sacrifice of the medium was the message. In the person of Christ, medium and message are one and the same, immutably so. There is no distinction between the two.

In the period leading up to the Transfiguration, the public message of Christ had begun to shift. Christ's words were cutting deep. "If anyone would come after me, he must deny himself and take up his cross and follow me. For whoever wants to save his life will lose it, but whoever loses his life for me will find it."

Christ was speaking with little time to spare. He would soon be condemned and nailed to a cross. The medium and message would be fixed, fastened for the world to see and ponder. Yet for Jerusalem, Christ would be a spectacle—a sideshow appearing on a ghastly hill during the Passover season.

VOICE: A sideshow—that's a peculiar thought. Don't you think?

READER: Oh, a sideshow indeed, Voice. Not for time and eternity, but for Jerusalem on holiday. Festive good heartiness abounded. Crowds swelled the streets grateful for law and order, for the rounding up of criminals. Christ, along with his loser-looking mates, would be lifted up on Gethsemane to die in agony. They would showcase what awaits those who disobey the law.

For Christ's followers, though, these were far from festive days. The mood was sullen and somber. It was all so different in the early days for the apostles, setting aside their fishing nets to follow. Aspirations swelled their hearts. They were to become fishers of men.

VOICE: What are "fishers of men" anyway? What do you suppose Peter thought he'd be when he first heard that line?

READER: Surely he was inspired, Voice. A change of vocation: Pulled from a life of bobbing boats and mending nets, he'd be something else. Along the shores of Galilee the apostles strolled, listening, loving, and learning from this curious and extraordinary figure from Nazareth.

Epitomes of commonality were Christ's apostles. Yet they had been drawn onto the divine stage. The common figures were caught up in the story of redemption. They were central characters in the drama that was thundering forth at the heart of the Father's plan. The story was being scripted by the hour, by the moment, by each turn and twist. Their every word and act was vital to the plot and would be inclusive in the story unfolding.

The story revealing Christ as the Messiah of God's redemptive plan is a long and winding saga, rapturously stunning. The mystery of Christ was hidden throughout the ages, like sand unseen, deep on the ocean floor.

VOICE: Sand on the ocean floor, like a hidden mystery.

READER: Indeed, sand lying there for ages. Pressed down deep, the mystery of Christ was hidden long in prophetic speak. Scrolled away, stowed away, life swam to and fro, not knowing the mystery latent in God's plan.

Astounding it is to consider all the collective facets and feats God directed in space and time to bring the message together. Barely believable is the idea that God would orchestrate Scripture and all its intricacies. St. Peter said it this way: "For prophecy never had its origin in the will of man, but men spoke from God as they were carried along by the Holy Spirit."

Redemption's story didn't come about simply because the stars aligned. The story is so precise that it synchronized time with eternity. It's no collection of silly notes, willy-nilly words, pulled from bottles cast out to sea. All the subjects—and the objects, too—were called and often coached by divine choice. Characters, settings, and scenes all mingled with "acts of God," shaping the saga of the Son.

Under history's enormous stretch rests a fulcrum in God's hand. Envision it, Voice. The fulcrum should inspire a certain reassurance, a sense of redemptive lift for man. History is not just about nations, wars, and such. It's about God in the midst of nations warring, striving, living, dying. In God's drama great, the past, present, and future perform as one. Their lines overlap with meaning.

There are, of course, those who detest the idea of God's involvement in the affairs of men. They want nothing to do with his dramatic stage, although, unknowingly, they stand upon it. Playing roles, they come and go.

I can hear them now as they speak: "Forget the fairy tale. God's an illusion, a needless infusion, a hopeless intrusion. God is nothing more than a deficit delusion, dulling man's true genius, making us dreary. It's all a parody, ruining our sense of self-clarity."

Can you hear the voices speaking, Voice?

VOICE: Your words seem most compelling. I do think I "hear" them, as you say.

READER: Proudly they stand onstage, modeling for orangutans seated in the stalls the potential held within them all. From stage left and right they enter, spit and sputter, then exit and fade away. They always go. They have no kingdom in which to settle. Restlessly they rattle on.

They seem so implausible, shouting out their lines upon the same life's stage where Christ lived and died. They cannot see that their script's not new. Their tares grow among the wheat; they're sowing seed, reaping self. There the delusion rests.

Leave them, Voice. Come again with me. To the Transfiguration let us go, where there's a different kind of light. The Transfiguration beams through the dusty, shadowy landscape of human achievement, transcending history with luminous hope. The Transfiguration story commences with Christ ascending a "high mountain" in the company of apostles Peter, James, and John.

VOICE: Why?

READER: It was once again time for Christ to pull away from the crowds, a time to seek solitude, pray, and find the stilling presence of God.

You are not against solitude, are you, Voice?

VOICE: No, but I doubt I'm as prone to solitude as you.

READER: Voice, what you are you may not always be. Look at the disciples. Christ says nothing to the disciples about the importance of the mountaintop retreat. All three versions of the story swiftly move to the point of transfiguration. Christ and the disciples ascend the mountain. Christ prays. The events unfold.

This brings us back to our picture and the worth of words. Moses and Elijah appeared in glorious splendor, talking with Jesus about "his departure, which he was about to bring to fulfillment in Jerusalem." Those words of St. Luke are loaded with meaning—his departure, which he would bring about. By his own volition, to Golgotha he would go.

Suddenly, Christ's face shone like the sun. His clothes were "bright as a flash of lightning." Christ's entire being was transfused with light, as bright as the "sun" or "a flash of lightning." The idea coming through in the original language is that of a metamorphosis, a complete change of being, like a caterpillar becoming a butterfly.

Flesh transfigured is not a flesh characteristic. The radiance of Christ in the Transfiguration story bears a message of its own. The luminous elements convey meaning; the light speaks a visual language.

VOICE: What does it say, this visual language?

READER: A great deal, Voice. Consider the disciples watching. Christ's divine nature instantly emanated through his flesh. What else could they think but that this figure before them was no normal man? This must be God, just as he claimed.

What an amazing sight for Peter, James, and John to witness! Christ transfigured with patriarchs Moses and Elijah—radiant, moving about on this earthly mountain.

Doesn't it make you wonder—not just a bit, but a great deal? What about the heavenly divide…just how far did Moses and Elijah travel when they got the call? Was it an instantaneous zip, and zap they were there? Or did they journey through distant lands before they popped in for their brief appearance? What say you, Voice?

VOICE: I'd better ponder the matter.

READER: Look, Voice. The words help you see. They paint a picture. To which is the greatest worth attached—the picture or the words that paint it? Consider the words as brush strokes, your mind as the canvas. Ah, it's all so wondrous!

Peter immediately recognized Moses and Elijah. He said, "Lord, it is good for us to be here. If you wish, I will put up three shelters, one for you, one for Moses, and one for Elijah."

Peter was no doubt stunned by the spiritually charged environment. Spontaneously he came up with the idea of shelters for Christ and his visitors. Christ gave no heed to Peter's suggestion.

No rationale can explain the appearance of Moses and Elijah. According to Scripture, Moses died in the land of Moab and was buried by God. The prophet Elijah is reported to have been caught up to heaven in a fiery chariot some 900 years prior to the Transfiguration.

Moses and Elijah were either present, or their appearance was a hoax, a fabrication. The latter point is destructive, like bulls stampeding through a pumpkin patch. It's no harder to believe in the appearance of Moses and Elijah on the Mount of Transfiguration than it is to believe in the transfiguration of Christ. One either believes or disbelieves. An event of this nature cannot be proven.

There is a factor in the push for proof that is freeing to consider. A bird with a twig in its beak too heavy to carry does not fly. Many things are too heavy to carry. It's a matter of letting go, Voice.

VOICE: I've never thought about birds with twigs too heavy to lift.

READER: Well, now you have. See how you change? Some loathe this idea of letting go, letting God be God. Instead they constantly flap their wings against the ground. Unbelief is easy to acquire and cultivate, Voice. The world is full of words, images, and sounds hawked from corner to corner, like a great scattering of twigs. There is plenty to fill the beak, as well as the heart and mind.

Howling packs run about with dubious doubts. Guess what, Voice?

VOICE: What?

READER: God's not on call. He has nothing to prove. He's not disposed to punch the clock, check in with humanity and explain his moves. Who would ensure that God's moves are right, anyway? Why not let God take care of the twigs too heavy to handle?

Human beings exist on the other side of the stained glass, where warm hues mysteriously filter into time and space. Why break the glass, Voice?

VOICE: I don't want to break the glass, Reader.

READER: Voice, I'm proud of you for that. I don't believe you do; you're not that type. Many do want to smash the windowpanes, Voice, but why? That's the question. Is the picture so demeaning, so unappealing? Or might the desire be to switch places, to call the shots, to be the one peering in rather than peering out?

Proof is extremely vital in so many ways, but in other ways not at all. There's an antidote for the relentless push for proof. The word is *faith*. Its cousin is a word called *trust*. Man needn't prove the spirit he possesses. The incessant push for proof has a way of belittling humanity, robbing the species of spiritual sensibilities. Faith and trust lift. They're a gift, not a formula.

The appearance of Moses and Elijah in luminous splendor defies everything known of what is knowable. Their cameo appearance, though, is a small matter for God to execute. With God, a thousand years are but a day. Moses and Elijah had only yesterday entered the heavenly sphere, where laws of time and space are requisitioned rather mysteriously.

Effortlessly Moses and Elijah came and went from their sphere to earth. In doing so, they stepped out of the Old and into the New. They were there tagged with Christ, and Christ was tagged with them. Instantaneously, characters old appeared onstage in the new drama being written. Their appearance gave the story new a beginning old.

To suggest that Moses and Elijah simply decided to drop in on Christ of their own volition is a proposition few would pen. The matter presses fast to the point to what is called *missio Dei,* a term, in short, suggesting that the mission of reconciliation is God's. Yes, that's the idea. God's on a mission—moving this, making that—so that factors fall together in place and time by his design.

VOICE: Missio Dei, what an idea.

READER: Yes, indeed. Moses and Elijah were called; they were staged. But they were not actors. They were characters perfect for the part.

God's message was clear. "Listen to him! This is my Son whom I love. I'm well-pleased with him," he said. The crux of the Father's message was this line: "Listen to him!" Moses and Elijah were present, but the plural pronoun "them" God did not use. Rather, God said "him." "Listen to him" were the critical words emanating from the cloud. Listen!

There's much to hear—here, there, and everywhere. There are words calling, vying for space. Just a little bit of the ear their destination is to be near.

What might the words say if they could speak about their mission?

VOICE: You mean words—just any words?

READER: Yes, that's right. Listen to how they speak, if you will. Hear them.

The word said to the ear, "Let me put down a bit of root. I live not to float with other words, but to be heard; that's why I've been sent. I need an audience to take me in, an ear. Don't worry so much about what I mean. Meaning is yours to make with the words you take. So, whataya say—let me in?"

Breath with syllables, thoughts in signs and symbols—that's what words are, Voice. Innocent they're not. Words matter. They speak to heart, soul, and mind. They speak of love and hate.

Listen! Listen!

VOICE: To whom does one listen?

READER: To someone—certainly you do, don't you, Voice? It's impossible not to. You hear me now. Is this what you choose? Choose. Listen.

Words forever flow. From deep within they flow. Unstoppable, they swoop and dive—sometimes in twisted form, but unstoppable they are. The Gospel story, too, flows with an amazing gait. The message was crafted largely by Christ on location.

The Transfiguration is an amazing part of Christ's story. "Listen to him," that's what Peter, James, and John heard. They didn't realize how soon Christ would be gone, even though he had told them he would soon be leaving.

"Listen to him." Those words represented a quantum leap in revelation. God had turned a page; a new chapter of luminosity had appeared. The awaited one was finally present, transfigured for the three to see…and the world to wonder what it was like for the three to have seen it.

The heavenly tour de force says much about the importance of the moment, about the mission of Christ. Doesn't it, Voice?

VOICE: I'm not here to argue.

READER: Their destination was exact. Moses and Elijah didn't pop into the Sanhedrin and pay a visit. Imagine Caiaphas announcing to the Sanhedrin: "We have a couple of special luminous guests with us today. Let me introduce…"

No, that was not to be. Moses and Elijah appeared on a mountain. The psalmist writes: "I lift up my eyes to the mountains, where does my help come from? My help comes from the Lord, the Maker of heaven and earth."

Up, that's where they were. There was an all-important message to convey: "Listen to him!" God, the Father, was speaking through his Son. God, the Son, was speaking on behalf of the Father. The Word had become flesh. The medium with God's message was present, luminous: "Listen to him!" Voice, he's the One with words for you to hear, words of life and not of death.

Ancient words from the letter called Hebrews spoke of God's messaging mission and Christ's radiance. Listen, Voice, the words are ever so important. "In the past, God spoke to our forefathers through the prophets at many times and in various ways, but in these last days he has spoken to us by his Son, whom he appointed heir of all things, and through whom he made the universe. The Son is the radiance of God's glory and the exact representation of his being."

The world awaited the Messiah, and when Christ appeared, the waiting stopped. He was the One in history's hold. On the Mount of Transfiguration, Moses represented the Law; Elijah, the prophets. Christ embodied the fulfillment of both. His message incorporated theirs in a new era of God's revelation.

Who else might have been privileged to sneak a peek at Christ as his face shone like the sun? Surely there were angels 'round about, on the move with Moses and Elijah. This amazing event might have also drawn other patriarchs out, as well, to peer down and see what God was orchestrating in the earthly realm. We don't know.

Who is to say how the forces of good and evil might have aligned that day? Certainly there were demonic forces down at the mountain's base. The Gospel narratives bear this out. As soon as Christ came down from the Mount of Transfiguration, he was drawn into a chaotic scene featuring a father with a demon-possessed son.

Suppose, with imagination's draw, that Satan might have been there, seeing what the three disciples saw. Always seeking, ever sneaking is Satan. The thought of Christ, the lead man, suddenly disappearing up a mountainside, would not settle well at all with the restless one.

Story raised his right hand and, with the motion of an orchestra conductor, gave Brother Legend a cue. It was time again for Lucifer to weigh in. Legend rose tall, and with a deep, deliberate voice, he began to speak from the back of the room.

LUCIFER: Where did the Word go?

DEVOTEE ON WATCH: Don't know, he was here and now he's gone with the three.

LUCIFER: The three—that sounds significant; let me sniff. Hmm, I have it. I have their trail. Up they've gone, climbing the mountain. Come with me, just you three. We'll head up the backside of the mountain. We'll see what's transpiring with the Word. Maybe he's getting ready to float up to heaven, pack it in.

Legend nodded back to Story.

READER: One can envision Lucifer on the prowl with a devoted demon on his back. Placing his heels under Satan's armpits, there Backrider sits. The perched demon rides backwards, always watching, scouting, and occasionally turning to whisper a word in his master's ear. Lucifer picks the backriders from his darkest dungeons. It's a very coveted position. He snaps them up on an irregular basis to keep all the demons guessing. When he feels their time is through, Satan shucks 'em. He likes to call it "shedding."

Lucifer, of course, has no right-hand demon, nor one to his left. He can't tolerate the thought of sharing power, of allowing clawing space so near. Just the same, there are always devotees 'round about him. They form his entourage.

Imagine how things might have gone. Satan, feverishly curious to find out what's going on, begins to claw up the backside of the mountain, with Backrider and three demons clinging to his tail. They make it just in time. Out of thin air, Moses and Elijah suddenly appear.

Story motioned with his script again towards Brother Legend.

LUCIFER: Whoa, old-timers—how'd they get here? Long past they've been dead, well and truly whisked away and shoveled under. This is suspiciously mysterious, maliciously messy. It's not fair, importing in the departed. It's just not fair, leaping over the natural elements. Dead is dead. I knew there was something significant taking place up on this mountain.

Quiet, imbeciles! Can't you see my mind treading, threading, through this scene? Didn't expect that, not them. Moses in the Promised Land, after all! Not so thrilling is it, ol' boy? Stick around awhile, and we'll show you the park—it's called Golgotha. It's a fleshy deal, fleshies murdering fleshies.

Promised Land, what a picture: Honey oozing out of the ground. Smell of bread waffling through the air, lambs roasting. It was all a gargantuan fabrication, a wayward waste of words. Spent on olden-day fleshies just to watch 'em move around on I AM's chessboard. Dumb fleshy pawns. They've got eyes, but they are as blind as teeth. Blinder, I'd say. I do say. See, I said it!

Brother Legend paused and once again offered a slight nod to Story.

READER: Suddenly Christ was transfigured. His face was radiant, shining like the sun. His clothes appeared as lightning.

Story quickly looked up at the center fan, and then slowly turned and nodded to Brother Legend. Brother Legend continued.

LUCIFER: You three see that? Don't answer—that's not a question! I know what it is. He's made that way. That's the Word in flesh. No wonder he's become so brilliant, all lit up like. Fleshy skin can't conceal the Word.

What did I hear you say, Backrider? "Can I do that?" Yes, you no good, rotten imbecile of a devotee. How dare you speak to me in question form? Who do you think you're talking to? I'm Lucifer, not God in fleshy skin. I'll shed you, you goofy nub of a demon! Who cares? Who wants to shine anyway on top of a dumb mountain, all luminous? So what's it all about? Who's here to see?

Legend nodded once again to Story.

READER: Into the scene enters the theophany. A theophany it was! A bright cloud came to rest on top of the mountain, and God spoke: "This is my Son, whom I love; with him I am well pleased. Listen to him!"

Story took a few steps back from the podium, fixing his eyes on Brother Legend.

LUCIFER: Hear that rumbling voice? Not a question! Hellish holograms! I've not seen anything like this since Mt. Sinai. I AM coming down on top of a mountain, speaking his mind, the Word blazing like lightning—what a spectacle!

Do you idiots know how revelational this is? Of course you don't! This is all fixing to be written up fleshy style—more scrolling, pasting on foreheads, reciting, memorizing. I AM doesn't do anything without thinking about words. He'll never say to fleshies, "Think as you wish. Stoke up your own storylines. Draw your own conclusions."

This is all in line with I AM's constricting ways of programming fleshies by way of select words and stories. Not me! You know my tune. You know how it goes.

Brother Legend smiled and began to sing the following lines:

> *Happenstance and chance. Flow and flap.*
> *Say what you wish and will, old chap.*
> *Mix up your words. Swirl 'em around;*
> *don't get precise when you jot them down!*
> *A tiddle here, a diddle there. Snip 'em up and pitch 'em in the air.*
> *Oh, what a wordy mix! Oh, what wondrous prose!*
> *Meaning on the run…all homespun.*
> *That's how wordy mixes should be done!*
> *A t here, an i there; dot 'em, cross 'em without the slightest care…*

Hey, wait a minute—this mountain air is making me giddy. This is serious business we've happened on to. What are you letting me sing for? We need to be growling, not crooning.

Old-timers showing up, walking, talking…this all points to a major deal, some kind of pinnacle, trouble—trouble, for sure. The Three is chiming, rhyming, symbolizing some kind of full-blown divine demonstration.

Look at the Word's three lackeys: all terrified, trembling, hitting the ground. Hey, you three—open your eyes, you cowards! Get your noses out of the dirt. Thought you wanted to follow, be fishers of men and all that…stupid, fleshy dummies! This is the spiritual world, nutcases, not some fleshy, featherweight kind of deal. Tremble on, you little wimps.

See what all this fleshy business has come to? The Word himself, putting on skin and climbing a mountain! Who needs a fleshy climbing suit? It's reprehensible. No surprise to me that fleshy skin would be luminous with the Word wearing it. What do you expect, a little candlelight glow?

I AM coming down as in the days of old. Moses and Elijah stepping out of eternity into time...what are they concocting? "Listen to him," I AM says. Well, I ain't listening. So what if he gets a million and one fleshies to follow? That's a million and one too many. Fleshies following—might as well have a virus following you around. They're nothing but walking mud cakes with a bit of breath.

Just mark my words: Those three trembling with their noses in the dirt, this is something they'll want to shout about, all fleshy style. I can hear them now down in the marketplace. "Thus saith, we seeith, upon said mountain, he shineith like lightning." But I'll be there to tell the truth. On said mountain they seeith not a thing. They hideith their faces in the dirt. They squirmed and wriggled, and no doubt piddled.

Go ahead, shout out your tales. We'll never let up. When they speak up, we'll speak over 'em, under 'em, and around 'em. Whatever they enunciate we'll reenunciate, lubricate, and elaborate. We'll give 'em barrage after barrage of biting enunciation. I've seen enough of this luminous extravaganza.

Now, you three devotee clingers, come up here quick. We're out of here. I'm scooting down on my belly just like I came up, but backwards. Get up here in front of me. As I start backing down, you do the same. Keep looking up. Those old-timers may still be around. With the Word near, they could be fierce. They're like old wolves. Backrider, you keep looking down; make sure no one is coming up. Quietly now, let's start our descending creep. We've seen enough for one day.

Luminous flesh on a mountain—what a way of reigning and ruling the cosmos! I need to get down and cough. This is all giving me a mean spell of spiritchitis. I'll luminate 'em all right—just give me time.

Brother Legend took his seat, and Story returned to the podium.

READER: Orchestrating the elements, the Transfiguration was not for show, but for effect. God was aiding the telling his own story. The initial audience consisted of the three apostles, Peter, James, and John. Years later, Peter included a synopsis of the event in a letter he wrote to followers of Christ dispersed throughout Asia.

St. Peter explains how the Transfiguration shaped his message. "For we did not follow cleverly devised myths when we made known to you the power and coming of our Lord Jesus Christ, but we were eyewitnesses of his majesty. For when he received honor and glory from God the Father, and the voice was borne to him by the Majestic Glory, 'This is my beloved Son, with whom I am well pleased,' we ourselves heard this very voice borne from heaven, for we were with him on the holy mountain."

This is the effect. "Eyewitnesses of this majesty"—St. Peter writes, tells, teaches, and testifies to what he has seen. Similarly, St. John writes, "We have seen his glory, the glory of the One and Only."

On the day, the three apostles were in shock over what transpired. They stood staring at Moses and Elijah, with Christ transfigured. Then the bright cloud enveloped them. When they heard God's voice, they fell facedown to the ground, terrified.

No wonder. When God showed up in Scripture in the form of a cloud, it was never a trite affair. Mt. Sinai with its ominous cloud brought not only the Law; it meant death to anyone who casually approached. This, however, was not Mt. Sinai; it was the Mount of Transfiguration, and the image of God was dramatically different.

In addition to the Father's words, there are also Christ's, which he spoke to his three disciples trembling in fear, as they lay facedown on the ground. Christ went over and touched them and spoke two impromptu lines. "Get up," he said. "Don't be afraid."

VOICE: What did they feel? What did they see? What did they hear?

READER: They felt the touch of God. They saw only Christ. They heard words of peace and comfort. Moses and Elijah were gone. The bright cloud had dispersed. Christ was alone on the divine stage. He was the One to see and hear. There was no God to fear.

Christ's two lines are recorded only by St. Matthew, yet they are extraordinary in their summation. Christ's entire mission to the human race may well be summed up by these two little lines: "Get up. Don't be afraid."

VOICE: Five words, all little. Reader, what do you think they're worth in terms of the picture they convey?

READER: Priceless they are, Voice, simply priceless. Christ's words to his terrified disciples did not fade with that eventful day. In time, they soared from the mountain, speaking far and wide. "Get up," he said. "Don't be afraid. The Father and I are one. There is nothing to fear."

These words beckon still through the valleys; on and on they go. "Listen to him," to the One who so long ago and far away was transfigured on a mountain, the Word Made Flesh with luminous essence. To him listen—that is what the Father said in his theophanous appearance.

The message of reconciliation required more than a human messenger from God, or even an angel. It required God as both medium and message. It required Christ. The luminous Christ had taken center stage. Christ was God seen, God heard. There was a face from beyond the clouds for humanity to see.

Listen.

VOICE: To what? What am I to hear?

READER: Listen again. Hear the echo?

VOICE: I hear it now, yes, I hear the echo. It's the words of Christ.... "Get up. Don't be afraid."

READER: Good, Voice. Very good.

Words do matter...the images they create can be priceless.

Get up. Don't be afraid.

JESUS CHRIST, MOUNT OF TRANSFIGURATION, CIRCA AD 32

—◦•◦—

"Okay, we'll break and then gather in twenty minutes," Story said.

Hollie and Goodwin strolled around outside for a minute or two.

"I think I'll just go back in," Hollie said. "The room is so inspiring."

Inside on the bench, Hollie sat alone, eyes closed, enjoying a faint breeze stirred by fans in slow motion. Her thoughts flowed, crisscrossing, intermingling. She prayed for stillness, for her spirit to be touched. Hollie allowed the words "Don't be afraid" to repeatedly flow through her mind, like ripples from a raindrop on water. She felt more than herself. She felt peace and rest.

She also thought of Mr. Ironbout and how the story of the Transfiguration seemed so radically different than what she had witnessed on The Point. Then she thought again: Perhaps Oban Ironbout would one day hear the voice of God and be unafraid.

At the allotted time, Scribe House was once again full of faces happily reflected in the mirrors.

"As you can see, I've only put three thoughts on the handout," Story said. "Yes, Sheila?"

"The point about listening to him, like him—what do you mean 'like him'?"

"Christ was an amazing listener, and his relational style of speaking was full of observations from what he heard and observed. As you can see, our fictional Lucifer is quite the opposite. You might wish to read the Gospels, specifically noting all the questions Christ asked of people.

"The group may be surprised to know that every six months we monks all come together on the mainland for a weeklong retreat simply to discuss what we're seeing and hearing. We spend time in prayer, in reading, and going over our messages, but we also use the week to discuss what we're observing—the trends, the messages flowing about.

"A lot of people are surprised that our aim at Estillyen is to help people live immersed in culture, not flee from it. People definitely need renewal, pilgrimages, and sabbaticals, but living more effectively in society is the aim. Estillyen is not a fortress *from* the world. We are a community *for* the world. Huge difference, that. Faith is personal but never private. It's a life shared in culture.

"You might hear us use the phrase 'threefold observation.' It means observing the words, images, and sounds resonating in culture at any given time. What are they communicating, mediating to whom, with what effect?

"The idea of creating a mass maze of cubbyholes labeled *secular* and *spiritual* is sadly, we feel, very limiting. I don't want to separate myself from the world's art. Christ never ran from culture; he moved within it.

"Anyway, let me pull myself back in. Yes, please, you have a comment."

"Hi, yes, my name is Crystal. I love the emphasis on 'Get up. Don't be afraid.' You spoke of those words as a kind of summation for Christ's mission. Do you have anything more on that point?"

"Yes, there is really quite a lot one could say. God appearing on mountains in Scripture is serious business. The disciples would have been terrified. The atmosphere was charged with God's divine presence. The disciples were mortal—they must have sensed their own inadequacy. They buried their faces in the dirt.

"Then the words of Christ are spoken: 'Get up. Don't be afraid.' Christ, the only begotten Son of the Father, infused a totally new image of God. Christ and the Father were one, but until Christ appeared, God's image was less clear. People wondered what God was like. This is why Christ repeatedly said things like, 'If you've seen me, you've seen the Father.'

"Said another way, before Christ was seen, the image of God in Christ was not seen. The image of God was certainly grasped by David in his psalms, and by Abraham and many others, but it was not expressly revealed as it was in Christ. That took the Incarnation: God walking, talking, touching.

"Therefore, in Christ God appears, saying, 'Get up,' not 'Get back.' He doesn't say, 'Be warned.' He says, 'Don't be afraid.' It was a new day for approaching God. There was a mediator present between God and man: Christ. Those succinct lines are, for me, a synopsis of Christ's entire mission and the gospel.

"The image we hold of God shapes us. We are somewhat fixed on this point here at Estillyen. I'm sure you have heard this coming through the readings."

"Most helpful," Crystal said. "I'd love to chat with you further at some point."

Story asked how many in the group had actually thought deeply about the meaning of the Transfiguration. Most admitted they hadn't. A young man commented that he had never seriously thought about Moses and Elijah appearing. "Like it was there," he said, "but not real—more like an aberration than a true happening."

An older gentleman, who introduced himself as Mr. Clarksburn, offered an astute point. "I feel that the appearance of Moses and Elijah foreshadowed Christ's resurrection," he said. "Moses was buried by God, as you said, but there he was with Elijah, both resurrected.

"They testify to Christ's resurrection. I would call them the silent witnesses in the Transfiguration story—not just talking to Christ about his departure, but standing with Christ as a testament to the ages."

"We better sign you up as a message maker—well done," Story said.

A young Miss Kelly wondered aloud, "Do you think the Transfiguration would have happened without the audience of three?"

"Good point," Story said. "What do others in the group think? Yes, Hollie?"

"I don't think so," Hollie said. "That seems to be the whole point. Take the example of Peter writing about the Transfiguration. I definitely feel that the event was for those three disciples. They were sort of like the grain of a mustard seed. From the three, the story was made known to the world."

This exchange, in turn, fueled considerable discussion regarding revelation.

It sparked off even more comments about the Gospel of Christ being written as he spoke and moved in community.

Story used the phrase "present speaking for future hearing" in elaborating on the topic. He talked about how Christ spoke into a specific culture and time, but also to all cultures at all times.

The conversation lasted just shy of an hour. The whole notion of God orchestrating the event, choreographing and directing the scene, consumed considerable time.

A young man by the name of Baxter said, "I never thought about God becoming so involved."

Baxter's comment produced a good chuckle. Everyone seemed to agree that they would never again consider the Transfiguration in the same light.

Soon Hollie and Goodwin were on their way. As they strolled away from Scribe House and through the meadow, they agreed to forego lunch. Goodwin wanted to check out the prospect of fishing, and Hollie wanted to read.

Alone they found their niches, but feeling not alone in any sense.

NINE
Framing

"Well, welcome, Hollie," Sister Ravena said. Please, have a seat."

"Great office," Hollie said. "Wonderful lighting.

"Thanks for making time to meet with me, Sister Ravena. I know you're really busy. I'm not exactly sure what to say concerning The Point and Mr. Ironbout. We did go up to The Point on Friday. I got to meet the mystery man. I think I mentioned that Goodwin, my husband, met him a couple of days ago.

"It was a very different conversation this time. What we discovered was truly amazing. Just like you said, there's a lot of pain up there on The Point."

"I'm nearly bursting with curiosity, but first, please tell me, how's it going, your time on Estillyen—are you finding it enjoyable, fruitful?"

"Oh, incredibly so. The Isle of Estillyen is such a fantastic place. It's so full of surprises. Just like this office. I didn't expect to walk in here and see such incredible art. It's wonderful," Hollie said.

"The old structures add a special depth to the art, don't you think?"

"Definitely. Do you mind if I take one minute to look at a few of the paintings?"

"No, not at all. The more I'm out from behind the desk and on my feet, the better I like it. I'm not pressed for time today anyway."

"That large one next to the far window—that has to be Lakes Three. We were just up there on Sunday. Stunningly beautiful. I think I could have stayed a week."

"Yes, bit of age to that one. Very nicely done, it is. The painting shows all three lakes, which, of course, you can't see unless you're in a plane. The other place to view them is here in the painting. The lakes hide from each other behind the pines, the locals say. Anyway, I'm glad you like it. It's called *Hidden View*. I often refer to that painting in talking about art. I like to emphasize art's extraordinary capacity to bring to life that which would otherwise remain hidden, unseen."

"I know, that's why I love being an artist so much. I'm often surprised, even stunned, by what appears on my canvas. Never thought about the subject or some aspect of something, and then there it is. It's almost scary at times."

"I view art as framing. By that I don't mean something framed. I like to think of art as framing life and imagination: a piece here, a piece there. I have nothing against frames, though," Sister Ravena said with a smile.

"For example, the painting behind you is perfectly framed. It's called *Rooster's Call*. The frame is simple, very clean. It allows the vivid image of the rooster a place to stand. It's almost as if the proud fellow were captured and hung on the wall, where he just froze. I do expect him to crow someday—I hope not due to my denial. Really, I love that rooster.

"When you look at the painting to your left, *Mary's Face*, it's different. The painting depicts Mary gazing at her son dying on a cross. It doesn't want a frame. It shouldn't have a frame."

"Oh, I agree. It's incredible, stunning. It looks like a masterpiece."

"The dramatic image is so full of life. The rich oils simply disappear into the wall unframed. It makes you want to take a knife and start chipping away at the plaster, expecting to see Mary's shoulders and arms. At the same time, the painting itself frames deep emotion, enormous pain, and enduring love. That's what I mean by framing.

"The small one over there—the abstract figure kneeling in prayer—is called *Surrender*. Kneeling. Bare feet. Seemingly no clothes. The rounded back, facedown. To me, it frames humanity. Nothing to offer God except surrender. The figure appears to be sacrificing his life. No wallet, no pocket for a wallet, no jewelry—nothing but darkness, obscurity, and humility. It can be so hard for people to obtain that position."

"Brilliant," Hollie said. "I so love the way you describe that. I think we have a lot in common. This large wall opposite the triple windows is great."

"It's perfect. The sun never reaches in this far, but the light is perfect."

"Is that Scribe House?"

"It has to be, don't you think? I love the flowers in the meadow. They're not all flourishing and perfect. Look at the trail where it bends—some are still buds, others in full bloom, but then you see a lot of stems with the flowers gone. They are equally beautiful."

"It's great, Scribe House. We were there yesterday. We couldn't believe the main room with the two mirrored walls. The reading was about the Transfiguration. It was called *Get Up—Don't Be Afraid*. Story was the Reader. Now I can't get the Transfiguration out of my mind."

"Story's real name is Apollos," said Sister Ravena. "Brilliant fellow. Don't tell him where you got that inside information, though. The Readers really do become their chosen names. Their work is very much a mission. I have something like that in mind for art. The readings, of course, are an art form of their own.

"That's one of the reasons I tried to approach Mr. Ironbout. Artists would love it up on The Point. It's such a beautiful place. We need more artists visiting Estillyen. I can envision courses, art auctions for needy causes, and a host of things as we look ahead."

"That sounds like a dream. And you're right, The Point is the perfect spot for such activity. Can I ask you about just one more painting?"

"Sure, which one?"

"That one—the young man in the green shirt with the black collar and cuffs. When I walked in, I could feel him staring at me. His fingers are so perfect—slender and full of tension, the way they're all pressing upon his chin with his thumbs pushing into his Adam's apple.

"I love the way his elbows wrinkle the fabric as they press down on the small table. He's just staring with that haunting look. He's in a kind of dressing room or something. The mirror on the table—did he just set it down, or is he going to pick it up? You can't tell."

"Both, I would think."

"But his look…it's distant, yet focused, like he's gazing far into the distance but at something near. Like he is staring at us, yet beyond us."

"That effect is extremely hard to achieve."

"And the expression on his face—it's what I'd call beautifully sad."

"You're actually not that far off from the name of the painting. It's called *Uncomfortably Numb*. It's inspired by a song with a similar title. Arthur Priestmoure is the artist. He comes to Estillyen every two or three years, and he painted it while on one of his stays. There's the date. Ten years, plus…that makes it fourteen years ago.

"I could have sold it a hundred times, but these are not for sale. That doesn't mean we couldn't hold auctions someday, with new or donated works earmarked as such. Not easy keeping Estillyen the way it is, though. We'll see. I agree, it's a beautifully sad, wonderful piece.

"The lyrics of the song are on the back. I think I have a copy in my desk. Let me see. Please have a seat again while I look. I've talked about it so many times I nearly know the lines by heart. I'm sure you know it. It starts with a question, sort of asking if the person is conscious."

"Oh, yeah, I know which one you mean. It's brilliant, the music, and such a haunting plea. Interesting. I never expected to be in a nun's office, viewing such incredible art and talking about that kind of music."

"It's important to do this. In faith communities like ours, we can become so insular, always talking about the world in such an objective sense. I had a great mentor who used to say, 'There is an enormous distinction between talking *about* the world and talking *with* the world.' It's a passionate subject of mine.

"Sorry, I can't find those lyrics right now. Anyway, I contend that there is one world of art, not two; one world of music, not two; one world of literature, not two; one world of people, not two. We can divide the world, and then divide it again and again and again. Soon we have a little fortress with the words and images we prefer, representing who we think we are or aspire to be."

"I know, I'm very much with you on that notion."

"And what have we done? We've barricaded ourselves into the world we have just selected. Certainly words matter. Images matter. Some are of little value, while others are invaluable. It's not as easy as eradicating this for that."

"I agree, I remember one of my professors talking about how an image poorly drawn may hang on a wall beside a masterpiece. Yet, the poorer image can cast light on the masterpiece due to the great contrast. The difference can be so stark, so startling. It's like a mournful, melancholy piece of music—how it can speak powerfully to my joy, or it can remind me of my journey, of why I'm grateful. You know?"

"Certainly. When we segment the world, selecting just our own cozy corner, in the end, who is it that is numb? We're cheated. There is so much to see and hear in the world of art, so much that's inspiring, provoking, and affirming. Does any of that make sense?"

"Definitely," said Hollie. "I really appreciate the way you think, where you're coming from. I hope we can talk more. We must, I think."

"Oh, dear, I'm afraid I've paddled the canoe too far away from shore."

"Not for me. And I've actually got something else I'd like to share with you, but not just now."

"Sure, I'm here. So, anyway, let's talk about Mr. Ironbout, shall we? Now that's a different subject. You say you went to his house? I've never heard of anyone getting that far."

"Yes, it's true. Win and I went up last Friday. I was full of jitters after Goodwin's first encounter. Mr. Ironbout actually shot a gun in the air, threw a barrage of walnuts, and threatened him. I still can't believe it."

"Not surprised."

186 | Messages from Estillyen

"There is a lot to the story, but Win's grandfather, who recently passed away, actually knew Mr. Ironbout. His grandfather's name was Raleigh Macbreeze. He was often called Sir Raleigh. Goodwin was given his grandfather's surname because he never knew his father."

"Win and Goodwin are the same person, right?"

"Oh, yes. Sorry, I'm just buzzing on."

"No, it's fine. Just wanted to be certain."

"Anyway, Win's grandfather once gave him an old photo of Mr. Ironbout's house. He had taken it while on a visit, decades ago. He used to come to Estillyen regularly back then, at least for a time. Win drew a sketch of the house from the photo. He was only ten or so at the time.

"I know this all sounds a bit strange. Win named the sketch *My Cottage Rare,* and he took it with him when he went trekking up to The Point, all unannounced. Goodwin was adamant. He wanted to see The Point and the house. Nothing could persuade him, otherwise. And believe me, I tried.

"His grandfather described The Point in detail, went on about it over the years, like it was one of the most unusual places on earth."

"I think this Sir Raleigh was right about that."

"Anyway, Win was certain the house in the sketch had to be the house on The Point. When Goodwin showed the sketch to Mr. Ironbout—that is, after he calmed down a bit—Win said his whole demeanor changed. Mr. Ironbout studied the sketch, and then stared into Win's eyes. He said it was kind of haunting.

"All of a sudden, Mr. Ironbout recognized Win's belt buckle, which had been his grandfather's. It has the letters Mac, with a large B below.

"Goodwin said that Mr. Ironbout stared at him with his penetrating eyes, and then looked again at the sketch. Win thought he seemed almost in shock. Mr. Ironbout's wife is depicted in the sketch, so I guess that jolted his memory. After a few minutes, Mr. Ironbout got kind of silent. He just told Win he shouldn't be there, that kind of thing.

"That's when he drifted over to the porch, pulled up a chair, turned his back to Win, and just sat there gazing at the sketch."

"Hollie, I don't know what this all means, but it's fascinating," said Sister Ravena.

"Yeah, I know. Wild, huh? And I'm surprised I agreed to go up to The Point with Win, but I did. When we got there, at first Mr. Ironbout seemed sort of normal…but peculiar. He acted like a foreigner on his own property, or something. It's hard to describe. He was restless.

"He was trying to be friendly and courteous, but it was as if he had just read a manual on how to behave. How can I put it? It was like he was an imposter, that's it, like he shouldn't be found on the porch being pleasant. That's what I mean by foreign. He spoke about getting back to his old self, how the sketch and everything caught him off guard. The inference was that bitterness and throwing walnuts was the real Mr. Ironbout, and being kind was not who he really was.

"I didn't buy it, though. In that brokenhearted man, I could see a man of kindness. You see how crazy this is? There is so much more I could say. We ended up viewing the burial plot of his wife and the twins.

"What a sight! There were short steel posts around the perimeter of the plot, with a black chain running through rings on top of the posts. The plot became a stage onto which Mr. Ironbout stepped. As he stood there amidst the gravestones, the mood became eerie and very sad. It was like he had entered a mist.

"With the grave markers as a backdrop, he stood there speaking words of anguish. He didn't just speak sorrowful words, he *became* the words. He was Burden, the character, true to form. The characters Misery, Bitterness, Defiance... he spoke for them all on that small plot. He knew their lines. He taught them their lines, as well as their moves. That's the way it felt, anyway.

"Standing there, with those black chains defining the perimeter of his stage, he breathed in bitterness and breathed out misery. He didn't speak so much from his mind as from his heart and soul.

"That's when it hit me. It sort of stunned me. I believe he saw us as the audience—the audience he never had, an audience of a lifetime. What we were observing no one else had seen, except his dogs.

"In torturous form, he performed, not as if we were just an audience of two, but as if heaven and hell were watching. He said, 'I'm a wounded man. Can't you see? I'm ruptured.'

"I could go on, honestly, but that's the gist of the story. We're so uncertain about what to do next, if anything. But Goodwin definitely wants to go back, and I think I feel the same. So that's kind of it."

"Remarkable, truly remarkable. Over the years, Mr. Ironbout has been the topic of numerous discussions, and there have been several attempts to reach out to him. The sisters used to take food parcels up to his signs, beyond the rock wall, and leave them there. He would always go out and bring them in, but it seemed he would grumble all the more, in the coming days. The sisters would joke, saying that kindness made him meaner, or that he hated the food.

"The time I went up there—it's been several years now—we hadn't seen him for awhile. He had walled himself off from the world. I just felt something needed to be done. He might have died, and no one would have known. We really wanted to see if we could help him.

"There's also the matter of the property. If he dies, and there's no will, what happens? We already know Source Telecom wants it, and money is not their worry. I think they are still after it. Our Abbey attorney heard they have been in contact with Mr. Ironbout, through solicitors. Not sure what that's about.

"It would be a tragedy, devastating, to have all those signal towers omnipresent, hovering over the community. What messages are they conveying? Certainly not the messages of Estillyen. Anyway, it would be a messy legal fight, and we would probably lose.

"A year or so ago, a Mr. Gerkawin and a Mr. Yarnes actually came to visit me. No one here knew them, or had ever met them. One of them, the tall one, looked down at me, the other up. Strange pair.

"They had a big scheme all figured out. They were looking at Lakes Three, and they offered to build The Abbey a new chapel in exchange for fifty years access. They started talking about trusts and what they called veracious charity, some kind of performance-giving scheme.

"They laid out their plan. They talked on and on about how a percentage of Source Telecom revenue would go to Estillyen. They spoke about a public relations campaign, showcasing Source Telecom's commitment to historic communities like Estillyen. I told them there was no community like Estillyen, but chatter on they did.

"I tried to interject. I listened, and then I listened some more. They finally sat back with smug smiles. I said, 'Thanks for the words you've expended today, and the layout of your proposal. However, we never work from formulas. It's all about people. We consider our work to be serving God. We believe that God takes care of Estillyen and its mission, and I have a very strong impression that God's not interested.' I thanked them, and told them there was nothing more to say.

"They were so dismissive, so infatuated with their own ideas. I felt that they were a true counterforce to good. Seldom do I ever get that feeling. People get hurt by people like that. We have a number of folks who come to Estillyen who have been run over by corporate tanks. I saw those two as tank drivers. Not a good pair, not at all.

"Well, back to Mr. Ironbout. I didn't get far the day I went up to The Point. Two of the younger nuns were with me. We went past the warning signs. They trailed just a few meters behind me, all three of us praying. It was cold, the grass and weeds dormant. We were about halfway to the house when the dog began to bark, and then Mr. Ironbout appeared.

"He screamed and hollered, spouting words that startled the young sisters. My younger days, prior to joining the Order, were not so sheltered, and I was not bothered—that is, until he fired his rifle and starting throwing walnuts.

"We've sought legal counsel, and even though Mr. Ironbout has certain rights, that incident alone could get him in major trouble. We know that, but what can be done isn't always the thing that should be done. Certainly, in our case, it isn't.

"We're an order not to ourselves but to the world. Estillyen is a retreat, a place of pilgrimage from the buzz of life, but for the reason of going back to it. We are to live in the world. Christ didn't stay on the Mount of Transfiguration; he came down.

"Mr. Ironbout is part of the world. Our world starts at Estillyen and goes out from here. The people who come here on pilgrimage are not angels who need to dust off their wings a bit. Well, there may be a rare one or two, but many come here on the brink of exhaustion, emotional breakdown, or tremendous heartache.

"You speak of characters. We see Confusion, Heartbreak, Rejection, and others regularly walking these paths. We're here to help people along, to help them move on, not escape into our fortress.

"So, what do I suggest about Mr. Ironbout? Let's wait. Think. Pray. We can speak again in a couple of days. You're here through the rest of the month, right?"

"Yes, we've signed up for the whole of *Redemption*—all twelve readings."

"Somehow, I don't think this is just a coincidence. God could very well be in it. You used the word *rupture*. Perhaps what you saw on that burial plot was a kind of bizarre confession, by a man so deeply buried in his own pain that he had no other words.

"Maybe, just maybe, he will rupture into grace. When people age, they tend to go one of two ways. They can become more gracious and kind, or they can become entrenched in the self, which can make them very bitter. Perhaps Ironbout is turning. We'll see."

Hollie was grateful for the advice. She agreed to lay low for the next few days and pray about the whole matter. She was getting ready to go, gathering her things, when Sister Ravena asked a question.

"You mentioned in passing there was something else you wanted to share?"

"Well, with all of this, it's really a topic for another day. I was thinking we might connect for tea or something. It's just that not long ago I discovered I have a medical condition, and it's weighing on me. I thought maybe you might help, I mean, you know, offer a bit of perspective."

"Oh, I'm so sorry to hear that," said Sister Ravena. "Of course I'll help in any way I can."

"Thanks. In a nutshell, it's something called polycystic kidney disease. It could get rather severe in time. I feel like it's changed everything. I know I'm still Hollie, but I carry something, and when I look in the mirror, I can't see my face without it reminding me that it's there. Anyway, not now, but if you wouldn't mind, maybe I could come back and we could have a chat. I'd appreciate your prayers, too."

"You are such a special one. I'm so delighted you felt comfortable enough to share that. We're very glad you're here. Estillyen needs you as much as you need us. God bless you. Of course I will pray. Maybe Friday…could you come for tea around four? We start early around here. I'm not going down to the village for the rest of the summer, so Fridays are really good for me."

"Wonderful. I'll be here."

"Here, let me move around from behind this desk and give you a hug."

"Thanks for everything, Sister Ravena. You have no idea how much this helped."

Hollie turned and began walking toward the door. As she did, she once again felt the peering eyes of the young man she had described as beautifully sad. Through the door frame Hollie stepped, as she turned and said good-bye.

"See you soon," Sister Ravena replied, as she watched Hollie slip away.

TEN
Tunnel House

"This brownie is too much—great chocolate," Goodwin said.

"They are quite scrumptious," Hollie admitted. "But I'm eating too much. Hand me your knife and I'll cut this in half. Here, go for it. I need this espresso, though. I think Tunnel House is the only reading house with a coffee bar. I suppose most everyone here will be going upstairs to the reading."

"So, you were encouraged by your chat with this Sister Ravena."

"Why did you say 'this' Sister Ravena?"

"Don't know—maybe because I've yet to meet her."

"You will. And yes, it was great sitting there with her in that room surrounded by beautiful art. The conversation flowed so well. She said The Point and the whole Ironbout saga have been a matter of concern for years. She was utterly amazed we made this connection. She called it remarkable. This has never happened before.

"Her idea was to give it a bit of time. But she didn't discourage our involvement, whatever that means. Maybe we really can be part of the solution. Wouldn't that be strange—come to Estillyen on a pilgrimage, and get pulled into the drama on The Point?"

"I know, it's crazy in a way. We've come here to remove ourselves from all the distractions, and we end up in this major ordeal. It isn't stressing me out, though. If we're going to be distracted by something here, this business on The Point seems to be worth it. Almost like a calling."

"I totally agree," said Hollie. "And, as for distractions, I am really glad they don't have Wi-Fi. We thought that was going to be a big deal, remember, but it's just the opposite. I think it would ruin our time here."

"I know, and it's not in any of the guest rooms either," said Goodwin. "I asked. It's only in the offices and that one room off the library. The sign says something about it being for those who find it essential to connect while at Estillyen, or about contacting their offices in case of an emergency."

"I think it's good. I mean, how can you honestly let go and move into the spirit of Estillyen if you're constantly online? Me? Right now I'm just loving this espresso and looking forward to the next reading.

"By the way, see the two small speakers on the wall over by the fireplace, on either side of the mirror? I asked the young lady about them, on my way to the loo. She said that area is for anyone who can't make it upstairs for the reading."

"Hi, are you here for the reading?" Hollie asked as she turned her head towards the three young ladies seated at the next table.

"Yes. They'll ring the bell soon," said a trim, dark-haired girl wearing trendy red glasses. "Should be any minute."

"Thanks. I love your green sweater," Hollie said. "And your white jacket—I like that, too. In fact, all three of you look as if you are going off on a fashion shoot."

The three smiled, just as the bell rang.

"Well, here we go to the reading room at Tunnel House," Goodwin said.

"Tunnel House…that's the coolest name," Hollie said.

Next to the coffee bar there was a very narrow wooden staircase that wound up a single story to the Tunnel House reading room. Directly below the room was a long, narrow tunnel, large enough for a hay wagon to pass through with a team of horses.

In the reading room, black curved-back wooden chairs added to the artistic feel of Tunnel House. The chairs formed three circles, each with twelve chairs. The circles had symmetrical gaps for access. In all, there were thirty-six chairs, plus a straight wooden chair in the corner farthest from the steps.

In the four corners of the room, there were short, square windows set low against the floor. The side walls of the room were short, only shoulder height, and rose to intersect a rough-textured cathedral ceiling. The ceiling was plaster, with the exception of the single center beam running the length of the room. The end walls helped open up the room, making the space available for meetings.

Two dark-green fans were mounted on the ceiling beam at equal distances from the end walls and each other. Each fan had five metal blades, which turned so slowly that the fans appeared to have just been switched off, with the blades making their final turns before falling still. A rustic, hand-waxed, pine floor gave the room a homey, historic character.

"I love all the dents and stress marks in the floor," Hollie said. "And look at the deep, golden shade on the walls. Now that's the way to paint."

"That's tint mixed with time; you're talking age."

Within the space of five minutes, twenty-eight people had settled into the smart-looking black chairs, waiting expectantly for the Reader to arrive. Everyone was chatting softly, when suddenly the sound of creaking stair treads hushed the conversation.

The quiet group cloistered in the Tunnel House reading room became quieter still. They listened to the dominating sounds of stairway creaks. Creak after creak, step after step, the sounds rose. The extent of creaking was beyond the capacity of a single pair of feet. Midway in the stairway ascent, male voices, speaking, joined the sound of footsteps creaking. For seconds fleeting, the stairwell was filled with intrigue.

Soon, a blonde, curly-haired, middle-aged monk appeared, wearing a brown habit with a red, woven cord belt. Behind him was a slim, gray-haired monk exhibiting a broad smile. He wore a black habit with a white belt. The creaking continued as the red-belted monk stepped into the center of the room. The white-belted monk made his way to the lone chair in the far corner and took his seat.

"Hello, everyone. My name is Drama. It's great to have you here at Tunnel House today. My colleague in the far corner is my dear friend and brother, Chronicle. He's supposedly now retired, but have you ever seen a retired monk? Brother Chronicle will be assisting me with a bit of the reading.

"Concerning Tunnel House, we're not sure why the house was built as it was, with the tunnel below. We know carriages have passed through, and it's an obvious shelter from a storm.

"We like Tunnel House for readings because a tunnel is a space for going through; from one side you pass to the other side. One end of the tunnel may show through to clouds and rain, the other end sunshine. Smiles may populate one end, sorrows the other. Tunnels are an experience. Some people simply dash through them, while others tend to plod along. Tunnels have a way of silently transmitting to travelers the pace prescribed.

"In life, sometimes it can be difficult to discern one's direction. In a tunnel, there are only two directions: this and that. But that can look like this, and this, that. Tunnels are funny that way. They can lead you in, or take you away. In and out you go.

"A tunnel is a tunnel true—never a passage or a pass. Calling a tunnel something else is like suggesting a crevice is a cave, or a canyon a crack. No, a tunnel is that which surrounds you. You see it all. There's no denying you're in it. Encased within you are; through its artery you progress. Whether short or long, you are the life within the tunnel. Yet the tunnel is not you. This you must always remember.

"And residing in a tunnel really does not work. A tunnel is not a place of residence. A tunnel may be quite short or expressly long. Certain tunnels have been reported to grow. Once you enter a tunnel of this description, the light at the other end does not grow brighter, as you might think. It looks as if the light is diminishing, but it's not. It's moved. The tunnel is growing longer.

"If you find yourself in a growing tunnel, let me suggest the slightest bit of advice. It's not wise, particularly when inside a tunnel deep, to start racing towards what appears to be a dimming light. For if you do, the light can go out; it can disappear. Before you get to the end, another tunnel has begun, and tunnel two may be twice as long as tunnel one.

"It's always best when in tunnel space to move at tunnel pace. Respecting the sense of tunnel enclosure is the mode. See it as a kind of caregiver, a respite from the elements that will bring you through, in tunnel time, to the life God has for you.

"Well, that's a word on tunnels."

"These guys are truly amazing," Hollie whispered to the young woman seated next to her.

"I agree; I'm not accustomed to hearing such things, spoken in such a way," she replied.

"Well, I do think it's that time—just a little past, actually," Drama said. We have three circles of chairs, so it would be good to have three volunteers for our Voice. This circle first. Great, two hands, but let's just take one. Your names are?"

"I'm Sherry, and this is Allie."

"We'll let the letters decide. Going with the beginning of the alphabet, this means Allie it is, unless you wish to swap. Good, circle two—one hand, thank you, Sir. Did I see three hands raised in circle three? We will let the numbers decide this time. Please determine among you who is the youngest in your circle.

"Your three voices will become our audience, our Voice. The wonderment of public sentiment you are. As I move along, my nod will be your cue. Raise your voices with true intent, with a tone of inquisition. Don't worry about making a mistake—you can't. We don't like rules. It's not allowed," Drama said with a smile.

"Our intern, Context, here in circle one will pass along the Voice bits. See, you never know who is sitting with you in an Estillyen circle. She's a very bright young lady. Thanks, Context.

"Okay, let's settle for a moment before we begin." Drama closed his eyes and quietly stood. Noticeable were the creaking sounds of Context moving about. To circle two and three she went, before quickly returning to the circle from which she had begun. Creaks ceased when she took her seat. Stilling silence filled the air, punctuated only by the tick and tock of the massive, tall clock swaying its pendulum at the bottom of the stairs.

"So then, if we're not asleep, we'll begin. The title of today's reading is *A Cry in the Crowd*. Let's listen to a few lines from St. Mark concerning this cry."

A Cry in the Crowd

Jesus asked the boy's father, "How long has he been like this?"

"From childhood," he answered. "It has often thrown him into fire or water to kill him. But if you can do anything, take pity on us and help us."

"If you can?" said Jesus. "Everything is possible for him who believes."

Immediately the boy's father exclaimed, "I do believe; help me overcome my unbelief!"

MARK 9:21-24

READER: Down the Mount of Transfiguration Christ moved, no longer mysteriously incandescent, far above on the mountaintop. With his disciples Peter, James, and John, Christ made his descent with divine intent.

Toward the plain below he headed, drawn down by humanity's gravitational pull. Want and need were ripe for harvest. People were in pain. The oppressed and possessed mingled in the lowland that day, waiting to see in Christ a bit of hope they might profess. A day earlier he was secretively absent, meeting with special guests.

VOICE: Who were these special guests? Were they foreigners from another land?

READER: Oh, Voice, from a distant land they surely were. Special, indeed, in the whole of human history, there had never been such a meeting. From the corridors of heaven, his visitors traveled.

VOICE: Heaven?

READER: Certainly. No doubts do I possess concerning what the story professed. Christ had stood on the mountaintop in luminous splendor, speaking with Moses and Elijah, beneath a heavenly canopy, a theophany.

VOICE: Moses and Elijah…doesn't that jumble the past with the present, the improbable with the impossible?

READER: Ah, Voice, that is a bit of fuzziness speaking. Remove the word *jumble* and clear your disposition. Past with present, yes. Improbable with impossible, yes—but it was not a jumble. Consider it rather a divine directive. God being God it simply was. With God, jumble does not exist.

VOICE: I see… sort of, I think.

READER: With Moses and Elijah on their way and the theophany departed, it was time for Christ to head for the mountain's base and walk among the crowds. Peter's impetuous plan of constructing three tabernacles to capture the glory on the Mount of Transfiguration so differed from divine wishes.

This notion of staying up, not coming down, was not an option. Christ had been designated to appear for all eternity. The subject of Mary's song he was born to be. Down was where the drama called, incarnated to be near, not beatified, and resting glorified under a tabernacle on a mountain high.

St. Paul captured so brilliantly the appropriate trajectory of Jesus Christ when he penned this line, "Who, being in very nature God, did not consider equality with God something to be grasped, but made himself nothing, taking the very nature of a servant, being made in human likeness."

How is it, Voice, that St. Paul was so perceptive?

VOICE: Not quite sure.

READER: St. Paul's words so valiantly written. Words woven behind prison bars bearing fruit even now. Ancient but living, past but present. Are you not thrilled by that prospect, Voice?

VOICE: The way you put it, I think so.

READER: Not grasping to stay away, not holding on staying up high. This is the way the oracle was written. At the very heart of the drama is the wonder of letting go, of coming down, of descending far, of revealing the mystery hidden throughout the ages. There was a great tale to tell—all about a shepherd seeking sheep.

READER: During the descent down the mountain, Christ instructed his chosen three: "Don't tell anyone what you have seen, until the Son of Man has been raised from the dead." While they didn't know it, this milestone of rising was just down the road.

Isaiah's prophecy foretelling how Christ would bring welcome news to the marginalized, the victimized, and the stigmatized spread a net far and wide among the populace. Among throngs of both the curious and the suspicious, Christ moved, casting words into unforgettable lines. Navigating the crowds was a serious issue, Voice. Listen to how St. Mark describes the scene on one occasion:

"Jesus withdrew with his disciples to the sea, and a great crowd followed, from Galilee and Judea and Jerusalem and Idumea and from beyond the Jordan and from around Tyre and Sidon.

"When the great crowd heard all that he was doing, they came to him. And he told his disciples to have a boat ready for him because of the crowd, lest they crush him, for he had healed many, so that all who had diseases pressed around him to touch him.

"And whenever the unclean spirits saw him, they fell down before him and cried out, 'You are the Son of God.' And he strictly ordered them not to make him known."

Among the masses, the populace, it does appear there was a substantial labyrinth, a major muddle of marked souls, which evil spirits possessed. Once inside, the spirits clung tight with demonic grip.

At the mountain base, Christ and his three companions quickly rejoined the other disciples, who had remained behind during the Transfiguration. The disciples were in the midst of a crowd when Christ approached. "As soon as all the people saw Jesus, they were overwhelmed with wonder and ran to greet him."

Christ's presence was like a lightning rod drawing people in his direction. A cry was heard. It came from the middle of the crowd. It was the cry of a father with a demon-possessed son. "Teacher, I beg you to look at my son," the father cried, "for he is my only son."

The boy was ill. He was severely afflicted, suffering from seizures, fits, and wicked spells. The torturous condition sorely affected the father's state. He had come to Christ's disciples, begging them to drive out the evil spirit. The disciples were unable to break the demonic curse and set the child free.

The spectacle had drawn a large crowd, along with teachers of the Law, who were debating and arguing with the disciples. Into the squabble Christ stepped. Without hesitation, he moved to the center of the dispute and asked his disciples, "What are you arguing with them about?"

Before they could answer, the father with the child said, "Teacher, I brought you my son, who is possessed by a spirit that has robbed him of speech. Whenever it seizes him, it throws him to the ground. He foams at the mouth, gnashes his teeth, and becomes rigid. I asked your disciples to drive out the spirit, but they could not."

Christ gave a rather unexpected reply. It wasn't an answer at all; it was more of an open public confession. "O unbelieving generation," Jesus replied, "how long shall I stay with you? How long shall I put up with you?"

VOICE: Reader, why such words? Do they truly belong to Christ?

READER: If not, then to whom, Voice, would you like to attribute these words?

VOICE: I don't know. They just seem rather at odds with Christ's manner of speaking.

READER: Voice, I hope you're not going back to that word *jumble?*

VOICE: No, not that. Do the words reveal a divine sigh, or something else?

READER: Perhaps it is a hint, or maybe a slight distraction. After all, in only a matter of days, Christ's speaking among the crowds would cease. Christ would be dead. This he knew precisely.

Consider it, Voice. Only yesterday it was that on the mountain, Christ listened to his Father's voice emanating from the brightly glowing cloud. Now Christ listened to the voice of another father, one not coming down from heaven. The father's cry came up from the muddle, the scrum, and the squabble of unbelief.

Christ could not move about in public for long without incident. Human need was great. As Christ acted, sending evil forces swirling, the curious flocked.

"Bring the boy to me," Christ said. They did. "When the spirit saw Jesus, it immediately threw the boy into a convulsion. He fell to the ground and rolled around, foaming at the mouth." Christ displayed no alarm, no sudden gestures, or words one might expect to hear like, "Stand back! Give us room; the boy is ill, can't you see?"

On the contrary, Christ engaged the boy's father in conversation. In the middle of the pressing crowd, Christ moved into conversational mode. The eyes of both Jews and Gentiles were bulging; everyone was listening with rapt attention. They inhaled, exhaled, and watched. "How long has he been like this?"

Christ asked. "From childhood," the father answered. "It has often thrown him into the fire or water to kill him."

This was not some mild form of epilepsy or minor malady. The demon dwelled deep within, possessing the recesses of the child's body, mind, and spirit. There the evil spirit made its nest, its dwelling place in the borrowed soul of a child. Everything on the inside was misaligned, twisted into a demonic state.

Deep down inside the child the evil spirit hid. From inside, it festered and erupted, tormenting the creature small. One symptom the father described was foaming of the mouth. Consider it, Voice: the toxic-looking fluids bubbling up, as if the child had eaten a poisonous substance.

VOICE: Reader, hold on please. I want to go back a bit, if we might. A minute ago you said something about the muddle, the scrum, the squabble. Is that how you really see it?

READER: Ah, now you've got it, Voice. That's your jumble rightly placed. Into the jumble of humanity, Christ willingly moved.

VOICE: These evil spirits, Reader—who or what were they, anyway?

READER: Angels they were, Voice. Ancient angels led astray who have no way to be born again someday. Their mode, their propensity, is to steal away in the souls and spirits of their victims. Behind ribs they hide, encaged in the darkened interior of those they possess. There they hope eternity will forget them, drop them from the ledger, count them missing, like falling stars. All the while, in souls deep they seep and creep around with tortured moves. Within the entrails of man, woman, and child, they seek to abide.

Immediately the demon within the child would have been aware of Christ's presence. The boy's condition was grave. He was thrashing on the ground; at the feet of Christ he laid. The crowd watched intently, listening to the exchange between Christ and the father. The welfare of the child was the paramount issue.

At the same time, Christ was also crafting the Gospel message. Word-by-word, sentence-by-sentence, parable-by-parable, the Gospel was being storied.

VOICE: Pardon me, Reader, once again. I've always wondered why Christ would tell people not to say who he was. You've made me think of it. Was it because he needed to complete the story?

READER: Oh, Voice, why is it I feel you are growing wise before my very eyes? You are not alone in wondering why Christ said go not and tell. His news was good, was it not, Voice?

VOICE: It was.

READER: So right you are. It has to do with pacing, harmonizing divine revelation with reality. In space and time Christ made his way from day to day. His moves were paced. Too much fuss, too much rush, and divine time and trajectory might be threatened. Then what would have happened? Heaven forbid, but it does make you wonder.

Back to our tale, Voice. As I said, the Gospel was being storied by Christ. Every word Christ spoke was part of that message; every question, every glance or gesture, was part of the message. On this day, the immediate audience included the father, the boy, the disciples, and the crowd. Christ knew, however, a vast and exponential audience was on the horizon.

No doubt Christ knew how critical it was for the storied message to be heard. Throughout the centuries, innumerable people have come to know what this father said, how the boy convulsed and foamed at the mouth, and how Christ responded. It's implausible, is it not, to think Christ would have no awareness of the Scriptures that would attest of him?

In speaking to this father, Christ spoke to one man, with the crowd listening. That's the way it is with Christ's revelational speak. When Christ spoke to an individual, he was also speaking to the world. The audience of one is inseparable from the audience of everyone.

The father is a central character in the drama. The possessed boy was his only child, and the condition had plagued the child since infancy. There is no mention of a mother. She may have been there, but then it seems she would have been noted. This we'll never know.

The begging and pleading speaks of the father's determination and sense of desperation. Likely, the father had gone to great lengths searching for a cure. The narrative reads as if the man is consumed with his son's condition.

Somehow the news of Christ's whereabouts had reached this father, who then made his way to the disciples. The concerned father had begged the disciples to drive out the evil spirit, but to no avail.

Instead, the father ended up in dialogue with Christ, the Redeemer. In answering Christ's question about the length of illness, the father went on to say, "Have mercy on us and help us, if you can." The distraught father uses the pronoun "us," not "me," in pleading for the boy.

In the father's words we see joint suffering, joint anguish. The plea is for a joint cure. In possessing the son, the evil spirit also held captive the father. The two were shackled together, as if wearing leg irons. Immediately Christ picked up on the father's qualifying phrase and repeated it. "If you can?" Christ said. He then continued, saying, "Everything is possible for him who believes." At once, the father counters, "I do believe; help me overcome my unbelief!"

The question posed and answer given are an integral part of both stories. His response is credible, confessional, memorable. Looking into the eyes of Christ, he floats between belief and unbelief. He wants to believe, he does believe…but he doesn't believe. He is both a believer and nonbeliever. Is that you, Voice?

VOICE: Well…I mean, you say…

READER: Please keep listening, Voice. He and the boy had suffered long. The father was sincere in wanting to cast his faith to a higher plane and break free from his state of unbelief. Just as the conversation was occurring, Christ saw another crowd racing in their direction. Christ turned his attention to the boy, and, without further comment to the father, spoke directly to the evil spirit. "You deaf and mute spirit," Christ said, "I command you, come out of him and never enter him again."

The spirit shrieked, causing violent convulsions, and came out. The boy looked so much like a corpse that many said, "He's dead." Christ then reached for the boy and lifted him to his feet. In so doing, Christ lifted the father, as well. The affliction that had shackled them both was broken. They were cured. The evil spirit was driven out.

Demons never mistook the identity of Christ nor doubted his power over them. Once Christ encountered a very violent man, while he was in the region of Gerasenes across the lake from Galilee. This poor soul had been demon-possessed for many years. He was homeless and roamed the countryside, violently taunting and threatening anyone who came near. Most often he could be found wandering among the tombs. Among the graves he reckoned with his identity.

The day Christ arrived, the demon-possessed man of rage ran to see him. To his knees he fell, and he cried out at the top of his lungs, "What do you want with me, Jesus, Son of the Most High God? Swear to God that you won't torture me!" The demon began to plead and beg with Christ, though Christ had already commanded the evil spirit to come out. Deep within the soul the demon clung.

St. Mark describes this man's tortured existence: "No one could bind him any more, not even with a chain. For he had often been chained hand and foot, but he tore the chains apart and broke the irons on his feet. No one was strong enough to subdue him. Night and day among the tombs and in the hills he would cry out and cut himself with stones."

The evil spirit clung on, not yet obeying Christ's command. "'What is your name?' Christ asked. 'My name is Legion,' he replied, 'for we are many.' And they begged Christ that he would not command them to go out into the abyss."

Into the abyss they begged not to go.

VOICE: The abyss—it's real. How do you see it?

READER: Real it is. See it I do, Voice. That great void—the chasm of emptiness where nothing finds nothing. There's nothing in the abyss—it's a kind of spiritual waste, never to be erased. The abyss is a limitless expanse, where words, images, and sounds have no meaning. There is no casting broad or narrow, no symmetry of sight and sound.

No one is there—no one to call, nothing to see or say. It's a vastness in which spirits forever float. They tumble, twist, turn, and tumble on. No exit, no door, no edge, no middle. Not a single wall or window. No tree on the lawn, no lawn, no outside, no air to breathe. Only fear to feel, dread to sense, gloom filled with doom—that's the abyss. Forever to be lost, never to be found. Nothing to seek, no one seeking.

No one enters the abyss. No one can. There is no entrance, no path in and out. No shepherds hunting sheep. Not a single whisper is uttered in the abyss. There are no utterers. There are no listeners. The abyss is beyond the mist, where only evil spirits go. In the abyss, there's never a time of planting, no seeds for growing, never a time of sowing, only nothingness to reap. No reward in reaping nothingness—no grist to grind, nothing to touch, nothing to feel.

In the abyss, there are no residents, no registers to register, only castaways, evil spirits flung to stay. The spirits in the abyss know beyond the mist they'll always be. Rolling forever restless is their unconditional state, their fate. On and on into nothingness they roll.

It was by boat Christ reached the Gerasenes. As soon as he stepped ashore, this man of manic mind and tortured flesh appeared. From out of the tombs, this stricken creature approached. He moved toward Christ not shyly, but loudly crying out.

This man of pathetic state must have had a name someone knew; he did not say. For him, only Legion spoke. It was Legion, one and all, who cried not to be cast out into the great abyss. Legion, a force of demons bound together with destructive might, begged. To Christ alone they begged.

Driving out a demon—to what might it be compared, Voice?

VOICE: I think it's hard to compare.

READER: It must be akin to driving a rabid wolverine from a den, is it not? Out of the soul, heart, and mind the demon is driven. It must go, no more clinging on; out is the command.

The fate of Legion was on the line. Not a single demon, but an entire legion, occupied this man. Perhaps somehow the demonic waves flowed, and the news filtered 'round to Satan's ear. Imagine, just suppose and nothing more, that as Christ came sailing o'er to the Gerasenes, Satan raced 'round by way of shore.

At demonic speed, peeling bark off trees, he raced, spraying sand, as Backrider watched the tiny particles trickle through the air. To the tombs he sped, to coach Legion, just as Christ arrived.

Those gathered in the upper room of Tunnel House were pressed to peak attention when, in the corner, Brother Chronicle rose and cleared his throat. A shaft of light streamed up from the low corner window beside him and filtered across his wrinkled face. With the countenance, clarity, and cadence of a poet, Brother Chronicle began to speak.

Chronicle's enthralling lines all linked in telling a story of Lucifer, Legion, and Christ, in a desolate place called the Gerasenes. Chronicle's narrative drew, in part, on the tale of the tombs, found in the ancient text of Scripture.

LUCIFER: Get off, Backrider. Lay low. You're shed; I'm through with you. Lucifer has Legion on his mind. Don't give me any pathetic play, walking 'round backwards, bowlegged with a sour face. Be grateful I shed you in such a wondrous place. Sniff. Ah, the tombs, the greatest of scents. Decay—it brings out my best of moods.

Chronicle sniffed the air in the room, looked up, and moved his dramatic eyes across the beam. He watched the twin fans slowly rounding their blades. As he stood there, the movement of the audience stilled further into silence. Only eyes were free to race and dart. With curiosity, everyone watched and listened.

LUCIFER: You'll find your way into some troubled soul. Just wait till you hear one of the fleshies sobbing around the tombs, saying, "I'd do anything if only…" That's your cue. They mean it. Promise 'em a chat with the departed, a little turning back of the clock. Now beat it—don't let my eyes see you. Your rank clouds my mind. This is an important day. Gotta think. Legion's now the optic of my diffusion. Scram—get lost among the lizards.

Now, Legion, I know you can hear me. This is Lucifer speaking. Yes, it's me, the one and only Lucifer. In my image there is no likeness. I've come to give you my support, help you thread your needle. Forget not: It's easier for a camel to fall into the abyss than for a demon to buck the words of the Word.

Fear not, that's why I'm here. You can ride this out, buck this wave. You can do it, Legion. I'm here, near, in the tombs watching, abiding. I see what you're up against; it's formidable. Heed my instructions, or the Word will have you cast into the abyss in a flash. Do you want to forever fall, twist, and tumble?

Listen up. Listen good, you hear? You're not without training. Consider what you've learned from me, Legion. Listen, there's a chance the Word will wane a bit. He is, after all, half flesh. Somehow he may become distracted and let you slip.

You know the drill, Legion. I know his power is enormous, but you've got me in the shadows of the tombs. I'm looking in your direction. I'm breathing in your direction. I'm contending in your direction. Fear not, this one called the Word.

Now, here's what to do. Remember, you always start with the inner core of three. There's amazing strength in that configuration. Heed my instruction, sharp, fast, Legion. There's not a second to lose.

Three of you demons in there get onto your sides and bend around, forming the inner circle. Then each of you reach out and grab the ankles of your fellow demon. Bite down on the toes ferociously while bending back the feet. I know some of you do not have feet. Just form them. Quick! There's little time. The Word's eyes are intensifying, rectifying, scrutinizing the form of your wayward fleshy.

So you've got the inner core of three. Remember, grab the ankles, bite down on the toes, bend back the feet. From the core of three, the ball of demons grows. The next circle is four, and it runs 180 degrees to circle one. Circle five then runs the same way as circle one. The circles crisscross; that's the strength. Grab the ankles, bite down on the toes, bend back the feet, until the last demon is locked in place. Crisscross, cross-criss, go, go, go!

Got it? Sure you do. Hurry, you imbeciles! I didn't come all the way out here to watch a maniac fleshy nut wander around in the tombs. I get the whole tomb idea; good choice, but how do you Legion loonies pick such a miserable-looking fleshy? Anyway, that doesn't matter now.

Legion, listen to me. When you hear the Word's command again, clench and bite with all your might. Maybe somehow you'll survive intact to roam another day, not entering the abyss all disarranged. You are Legion. Grab, bend, bite. Do you hear me? I command you! I demand you! Ignore the Word; listen to me!

Don't worry about your toes. What does it profit a demon to save his toes and enter the abyss intact? By the power resident and swirling in me, I command you: Listen to me!

What's that? Legion, don't say that, you stupid imbecile. Never! Don't speak of swine, you crumpling idiot. You're there to swell, swell from the core, all backs against old fleshies' ribs. I command you. Hold your possession, your position, hold. Clench, bite, bend, with all your might, like great demons do.

With a profound look of satisfaction upon his face, Brother Chronicle nodded gently to Drama, who was ready with his lines.

READER: As Legion trembled inside the kneeling man, Lucifer's command became lost. Legion could not hold back his words when the contorted band of demons spotted pigs grazing on a hill. The clenching demons begged Christ, "Send us among the pigs. Allow us to go into them."

St. Mark provides a glimpse of what happened next. "And at once Jesus gave them permission. Then the unclean spirits went out and entered the swine— there were about two thousand—and the herd ran violently down the steep place into the sea, and drowned in the sea."

Drama returned a nod to Chronicle.

LUCIFER: What a mess! Water…how revolting.

And Chronicle nodded again to Drama.

READER: People from the town came to see the effect of demons entering pigs. "Then they came to Jesus, and saw the one who had been demon-possessed and had the legion, sitting and clothed and in his right mind. And they were afraid."

Drama smiled, nodding in Chronicle's direction.

LUCIFER: Wholeness, how I hate it! He was so much better off with us. At least he had power, could snap chains. He was free to roam in delightful places.

Slowly the age-worn face of Chronicle descended through the filtering light, as once again he took his seat. Drama continued with the reading.

READER: Then Lucifer—who was and wasn't there—backed away. Step-by-step, he slowly moved, growling, grunting as if speaking to the dead, while through the tombs he backward swayed. Sliding along on his massive, bristly feet, he soon began to trail away. Shadow upon shadow did the trick, eventually veiling him in darkness, his desired abode—particularly after such a contrary and costly day.

However it came to be, Legion knew a pig was a pig and not a sheep. Seemingly, to Legion, it did not matter. Being *disclosed in* and not *exposed out* is all that mattered—anything but the abyss.

Behind the skin of pigs or human flesh, demons creep. Treading there in the darkened marsh of soul, in madness they cling, yearning not to be cast out into the vast abyss. In the abyss there are no ribs to hold. In the great expanse of nothingness there's no place to hide. There's nothing but abyss exposure.

Angels in the exalted realm once these clinging demons were—until in that hour of great calamity, of repulsive reaching and wanton wanting, they were cast out, descending. How they must hate that little word: *cast.*

The demon-possessed souls encountering Christ never spoke a quiet word. They came not alongside whispering, as if speaking to him in private. Satan seemed to be the only one to master the conversational tone. As he tempted Christ in the wilderness, he did not come out shouting and screaming, "Holy One of God!"

The master of subtlety he was. "If you are the Son of God," he said, "prove it: turn a bit of stone into bits of bread; jump and you will not get hurt. That is, if you are the Son of God...."

Perhaps on that mountain, there transfigured, the luminous figure seen by Peter, James, and John is what the demons always saw. Just suppose, beyond the flesh, they saw straight to the Word, and seeing the unmistakable, they could not help but scream and shout.

Christ's message was both humanly crafted by Jesus of Nazareth in culture's grain, and transfigured in a manner only the Son of God could deliver. In the crowd, in the midst of curious eyes, a father cries; that is how the messages were made. A question here, a comment there, and all the while revelation flowed.

This intertwined weaving of incarnational revelation can, for some, make the whole Gospel story appear too circuitous, too bogged down in the human condition. Arguably, this is why some people hate it so, despising it as preposterous, rendering it foolishness. Revelation, redemption, so embedded in humanity's wail and way—where's all the sanctity? How could God be so far removed from a celestial home? In a human scrum—surely that's not the way God should be?

There, in the scrum of humanity, Christ is found exchanging lines. A father watches his convulsing child rolling in the dirt and begs, "Have mercy on us and help us, if you can." He believed to the point of seeing mercy in Christ's eyes. In this discourse between a distraught father and Christ, few words were actually spoken. From these short lines, quickly exchanged, however, revelation flows, roaring deep and wide.

"If I can," Christ said. "Everything is possible for him who believes." At once, the father counters, "I do believe. Help me overcome my unbelief!" How does one place a value on these buoyant words, these little lines that speak, flowing through reservoirs of time?

Preferring the requisition of other words, many look at Christ's words and turn away. There's no thought of unbelief as something to overcome. Ancient words from history's dusty patch seem so distant. The prospect of formulas clear is much preferred over mysteries old, appearing as they do through panes of time with such storied hues.

The ancient panes, though, are not meant for glancing. They're for peering through. The more one peers, the more one sees. Images seemingly obscure and opaque at first have a way, in time, of dispelling doubt. Christ's words begin to flicker with light certain.

Through the glass dim, it can even appear that God seeks a kind of solace among the scrum-troubled sheep, those wandering and wondering after him. His face divine peers through, though it is impossible to tell whether it is the face of the Father or the Son.

Out of the crowd, the cry of a father is heard. He calls out with words. With words he begs, he hopes. Words he does not expect, he hears: "Everything is possible for him who believes." These words he does believe.

Words matter…Christ's words matter most of all.

I do believe, help me in my unbelief.

DISTRAUGHT FATHER WITH DEMON-POSSESSED SON,

NEAR JERUSALEM, CIRCA AD 32

———❖———

"Well, there's a bit of drama in Tunnel House," Drama said. "Please, no tossing of eggs."

Everyone stood and applauded, turning in the direction of both Drama and Brother Chronicle. Drama was quick to say, "And what about our Voice? Weren't they great?"

Hollie turned to Goodwin, amazement again on her face. They sat back down, perched on their seats, as the group began to mill around and filter down the stairs. Several people passed by Brother Chronicle and Drama to shake their hands and offer a quick word.

"What about a stroll across the lawn?" Hollie asked. "Sounds good, don't you think?"

"Sure."

Down the steps they happily descended and moved out onto the lawn.

"Well, Lee, what did you think?" Goodwin said.

"I really like Drama and Brother Chronicle. They were both great. The reading was incredible. And just Drama's opening comments, about going through a tunnel, at tunnel pace—that little bit right there really hit me. I'm gonna have to pace myself, you know, Win. That's such a good perspective.

"Drama's so eccentric and so interesting. The idea of God being in the scrum— you can see that's so right. I feel very close to these people. It's strange—kind of like what you were saying about being at Ironbout's place. It's sort of uncanny.

"This place—just how cool is it, with this tunnel running through it? I think I'll come down tomorrow and start painting it."

"Sounds perfect," encouraged Goodwin. "But we also really need to talk about The Point, and what we think we should do. I'd like to go up there, maybe tomorrow or Saturday."

The minutes quickly passed. Drama, Brother Chronicle, and the audience of twenty-eight soon regrouped in the Tunnel House reading room.

There was no chore in engaging those there assembled. Eagerly questions and comments flowed, from Cristal, Beverly and Trevor, Kurt…

Like all the readings Hollie and Goodwin had attended, it was time that pushed for a conclusion, not lack of interest.

The last line was Drama's: "Again, thanks for being at Tunnel House today."

Soon the creaking steps fell silent, while the tall clock stationed at the bottom of the stairs ticked on. In perfect tunnel time, it ticked and tocked, metering another day on the Isle of Estillyen.

ELEVEN
Speaker's House and Destiny

"Want me to help carry your kit, Lee?" Goodwin asked.

"So you're painting Tunnel House today—that ought to be fun. I'd like to see you paint all the reading structures."

"Estillyen is incredible for artists," Hollie said. "It's not just the structures, but nature and the zany characters. Everyone would love Estillyen if they could just see it."

"Show it to them. You've got the talent. Seriously—I'm not kidding. Why don't you?"

"When you paint Estillyen, you just let it present itself. Its own magic comes to life. It's real. No need to put a fairy in the tale."

"I know what you mean. I could try a few pencil sketches, but not one of your oils. That's your gift. Why don't you consider a whole Estillyen collection? Think about it, really. Sign them 'Red Factor.'"

"I should clobber you with this, but I don't want to bend it. By the way, I love this folding seat. Thanks for encouraging me to get it. It's perfect for Estillyen, doubling as a walking stick. I'll carry this. Everything else folds into my canvas carrier. That carrier was expensive, but it's worth it.

"What about you?" Hollie continued. "Are you really thinking about going to The Point today to see Mr. Ironbout?"

"I'm not sure now. I think I'll go tomorrow—you know, after lunch. Maybe we *should* just let things settle down a bit. There's no telling what state of mind he's in."

"That's probably a good idea. I'm planning to see Sister Ravena around four tomorrow, and we could meet up at The Abbey for supper. They'll have fish. You'll be starving after a trip to The Point."

"Yeah, maybe you're right. I think I'll bike today then. I want to go back up to Lakes Three and all around."

"What, without me?" Hollie teased.

"Maybe we can go up Sunday."

"No, that's fine. You go. Well, I'm ready. I think that's everything: paints, brushes, bag, water, chewy bits, and easel. Here, take this apple with you. Throw it in your pack. I'm taking my little backpack. My water and everything's in it. Walk down to Tunnel House with me, though. On the way, we could go by the ponds and see if One is still drawing the crowds. Why don't you carry the case, muscles?"

Hollie and Goodwin moved along the interconnecting paths that led to the backside of Silo on the Mound. They were just passing the Silo when a yellow calico cat strolled across the path, followed by a small pig.

"Pinch me, Goodwin! I must be losing it," Hollie said as she squeezed Goodwin's forearm. "That's a cat followed by a little black-and-white pig, isn't it? The pig is shadowing the cat's every move."

"It appears your mind is still with you. That's definitely a calico cat and a black-and-white pig."

"Where do you suppose they're going?"

"It looks like they're headed for the lean-to on the other side of the barn. Let's go around the front to see if we can spot them—this way, through the gate."

Hollie and Goodwin scurried down the path and across the barnyard.

"Is it okay to be here, Win, with all these animals? They look wild."

"Come on, the front of the lean-to is just over there. It's the one with the red wooden gate. Let's take a look," Goodwin said as he moved over to the gate. "There's the cat up on that crate, and the pig is beneath it in the straw. Amazing."

As Hollie and Goodwin stood there staring at the two creatures, a slim, older gentleman approached from behind.

"Hi there," he said.

"Oh dear, you scared me," Hollie said.

"Sorry, Miss. I suppose you are curious about Tiptoe and Spook. We call her Tiptoe 'cause of the way she catches prey. Tiptoe learned that to catch a mouse you gotta be quieter than a mouse. She moves like she's got cotton balls glued to her little paws. That's it, cotton balls. Then she sticks out her claws, and no more moving mouse."

"Really, well, that's a talent," Goodwin said.

"Tiptoe's had several litters. She had one when Spook was born, two years ago, I believe. The pigs are across the yard. When this pig was a couple months old, he got out. They were moving sheep through here that day. Sheep make a lot of ruckus; they bellow and chatter and twitch all around with nervous eyes. The sheep scared the pigs dizzy."

"I'll bet," Goodwin said.

"Spook took off—of course, he wasn't Spook then 'cause he didn't have a name. A day or two later, I spotted him following Tiptoe into the stalls, so I followed them. I took him back to his pig relatives, but every time he heard noise, machinery, somebody hammering, he'd get frightened and run off. That's when I named him Spook."

"Amazing," Hollie said.

"Sure enough, a pig on the run…. He loves Tiptoe—think's she's his adopted cat mom. I can see the calmness in his eyes when she's around. Just waddles and follows.

"To be honest, we think he's not quite right—you know, sort of demented. I suspect the first time he got out, he felt lost, maybe went into shock. I figure Tiptoe came by and found him, and her quiet ways calmed him down. Tiptoe licks him; she tries to clean him up like Spook was a kitten. Did you ever see a calico cat licking a pig?"

"It's definitely a first," said Goodwin.

"Oh, forgot to say, my name's Mr. Statter. What's yours?"

"I'm Goodwin, and this is my wife, Hollie."

"You here on a pilgrimage?"

"Yeah, I guess you might call it that," Hollie said.

"It's good to reckon with your soul," Mr. Statter said. "When I was young, my inner spirit got all belligerent; it got to where I hardly knew it, sort of remorseful-like. It started bossing me around, all ruthless-like. Then one day I said to my inner me, 'Hey, who do you think you are?' There was no answer. That's when I figured it out."

"What?" Hollie asked

"My spirit was moving in its own direction, making its own plans, charting its own course. Wantin' me to tag along, as if I had no say in the matter. Well, I was having no part of it. I spoke to my spirit—called it up short, sort of twisted it by the ears, in a manner of speaking.

"That's when a friend suggested I visit Estillyen, spend a week or two. Said I should listen to the words that the monks weave into messages, take in the trails, meet the Estillyen people. That was forty-seven years ago."

"That long ago," Goodwin marveled.

"Yes, siree. I began to contemplate, reflect, and read a bit, you know, some of the *Redemption* material. It wasn't long before me and my spirit got in sync—got to knowing each other again, but better than before. It never wanted to act up again. My spirit became the true inner me. Found myself, I suppose.

"Say, I hate to rush, but I'm running short, a bit behind today. Got to be going—eggs are waiting. Then gotta kiss a dog, pet a hog, and go downtown. Good meeting ya—gotta run. Come back anytime. Tiptoe and Spook will like your company. Give 'em a pet if you wish."

Quickly, Mr. Statter turned, headed for the small barn at the other end of the yard, opened the sliding door, and disappeared. Hollie and Goodwin just stood quietly, watching him vanish.

"See what I mean, Win? Estillyen has all the characters an artist would ever need. Tiptoe, cotton balls, and a pig named Spook—it's unbelievable. Let's head on down to the ponds. I want to get over to Tunnel House soon; the light's perfect."

Hollie and Goodwin made their way past the ponds. As they walked, they spotted One, who was drawing in the curious. A group of schoolchildren were up from the village. They busily raced around the ponds while an instructor photographed One.

Both Hollie and Goodwin were in similar moods. They tended toward deeper thoughts. Hollie went down to Tunnel House, set up her easel and began to paint. Goodwin peddled off to Lakes Three on a rented Estillyen trail bike made of carbon steel. Each in their own zones of individual expression, they felt no disconnect as they drifted through the day.

Later that evening, their words linked all manner of subjects as they explained their adventures and especially their dispositions. Neither could quite describe what they felt, but equally they felt it. They spoke of destiny.

"It's hard to describe, this matter of destiny," Hollie said. "That intangible quality of life, that pulling force. Somehow being here, I certainly feel its draw. You know what I mean, Win?"

"I'm with you. I didn't expect this visit to stir up so much emotion."

"I feel for people who seem to have no sense of destiny," Hollie said. "Like it doesn't exist. There's no force, no tug, just a life of consumption, with no true life-giving aspirations.

"Then we come across a person like Mr. Ironbout on The Point, once so full of dreams. What a tragedy a worn path is to the graves."

"I know, 'forty years' he said, and, of course, it's more than that for him up on The Point. I suppose to him life must seem pointless—dropping dead sheep from the edge of the cliff, listening to the waves, moving about in the graves.

"The costly part of seeking destiny is the thinking, parsing, failing, finding, yet never letting go of destiny's draw. But that's incredibly hard to say to a man like Oban Ironbout. Now that I think about it, I should have just said nothing the other day."

"No, your words were important, Win."

Hollie's artistic mind began to flow. She decided to journal a few lines.

Even in the arena of great disquiet, when the breeze of aspiration barely blows, destiny calls. Destiny's music may be faint, yet it never completely fades.

Destiny calls from within the arena, "Draw near, step into the ring." At times, the notes may sound deranged, but the melody is always that of destiny. It calls to the spirit, pulling beyond the gravity that is humanity. "What is this force?" she asked. "For some it's a cousin of insanity; for others, sanity it is."

As Hollie and Goodwin had painted and peddled into their respective zones that day, they felt that destiny was near, not far, distant. They felt that its call had moved close enough to whisper.

A stilling quiet settled into their hearts and minds, as another Estillyen day departed, and the sun slipped over the sea's horizon. Soon the moon's glow graced the waves, and Hollie and Goodwin laid their heads upon fluffy pillows. Into sleep they fell, buoyed by destiny's touch and call.

The following morning, the tugging revelations lingered. They were eager to make their way to Speaker's House for the reading.

"I want to look at the stone foundation of Speaker's House," Goodwin said. "Like a lot of the construction on Estillyen, the stones are from the isle."

The foundation of Speaker's House was massive. It anchored the structure solidly to the ground and easily supported the weight of its beam-and-mortar construction.

Goodwin wandered over to a commemorative stone near the front entrance. Engraved in large print were the words: "On the 500th anniversary of Speaker's House, this inscriptive stone was carved and set by Estillyen's Order of Message Makers."

"Lee, listen to the cool history of this place," said Goodwin to Hollie, as he read the stone's words aloud:

Speaker's House is the oldest structure on the isle. The original part of the building dates back more than 600 years. It was built not unlike an ancient theater, where audiences stood on narrow circular balconies and watched theater troupes below. Speaker's House has a single balcony constructed in this manner, which also provides passage to eight sleeping chambers.

The admired building is very rarely without full occupancy. It has become a favorite of longtime Estillyen visitors. Speaker's House is the sole property connected to The Abbey or monastery that runs its own kitchen and dining area.

Speaker's House is primarily a lodge. Readings are given just once a week. Guests don't seem to mind scooting chairs around or standing on the circular banister. A first-time visitor might assume that a reading at Speaker's House would be more for show than substance—that is, until the reading begins to unfold.

"What history," Hollie said, as she and Goodwin made their way inside. They were immediately greeted by an enthusiastic voice.

"Hello, everyone. Welcome, indeed, to Speaker's House. My name is Writer. I know that sounds all wrong. My name should be Speaker, or at least Mr. House. But really, I am Writer, who has come to speak. Well, read, even if it's really speaking. See how confusing it can get on Estillyen? Reading, speaking…what do I know? I am just Writer."

Hollie and Goodwin were fortunate to spot an unoccupied, high-backed two-seater. The well-preserved, tapestry-covered settee didn't require the slightest scoot or positioning. Seated against the wall, they could see more than half of the circular rail above, yet were tucked neatly below the landing. Writer stood unobstructed in the middle of the open space.

"Let me introduce my colleague, Brother Testimony, who will be assisting with today's reading. Brother Testimony has been a resident of Estillyen for more than fifty years. We are honored to have him with us today."

Brother Testimony was seated in an armchair near the hall at the far end of the room. He was farther away from Writer than anyone else. Brother Testimony wore a black habit. His head was bald, and his eyelashes were snow white. Next to Brother Testimony was a roped-off hallway with an inward-swinging door, slightly ajar. Light from the main room shone around the door, but traveled not far, before the darkened hall absorbed it.

"In addition to Brother Testimony, we'll need three voices to read a few lines in unison. Adjective, our smart-looking intern, will hand out the lines. I see one, two, and over there, that makes three.

"When you see me nod, that's your cue. As the Voice of the audience, speak slowly, and let the room fill with the sound of your voices. The questions and comments are being called out from the crowd. If we might, let's have your names. It helps give a bit of identity to the Voice."

"I'm Anthony," said a young man seated alone, not far from Writer.

"I'm Eleanor," offered a woman neatly dressed in traditional plaid. She was sitting with two young ladies, a third her age.

"And I'm Hollie."

"Thank you so much. Just before we begin, let's pause to let our thoughts settle and still."

"What did I do?" Hollie whispered to Goodwin.

"I don't know, but you did it," he replied.

Not much could be heard during the fifty-odd seconds that soaked up the room's silence. There was a cough, and then another. A throat cleared, a distant door shut, and beyond the room's main entrance, muffled conversation could be heard from the reception desk.

"Okay, then. The title of today's reading is *Remember Me*. We'll begin with one simple and ancient line from St. Luke."

Remember Me

Jesus, remember me when you come into your kingdom.

LUKE 23:42

READER: Christ's figure shone expressly bright when transfigured on the mountaintop. Still more brilliant did his glory show when the sacred One was lifted high upon a hill called Golgotha.

Golgotha, the wretched place of misery and pain, the hill of crucifixion. That's where the Son of God was lifted up.

VOICE: Why was he lifted up? The simple truth, that's all.

READER: For sins he was lifted up.

VOICE: Whose, precisely?

READER: Not his own. Sins committed then and there—sins stretching back in time, and those yet to be. Yours and mine. Great and small, the lifting up was recompense for them all.

Golgotha is the place where spikes were bunched.

VOICE: Where were those spikes? What do you think—perhaps in an old rusty pot or lying on the ground?

READER: You're right to question and consider, not skip through the story all hither and thither. They may well have been recycled and bent, harboring all manner of menacing particles. Bunched, they waited for their thudding blows to drive them through, until solidly set, embedded deep within the cross. Piercing skin and bone, instantaneously they released infectious residues into the blood of the crucifix.

VOICE: The atmosphere on this renowned killing day…what was it?

READER: The atmosphere on this chilling-killing day was mournfully convulsive.

At least it was for some, but certainly not for all. It was a day of retribution for the religious elite. Their fortitude had paid off. They had won, or so they thought. Good riddance was the mood, a chance to finally shake their fists at this dangerous zealot threatening to destroy God's temple.

For the disciples, *bewilderment* is the word most appropriate. They had left everything to follow, to learn, to become disciples. Their Redeemer was destined to die. They watched and listened as their Lord, so confessed, hung before them, dying.

On their journey with Christ, there were many private, joyful moments. On one such occasion he said to them, "Blessed are the eyes that see what you see. For I tell you that many prophets and kings wanted to see what you see but did not see it, and to hear what you hear but did not hear it."

Voice, what do you want to see and hear?

VOICE: Your question sounds important.

READER: Consider the question, as long as life, if you wish. The disciples were, indeed, blessed to see and hear, but on this day, bewilderment and brutality teamed up to wrench and test all they'd come to know.

VOICE: Reader, for Christ's family watching, what did they see when their eyes looked up to Golgotha's hill?

READER: You ask what they saw the day on which history was repurposed? They saw much of love, grace, torture, and disgrace. Utter heartbreak and sorrow was etched upon their faces.

Into the hands of men the Son of God fell. Almost utterly unbelievable, is it not, Voice—God spiked by men? In their grasp they had the King of the Jews, Jesus of Nazareth. Spiked to the cross by sinners, Christ died for the residents of the world so loved by God, sinners all.

VOICE: His condition on the cross—was it as terrible as you say?

READER: Worse! Far worse. Worse than any cursed verse. How can truth die? The Light of the World be extinquished? If you were the light, how would it feel? Smothered in thick darkness, the eyes grow dim, until there is no more sight of seeing.

Voice, let the words of the psalmist speak: "I am poured out like water, and all my bones are out of joint. My heart has turned to wax; it has melted away within me. My strength is dried up like a potsherd, and my tongue sticks to the roof of my mouth; you lay me in the dust of death. Dogs have surrounded me; a band of evil men has encircled me, they have pierced my hands and my feet. I can count all my bones; people stare and gloat over me."

Time neither lessens the severity nor overshadows the butchery. The psalmist, with prophetic prose, sketched out this vivid image of misery.

An aging poet once said, "Heaven's angels pulled in their wings that day, kneeled and went to weeping. They wept and wept till all of heaven's fountains overflowed, and tears a river wide gushed through heaven's gates. Three days long it rushed, until upon the rising tide they saw their Lord appearing."

VOICE: Is it true?

READER: Why shouldn't it be?

Stunned was the universe, surely, staring down at creation's architect impaled on a tree between two thieves. Gone were his dwelling days, all spent. The Word Made Flesh, Mary's child, was to be no more in his natural state. No more bringing news, walking among the pressing crowds, lifting up those burdened down.

Hoisted high before bulging eyes and clenched fists, the message hung. Blood was his garment. Drenched red he was. From tissues deeply torn, blood flowed. Blood of head joined blood of face, moving down the neck. Over the shoulders, blood trailed to his chest and back. Around the waist and down the legs, blood flowed.

Around the knees, from chinbone to ankles, the warm crimson fluid trickled on. Across the feet it advanced, past the spikes, before the toes it reached. From there it dripped, moistening the ground, the blood of God and man mixed. It dripped. Sacrificial blood dripped, drop by drop, into soil soiled by sinners. On Golgotha, many had been crucified for sins. Yet for others' sins they had not died.

Christ's plaque was nailed, not below his feet to be obscured by blood, but above his head, clearly labeling this figure so mistakable. The one dying there in the middle was Jesus of Nazareth, identified as the King of the Jews. In Amharic, Latin, and Greek, those words were written upon the plaque.

Before the watching world, the Word Made Flesh was spiked. The Alpha and Omega of divine verse hung, his shredded flesh dying, but his words ever living, never dying.

This drama of the Lamb of God sacrificed by the world, for the world, was scripted before the world began.

VOICE: How can that be? Is it so?

READER: It is, Voice. Listen to the words of St. Peter: "Like that of a lamb without blemish or spot, he was destined before the foundation of the world, but was made manifest at the end of the times for your sake."

*Made manifest...*what curious words, Voice. But right, so right, they do seem. Out of the eons of time, Christ's days had finally arrived, pushing the manifest into present's place. Prophetic words sewn in centuries past burst forth with detailed precision.

Voice, I implore you to grasp the significance of these prophetic words. There is no precedent for words acting as these words did, to tell a tale, to draft a drama. In they came. From here and there, they came. At the assigned time and place, they converged, joining the lines for Christ's message in the making.

Ancient prophecies, once penned, had long abided. They waited incomplete, unfulfilled. Words past spoken waited for their stories to arrive so they could be folded into present verse. Once folded in, the prophecies settled into the message. They spoke full with meaning, never again just foretelling.

Like ornaments without a tree, the prophecies had long waited to be hung upon their stories. Ornaments brought their gifts to the message—credibility, connectivity, certainty. The storied message of Christ would not be bare.

Isaiah's words were there to do their part, showing up to be unfolded and folded in: "He was oppressed and afflicted, yet he did not open his mouth. He was led like a lamb to the slaughter, and as a sheep before her shearers is silent, so he did not open his mouth."

That's the way these ancient words worked: converging, joining lines, making messages that matter most. As the story broke, characters also got their call. Emerging, they rushed to and fro in this great pageant. Most had no idea that their hour of scurry was being folded into the story for posterity and eternity.

Judas was there, grasping thirty pieces of silver and his hanging rope. The priests were there, grasping Judas and the silver coins he scattered on the temple floor. With the pickings, they eventually grasped a plot of land. A malicious mob, wielding knives, swords, and clubs, grasped Christ. Pilate grasped his towel. Barabbas grasped freedom.

A rooster grasped morning light and a deafening crow. Peter grasped sorrow in the hours of early morn. Simon the Cyrene grasped a cross, one not his own. Soldiers grasped clothes and cast lots. Two thieves: One grasped the kingdom of God; the other grasped defiance. One grasped redemption, the other retribution.

Christ grasped gasps and final words: "Father, into your hands I commit my spirit." With that, Christ grasped his final breath.

VOICE: Reader, it seems so utterly bizarre to consider the Son of God being beaten, spiked, and crucified for an ancient rendezvous between Adam, Eve, and Satan.

READER: Dear Voice, St. Paul perceived this to be the case and wrote, "For the message of the cross is foolishness to those who are perishing, but to us who are being saved it is the power of God." That's the word he used: *foolishness.* Let's not reject this word but accept it.

VOICE: Yet why such an extreme price for fruit plucked—a reach, a single breech of divine protocol?

READER: The fairy-tale portrayals of forbidden fruit, it seems, cheat the severity of the matter. The fall of Adam and Eve is not about the sound of crunch from fruit bitten. It is about the sound of words and a message believed. Grasping hand followed grasping heart. That's the part that spun humanity into an inordinate orbit.

Ever so quickly words flowed into lines, inspiring thoughts and changing hearts to believe what should not be believed. That's the way of words. Words jump into lines; lines jump into minds; thoughts jump into hearts. In the heart they vie for space with other words placed by other thoughts. Adam and Eve became sinners, new believers. They believed Satan's words over God's.

"Oh, yes, I am a believer," it's often said, as if there are others that do not believe. However, everyone is a believer—believing in this or that, or both. Disbelieving is a form of belief. Not believing in God is to believe in disbelieving. Arguing that people do not believe is like arguing that people do not breathe.

Do you get my point, Voice?

VOICE: Yes, I think I do.

READER: Unlike in the vast abyss, the world reverberates with messages, attractive and alternative, pure and perverse, true and false. Messages come forth in words, images, and sounds. Into culture they float, playing games of tug-of-war. They pull at unbelievers to believe and beckon believers to disbelieve. They call out to buyers to switch and try to plead with pundits to place their bets.

To be "like God" was the pull of Satan's line, spun so attractively for Eve. So wondrously autonomous, sovereign, and free—that's the prize. Switch and try; change your vote; cast your lot. Grasp a bit of fruit; never mind, it's really a bit of rope. Give it a tug.

Not a hint from the ancient tale suggests that Adam and Eve paused, even slightly, to consider where this newfound God-grasp might lead. This pair, newly formed from earth and rib, were ready, they thought, to rule like God. How implausible was the notion!

What about sculptor God, the breather of life, the One that hung the stars in place? Did Adam and Eve not consider that he would need a job, perhaps something light in his semiretirement? Was he to be in their care? Could they offer divine security in their new plan? Perhaps he could join their team, offer some wise old sayings now and then.

It was not due to force, threat, or consequence that Satan's lines were believed. The message was embraced because of its appeal. Satan's words were few. They formed a brief message that appeared to be genuine. The challenge with words is to know their intent, their dispatch, and particularly the spirit that helped them hatch.

Adam and Eve engaged a dastardly message. Its evil intent was cooked up in the cauldron of Satan's spite. In his darkened spirit, the ingredients of the message were sifted, until just the right words crept out of the mediator's mouth. Once the message was embraced, there was no sovereignty for Adam and Eve, no liberty. They were frightened, transfigured.

Their act resulted in a severe stab to creation's side—Satan's knife was deeply plunged. A horrid howl was heard, dissonance wrecking harmony, trouncing tranquility. The horrific scream echoed thunderously throughout the kingdom grounds. Beasts roared, stalkers stalked, killing commenced. Everything changed, bearing the mark of sin. Man was out, not in.

Out, not in, separated by sin—that's what placed Jesus Christ on the Via Dolorosa. That was the compelling unction of his zeal, his cause. His focus was not to stay up in heaven looking down, letting man fix the fix he was in. Man's fix was unfixable by man. Instead, Christ embarked on a journey long, taking him from a manger stall in Bethlehem to that wretched hill, Golgotha.

The final leg to Golgotha's hill was along the Via Dolorosa, the way of suffering and grief. Compelled by grace, Christ made his way down the notorious road to meet the frozen face of death—his own. Heaps of wily schemes were piled high along this infamous road. They were placed there by darkened hearts that had longed for such a day.

Along the Via Dolorosa, Christ did not walk alone. He staggered along with two condemned criminals. The companions three made their way to find the hill of death and frozen faces. When these two criminals first caught sight of Christ, the story does not tell. It may well have been when Christ was first adorned with a crown of thorns.

VOICE: Where was that?

READER: In the fortress, Voice. Once Pilate had washed his hands and freed Barabbas, Christ was led away to the Fortress of Antonia, where the eternally begotten Son of God was used for sport. A hundred Roman soldiers, maybe more, were stationed in this fiendish garrison of known brutality. Inside the fortress, Christ was stripped and beaten with a staff.

He received repeated blows to his head and face. It was in this holding pen, this perverted place, that Christ was awarded thorns for his head and spit upon his face.

Voice, there is something terribly sinister about unbridled authority in the hands of collective evil with no fear of retaliation. Evil spurs evil. Most eyes do not care to see the site of frenzied hounds ripping apart a defenseless fox. Yet some sinister eyes do. They find sweet delight soaking in pain they do not have to bear. Pummeled, as the sport of soldiery and brutality, Christ was readied for crucifixion.

Along the way of suffering and grief, Christ was led. One wonders if the evil one might have been about, to see what others saw: the Son of God staggering along with his cross and bloodied flesh. Suffering and grief, after all—that's the central tenet of Satan's game. Surely Satan could be counted on to drop in, dash about, and move in and out of the heaps of garbage roundabout.

Satan would not want to miss this defining act on Golgotha's hill, this spectacle of dying on view for the living. Just maybe, it would all prove too much for the one foreordained as the Savior of mankind. If the soldiers at the Fortress of Antonia couldn't make him break, then possibly the sheer pain of the crucifixion would do the trick.

Satan may have thought that when the spikes were driven through the skin, ripping muscles, cartilage, and veins, perhaps that would be the moment the angels would be called.

Writer raised his right hand and extended his palm in the direction of Brother

Testimony. Brother Testimony rose to his feet and took three small steps towards the room's interior. Apart from the audience, he stood. More in the shadows than in the light, he began to speak. His voice resonated with clarity, and his white eyebrows appeared to be jumping along to the rhythm of the words.

LUCIFER: Let me tell you, my devotees, listen up to Lucifer. When the Word hears his own bones crunching in his hands and feet, this whole redemption deal set forth by I AM is gonna unravel. You think I AM is gonna stand by and let dummy fleshies kill the Word? It's like long ago, when I AM told Abraham to kill his son, knife him, and then at the last minute called it off, got a ram in the thicket to take the fleshy kid's place.

That's what we've got here—some kind of trick, a bait-and-switch deal. Maybe that's not even the Word. Who knows, I'm just saying. Oh, brilliant, here he comes. They've got a couple of criminals with him. I know the one on the left. How perfect—the Word's blood is everywhere.

Oh, did I tell you, or have you heard, it was a staff to his head. How right! Did we inspire that, or did that come from the fleshy text? It doesn't matter. All that matters now is pain and the prospect of divine disruption.

Beautiful—look and learn something, my demon devotees. That's the way! That's what you're supposed to do when you get fleshies in your clutches. No mercy—just think slaughter, slaughter. Keep that word in the forefront of your minds: *slaughter*. It's a good, robust-sounding word. You imbeciles are too untoward, too twitchy, too cliché. You need to be more ruthless and horrid like me.

Look to me, Lucifer. Look to me so intently that, when you look in the mirror, you'll see my face. Get some grumble in your rumble. We've got to pull together in pulling things apart. The divine wards are on full alert. Hey, stop that! Watch it, imbeciles—don't gesture upward, not now. This is not the moment for provoking the heavenly forces. I'm told I AM is really worked up over this whole affair. Anything could happen. Even if he goes through with it, I AM can change his mind and obliterate the whole planet.

Delightful it must have been for the soldiers to knock him about. If only they could have killed him, then I AM's prophetic words that have to be couldn't be, and this grace thing would all be over. Don't you rotten core of fools know how vital this day is? Then *show* me you do—look all full of eagerness and angst. We need to disrupt, distort, and dislocate. Got it, idiots?

Later we need to check out that soldiering lot at the fortress and see how many souls can be bought. Got to be a high percentage. That goes for everyone down the line, from Pilate's palace to the ones that make the crosses.

Especially check out the spike drivers. They'll not be the same after this affair. There must be a lot of Judas hearts around here. The spilling bowels—oh, he was of our ilk, but he was a stupid fleshy just the same. There are plenty where he came from. Sneaky fleshies—they're all sickly made. Redemption, why them? What a waste.

I'm just saying, it's all down to I AM. Why he's bent on killing the Word over fleshies is beyond me. I AM has become downright delusional. Even if it was possible for me to feel sorry, I wouldn't. It's his own mess, making fleshies. The Ancient of Days has stumbled, just like the Word. Look at that! Good, lash him again! Who's that fellow picking up his cross? Giving the Word a cushy break—how pathetic.

Look to me, my devotees. I've chosen you. You're here on this momentous occasion because you're my worst demons, but you need to get a heap worser. I mean worser than worse, so you won't be so worthless. You twelve must stay alert—I command it. I demand it. Any slip-up in this divine plan, and we'll make a move. We'll capitalize, maximize. He's got a long way to go before any rising from the grave takes place.

Now listen to me, you imbeciles. When you get my call, begin to chant with me. You know, the Word can simultaneously hear angels in heaven breathing and the hounds of hell growling.

He can hear anything. On this occasion, we want everything groaning, howling, and growling—nothing less than full-force travail. If we can get him to throw in the towel, the glorious victory will be ours.

Why I AM ever concocted fleshies is beyond me. What's the Trinity see in 'em? Don't answer…that's not a question! Mud with breath, that's all they are and nothing more, big deal. You devotees can go through walls, soar through space; they can't.

He almost got it right once, I must admit—the flood. What a sight it was—all that choking and drowning. Those fleshies can really paddle and claw. Then he had to ruin everything by making that stupid boat. Talk about dumb…

There's something wrong when I AM gets so involved, gets all worked up over fleshies, as if they were some kind of an extension of him. *Amputate, annihilate, extricate*—those are the choice words I AM refuses to hear.

That's what I do with my backriders. Once shed, I snap my fingers. If they're not gone, I erect a firewall as thick as a mountain. They're never allowed to see me again. If they try to sneak through, I toss 'em into the middle of the firewall, straight into the roasting pit.

Oh, where was I? That's right. Now, if this turns out our way, and the Word and I AM fail, pull out, the fleshies will be left in our domain. We'll need to harness our hate, not obliterate 'em. Our slaves for eternity they'll be. See, like I have been telling you, there's a future. There's reason for hope!

Now the optic of my collusion will be on that center cross. I've already received word that's the one reserved for the Word. If he comes down before he dies, celebration all around. You can go out and kill any fleshy you want. Our job is to get the travail going, let the Word hear the howling of hell, hear all the misery he has caused. Maybe that'll break him down.

Sometimes it's not the created that's at fault; it's the creator. Adam and Eve are no different than my devotees were in heaven. We were not to blame for the impulses planted within us. 'Course, we're so superior to fleshies, it's hardly worth the comparison.

Pathetic it is, this whole idea of grace, redemption, and reconciling the world to I AM through the Word. Well, he wouldn't be dying to reconcile it if he hadn't made it in the first place. He just couldn't keep his creativity in bounds. Forgiveness, too, makes me spit. What a sick word it is, a pathetic notion. Gives me chills, brings steam to my throat. No talk of that when I was moving around in the heavenly realms.

Now, keep your spirits down, deep in discouragement, and try to spread around as much hate and bitterness as you can. I'm counting on you to be at the bottom of your game. Turmoil is what we need. Grasp that word: *turmoil*. Anything can happen in the spirit of turmoil. The more people stumble and fall, the better.

Now, here's our three-word chant: *Turmoil, travail, tribulation…turmoil, travail, tribulation…whataya hear, whataya get…turmoil, travail, tribulation.* Isn't that great? That's what we want the Word to hear, over and over, as he's spiked up there dying.

Here's what we do. We start very quietly. We let him wriggle for a while, and then after hours of suffering, we'll start to pile it on, fill his ears. Each hour we raise the volume. I want you three to chant bass, you three double bass, and you three triple bass. Everyone else chants whatever your dumb throats allow. Off-key is good.

We will all chant together three times. Then, only the double basses chant, followed by the triple basses. When you triple basses chant, chant the same words, but very, very, slow. So nice it will be!

Ah, isn't it marvelous, the way of suffering and grief? Do you suppose they named this street after me? Can't you just feel the heartache, the anguish of this place? For sure, this is one of the choicest places on this planet. Someday, when we get the world for ourselves, the capitol park will be Golgotha. I can already see it. The Way of Suffering and Grief will be the main thoroughfare.

Only I can dream so stupendously. You know, just occasionally, the pot is superior to the mold—and even to the potter. That's what happened in my case. Oh, with all this treachery about, I feel so benevolent. I shouldn't, but this is a special day.

I'll tell you what I'll do, my devotees, I'll let you gaze. All twelve of you to the left, quick, come around and get on your knees. See my profile, my face. Go ahead, gaze, a full minute is yours. Good, now rush around to the right and gaze again. Which side is most beautiful? I already know—it's impossible to tell.

Okay, enough. Many are the eyes that have longed to see what you just saw. We need to focus. Don't forget, like I keep telling you, he's half flesh. He's a carpenter. When they start spiking him to the cross that could be our finest sunset. Oh, think of it: the carpenter spiked to wooden planks.

At any point along the way, life on earth could pause; God could pull out, call it quits. All this cosmic struggle is down to fleshies, the little, godlike beings that never should have been. Such heartache they have caused their Creator. That's the only good thing about them.

Now shut it—he's coming closer down my street. Let's watch.

Brother Testimony paused. He slowly nodded to Writer, and his eyes blinked. He turned around, moved toward his armchair, and took his seat.

READER: Christ made his way along the Via Dolorosa to the destination Golgotha. In tow were the two criminals who would die beside him—one on his left, one on his right.

VOICE: What do you suppose they must have thought of Christ, this mysterious one in their midst?

READER: The criminals were destined to be there, for ancient words speak of them as transgressors. "He poured out his soul to death and was numbered with the transgressors; yet he bore the sin of many, and makes intercession for the transgressors."

On the Mount of Transfiguration, he might have fled, disappearing swiftly in the company of Moses and Elijah. He could have shown his back to the earth, not turning around, fleeing safely to kingdom grounds. Without a trace, he could have left humanity far behind to deal with its own predicament. Yet he chose not to flee.

Christ came down the Via Dolorosa in the midst of sinners' gaze. Surely he would die. As the sacrificial lamb, he walked on feet unswerving. A lamb's feet they were—feet of the Shepherd, too. He was true to course. For redemption's plan, the Son of God came to die.

Down the Via Dolorosa and beyond Jerusalem's city walls, the condemned three walked on feet with numbered steps. Their final steps they used. At Golgotha, their feet were clutched and spiked. No more would their soles press upon the ground.

On crosses, their feet were pressed hard against splintered wood. They were spiked in an act of full disgrace. "Numbered with transgressors"—these are the words that placed scars on Immanuel's face.

Crucified as objects of public scorn, the three were hoisted high so all could easily see the cost of human disobedience. Spiked to their crosses, they hung in trembling pain, waiting for death to drape its freeze upon their faces. They waited for death to close their eyes and halt the morbid public stare of piteous disgrace.

One of the criminals could not contain his hate; he hurled insults through the air. The object of his hate was at his side, the one with the placard that read "King of the Jews." The criminal shouted out, "Aren't you the Christ? Save yourself and us!"

Simultaneously the crowds jeered. "Those who passed by hurled insults at him, shaking their heads and saying, 'You who are going to destroy the temple and build it in three days, save yourself! Come down from the cross, if you are the Son of God!'

"In the same way, the chief priests, the teachers of the law, and the elders mocked him. 'He saved others,' they said, 'but he can't save himself! He's the King of Israel! Let him come down now from the cross, and we will believe in him. He trusts in God. Let God rescue him now if he wants him, for he said, I am the Son of God.'"

Hate was hurled at all three, but particularly at the one in the middle, the one important enough to receive a plaque as well as a crown. Moving closer was death's freeze. Minutes pulsed, the criminal without remorse hardened steadily to the core. His heart would not heal before his body died. Fearless, the condemned criminal became a spokesperson for sin, striking out at God as the reason for his condition.

Hating what life had dealt, the man of misery spoke with a spirit of damnation. He despised the figure his eyes beheld, this self-acclaimed redeemer of man. No reason for hope—the criminal's eyes had seen all there was to see; he was blind. He did not want to believe. He would not believe. He did not believe. Sin he was. Sin he would be, unto death.

Equally in the throes of the agony of death, the second criminal could see. His repentant eyes somehow saw a figure his heart did not despise. He saw this Jesus hanging there beneath the sign Pilate had prepared. It was to him he called, saying, "Jesus, remember me when you come into your kingdom."

Through swirling chants and the sneering of the crowd, Christ prayed, "Father, forgive them, for they do not know what they are doing." These words the repentant thief may well have heard. In a rebuke to the insolent thief, the repentant thief openly confessed, "We are punished justly, for we are getting what our deeds deserve."

The end was near—the worst kind of end, a miserable death of dying, with the living watching, gawking. Quarantined from the living, on show for dying, is a wretched way to die. Crucifixion was not death by hanging, where suddenly the neck breaks and eyes see no more watchers watching. Crucifixion is to die rejected and deserted by the world; it's to die in public all alone.

Stretched out on a cross between criminals of contrasting fates, the figure in the middle was the supreme message from God to man. Every word, every sigh, every motion added meaning to the message. "To see the Father, look only at me," Christ taught. This truth did not fall away when, upon the cross, Christ was crucified. The image of the Father and the dying Son are one.

The hardened criminal spoke for sin, not bowing will or wicked heart. The criminal of contrast spoke for sinners throughout the ages, who have recognized that sheep lost need a shepherd to be found. "Jesus, remember me when you come into your kingdom" was his famous line, tenderly spoken. The repentant thief wanted to believe, he did believe, and he willed his belief to Jesus of Nazareth.

In response, Christ promised, "Today you will be with me in paradise," and that promise was swiftly approaching. Christ was in the final throes of death. "Knowing that everything had now been finished, and so that Scripture would be fulfilled, Jesus said, 'I am thirsty.'" Another prophecy unfolded: "They put gall in my food and gave me vinegar for my thirst."

The end was close and closing in; death was moving up the crosses three. On the middle cross Christ hung. Isaiah foretold what those present saw as they gazed up at this figure torn. "Just as there were many who were appalled at him, his appearance was so disfigured beyond that of any man and his form marred beyond human likeness." One more prophecy had unfolded and folded into its story.

The Holy Trinity alone knows the depth and breadth of what actually occurred on the cross. Prophets saw sketches of what would be. The disciples were told what to expect, but they were overrun by events. They could not comprehend what had never been. Characters, the entire troupe folded into the Gospel narrative, saw only facets of the drama of which they were a part.

On the cross Christ hung until he was certain Scripture was fulfilled. Alone was Christ in understanding the scope and significance of what was taking place. The idea that Scripture's prophetic words must be fulfilled is spellbinding, is it not?

Prophecies from a distant past act not unlike stars, long ago sent on their way emitting light. At exact intervals the prophecies were sent. With precision, the words beam toward the events for which they were destined.

Eventually, past words meet present story. In a divinely inspired embrace, they intersect, fuse, and move on into eternity. Prophecy is no chess game of matching bits. It is actually God speaking, overlapping lines throughout history, at various times and in various ways. Though appearing as disparate as taps can be, the fulfillment of Scripture is the fulfillment of God's thoughts, which come forth as words tapping through the ages.

The mystery "hidden for ages and generations" was being revealed on that patch of ground called Golgotha. There, in that place, with blood dripping and time ticking, the mysterious Message á Medium of God hung. He spoke with words and without.

As all prophetic Scriptures found their storied places, it was time for Christ to die. His death spoke with universal awe, as the Father's beloved Son died in love laid down.

Mary, peering from the hill, watched the flesh she bore give way to death. Which words he spoke as his last, no one knows for sure. St. John records, "It is finished." St. Luke reports that Christ took his last breath after saying, "Father, into your hands I commit my spirit!"

With death, the pumping of blood and its dripping swiftly stopped. The medium was now silent—but speaking still. Death silent spoke meaning into life. Death silent was the sign signifying redemption's price was paid.

St. Luke wrote, "It was now about the sixth hour, and there was darkness over the whole land until the ninth hour." God's thoughts were then rendered not as words, but acts. Matthew's account provides the greatest detail:

"At that moment, the curtain of the temple was torn in two from top to bottom. The earth shook and the rocks split. The tombs broke open and the bodies of many holy people who had died were raised to life. They came out of the tombs, and after Jesus' resurrection, they went into the holy city and appeared to many people. When the centurion, and those with him who were guarding

Jesus, saw the earthquake and all that had happened, they were terrified, and exclaimed, 'Surely he was the Son of God!'"

VOICE: What do you suppose Satan said?

Writer turned in the direction of Brother Testimony, who had already quietly stood up and moved to his prior position. His lines were brief.

LUCIFER: Darkness, earthquakes—what's happening? This can't be. This is not what I expected. It's too soon. He died too quick—it's a trick.

This is not fair. Tombs breaking open, hear that, and that. Silence, imbeciles! Stop your chanting—can't you see the Word's really dead?

Testimony nodded back to Writer.

READER: The curtain in the Temple was torn. The way to God had been opened. The Son of God was crucified, not only between two thieves, but also between God and man. God reconciling the world through Christ was a reality.

VOICE: Where did Christ go? What happened at that precise moment?

READER: This we do not know for sure, and, of course, the story is not yet complete. We do know this: When the repentant thief cried out, "Jesus, remember me," there was a reply; there was a promise. Did Christ not say, "Today you will be with me in paradise?" He did!

Therefore, among the vast sum we do not know, we know that Christ died and was, that very day, with a repentant thief in his Father's kingdom!

Words matter…words from the cross matter immensely.

Jesus, remember me when you come into your kingdom.

THIEF ON THE CROSS, GOLGOTHA, JERUSALEM, CIRCA AD 32

⬥

"Well, there we are," Writer said with a gentle smile.

Spontaneously, everyone in the room rose to their feet and applauded. Writer quickly turned and extended his right arm in Brother Testimony's direction. Testimony smiled and bowed modestly. With both hands raised, Writer then acknowledged each member of the Voice. Still smiling, he nodded first to Eleanor, then Hollie, followed by Anthony. There was more than one tear in Hollie's eye. She was not alone.

"*Remember Me* can be rather moving, I admit," Writer said. "But that is good, not bad. We are created with such capacity.

"The Gospel is actually a tremendous love story. The full scope of how this played out in the heavenly realms is something hard to grasp. The relationship between Father and Son…well, yes, there's a great deal to ponder. Let's take a few minutes to contemplate the message. Then we'll have a brief chat, for those who wish."

Hollie and Goodwin made their way down the broad front steps, out to the low stone wall, and chose a place to sit. The wall bordered the back and sides of Speaker's House.

"Do you know what that was like?" Hollie said, her face glowing. "It was incredible. All of a sudden, you are caught up in this story, this amazing reading. My heart was racing. I still can't believe I raised my hand."

"I thought it was brilliant—all of it, everyone. You were great," Goodwin said.

"That was so powerful, the way Writer carried the story along with his artistic flow and gracious sincerity," Hollie said.

"And Brother Testimony—he's a cool old dude with his black habit and white eyebrows."

"Oh, absolutely," Hollie said. "They're so dedicated, it's amazing. The story was so real. I feel challenged after hearing it like that today. I should have considered all of this much more than I have in the past. Sometimes I feel like the painting I told you about, the one in Ravena's office called *Uncomfortably Numb*."

"I hear you, but that's why we're here, you know. Don't beat yourself up about it. There's a lot to consider. I think we're all numb in some ways."

"I suppose I'm just thinking about it more lately."

"I think I'll take a walk around the house and meet you back inside. Okay, love?"

"Sure."

Hollie sat, her mind revolving around the subject of suffering. She thought about how embedded suffering is in life. How it can abide with joy, and joy with it. A kind of strange tranquility came over her.

She thought about staying outside, not going back in. She was aware that everyone was heading through the front door to reassemble. Hollie wanted to be with them, but she also wanted to be alone. She stood, dusted off the back of her white jeans, and looped the handle of her purse over the shoulder of her chocolate-colored blouse. Making the decision to rejoin the group after all, she slowly crossed the lawn, watching the tiny dew drops cling to her dark-green flats.

"Okay, just for a brief time, we'll open it up for a bit of conversation," Writer said. "Don't feel obligated to comment, but please do if you feel inclined. A few thoughts to start you off: There's the image of Christ on the Via Dolorosa. The word *grasping* sort of popped out of the reading. And, of course, there's the whole subject of redemption."

Back and forth the comments flowed, as words winnowed their way into hearts and minds.

Just shy of thirty minutes the clock had changed its face when it was Writer who said, "I think that covers the main points. Remember to keep an eye out for those themes. Anyway, I guess that's enough speaking—or should I say reading—from Writer. So, from Writer to you, one final word: Peace."

As the gathering broke up, Goodwin said, "I want to get a copy of the reading."

"Sure, I'm planning to get the full set of *Redemption*," Hollie said. "You know we talked about it."

"I know, but I'd like to get a copy now, to take with me up to The Point and give to Mr. Ironbout."

"Oh, are you sure you want to do that? Don't you think that's too pushy, maybe too much? I hope he doesn't suddenly turn on you and throw it in your face."

"Yeah, I hear you. And it's not the kind of thing I normally do, you know that. But the whole grasping idea, the suffering…maybe the pain will speak; maybe he'll not feel so alone. I don't know…it might be a way of connecting."

"Well, okay then, let's get one. I'm going to head back to The Abbey, and then later I'm planning to see Sister Ravena. Do you want to go up to The Point now, straight away?"

"Yeah. I'll bike up, so it won't take too long."

"Be careful, won't you, Win? He could still lose it. We really don't know who we are dealing with."

"I know—he might grab me and throw me off The Point."

"Oh, you're impossible! Let's go."

TWELVE
The Visits

Trip dashed off the porch, down the front steps, and across the lawn. He barked with a rapt, deep tone, as if a ferocious preadator were approaching the house. He raced over to the walnut tree and halted, but he continued his intense, steady bark. His black-and-white tail curled upward, so tightly wound that its tip touched the middle of his arched back.

The front screen door opened, and Mr. Ironbout appeared. He moved onto the porch and paused at the tapered boxed column to the right of the steps. He placed his coffee cup on the brick ledge surrounding the base of the column and reached for his glasses in his shirt pocket.

"What is it, Trip, a monster? Good boy…yeah, you're getting 'em, but shush. No, no walnuts today—least I don't think so. Oh, I see, a shiny monster with wheels, pedals, and a handlebar. Haven't you ever seen a bicycle carried through the weeds? What kind of dog are you? I thought you were smart. Sure you are, don't worry. Strange sight, for dog eyes."

Mr. Ironbout moved down the steps and walked a few meters in Trip's direction.

"Come here, Trip; it's okay. I think I know who it is. Come on, who else would it be anyway? Nobody else would be so brave. Come on, get over here."

With the wheeled monster only a few meters away, Trip headed for Mr. Ironbout. Trip's head was bowed, and his tail wagged anxiously. He readily looked up at his master for assurance.

"Good boy. Sit. Now stay. Hmm, there he is."

Goodwin reached the end of the path, lowered his mountain bike, and leaned it against the walnut tree. He quickly looped the strap of his backpack over the seat.

"Come here, Trip," Goodwin said. Trip's hair still bristled high on his upper back.

"Go on, it's okay," Mr. Ironbout said. Trip moved in Goodwin's direction, strongly swaying his hindquarters, in a shy, rhythmic dance move.

"Hello, Mr. Ironbout! I hope I didn't startle you or anything. Just thought I would ride up and see The Point again. I see Trip's still on guard duty."

"No bother at all. It's sort of good to see you. I was just having some coffee and a bit of cheese on toast. Come on up to the porch. Want some coffee or water?"

"Thanks, I've got a bottle of water in my pack."

"Your pack's resting over there; leave it be. Come in and get some well water, the best water on the whole of Estillyen."

"Okay, sure," Goodwin said, as he followed Mr. Ironbout up onto the porch.

"You can work up a thirst coming up The Point," Mr. Ironbout said while he opened the screen door, allowing Trip and then Goodwin to enter. Goodwin stepped into the same time capsule Hollie had entered the previous week.

"Wow, I love the clean lines of this place," Goodwin said. "It's such a true arts-and-crafts feel—very understated, very classic. Very nice, Mr. Ironbout."

"Yeah, I'm not one for frills or Victorian twists and turns—actually hate 'em. I like things honest. Meaning if it's there, it ought to be doing something. You know what I'm tryin' to say? Brace something, hold something up. If you're gonna put trim on a window, I figure make it straight, out of oak, five inches wide and thick, proper-like.

"You see these baseboards? Look at the top edge; it's flat halfway across, and then there's a slight thirty-degree taper. The base shoe does the same. In the baseboard, there's just that one simple horizontal bead, an inch down from the top. That's what I call utilitarian art. Never tire of looking at 'em; they don't make you all dizzy, or try to yell at you when you walk by. You know what I'm sayin'?

"Doesn't mean I didn't do lot of figuring when I built this place. Often, it takes more time to figure simple than it does complicated-like. The floors are all white oak, 'cept for the kitchen—fir, you know, a type of pine. Here, get yourself a glass, there in the right cabinet. Let me draw it for you."

"Your coffered ceiling in the front room is terrific. I really like the low profile of the beams. They look really nice painted."

"Ha! Painted. All the paint inside here was done over forty years ago. Me and Leslie painted it. One day I gotta do some sprucing up, but that sprucing day hasn't made its way onto the calendar. When I see it penciled in, I'll get to doing, know what I mean?"

"Since Trip's so smart, maybe he could be in charge of posting projects on the calendar."

"Now, you've got that right. If Trip spoke English rather than his dog language, I could teach him how to wire the house. He may act as nutty as a drunken reindeer, but don't let him fool you—he knows everything I do and why I do it. He's probably decipherin' our conversation right now."

Goodwin smiled and reached down to give Trip a pat on the head.

"How many bedrooms do you have, Sir?"

"Two upstairs that no one's ever slept in and mine. Off the living room, there's an office sort of room facing out to the side garden. Hollie saw it the other day. That's Trip's bedroom. Say, she's a fine one, by the way; you sure got something there in that wife of yours.

"Good water, isn't it? Help yourself. Want a gingersnap? It's 'bout all I got. They're in the jar there."

"Sure."

"Don't mind the stack of papers on the table. Trip and I've been scouring every nook and cranny in the house. I've been through that pile of papers two dozen times, at least. Here have a seat."

"Thanks. What are you looking for?"

"Ah, it's a long story, kinda like a porcupine that keeps popping up and shootin' darts. Thought this porcupine was gone, but it has a way of coming back around. Got this important-looking letter the other day…all official writ, making claims about The Point."

"I see, that doesn't sound so good."

"Yeah, been gettin' letters of this ilk for quite a spell now, just been pitchin' 'em, but that one in the green envelope is menacing, more so than all the rest, official-lookin' seal on it and all."

"Sorry to hear that, Sir."

"Needn't bother you with such."

"No, please, if there's anything I can do…"

"Well, it's a complicated bunch o' nasty business, actually. Has to do with that rotten wayward Source Telecom and my rotten wayward second nephew, twice removed. His dad's dad was my cousin Jarrod, on the Bentley side. My cousin's dad's dad was my great uncle, Rufus. Uncle Rufus was a fine feller, treated me like a son, or grandson. Neither Jarrod nor Jarrod's father cared for Rufus, though. They were both pale, frail, sickly types—never wanted to venture out of doors, always tinkering with electricity and soldering irons in a damp basement.

"Uncle Rufus, well, that wasn't him. Every now and then he'd light out for Estillyen, come up here to The Point, spend a week or so, go fishing, hike all around. Three times, when I was still a wee tyke, I got to go along. Naturally, I fell in love with the place—The Point.

"Anyhow, to make a stretched-out story less yeast-like, I stayed in touch with Uncle Rufus, right up till he died. Ninety-four he was when he passed.

"When he turned ninety, there was a big birthday celebration over at his place in Druhms Key. I went, of course. That evening, as things were settlin' down, he asked me to step out on the porch for a minute. We sat in the swing. Rufus lit a cigar and said, 'Oban, I want to give you something. Want to deed you The Point.'

"I was stunned—couldn't believe what I was hearing. 'The Point?' I said.

"'Sure enough,' he said, 'you are the only one that appreciates it same as me. Therefore, before I'm no longer 'round blowin' birthday candles, I want us to get over to Port Estillyen, sign it over legal-like. No fussing about, want it done,' he said.

"And that's what we did, the very next week. We went down to Hatter & Sons. Course, truth is, old Hatter never had any sons—he was a lifelong bachelor. When we showed up, I could tell Hatter himself was well along in years. Not quite as old as Rufus, but up there.

"You see, all the land holdings for the Isle of Estillyen, the highlands and lowlands, are in private hands. That is, except for The Abbey community, which takes in the monastery and all the related structures. Port Estillyen has no legal jurisdiction for the holdings up here. So they don't keep records.

"And that, I'm afraid, is sort of what centers on my problem. Uncle Rufus and I signed the deed, sure enough, and old Hatter witnessed it, wearing his wire-rimmed spectacles. He stamped the documents, gave 'em the official seals, and that was it. Uncle Rufus said, 'I don't even want a copy, just send one to Oban, and keep the other one on file.'

"A few days later, a brown envelope arrived in the mail. In the upper-left corner was Hatter & Sons' logo, dark-green and gold. I can remember it like it was yesterday. It was a regular-sized envelope—say four by ten, but special paper, and fairly thick.

"When Leslie and I built the house on The Point, we stowed it away in the closet, the south bedroom. At least I think that's right.

"Then, as you would have it, one night old Hatter's cat knocked over the space heater and caught his place on fire. At least that's what everyone surmised. Hatter & Sons burned to the ground and smoldered until nothing was left to burn. Nothing at all. And that meant the original documents for The Point were somewhere among the ashes.

"Leslie and me thought about makin' another copy, but we never got 'round to it. We had ours here and just forgot about it.

"No problem, ever, until a fews years ago. Shortly after the Source Telecom people started poking around, I began to receive these green envelopes. Seems this second cousin, twice removed, Brad Bentley, linked up with Source Telecom in some way, claiming there's a letter from Rufus to his great uncle Jarrod, saying he'd like him to have The Point.

"Nothing legal, mind you, just some handwritten note. Probably fake—Brad Bentley had spent a lot of time in the pen honing his thieving ways. The Bentleys have always had a lapse in their lineage, quirk in their quiver.

"Well, I said all that to say this: The envelope has vanished. I've searched everywhere, and everywhere again. Then I started all over again. Been lookin' for weeks.

"It's possible one of the dogs grabbed it and carried it outside. Trunk's mother, Track—that'd be Trip's grandmother—was always carrying stuff out on the lawn, particularly newspapers. There they'd go, blowing off The Point. It was like a game for her. I suppose she could be the culprit."

"An amazing story, Mr. Ironbout. It sounds rather serious and complicated. But what exactly are they saying?"

"Well, without that envelope, I could be in a heap o' trouble. Can't prove anything about Uncle Rufus' wishes. They're talkin' about some judge sitting in on a discussion, 'bout six weeks from now. I'm sure it'll all work out...not to worry."

"I certainly hope so," said Goodwin, at a loss for what else to say.

"Yeah, well, we'll see. Meantime, let's go back out on the porch. Trip's looking suspicious; he's not sure what he's seeing, another person sittin' inside the house with me.

"Lots of company, Trip is. We listen to the radio together every night. He really likes *Tunes Spun* on Saturday evenings. Mostly he likes jazz—can you figure that out? When I get a bit tipsied up—nothing serious, mind you, just rosy cheeks, you know—we'll do a little dance there in the front room. I just hold his front paws and take a step or two.

"Good boy, come on Trip. Let's go 'round the side, where we was before. It's a good spot. Have a seat there on the swing. I'll take this worn-out thing. You know, I like wear. You like wear? Ever think about it? I like to go into a place where I can hear the floors creak, or go up creaking steps. Makes you feel like you are part of what was, and still is, you know what I'm tryin' to say?"

"I do know. Modern engineering methods have a way of fitting things so tight," Goodwin said. "A lot of it's good, but the days of true carpenters are nearly gone."

"So right. Well, this has been nice talkin' to you, but I guess you came for your sketch. I must have stared at it fifty times. Nice mood—I like to view it with a bit of distance."

"No, why don't you keep it for a while longer. I might get Hollie to come up again, and we can get it then. This place is just so completely amazing. It's such a great setting—the lot, the house, and all. Drawing it when I was a kid, it's strange to be here—like I'm in the sketch. Before it was an imaginary sketch; now it's real as life."

"Yeah, there are ten hectares up here. Nice…except for all the tragedy that came about. Well, anyway."

"Hollie and I understand you've gone through some really tough times, Sir. We just felt we should let you know we're around, even though we've just come to know you."

"That's kind of you, young fellow. There's a lot I've got to get my head around before I sort out my directional thinking. I suppose I did sort of speak open-minded thoughts to you two the other day. Hollie kinda shocked me, got me all Leslie-minded. And your sketch—there's something I'll tell you about that, something you wouldn't have known. Not today, though. Like I said, I need to get my directional thinking redirected."

"You know, Sir, one of the main reasons we came to Estillyen is for Hollie. She was recently diagnosed with something called PKD, a kidney disease. It can be a tough one. No cure, really. If it starts progressing, it can take over. Not sure what it means in terms of children for us."

"I'm sorry to hear that. Really, I don't like hearing that at all. No, not at all."

"But being here on Estillyen has been great. A real breath of fresh air. We're here a good while yet, so plenty more time to soak in the peace.

"By the way, I was thinking of you earlier and brought you one of the readings. It's in my backpack, if you want it."

"You mean one of them monk readings?"

"Yes, it's one of those. In fact, it was from today's reading. Just thought I would bring you a copy."

"Never read one…don't suppose it would hurt. Doubt I can make much sense out of it. Is it written in Latin?"

"No! That's a riot."

"Always thought them monks were a bit loony, you know what I'm tryin' to say? They have a peculiar way of looking at you, like they're peering through wavy glass—like they're here but not here.

"They remind me of birds in a birdbath splashing all around and then suddenly pausing and twisting their heads peculiar-like. Years ago, before I ran everyone off, a few of 'em would come up this way for walnuts. Used to talk with them a bit, back then. You may not believe it, but I was quite inclined toward the spiritual side in those days.

"Anyway, speaking of walnuts, I'm gonna saw the big branch off that back walnut tree within the next couple of days. It's taking privileges, extending itself all the way along like that. Look at it, reaching way out over the plot. Those end branches are starting to stretch down and scratch the markers, all deliberate-like.

"That big branch should have grown upward, but for some reason it kept growing sideways. The tree probably had a double trunk in the beginning, and that branch sort of got shoved over. Doesn't look right; it ain't right. It's nearly the same size as the main trunk.

"Nope, that limb's days of liberty-taking are gonna come to an end. It'll soon be firewood."

"That looks like it will be a fair-sized job; I hope you've got help and a good saw."

"Oh, yeah, it shouldn't be a problem. I'll get Trip to help me."

"Well, Mr. Ironbout, I wasn't planning on staying too long. I just thought I'd bike up and stop in for a few minutes. I'm so glad you weren't pitching walnuts today. By the way, you've got a good arm."

"Thanks for the compliment, but I'm not sure that's the kind of compliment I ought to be a-warranting, you know what I mean? I suppose I need to reassess this whole manner of meanness and walnut pitching. I've not been myself since you showed up 'round here. Dearie me, it twisted my head all around on the inside."

"Well, don't be hard on yourself, Sir. No harm done—I know how much this place means to you."

"Appreciate that. Just the same, I think I'm due for a bit of peering into the mirror. Got to do that now and again. I've just been dashing by, so to speak. You know what I mean—shaving, plucking, grooming, but not peering into my eyes more deep-like."

"Reflection is definitely a good thing sometimes," said Goodwin. "I've been learning a bit about that during our stay on the isle.

"Well, it's sure nice to talk with you again Mr. Ironbout. I guess I'll go get the monk's message out of my bag, while I'm thinking about it."

"Trip and I will go with you. Come on, Trip, let's go get a monk message, see what it looks like."

Mr. Ironbout and Goodwin leisurely walked around to the front of the porch and across the lawn. When they got to the bike, Goodwin reached for his backpack and pulled out the rolled-up message.

"This is it," Goodwin said. He unrolled it and extended it with both hands to Mr. Ironbout. "The reading's called *Remember Me*. Hope you like it."

"Sure, I'll try to remember to read it. I'll even clean my spectacles. Nice visiting with you there, Goodwin. You say you might come back up with Hollie?"

"I'm pretty sure she'll come along. I'll definitely be back before we leave for home, though. Well, I'd better get moving. I'll get the sketch next time."

Goodwin reached out his hand to Mr. Ironbout, who responded with a firm handshake. Goodwin turned, picked up his bike, hoisted it above his head, and began walking through the tall, weed-covered path.

"I need to sickle that path a bit, I suppose," the old man shouted to Goodwin. "Maybe before your next trip up here. See ya. Take care."

"Same to you, Sir."

Goodwin soon disappeared. Mr. Ironbout rolled up the message and stuck it in his left hip pocket. He began walking back to the house with Trip.

"Ah, looks like we'll have a bit of reading to do, Trip, along with some tree cutting. You think you can handle a saw, carry some logs? Hmm, whataya think? You don't look much like a lumberjack to me. I'm too easy on you, ya know that?"

Goodwin peddled down The Point, veering off on a few inviting paths along the way.

Meanwhile, Hollie made her way over to Sister Ravena's office.

"Hi, there," Hollie said to the young girl seated nearest to the office door, as she pulled the door shut behind her. "My name is Hollie. I'm here to see Sister Ravena."

"Oh, yes, she's in. Please go on through. I just saw her making some tea. Go to the open doorway, make a slight jog to the right, and then straight on to the end. Just give a wee knock."

"Sure, thanks. Where'd you get that complexion anyway?" There was no reply, only a blushing smile as Hollie passed.

Hollie swiftly found her way and gave a couple of taps on Sister Ravena's door.

"Please come in!"

Hollie entered with a smile.

"Hi! Will you join me for a cup of tea? It's green. I'm just winding down after a very busy week and a great, productive day. How's the artist?"

"Good, I think, said Hollie. "I feel productive, too. I spent most of yesterday painting at Tunnel House. And yes, a cup of tea would be great."

"Here, let me pour it while it's good and hot. Do you want sugar?"

"No, just as it is, please."

"Are you painting something on the inside of Tunnel House or the structure itself? Isn't that a unique place with those corner windows?"

"I'm painting primarily the tunnel, with some of the structure worked in. I've already got what I need, and I can fill in the rest. I want to complete something while I'm here, like we were saying about the artist who did the painting of the young man. Oh, the tea hits the spot."

"Funny you should mention that painting again. You know, I had someone else looking at that earlier today, one of the longtime contributors to Estillyen. Anyway, the tunnel, that should be interesting. Can't wait to see it."

"Yeah, I want to put myself inside the tunnel—I think a back view, going through it. That's one of the many inspirational insights I've had since being here. I feel so connected to this place. It's incredible. Honest."

"I'm really glad to hear that. We're getting more and more people your age coming over. It seems things spiritual are swirling again. I like the creativity and enthusiasm they bring. That's one of the main reasons I was so keen to explore The Point. Still am.

"Like I mentioned, I could see artists up there, on-site instruction, all kinds of things. Some people, I'm sure, would be interested in donating their work for a good cause. The paintings done on Estillyen would be special, I think. I'm biased, I suppose.

"We could have an annual auction. The infirmary is always in need. There are plenty of options. We're also connected to a very big world, a great deal of it hurting."

"I'd love to be involved in something like that, Sister Ravena, truly. That's kind of why I wanted to chat with you just a bit. I hope that's all right."

"Certainly—that's very much a part of Estillyen. Please."

"Oh, first, I almost forgot! Goodwin's gone up to The Point this afternoon to see Mr. Ironbout. I think he's there now, or maybe on his way back. He took one of the messages with him—the one we heard today at Speaker's House, *Remember Me*. Writer did the reading—that sounds funny, doesn't it?"

"Oh, I'm aware of that one…gripping. He read it last year for the community chapel during Holy Week. That should be quite interesting for Mr. Ironbout. I do wish things could change."

"I know. You can just see the potential that's there—potential he has tucked all away. If only he could work his way through the pain. Maybe Goodwin will make some headway. Writer's reading certainly can't hurt—if he reads it.

"Anyway, as I was saying, it seems I've got a bit of a health issue—this polycystic kidney disease that I was diagnosed with about a year ago."

"I know—I was so sorry to hear it. Is there more that you'd like to share about it?"

"Well, I feel fine just now, actually great. So far, the doctors have only detected two small cysts. There's not much they can do in terms of treatment. It's more the kind of thing you monitor. It could stay like it is or go dormant—anything is possible—but the percentages are not very encouraging.

"Ten years from now, or anytime, it could go full-blown, taking over the kidneys, moving to the liver. The worst-case scenario would be a kidney transplant. The disease clearly threatens life as normal. It's what I describe as being curiously ill.

"I guess I'm coping better than I thought I would a few months ago, but it hits me when I'm not suspecting it. Then all the anxiety about the future comes rushing in. It's not so much a fear of pain, but of not having a regular life. Since I've been here, that fear has captured me a couple of times.

"Goodwin is great, caring, but I honestly don't think he realizes how different his life may be because he's married to me. This disease—by the way, I hate the word *disease*—has turned life upside down. Nothing is normal anymore."

"I'm honored you would share all this with me, Hollie. I can't imagine how you must feel, how challenging this is to cope with. I'm so sorry you're having to face this. Do you have a good support group back home?"

"Well, Goodwin and I are a bit dislodged right now. We've been 'exploring' before settling in. Estillyen is kind of the last stretch of our journey. Win calls it a journey of sourcing.

"Estillyen is proving to be incredibly important—very valuable, I believe. I'm feeling a different sense of self, something kind of revealing, like destiny and reality are coming together. I'm not sure if that makes any sense."

"It makes perfect sense. I've never faced a real health issue personally, but in my work I've been around a lot of people who have. Many of my colleagues have been very involved in providing care and support.

"You'll need support. I think the people who cope best are those who sense true worth. That may be what you're experiencing; it sounds rather like that."

"It's just that I so didn't want this—not this. You know what I mean," Hollie said, as she began to blot the tears welling in her eyes. "I'm sorry."

"Hollie, you're such a talented, brilliant young lady. It's fine—tears are a gift; they have a reason. You know not all nuns start out in the children's choir. Many have gone through bitter trials and heartaches before, then one day, they find themselves answering God's call to a different life.

"I was like that, some thirty years ago. I had gone through some turbulent waters. I was looking out over the vista at a new life, what you might describe as a normal life. I had just gazed across the horizon at what I thought was an ocean blue, when I heard God say, 'Follow me.' I knew what that meant: It meant letting go. It meant grasping hold. There was a call.

"Letting go made answering the call possible. You, too, have a calling, and you will have to let certain things go, as a greater sense of worth takes over. The aspiration of normality is not always best. Consider Mary; she was hardly normal.

"She was chosen for the highest honor bestowed on any human being. Mary also suffered greatly. The second the angel arrived, with the message of good cheer and announcing God's favor, normality was no more. She watched her son, the Son of God, die on a cross. What's normal in that scene? Nothing.

"I'm really glad you are an artist."

"So am I."

"The reason I say that is because artists possess that special sense of perception, coupled with imagination. When directed towards the stories and characters you find in Scripture, artists can be a source of surprising comfort for the world.

"If I can suggest anything, I encourage you to look at the future not as a path measuring how far you can go. There are some people who come and go very quickly, yet add so much worth to the world. What they say and do lives on, helping, healing, and inspiring others to carry on. Others live long, only to live not knowing what to do.

"Art brings worth to life. Life is about the worth you discover, the worth you give, and the worth you leave. I'm confident, totally confident, that you can be remarkable at all three."

"I really like that," Hollie said. "The worth you discover, the worth you give, and the worth you leave."

For more than an hour The Abbey visit lingered. Eventually the tea was gone, and Hollie found herself giving Sister Ravena an affectionate hug.

"Thanks so much for the visit. I'm so grateful for your time. I wish I had a big sister like you."

"You do," Sister Ravena said with a smile.

Through the office door Hollie exited. Down the hall and outside onto the path she stepped. She gazed at the left fork of the walk, the *Y* that turned into a *U*. Then she considered the right fork that led back to The Abbey.

She chose neither. Instead, she strolled on the grass, enjoying the warmth of the sun, as she watched the reflection of the clouds dance across the lawn.

THIRTEEN
The Message and the Appendage

"It's Saturday night, Trip; you know what that means," Mr. Ironbout said. "It'll be time for *Tunes Spun* directly, in a little over an hour. We'll listen to it, but I'm telling ya, you've got to be fit tomorrow. We're gonna deal with that appendage.

"We've let it go too long; that branch has taken all the liberties it's gonna take. Why didn't you go out there and saw it off, hmm? I would of helped you, silly. I wouldn't have left you on your own.

"Say, what about a reading? You look like you're up for it. You'd make a good audience. Your new friend Goodwin brought me that monk message, you know. It's pulled from that book in your office. Don't see you readin' it much, though. Little confusing, isn't it? I understand, those are pretty ancient stories.

"Let's have another little shot to wet the whistle, before we get too embedded in all this reading and thinking. Come on, I'll give you a biscuit. Let's see, here we are. Good, isn't it? Keeps your teeth white. Well, this keeps my innards fit, my mind tickin'.

"Whataya thinkin' about so serious-like, the price of my scotch? Sure, I know it's a bit pricey, but it's single malt, aged ten years. Just think what I'd be spending on doctors' visits and pills to ward off colds and such. When was the last time you saw me with a cold, down on my back? Hmm, can't tell me, can you?

"Let's take a little shot with us. We're gonna need straight eyes sorting through those monk-stitched words. Come on…come on, boy. Let me just settle in here. Go on, get comfortable in your chair. Good boy. Now, let's see, whatta we have in the way of a message? You got your good Trip ears on? Let me just set these spectacles. Ah, nice scotch.

"Okay, listen up, audience. The title is *Remember Me*. Now, that's a good one, isn't it? Wonder if God remembers me, Trip? Hope he doesn't fall off his throne when he sees me reading this message to you. Yeah, it's me, God, Oban Ironbout; I know, amazing, isn't it?

"I realize you ain't heard from me in a long spell, but factors are a bit different, sort of flipped up lately—a bit surprising. Been shocked a bit; my thinking's been sort of rattled since that unexpected visit. Anyway, Trip and I are gonna take a listen to this message. I'm sure you won't mind. Trip's all built up about the reading.

"Trip, what we're gonna do is this: I'll read a sentence or so. Then, while you absorb it, take it in, I'll carry on kind of quiet-like. Now and then, I'll cast you another line or so. You reckon that'll be all right? Sure, I thought you would agree.

"Now, here's the opening line…"

Christ's figure shone expressly bright when he was transfigured on the mountain. Still more brilliant did his glory show when the sacred One was lifted high, upon a hill called Golgotha.

"Whoa, Trip, I know you're no dummy, but that may be a bit much even for you. Let's continue—it seems to be a dialogue."

"Why was he lifted up?" Voice asked. "The simple truth, that's all."

For sins he was lifted up.

"Whose sins?" Voice asked.

Not his own. Sins committed then and there—sins stretching back in time, and those yet to be. Great and small, the lifting up was recompense for them all.

"Trip, I'm afraid this is gonna twist your head a bit. Let me read on and see how it flows."

Golgotha is the place where spikes were bunched.

"Where were those spikes?" asked Voice. "Perhaps, in some rusty pot or lying on the ground?"

You're right to question and consider, not skip through the story all hither and thither. Recycled and bent they may well have been, harboring all manner of menacing particles. Bunched, they waited for their thudding blows to drive them through until solidly set. Instantly they released their infectious residues into the blood of the crucifix.

"Hmm, it continues on about this Golgotha place. Sure glad we don't have a Golgotha 'round here on Estillyen. Bad deal it was. Feller who stuck these words together was kinda seeing full force, Trip, sure was."

"His condition on the cross—what was it, really?"

Voice, let the words of the psalmist speak. "I am poured out like water, and all my bones are out of joint. My heart has turned to wax; it has melted away within me. My strength is dried up like a potsherd..."

"Now, Trip, that word there, *potsherd*, has nothing to do with herds; it's not saying pots and herds. It's like a shard. Guess you don't know what that is, either. It's a fragment of pottery. That's what this is about, how a broken piece of pottery feels, all disconnected, broken. You know, I used to know a good bit about this stuff, Trip.

"If I read anymore of these messages, I'll get you something from the Psalms—a bit mellower, though. There's a lot of talk about sheep; you'd like that.

"Whoa me, this is turning a bit macabre-like, Trip. You're too sensitive for some of this, I know. Listen..."

Hoisted high before bulging eyes and clenched fists, the message hung. Blood was his garment. Drenched red he was. From tissues deeply torn, blood flowed...
Around the knees, from the chinbone to the ankles, the warm crimson fluid trickled on. Across the feet it advanced, past the spikes, before the toes it reached. From there it dripped, moistening the ground...

"I see...hmm, that kinda presses hard on your mind. Oh, here's a line you'd like, though."

Like ornaments without a tree, the prophecies had long waited to be hung upon their stories.

"Kinda nice, different don't you think? You just put your head down, and I'll carry on throwing out interesting bits.

"Oh, this part's about Judas. I remember him. He's a character you wouldn't like at all."

Judas was there, grasping thirty pieces of silver and his hanging rope....

"That Judas fellow would have stolen a dog's collar, if he thought he could pawn it.

"You want another biscuit, Trip? I think I could tolerate another sip; my lips are getting out of sync. Just watch this message and don't eat it. Remember, when I'm in the kitchen, I can still see you in here. I'm watching you. Don't move. Good boy.

"Okay, I'm coming. Here we are. There, that's better. Where were we?

"Yikes—Satan. This won't make sense to you, but I'll read it…it's fascinating."

Lucifer began, "You know, just occasionally, the pot is superior to the mold—and even to the potter. That's what happened in my case. Oh, with all this treachery about, I feel so benevolent. I shouldn't be, but this is a special day.

"I'll tell you what I'll do, my devotees; I'll let you gaze. All twelve of you to the left, quick come around and get on your knees….

"Benevolent, my uncle. He's the devil. Dear me, Trip, this doesn't let up one bit. Those monks got some kind of way of stitching words together. They've got time, though; it's not like they're hanging out in the saloons. Here's another bit that would surely confuse you, if you knew what it meant."

Christ came down the Via Dolorosa in the midst of sinners' gaze. Surely he would die. As the sacrificial lamb, he walked on feet unswerving. A lamb's feet they were, feet of the Shepherd, too. He was true to course: For redemption's plan, the Son of God came to die.

"This was an important place, Trip; I sort of forgot about all that."

At Golgotha, their feet were clutched and spiked. No more would their soles press upon the ground….

Crucified as objects of public scorn, the three were hoisted high….

"Deary me, Trip…I should have read this in a couple of settings. There were criminals involved."

Moving closer was death's freeze; minutes pulsed, the criminal without remorse hardened steadily to the core. His heart would not heal before his body died. Fearless, the condemned criminal became a spokesperson for sin….

Hating what life had dealt, the man of misery spoke with a spirit of damnation. He despised the figure his eyes beheld…no reason for hope—the criminal's eyes had seen all there was to see; he was blind.

Equally in throes of the agony of death, the second criminal could see. His repentant eyes somehow saw a figure his heart did not despise. He saw this Jesus hanging there beneath the sign Pilate had prepared. It was to him he called, saying, "Jesus, remember me when you come into your kingdom."

"You probably won't sleep a wink after this, but I'll read you this part anyway. Pretend I'm one of the monks."

The end was near—the worst kind of end, a miserable death of dying, with the living watching, gawking. Quarantined from the living, on show for dying, is a wretched way to die.

Crucifixion is to die rejected and deserted by the world; it's to die in public all alone.

"Here's another one."

With death, the pumping of blood and its dripping swiftly stopped. The medium was now silent—but speaking still. Death silent spoke meaning into life. Death silent was the sign signifying redemption's price was paid.

"Ah, Trip, listen to this evil slug—it's Lucifer again."

"Darkness, earthquakes—what's happening? This can't be. This is not what I expected. It's too soon. He died too quick; it's a trick.

"This is not fair. Tombs breaking open, hear that, and that. Silence, imbeciles! Stop you're chanting, can't you see the Word's really dead?"

"Then it comes to an end. There's a line about words."

Words matter. Words from the cross matter immensely.

"Well, dear, oh dear, Trip, what are we gonna do with that all that rolling 'round and contorting the mind, hmm? Now if a man wanted to ponder, that's a stretch of words on which to ponder.

"I wish you drank Scotch. We could ponder together. Being a dog is not so bad, though. All this considering of God and such is not as easy as you may think.

"*Tunes Spun* will be on in less than ten minutes. Let's have a snack. You want some peanut butter and some of those stone-ground crackers? What about a tangerine? Dear me, we need to shake this off. We'll have to tap our toes a bit. Come on, now remember tomorrow we're up early; gonna rid ourselves of that appendage."

It was a quarter past ten when Trip slowly walked down the hall, turned left into the office, and curled up on his green-and-blue plaid blanket. At twenty past ten, Mr. Ironbout placed his toothbrush back in its holder and shut the medicine cabinet door. He peered into the mirror for a moment, thinking about the reading, Goodwin and Hollie, and himself alone. He turned off the upstairs bathroom light and walked sleepily down the hall and into his bedroom.

He pulled back his pale green sheets, fluffed up his pillows, lay down, and fell fast asleep. The reading, though, filtered into his dreams.

Morning dawned.

"Trip, you want this last bite of sausage? Let's split it. I'll cut it with my knife. Here's your half. Good, isn't it? We needed a proper breakfast, you know. We're gonna be like a couple of lumberjacks today, working up even more of an appetite. You've got the easy bit—just picking up branches. Let's get to work, no slacking off now."

Soon Mr. Ironbout and Trip were out on the side lawn.

"You see, Trip, look at it. That branch already swings down and touches Leslie's marker. We're not having it. Watch this, Trip. Here, take that, you appendage! Ah, there, the first branch. Let's start making a pile out in the middle of the lawn.

"Does this saw hurt your ears, boy? It's just a lot of buzzing. Watch, Trip, it's easy—zip, zip, two more, three more; that's the pace. Confounded branches, who do you think you are, stretching out over the graves like that, reaching out with the wind all scary-like at night? Well, I ain't afraid of you.

"Trip, let's take all the branches and cut 'em up into chunks as we go. I want to lop off all the branches on this main trunk of a limb, or whatever you call this blasted thing. If we let the branches fall with the limb, we'll end up fighting 'em; they'll sprawl all over the yard.

"I can't believe how far this limb stretches. It looks like a tree growing out of a tree. I make it about ten meters, just stepping it off. You want to step it off? Dumb-looking thing, isn't it? I won't be looking at it much longer. Glad there's no bird nests.

"It's a good thing we've got both our ladders, Trip. I think I can use the big step ladder all the way along. I'll put the extension against the main trunk. Will that work for you? Why can't you climb a ladder? You can climb everything else.

"Last night's rain made the ground a bit soggy. That won't stop us, though; we're lumberjacks. Real deal, we are. We'll take a break around eleven. We'll eat one of them raisin muffins. You'd rather not, you say? What about a carrot, then?"

Along the massive limb Trip and Mr. Ironbout progressed, starting at the graves and working back to the main trunk. That was the plan. The more Ironbout cut, the more intense was his mood. It was as if the limb became a living figure. The more he sawed, the more engrossed he became. For him, the limb was an intruding force threatening to overpower his world, the world he'd worked so hard to preserve.

The eleven o'clock hour came and went. Mr. Ironbout didn't notice; he was too absorbed to stop. He reckoned he'd get the whole limb down and then have lunch. Solely on the appendage was his mind engaged. He skillfully focused on the cuts, calculating where each limb would fall.

Trip watched, as sawdust flew through the air and settled on the lawn. Anyone watching would have realized there was more going on in Mr. Ironbout's mind than the removal of a giant limb from a walnut tree. He was focusing beyond the appendage to what it represented.

That limb was like time. It could never have stretched so far without the aid of time. Its very existence meant years had taken flight; decades had whiled away. The longer Oban Ironbout lived, the further those blocks of time had fled, stealing memories that were different, kind, and hopeful. Images once vivid had become less clear; they had taken on fuzzy edges. They were fading from his mind.

It was that first bitter block of time that had stolen Leslie and the twins he never knew. Now the appendage of time was waiting for him, not yet achieving the prize of its reach. But he could see the appendage; he was not blind. Each year it reached a little further. He knew that one day it would reach across his own marker, mocking him in his grave. He would be gone, and on and on the appendage would reach.

Time could not be stopped. The limb would not stop. The appendage of time, however, could be chopped, removed, eliminated. Mr. Ironbout would chop the appendage into decade hunks, then yearly chunks, all to be burned on wintry days.

Mr. Ironbout knew that, for him, winter had arrived. He felt his age, along with a sense of his own madness. He realized he was on the losing side of time. He thought that in some strange way, this act of chopping up the years would prove cathartic to his soul, rendering a little peace.

But time would not give back what it had stolen; this Mr. Ironbout knew. In his heart, he wanted to change before he died. Although how could he ever rid himself of himself? This is what tortured him. He was Oban Ironbout, a man molded through decades of bitterness and hate. How could he surrender such a menacing mold? Who would he become?

When he held Goodwin's sketch, he had been utterly surprised to feel that glint of light touch his heart. It was such a strange sensation, that sudden glint and rush, that sense of life and lift. He imagined a nightingale in song suddenly perching on his shoulder. From its beak a feather dropped and gently floated down into a cauldron of hate. Should he lift it up, try to grasp it, consider it more dearly?

The notion was maddening. No, not now in life's winter. Kindness could not appear, bringing unforgotten spring showers. Not for him. For such showers he had no reservoir; his heart was too sealed and hardened. Alone he had walked. For so far and long he had walked with hate. The very idea of kindness now appearing, was this not itself cruel? It was so late, so very late, he thought. How could he now be blessed, after knowing only curse?

He was Oban Ironbout, the man of cursing verse, the cursed. He was a man of hammered heart. *Glint of light, why did it wait so long?* he thought.

Oban Ironbout felt the appendage was mocking him, taunting him. He had spent his life stretching, reaching out for those he laid to rest so long ago. Now, in winter, was he to reach beyond the graves and touch a bit of joy? If he did, who would he be? He thought the glint of light was cruel to tease him.

I mustn't let go of my reach to grasp a glint of light, he thought. *What if I do and it flees? I'll be doubly darkened.*

More darkness he could not bear. He felt it was better to hold on. It was winter now, this he knew, not some fairy-tale spring. Further he mused, *I'm Oban Ironbout; I've become too devoted to death. To embrace the glint, to let go, would brand me a traitor.*

He shouted aloud, "Don't mock me, you blasted appendage! How do you feel now that your limbs are all lopped off and your leaves are starting to shrivel on the ground? No, you'll not live on to mock me, to show me what my life has been. A life lost, you say? A lifetime of only reaching for the graves, you say? Do you know how it feels? What have you known of loss? You're just a tree—and just an appendage at that.

"Like you, I've grown bent, it's true. Too far I've grown—stretching, reaching. I'm an appendage of death, I confess. That's all I know. I also know this: I must rid myself of you before I die, or before I live. That's all I know.

"You know what I'm gonna do now? I'm gonna cut under your armpit, you monster without feeling. Let me set my ladder on your fellow trunk. How does that feel, you heartless appendage? Your main arteries are being severed. Oh, it won't be long.

"You're up so high, you are, you blasted appendage! Don't worry; I can still stretch. You think I can't reach like you. You think I'm through? Lop! Did you hear that sound? Do you know what that was? It was your armpit. It looks like a giant piece of cheese lying on the ground. Like a quarter moon, there it lays.

"Now let me just climb one more step. I'll cut you loose from the shoulder; right on top I'll cut, just slice straight through. Then you know what'll happen to you? Your long, miserable reach of barren limb will slowly descend. In the end, where your reach sprouted out over my graves, you'll now be a stump. You, the appendage stump, will now slowly bow in reverence to the graves and then touch the ground. You will show respect, appendage.

"Your shoulder is half-severed and still you hold you fast. Not for long—like the hands of a giant clock, you'll go from pointing three to five. Your trunk mate points to twelve. Your hour will swoop down to five. Twelve twenty-five will mark your fate, the moment you died. That's where your sweeping reach will touch the ground. When you bow, you will seep and weep from your wounds in reverence. You hear me, appendage?

"Tick, tick, tick—your time will soon be gone. No more swaying through the seasons. Your great pointer will angle down in silent respect, no more mocking. Then you know what I'm gonna do, when you're all severed? I'm gonna chop you up, decade by decade, year by year, chunk by chunk.

"That's what you think should happen to me, isn't it, appendage? No pretense of sprouting out beyond the graves. I should be cut down, bow one last time, and die, so you can hover over me. We'll, I'm not dying today—you are!

"Trip, stand clear. Go on down to the end, boy, and watch the appendage slowly bow. Just a little more—hear that, Trip? That was a crack; there's another. See, appendage, your mocking spell is coming to an end. Let me just twist around, give you one last cut."

With the saw buzzing away in his right hand, Mr. Ironbout reached out for the appendage. He held onto the ladder with his left hand. He stretched to make his final cut, and as he did, the ladder unexpectedly slid on the bark of the tree and twisted.

"Oh, watch it—oh, no! Oh, Trip, what's happened? I've hit the ground hard, really hard! Think I've cracked my ribs. This is not good, boy; daddy's hurt. Trip, my left leg…I think it's broke—oh, it hurts. Oh, we gotta get help; there is no help. Oh God—look out, Trip! The limb's…"

A loud crack rang out. The appendage suddenly broke loose from the trunk. Instantly the giant limb thudded to the ground, pinning Mr. Ironbout beneath it.

Hours passed.

"Oh, oh, oh, what is it? Where am I? Trip, is that you? It's nearly dark; I'm cold… my teeth are rattling. This is bad, Trip, really bad. Oh God, I'm pinned. My leg, I can't move it. Come here, boy, come here. Trip, Trip…God, oh God, what happened? How did I get on the ground? I'm gonna die here. Oh, my leg…Trip…this is serious, boy. The appendage has me trapped. I can't move, Trip. We're alone, Trip.

"I shouldn't have mocked the tree that way—I know, God. I was thinking it might help clear this hate out of me, God. Trip, don't leave me! Don't leave me, boy. I think I'm gonna die. Oh, the pain! Oh, what happened? Oh, no, I don't think I'll make it. The limb was supposed to bow. It snapped, Trip. It bounced. I can barely see the markers. Looks like it's in the plot. Trip, Trip, come here! Touch me, touch me. I've had it. I'm in a bad way, boy.

"Ain't nobody coming up here, Trip. I'm sorry, God, about me...how I wasn't, couldn't be different. I blamed you, but I knew you once. I'm like them thieves. I'm both in one. I'm gonna die before I can get rid of the one and be the other. Oh, oh, oh. The bad one is not how I really am. I was wanting to be the other. That's what I was gonna talk to you about...oh, no, this is bad, Trip.

"This is it, Trip. Give me that saw. Can I reach it, Trip? Little finger...oh, oh, get it; get it, tiny bit, an inch more. Two fingers I got, Trip. There, come here, saw. Trip, Trip—I'm gonna try to gouge out some of the limb below my knee. Come here, boy, can I sit up? Oh, oh, uh, uh...I'm on my elbow. Oh, Trip, not sure...I may have to sever the leg. Can I get in the Rover? Would I be able to, uh, uh...

"If I can get the leg free...There's not much chance either way. I'm gonna die, Trip. Oh God, it shouldn't be like this. I just got ruined. Here, Trip. I'm pulling the rope. Oh, the pain, the pain—it's something fierce, Trip. Another pull; there it is. Don't, Trip; don't run. Don't leave me, don't leave...please, boy.

"Oh God, it's too heavy; I'll just have to kind of use a throwing motion. Here goes, Trip..."

FOURTEEN
Worth

"Win, I can't tell if exercise helps or hurts my condition," Hollie said. "I do feel better when we get out and walk like this. It could just be mental, but that's part of it, I guess. There must be benefits. It's a long trek, but I'm glad we decided to come back up to Lakes Three. I love it up here."

"Look at those squirrels chasing each other around the pines," Goodwin said. "Do you see how fast they're going? Why didn't I bring the camera? We buy a camera and don't use it. I can't believe we saw that solid black one with no tail."

"I know—he looked like he was impersonating a rabbit. Fat little stomach and bulging cheeks. Adorable."

"Perhaps that same fox that got One's foot bit off his tail. Maybe that's his thing: a mad fox stalking Estillyen critters. He just gets a tail here, a duck foot there, and decorates his Estillyen fox den. You know, like hanging up antlers."

"If you stick around Estillyen much longer, you'll sound like old Mr. Ironbout, sort of in your own world. You know, I was just thinking about Mr. Kind—the way he talked about Lakes Three; the way his eyes sparkled. I could see him walking up right now."

"Yeah, I wonder what that little fellow's up to? I think he's going to try to meet up with us at Blyer's Café on the return. That seems like ages ago, doesn't it? I can't believe we're heading back a week from Tuesday."

"I know. It feels like forever since we got on the ferry. Yet time has also flown. I don't think I've been bored a single minute. I know I haven't. It's interesting coming here, not knowing anyone and meeting so many people. You have this vague idea of Estillyen before you get here—at least I did—but it's nothing like what I thought it would be.

"The people are real. The whole thing with Mr. Ironbout and The Point... did you ever expect to come here and meet someone like him? I didn't. Wonder if he read the message you gave him."

"Not sure with him. He might have burned it. But he does seem changed somehow—didn't say anything offbeat to me at all last time. There is something deep about him. He's a real mystery."

"I think you're right," said Hollie. "He has that strange way of talking. Some people talk that way, knowingly masking their intelligence. He's very much that way, I feel. Ironbout's had a blunt trauma kind of life, but if you look at that house, it must have been so amazing when it was first built. Just think about it new, all freshly painted, when he and his wife were young. It's got the touch of an artist. That is a very crafty bit of architecture up there on The Point."

"I know. The coffered ceiling in the main room is superb. All the trim is perfectly straight and tightly fitted. He talked about the baseboards like he put them in yesterday: 'They have this one simple bead on 'em. On the top, halfway across, there's a thirty-degree slant.' Everything has this meticulous detail. It's all understated, though—nice."

"How old do you think he is?"

"To watch him pitch walnuts, you'd think he was young. They whizzed past my head like they had been fired from a gun."

"Think about his wife; she died, what, forty years ago?" said Hollie. "So add that. We don't know how old they were when they got married. Something he said made me think they didn't try to start a family right away. I know what it was; it was when he was talking about the sheep. He said that he and Leslie started with four sheep, remember? Then, when he was talking about her death, he referred to the herd.

"Her birth year is on the marker, but that whole experience was so rattling, I didn't really concentrate. That was such a strange scene. I have the feeling she was in her late twenties or around thirty when she died. So I'd say he's right at seventy, or somewhere around there."

"Must be," Goodwin said.

"Sister Ravena brought up the subject of the telecom company and how they would love to get their hands on his land. From what you've said, that sounds like a very serious matter."

"Well, I didn't read the letter or anything, but something is clearly up. Those legal issues can drag on for years, though."

"A telecom tower on The Point is certainly not Sister Ravena's vision for Estillyen. She sees The Point as a place for artists painting, retreats, seminars, special events.

"Sister Ravena's fantastic. I appreciate her openness. She's not weird, all down on the world or anything. She views art as part of the ongoing process of creation. I do too, of course—the whole idea of continuing to create in God's image."

"I hear you, but a lot of creative expression is not so creative, don't you think?" said Goodwin. "A lot of it is pretty far from getting a thumbs-up from God."

"Yeah, sure, but that's part of what I like about Sister Ravena. She wasn't trashing anyone. I hate when people do that, and it's so pervasive. Anyway, that's not the point she and I were actually discussing. We were talking more about the way art is part of our innate expression—and how art can be therapeutic.

"Somehow we got on the subject of media. She was talking about Christ as the mediator between God and humanity. She's bright, I tell you. She mentioned that the root word for media is *medius*, from the Latin, meaning "middle," and how the root word for *mediator* is actually "media." That's the way Sister Ravena sees art functioning. It's in the middle, between the artist and the audience.

"She really puts her mind into the subject. When you think about it, all forms of art, and I guess all media, are in the middle. That's where the monks are coming from, focusing on words and competing messages. She wants that kind of direction for Estillyen art. Art at its best, doing its best. I told her I'd love to be a part of it somehow.

"I so appreciate what she said to me. I don't know how, but she spoke right through me. Well, not actually through me, but more to my spirit. I can't get the whole *worth* idea out of my head: 'Not how far you travel in life, but the worth you discover, the worth you give, and the worth you leave.' I love that. I've embraced it, locked it in.

"Really, Sister Ravena is special. I think she was planning to get married once. When she was talking about looking over the ocean to the horizon, that's what she meant, I'm fairly certain. I didn't press it; I didn't feel it was appropriate. Anyway, it wasn't important. She seems totally complete.

"You can see the soul-centered peace she has. She knows who she is; her sense of worth flows from her faith, her calling. Maybe we were supposed to come to Estillyen just to meet her."

"Do you think Oban Ironbout is in that category, someone we were supposed to meet?" asked Goodwin.

"Don't know. He might be. He's certainly a character, and it's interesting, this long-ago link between Mr. Ironbout and Sister Ravena. It would be great if they could connect—for the good of The Point and the whole community. Especially the artists; it would be incredible to paint up there.

"Speaking of painting, do you like my tunnel painting—I mean, what you can see of it?"

"Awesome, honest. I think it's superb already. I'm really glad you put yourself in it. I know you don't like to do that. Have you ever done that before?"

"No, not really me. I mean, actually meaning to be me."

"I also like the real-life size in relation to the tunnel. I bet if I'd measure you in the painting and calculate it out, you'd be spot-on in terms of size. The back view—that's dramatic, a bit mysterious, and great with the orange raincoat against the dark tunnel."

"You don't mind not being included, do you?"

"No, you know I'm not like that. It's right. It would change the entire mood of the painting if I were in the tunnel with you. I'm there with you, just not seen."

"I'm going to bring in soft light along the base of the tunnel, down at the bottom of the right wall and onto the cobblestones. It's there in reality, when the moon reflects off the ponds. The little ripples in the water make the light shimmer. I saw it on Friday night when we walked through the tunnel. You remember Plot talking about God's image reflected on a meadow pond? That's what sparked for me when I saw the light in the tunnel.

"I'm glad I could spend most of yesterday working on it. I must finish it before we leave Estillyen. What do you think I should name it?"

"Don't you always say you can't name it until it's done?"

"That's true. I'm just eager to finish. You know, as I think about it, if it's okay with you, I don't think I'll go with you up to The Point tomorrow. I definitely want to go again—say, Wednesday or so—but if I dedicate tomorrow afternoon, I think I can finish this."

"Go for it. I'm going to bike up. I can be there in no time—that is, if I don't wander too far from the path. I really like that old fellow, Lee. I agree with you about his manner of speaking. The guy is smarter than a mountain lion."

"Win, if you lived in a place like this, do you think you would miss the urban buzz?"

"Not sure…probably not. The line you were on earlier about worth—I feel that's right. I suppose it all depends where that pursuit of worth leads."

"Those sailboats on the first lake earlier today—they were so picturesque, the three of them just brightly sailing through the water. Some people spend their entire lives wanting to come to a place like this. We've got to make another trip up here before we leave. Can we go by Fields and Crops on the way back?"

"Great idea, but it's Sunday; they're closed."

"Oh, I totally forgot. The service this morning was so early, it seems like yesterday. It was nice, though. That small choir is so good it probably attracts angels. I can see them pausing, peering down to listen. There's so much talent on Estillyen."

"Where are we headed tomorrow, by the way?"

"Dairy House again, with Plot. He's so intriguing. We'll have to tell him about the tailless squirrel that looked something like Tremble."

"You're right, Plot would get a real kick out of that. For now, though, we better get going."

The following morning, the reading room at Dairy House was packed. More than ten minutes beyond the allotted starting time of ten-thirty had already ticked away, but Plot was nowhere to be seen.

People were quietly exchanging bits of conversation, when sounds began to emanate from the kitchen. The back door opened and shut; there were voices. In a matter of seconds, Plot appeared.

An elderly monk followed him, carrying a folding chair. The older monk placed the chair at the end of the short hall between the kitchen and the reading room. The bulk of the chair opened into the hall. Only the tips of the front legs extended into the room's interior. The monk calmly took his seat.

Meanwhile, Plot stepped into the reading room. "Welcome to Dairy House, everyone," he said. "My name is Plot. Sorry I'm running a bit late. I was down in the village early this morning for a meeting. I'm not sure who to blame: my mouth for ushering too many words, my ears for listening to too many words, or my legs for not moving a little faster. Regardless, I'll take the blame, until I can find which one caused me to be late."

Plot's cheerful demeanor quickly set everyone at ease. Smiles graced faces as the assembled audience waited to hear what Plot would read.

"Well, since those three characters stole nearly fifteen minutes of our time, we'd better push along. Oh, let me introduce my colleague, Brother Witness, who has graciously offered to assist with today's reading."

Plot turned to his left and smiled at Brother Witness, who rose slightly, smiled, and nodded to the room.

"It's good to see some friends here today. Elizabeth, Sherry, Matthew—great to see you again. And Thurston—what a surprise! Wonderful to have you here. It's Hollie and Goodwin, right?"

"Yes," Hollie said.

"Thought I got that right. Let's see, we need a few volunteers to be our Voice. Three would be great. What about you three?" Plot asked with a smile, looking directly at three young women seated comfortably on a sofa. Their features varied: long, curly blonde hair; short black hair; and one in the middle, who was obviously fond of streaks. They all blushed in response to Plot's proposal. They looked at each other nervously and giggled.

The curly-haired blonde said, "No, I can't."

The one in the middle said, "Why not? We must."

And within ten seconds, the collective decision was made: "We'll do it."

"Great," said Plot. "Let me pass along these lines and we'll get started. When you see me nod, that's your cue to voice the questions or comments. Speak in unison, voicing your lines slowly and with a sense of honest appeal in your tone.

"Okay, I think we're there. The title of today's reading is *Stop Doubting and Believe*. Let's just settle in silence for a few seconds, and then I will begin with a couple of verses from St. John.

"The context is Christ speaking with the apostle Thomas. This is the second time Christ appeared to his apostles following his resurrection."

For twenty seconds, maybe more, the room was silent. Then with a full voice, Plot opened with lines from St. John's Gospel.

Stop Doubting and Believe

A week later his disciples were in the house again, and Thomas was with them. Though the doors were locked, Jesus came and stood among them and said, "Peace be with you!" Then he said to Thomas, "Put your finger here; see my hands. Reach out your hand and put it into my side. Stop doubting and believe."

JOHN 20:26-27

READER: Through locked doors Christ suddenly appeared: seeing, looking, touching, speaking. Words of peace he offered to his disciples. He had risen from the grave, where he had lain dead, so unquestionably dead.

This is not the way of the dead. They do not rise up to live again in light, once death's signatory, Freeze, has seized and fixed their faces.

Around the crosses three Freeze had surely crept, circling all their bases, waiting to leap, sensing time and pulses faint. Then upon the center cross Freeze leapt. Climbing up on crimson stain, Freeze moved to seize the One with the wordy plaque and thorny crown—the envy of the hill. It was time for pulsing to end its marathon of life. No more pulsing, no more coursing of the blood.

Thick darkness draped o'er the land, eclipsing the sun.

VOICE: Where did the sun go? Had it failed to shine, or fallen from the sky?

READER: Fallen from the sky, Voice, no—although this may have been how it seemed. Its darkened drape was a sign signifying that death's Freeze had leapt on the Son of God. Creation had never known itself minus God's Son. The earth trembled, rocks split apart, and tombs broke open. The dead awakened. Upright in their crypts they stood. They, too, were signs signifying that the impossible, the inevitable, could be overcome.

The dead had broken free from Freeze. Into this mysterious, darkened day, the dead, now living, stepped. On soil they walked, with soles miraculously warmed by pulsing blood. The dead were living. Walking, talking—Voice, were they not a peculiar message?

VOICE: Never thought of them as a message. They must have been alarming.

READER: Can you see them moving about in utter wonder?

VOICE: I can see them.

READER: They signified the beginning of the end had come for death. Death's unstoppable reign had been broken.

It was a centurion who stood near the cross on the swaying ground who saw it all. He watched as Mary's son fell silent, and Freeze masked the face of life with death. These dramatic acts occurring signified that the face on the center cross was not that of a normal man.

"When the centurion and those with him who were guarding Jesus saw the earthquake and all that had happened, they were terrified, and exclaimed, 'Surely he was the Son of God!'"

Voice, there on Golgotha's hill, amidst the desperate, dying, sobbing, crying, a surprise arose: A centurion believed in the dying Christ. At Golgotha's hill, amidst the spiking, crucifying, dying, his confession was heard: "Surely he was the Son of God!" *Surely* was the word spoken, Voice, meaning clearly this was not merely a criminal crucified.

Only three people did Christ address from his planks of pain hoisted high. Words he spoke to his mother Mary, the favored one Gabriel had visited in days gone by. Much older now, Mary stood on a hill; she watched her firstborn die. On Golgotha's hill he was openly manifest above the jeering, mocking crowd. Christ also spoke to the disciple standing next to his mother and to the repentant thief. These three, and of course God the Father.

Dying on the cross, Christ's words were few: "I thirst" and "It is finished." These are two quick lines the mocking, gawkers heard. Some words Christ prayed. Just before his death, he prayed to his Father in utter agony. *"Eloi, Eloi, lama sabachthani"*—which means "My God, my God, why have you forsaken me?"

With eyes of coal, death stretched across the figure on the cross. Freeze waited for Christ's departing words and the drop of his head. "Father, into your hands I commit my spirit." Freeze then settled in, drawing every trace of warmth from this One heaven-sent.

That's how it was, Voice. It was over, finished. It was time for the eternity's ancient hourglass, the vial of ages past, to be righted, turned upside down, so to speak. Do you know what I mean, Voice?

VOICE: What was over? What was finished? What do you mean "vial of ages past"?

READER: What was finished? The era without grace, which the blood of a billion goats and bulls could not buy—that was over. The time of ages past, with mystery clasped, hidden fast—that too was over.

VOICE: Mystery clasped...are you sure that's what you mean, Reader?

READER: Yes, Voice, the time of waiting and watching for the Messiah to appear was over. The mystery of redemption was a mystery no more.

VOICE: What else was over?

READER: The torturous pain throbbing through spiked hands and feet—that was over. Not a single word of accusation or bitterness was heard from this one so spiked. Not a syllable of this sort came down from the man who bore the thorny crown.

The supreme message of God was the Son. He was the medium chosen by the Father. A one-of-a-kind medium, a message of reconciliation, redemption, was Christ. In the words of St. Paul, "God was reconciling the world to himself in Christ."

In a word, the message was grace. Submissively, willingly, the Lamb of God died on the cross.

VOICE: What happened to Christ's body hanging there?

READER: Thank you for asking, Voice. It was claimed and taken down. A man named Joseph acquired permission from Pilate to remove the body. Not just anyone could run in and snatch the corpse of Christ.

VOICE: Does it have to be said that way, corpse and all? It sounds...so...I don't know...earthy or unheavenly.

READER: Listen further, Voice. Real it is. That's why the story's there. Joseph was an influential member of the Jewish Sanhedrin and lived in a small town called Arimathea. An unlikely person to claim the body, one would think. Joseph of Arimathea was a man of wealth, a devout individual. A man of smart attire, he surely was.

VOICE: So interesting to consider, when you think about it. What would he have worn on Golgotha's hill?

READER: You ask too much, but ask away. The story does not say. But I can imagine him there: climbing up, hoisting down, and resting the body of Jesus Christ on the ground.

VOICE: Did he believe in the crucified one?

READER: St. Luke describes him with brevity as one who "awaited the kingdom of God." Evening shadows had surely fallen by the time Joseph went to recover Christ's body. The man from Arimathea had an accomplice—a Sanhedrin colleague, a Mr. Nicodemus. He was another man who had been drawn to Christ. Joseph purchased linen cloth for the burial. Nicodemus acquired a "mixture of myrrh and aloes" weighing some thirty-four kilos.

What a peculiar sight they must have been. Minds set on self-imposed obligation, amidst watching eyes they moved, no doubt quietly respectful. For, their hearts were once warmed by the one they had come to lay to rest.

Together, it was they who climbed the wretched hill of death and took down the body. The distinguished pair had become a team. They were claimers, carers, anointers. Can't you see them on the hill, Voice, this Sanhedrin duo in the dim evening hues, moving about, dutifully determined? Their presence— does it not add a heartening lift to this mysterious story of injustice and anguish?

VOICE: Reader, I think you're right. I've never thought of it like that.

READER: This unlikely pair carefully wrapped the body in strips of linen, and then they carried it to a shallow cave—a tomb, it was called. They rolled a large stone over the tomb's entrance. That was their final deed; their job was done. This act of burial kindness admirably sealed these characters in the story.

The full extent of interaction between Joseph, Nicodemus, and Christ is not known. St. John records that Nicodemus once paid Christ a visit. He came around at night to ask some critical questions of this teacher he did not know— though Nicodemus was convinced that Christ was blessed of God. Nicodemus said to Christ that night, "No one could perform the miraculous signs you are doing if God were not with him."

This line prompted a most intriguing conversation between the two concerning the kingdom of God and how it might be entered. Christ explained that entrance to the kingdom of God required a rather radical procedure. He spoke of a spiritual transformation, and used the words *born again*. Ponder it, Voice— born again, born not just once, but born again.

VOICE: I shall.

READER: During their exchange, Christ also spoke prophetically of his crucifixion. He said to Nicodemus, "Just as Moses lifted up the snake in the desert, so the Son of Man must be lifted up, that everyone who believes in him may have eternal life."

Consider it, Voice. Stories, like the one of Moses crafting a serpent and placing it on a pole—how did they come to be? They were woven into ancient texts in a way that allowed Christ to pull and pluck, pick and place, in constructing his Gospel message.

VOICE: Never thought about it that way.

READER: You must, Voice! What is it you want to do with your thinking? Where are you going, Voice? Think while you live, before Freeze comes to seize. I implore you to see beyond your seeing, hear beyond your hearing. How, you may ask? Certain words will help you rise to the challenge.

Again I ask you, Voice, how did these stories old come to be, from which Christ pulled and plucked?

The ancient texts ensured that Christ's message would be layered rich with meaning deep. Ancient stories of this nature are exceedingly clever. A single story, rich with characters and meaning, finds a story of its kind and worth, and the two intertwine. Each story, already rich on its own, becomes exceptionally so when the two are woven together. Fused, they impart far greater depth of meaning than either could do on its own.

VOICE: I see what you mean, Reader; I do.

READER: Voice, this intertwining capacity of verses great says much about why Christ's message was both so radical and so powerful. Soaked in cultures rich, the ancient stories brimmed with meaning. They waited to be chosen, to be woven in, to go calling out.

VOICE: That is exceedingly clever. To think, they lie in wait in story's hold, some quite old, and then in time they intertwine in a story new. Can we talk about this some more?

READER: Certainly, but not just now, Voice. We've left our story waiting. In the tomb, remember, there Christ lay dead, wrapped in linen cloth.

VOICE: You're right. Please carry on. You will, won't you?

READER: In the tomb he lay until the Sabbath passed. Then a new round of God acts began to unfold.

VOICE: God acts, you say…what acts?

READER: Think, listen, and think again.

A violent earthquake shook Jerusalem on the morning of which we speak. Listen to the ancient words, worked into lines, woven into story. "And behold, there was a great earthquake, for an angel of the Lord descended from heaven and came and rolled back the stone, and sat upon it. His appearance was like lightning, and his raiment white as snow."

At this very hour, Mary Magdalene and Mary, the mother of James, were on their way to the tomb to anoint Christ's body with spices. When they arrived, they encountered a pair of angels, who appeared as men in "clothes that gleamed like lightning." The women were terrified and bowed down to the ground.

The angelic messengers said, "Why do you look for the living among the dead? He is not here; he has risen! Remember how he told you, while he was still with you in Galilee: 'The Son of Man must be delivered into the hands of sinful men, be crucified and on the third day be raised again.'" Then they remembered his words.

The women fled the tomb and ran to the apostles with the news. When the disciples heard the report, Peter and a fellow disciple raced to the grave to see for themselves what had taken place. When they arrived at the tomb, they found only strips of linen on the ground, and a folded head cloth nearby.

The two disciples believed what they saw, but it would take time for the ramifications of the event to sink in, to filter through with meaning full. In the words of St. John, "As yet they did not understand the Scripture that he must rise from the dead."

The story of suffering and grief was being divinely infused and choreographed with resurrection light. Throughout the centuries skeptics have scoffed and howled at believing a story that cannot be proven. The issue for many, though, is not so much about proof to be found, as it is the matter of faith that must be placed.

Truth rests in treasure troves, along ancient paths, ready to expend its rewards. This, however, it cannot do if the seeker demands that the treasure prove its worth before taking hold. Twins—skepticism and unbelief—are so easily born. They can chop truth away. Like sharpened knives they cut.

Belief that must pass through the prism of proof before being released can cause a strange disease, something akin to cataracts on the soul. When plucking petals from a rose, there comes a point when the rose is no more. It is the same with the words and story that flow forth from ancient texts of Scripture. Do you want to pluck them away, Voice?

VOICE: No, not me. You must have someone else in mind.

READER: Just checking.

It's often something along these lines that is said in deference to Scripture's offering full. "Oh, that? Don't bother; that's a line for disregard, and you might as well ignore that chunk and this one, too. Take what you want and leave the rest. I'm afraid that with these ancient troves there is more to disrespect than respect. We have other words; why worry? You must learn to skip around, taking in what seems to fit the mood and the circumstance."

Believe, Voice. Once resurrected from Freeze's brace, Christ appeared face-to-face in numerous settings over a period of forty days. Ranking these appearances in terms of importance is not possible.

Surmise and choose, rank the order we can, but it is a bit like twiddling with twigs in a forest. Look at the broader picture; look taller, higher, and consider. Interplay between heaven and earth shaped all the events with divine intent, and there was much at work beyond knowing. This was no one-time incident of minor note. Divine drama was unfolding in culture and time; the events were being storied for eternity.

The story was still being shaped as the resurrected Christ began to appear. The disciples, the chosen repository of Christ's message, were in a state of collective confusion and needed to be sorted out. The apostle Peter, only days earlier, swore he did not know Christ. At the time of the resurrection, he is seen as bewildered—running around, dashing about.

Many of Christ's disciples were befuddled and perplexed by the stories and rumors swirling around Jerusalem. This was clearly the case of the two disciples who were traveling on the road to Emmaus. They walked along, harnessed in discussion, when suddenly Christ appeared. These two were not part of the inner circle of twelve. They were part of a larger group of disciples that had come to follow Christ.

Christ suddenly slipped alongside them on the road and asked, "What are you discussing together as you walk along?" With downcast faces, they paused. Then the one named Cleopas said, "Are you the only visitor to Jerusalem who does not know the things that have happened there in these days?" With anonymity and brevity Christ replied, "What things?"

"About Jesus of Nazareth," they said. "He was a prophet, powerful in word and deed before God and all the people. The chief priests and our rulers handed him over to be sentenced to death, and they crucified him. But we had hoped that he was the one who was going to redeem Israel."

Christ bluntly said, "How foolish you are, and how slow of heart to believe all that the prophets have spoken! Did not the Christ have to suffer these things and then enter his glory?" And beginning with Moses and all the prophets, he explained to them what was said in all the Scriptures concerning himself. Christ still had not disclosed who he was.

VOICE: You mean, Christ walked right there beside them, and they had no idea who he was?

READER: That seems to be the case. The two disciples, in Christ's own words, were "slow of heart." Their spiritual perception was sluggish. As the three approached the village where the two disciples stayed, they invited Christ to dinner. While seated at their table, he gave thanks and broke bread. At that point the two recognized Christ.

Instantly he disappeared, and they were left asking each other, "Were not our hearts burning within us while he talked with us on the road and opened the Scriptures to us?" The two hurriedly returned to Jerusalem and found Christ's apostles and conveyed the news, saying, "It is true."

The forty-day period following Christ's resurrection may appear less crucial than all that occurred during Christ's ministry. These days, however, were as vital as all the rest. The prophetic word of Zechariah speaks: "I will strike the Shepherd and the sheep will be scattered." On the Emmaus road the first pair of scattered sheep were found.

With so many sheep being scattered about, it's hard to imagine that Satan would let such an opportunity go untested. Satan had to be somewhere—why not near the action of the resurrected Christ?

Plot turned around to his left and nodded to Brother Witness, who was already rising to his feet. He gently nodded in response, took a single step into the room, and began to speak. His rhythm was buoyant, his intonation precise, his pace lively.

LUCIFER'S DEVOTEE: Master, Lucifer, whatta we do now? The Word has up and resurrected.

LUCIFER: Shut up, you imbeciles, all of you, not a word. I've got to breathe. This resurrection surge has created some kind of vacuum in the spiritual sphere, some new strain of spiritchitis. I've got to cough. It's causing my membranes to flutter at lightning speed. This is too much.

Stand back! I'll go cough 'round those busted-up tombs. Maybe I can scare some of them come-alive fleshies back into their boxes. Did you see how stupid they looked? "What happened? Where are we?" Stupid dummies. Some of the religious lot was trying to put the blame on me. Talk about idiots! I put 'em down; I don't wake 'em up, the religious nut cases.

I'll be back in three lightning strikes. Meanwhile you two uglies go down to Golgo's dungeon and pull me out a new backrider. I thought we'd be camping out here for a while. Not so with the Word floating about all resurrected.

Now, form a circle. Get down on your knees and lock your arms. Everybody facing out. I want to see 360 degrees of demon eyes. Okay, now make your eyes bulge real big, like owl eyes. Ah, look at that, my defensive watch. If any of you sees anything, anything whatsoever, hum the code. Watch and wait. I'm going. But while I'm away, I'm watching. My eyes know no visual distance.

I'm moving, watching. I see you, as if I've never left. Oh, how pleased I am to see my band of chosen devotees interlocked arm-in-arm, obeying my orders. So stiffened tight they are, a single ring of bulging eyes. What a battalion, a buttress.

Now from a distance far, do you hear my whisper, devotees? I'm whispering, but watching, still. What a sight to witness—oh, how adoringly you recognize my whisper.

I'm watching. Can you hear the delightful sound of my cough? Like a huge mortar being fired through a wall of mud. Did you feel the vibrations?

Okay, I'm back. Good cough. Have you seen the Word?

Bad news, by the way. Get up, idiots. Relax your eyes. Listen. The come-alive fleshies that sprung their graves, they've heard that the Word went down, preaching, testifying to all the old fleshies stowed away. That's what woke 'em up in their boxes—his force swooping down and the exclamation of the underworld when he appeared.

They said legions of angels were stretched into infinity. It's not fair rushing in like that all unannounced, beaming light into all that rich, black-shelled darkness. He's probably already reached the other side of the abyss by now.

Does the abyss have a far side? Shut up—that's not a question! I was just having a fractional blink. A tiny blink...I've got the concern of the whole netherworld looking in my direction. There's a lot going on. Who else can they turn to when the universe gets all turned upside down? Hey, what's that quizzical look on your faces? That better not be doubt. The only thing I hate worse than a doubting devotee is a double-doubting devotee. Don't you ever be a-doubting! Devotees believe! Look to me—Lucifer.

I know what happens in the abyss. Who do you think you're looking at, imbeciles? You want to know about the abyss? I'll tell you about the abyss. The abyss is forever expanding, but the Word raced to the edge of the expansion; he turned around and spoke. The Word and I AM halted the expansion for an hour, just like they stopped the sun back in Elijah's day.

When the Word spoke, his words were like streams of light racing in the opposite direction. That's what happened. Imagine all those spirits tumbling and rolling in his direction! Forever they'll tumble, hearing: "I am the way, the truth and the life." It's ghastly. He's not playing by the rules. The Word should have telegraphed his message—taken it slow, not rushed in like that.

Look at me—Lucifer. I'm like no other. I'm the delusion, the deception, and the death, but I don't make a doctrine out of it. Narrow—who wants narrow? Not with me—broad are my gates, all manner of gates, with a plethora of signs and symbols so people can find their way in.

Come on in, that's my motto. I favor the inclusive approach. No sneaking around, hiding my message for ages in scrolls, like cages. Just think how much better my way is, so much more appealing, truly universal. A sprinkle of philosophy here, a scoop of superstition there, a dash of doctrine mixed in—that's what fleshies want. That's what they crave, not narrow gates, getting their sides all scarred up trying to enter.

It's not right making fleshies so they're able to see all kinds of ways, wanting all kinds of gates, and then torturing 'em if they don't go through the narrow gate. Why didn't I AM just make single-minded one-gaters? He let his creative prowess get out of hand. From the very outset, fleshies were out of whack. They're miserable creatures—malformed they are.

I'm just saying! I want spirits drawn by adoration—sure, just like I AM—but we have scads trailing in that don't even know they're following. That's the beauty of it, the liberty of it. A free-flowing kingdom…roam and romp as you please. That's the spirit. My followers follow by rejecting. Fleshies are a rejecting kind. That's all I ask: Just reject the ways of the Word and I AM, and you're in. Believe whatever you wish. Any gate will do.

All this spiritchitis will destroy the cosmos. Nothing will be the same. If too much of their way gets going, everything's gonna get off kilter. I AM, the Word, and the Third have come up with a master plan. I've figured it out. They're instituting this new deal called spirit and truth. Guess they're not satisfied with the fleshies doing sacrifices.

They made the rules, not the fleshies. As far as I'm concerned, that was the only thing they ever did that made any sense—the killing, the blood, the sacrifices. Ah, brutal butchery, all that helpless groaning and travail. It's been wonderful to watch down through the centuries. It's what I call real, honest misery. Not some flimflamsey offering of grain, but of blood. The fleshies have been awash in it for years.

We hate everything. Remember that. You know how you demons all gather each year to renew your vows and slash each other? Even that is changed. We'll have to add a new line, because of the Word rising up like he has. You're the first to hear it. After we chant, "We hate everything," we'll have to add the line, "And we hate this day most of all." This is a wretched day. This is the worst day I've ever known.

Got news for you, though. Just because the Three dreamed up this spirit-and-truth deal doesn't mean it's gonna work. Who was it dreamed up the Garden, hmm? They discussed it, all around. "Let us make man in our image." That's what they said. Right there, all three are implicated in the mess. Fleshies—I hate every one of 'em. I've seen a good number of 'em bearing my likeness, but that doesn't matter. They never should have been, stupid mud cakes.

I've got to figure out our next moves. We need to get some wars going on 'round here—shake everything up; get stuff buried in the dust. Resurrection: a bogus idea, it is. Ah, that's it! That's what we can begin to spread right now, right here, today.

See if you can say it with conviction—like this, slow with meaning: "Bogus, bogus, bogus." Push out your lips, and then say it with a deep, guttural sound. Try it, and don't look confused. You double basses, you try it. Ah, nice, I like that. We can fill the atmosphere.

Oh, you two back there. Come here, Backrider, you fool. Hop up, shut it. There's a bad case of spiritchitis going around. Train your dungeon eyes on anything that moves. This spiritchitis force is atomic in nature.

Here's what I want you to do. The twelve of you practice a new bogus chant. I want it simple, just: "Bogus, bogus, bogus, don't be a fool, it's not real; bogus, bogus, bogus, don't be a fool, it's not real." That's it—now you think you imbeciles can do that? I want lots of cadence, all low, and from there descending.

While I've been instructing you, I've received word that the Word has just been spotted. He was walking on the road to Emmaus. He must be confused; his bunch of brats are all around here, so what's he doing there? Come on, Backrider, let's you and me practice the chant as we chase.

You lot, form that circle. Start that chant. Surprise me when I return with the extent of your tonal mastery. I'm counting on you. You're the fount of my delusional flow.

Come on, Backrider, let's scoot.

Brother Witness ended with a smile, as he moved his piercing eyes slowly across the room. Without glancing behind him, he took one backward step and confidently sat down in his chair in the middle of the doorway.

READER: Within forty days after his resurrection, Christ would ascend. It was crucial to gather the flock and rivet their focus on carrying the Gospel message from Jerusalem to the ends of the earth. The disciples needed unswerving conviction concerning their message.

The story of Christ cannot be boxed in or left stratified among religions. The core of his message disavows it. The central message of the cross is that "God was reconciling the world to himself in Christ." Voice, the words speak of the world complete, do they not?

VOICE: Your point's well taken.

READER: The message is not merely about a peculiar people in a peculiar place. The story embraces everyone, everywhere—every human being, past, present, and future. The story is not small and limiting. It continues even now to unfurl and expand like the universe itself. Everyone is encompassed in the divine drama—even you, Voice.

VOICE: I am?

READER: Certainly—the story's scope is meant for everyone everywhere. The all-encompassing force of redemption rushes into the universe and all it contains. It cannot be stopped. It will not be halted. There is no void, no space, no other world. There is no place to go where the power of reconciliation does not flow. Certainly the force can be denied, declined, rejected, but that's not escape.

The story of Christ is not unlike the tale of the trees speaking to one another in the Garden of Eden. The trees used to love to call out to each other. In doing so, they'd always identify their location in proximity to the tree of life. Christ, who hung on a cross, is, as it were, the tree of life. Christ's story defines everyone's story, not pugnaciously out of a spirit of contempt, but out of relationship to God. God subsumes all of what religion is, and Christ is God.

After disappearing from Emmaus, Christ appeared to the apostles that evening in Jerusalem. The apostles had received the report by the two disciples from Emmaus. But when Christ appeared they still thought he was a ghost. Christ encouraged them, saying, "Look at my hands and my feet. It is I myself! Touch me and see. A ghost does not have flesh and bones, as you see I have."

During this first visit, the apostle Thomas was not present. When Thomas heard the news, he told the apostles that unless he could actually "see the nail marks in his hands" and put his finger where the nails had been, he would "not believe."

The following week Christ again appeared to his disciples, and this time Thomas was present. They were all gathered in a room, and the door was locked. Suddenly Christ was in their midst. Christ invited Thomas to examine his hands and his side, and then he said to him, "Stop doubting and believe." Thomas did not attempt to examine; he simply replied, "My Lord and my God."

Christ then addressed a magnanimous point. He said to Thomas, "Because you have seen me, you have believed. Blessed are those who have not seen and yet have believed." This was the great mission now apparent. Who out there among the vast unknown, having not seen, would actually believe?

Soon stories of Christ were reported, collected, and written down. Words would jump into lines; lines would form messages-making stories. The stories intertwined, fueling thoughts, filling hearts and minds. In this charted course of words newly scribed, it would seem most unreasonable to conclude that Christ would have adopted a laissez-faire approach.

The one who placed so much weight on the Scriptures knew all the elements that would come to be the Gospel story. There was no chance or happenstance. The events during this forty-day period, like all the rest, were gathered, and they entered the Gospel story with multilayered meaning and divine intent. Christ knew precisely which words would jump into lines, forming messages.

A line of no small import is, "Stop doubting and believe." Is it not so, Voice? It is. Indeed, it is.

St. John writes, "Jesus did many other miraculous signs in the presence of his disciples, which are not recorded in this book. But these are written that you may believe that Jesus is the Christ, the Son of God."

Those common men, chosen by Christ to tell the Gospel story, would soon be sorely tested. It was time for those who had been "slow of heart," confused, or somehow dismayed, to fully awaken. It was a time for doubt to flee and belief to rise.

Their opportunity would soon come. The day would be Pentecost.

Words matter...some far more than others.

Stop doubting and believe.

JESUS CHRIST OF NAZARETH, SPEAKING TO THE APOSTLE THOMAS,
JERUSALEM, CIRCA AD 32

Plot paused. There was warm applause from everyone in the room. Plot looked first in the direction of Brother Witness, who remained seated but acknowledged the applause with a smile and nod.

Plot extended his arm toward the voices three, and he too joined the applause. By now, the young lady fond of streaks was once again seated in the middle of the sofa, next to curls of blonde and hair of black. Their smiles were vivacious.

Soon a sense of satisfied calm settled in the room.

"Well, it looks like we didn't make up any time," Plot said, as he looked across the room to the hexagon-shaped antique clock above the fireplace mantel. "I think we've actually lost a little more. This time, I *know* who's to blame; it's the mouth with words.

"If you wish, we could have the time of conversation now, and then afterwards you could follow with contemplation. I'm easy. I'm just sorry for being late."

Everyone looked back and forth, making connections as a group. There were several nods in favor of Plot's suggestion.

"Okay, it looks like the nods have it, and the nods are going up and down, not sideways, so I guess that means we converse.

"Elizabeth, you have a comment?"

"Yes…"

It was Martin who followed Elizabeth. Mr. Scruggs got a turn, followed by Hollie, Allison, and Gregory. Around the room, conversation flowed, until Plot said, "Well, it seems that's a reasonable place to conclude, wouldn't you say?

"You're a brilliant group. It's always revealing. Thanks for being at Dairy House today. God bless you. Be of good cheer."

It was not long before the group had stretched, gathered their bits and pieces, and begun to slowly trickle outside. Hollie and Goodwin waited, hoping to speak with Plot.

"Goodwin and I were just holding back a bit, Brother Plot. Can we catch a word?" Hollie asked.

"Sure. Do you want to take a seat?"

"Just for a minute," Hollie said.

"It's good to see you two again."

"I really appreciated the reading today," Goodwin said. "I don't know how you think along the lines you do."

"Oh, before I forget," Hollie said, "yesterday we saw a little squirrel that reminded us of Tremble. He was solid black. We were up at Lakes Three, and all these squirrels were chasing each other around the pines, when this charcoal squirrel stopped and stared at us."

"You know, the black ones are quite rare on Estillyen," said Plot.

"That's not a surprise—everything seems quite rare here," said Hollie. "Well we thought he looked a bit curious, so we got a bit closer and then could see he didn't have a tail. Solid black, with just a little stub of a tail. Chubby little thing, he looked like a rabbit. We thought you would enjoy hearing that.

"We also wanted to let you know that Goodwin is headed up to The Point to see Mr. Ironbout and…"

The momentary word Hollie and Goodwin wanted to catch with Brother Plot didn't work out as planned, as the minute somehow stretched to forty-five. Plot could not resist offering them a cup of tea, and, of course, there was Tremble.

When their time at Dairy House was finally over, both Hollie and Goodwin headed out on their respective missions. Hollie went to finish her painting of the tunnel, while Goodwin peddled up The Point.

FIFTEEN
Pinned on the Point

"Hello, anybody home? Anybody around?" Goodwin asked, as he gave three knocks on the unlatched screen door, which slapped against its frame with each quick knock. "Mr. Ironbout? Trip?"

Goodwin could see the front door was wide open. He could see straight into the house but thought, *I feel uneasy about entering.*

He spotted Mr. Ironbout's old green Rover parked in the lawn on the east side of the house. Not a sound could be heard except the chirping of birds around the basin. Goodwin decided to head around to the side porch, when he noticed Trip easing up the side steps.

Slowly, tentatively, Trip moved. He seemed frightened. Goodwin knelt down and gently coaxed Trip to the center of the porch. Trip progressed cautiously, with his tail tightly concealed between his legs. The dog's chin nearly scraped the porch floor, as he gingerly made his way to Goodwin.

"Hey, Trip, why are you squinting your eyes? Come here, boy—what's wrong? What's that on your chin? Did you catch a rabbit or something? Where's your owner? Is he over this way?"

Goodwin stood and started walking towards the side porch. Trip's posture immediately changed. He raced off the porch, leapt into the yard, spun around, and began barking. Trip looked back and forth between Goodwin and what Goodwin had yet to see. Trip's eyes were vivid, his demeanor anxious, as if he were viewing a threatening predator on the property. Goodwin knew something was wrong.

"What is it, Trip?" Goodwin spotted the tree, quickly noticing its huge limb was missing. Next, he saw the reason for the alarm in Trip's eyes. Mr. Ironbout was lying flat on his back, pinned under the massive limb.

"Oh, my gosh!" Goodwin exclaimed. Swiftly he ran to Mr. Ironbout, knelt near his head, and placed his fingers on the right side of his neck.

"Mr. Ironbout, Mr. Ironbout, can you hear me? Sir, can you hear me? Trip, he's pale. Sir, do you hear me? Come on, Sir, wake up! Here, let me feel your neck. Mr. Ironbout, we're going to get you out of here. You're gonna be all right. You have a good pulse, a strong Ironbout pulse; that's no weak and waffling pulse, no sir.

"One second—you just hang in there. Trip and I will race into the house and get a blanket. You just hold on. Come on, Trip."

Goodwin raced across the lawn with Trip in the lead. They bolted up the steps, dashed across the porch, and rushed into the house.

"Where's a blanket, a wrap, Trip? What about in here—that must be yours. It'll do. Quick, into the kitchen! Just a little water, water, water...let's fill the kettle. Come on, come on...that's good. Let's go, Trip."

Through the screen door they bolted, with Trip again in the lead. In his left hand, Goodwin carried Trip's green-and-blue plaid blanket. In his right, he held a gray kettle filled with water. With the movements of a focused long-distance sprinter, Goodwin sped back across the lawn.

"Now, here, Sir, we'll just place this nice blanket over you. There, that was Trip's idea. We're teaming up on this, Sir. Trip wanted me to bring you some water, too. Here, I'm just gonna put the edge of the spout to your lips, right here on the side. Nice well water, Estillyen-deep. Do you hear me?"

Mr. Ironbout made a slight grunting sound.

"Thank God you are conscious, still with us. Now take a sip, a tiny sip. Good, good, that's it. Now we'll set that out of the way."

Mr. Ironbout suddenly blurted out, "We don't need potatoes.... Blake, the sheep are getting out..."

"Sir, very good to hear you speaking. Don't worry about the sheep just now. Trip's got 'em spotted. He'll have 'em rounded up in no time.

"Yes, Sir, you have good vitals," Goodwin said, as he thought, *Dear Lord, what am I going to do?*

"We'll get you right. Just keep that pulse beating now, strong Ironbout beats, you hear me. No weak beats now. Trip and I are here. We're going to pull this together.

"Trip, every move counts. Time's critical, Trip. Oh, how does it go? *Analyze, stabilize, mobilize.* That's it, Trip. Now, Sir, let me just take a quick look at that leg—that's a strong leg, an Ironbout leg."

"Appendage cursed me...ooh, ooh, I'm dying," Mr. Ironbout slurred.

"This big old limb sure has pinned you down, Sir. That part of your leg under the limb is a little hard to see. It could be a bit twisted. Let's take a look at this place just below your knee. I just want a bit of a closer look before Trip and I get you outta here. I'm tugging at your torn trousers, peeling back this twill a bit…I want to see…"

"Blamed tree…oh God, wasn't…" Ironbout moaned.

"Looks like you've been oozing a good bit of blood. That gash is deep, but you're still intact. I think Trip has been nursing you by the looks of his chin. Thought he'd caught a rabbit. Trip; you're a good wound-licker.

"I'm just gonna take my belt and tie it around your leg, Mr. Ironbout, just above the knee. Trip and I are teaming up on this. You just keep that pulse going, Sir. Good, nice and tight.

"Can you hear me, Sir? Let's just feel that pulse again. Very strong. Now we just need to get you moving.

"Let's see…let me think. Think, think…the saw? We must move…no time, time…*time*…

"We need to do a bit of engineering, Sir. What do we have? Let's see…

"We're just going to have a quick look in the Rover, Sir. I'm right here, Mr. Ironbout, just opening the back doors."

"Get the bat and the…I gotta know which way to go if I'm gonna get there… uh, oh, ooh," Mr. Ironbout rambled, with his eyes clamped shut.

"No chain in here, Sir, but you've got an S-hook and some heavy bolts."

Chain, chain, Goodwin thought. "The grave plot, Trip! We're just gonna look over here, Mr. Ironbout. You know…your black chain around the plot.

"Looks like the end of that limb caught it, Mr. Ironbout. It seems to have broken the chain, snapped it. Come on, Trip, quick, let's grab it. We're just pulling it through the loops. There we go; this long section is perfect.

"Now, don't go to sleep on us, Mr. Ironbout. We're gonna be leaving very soon. Keep that beat up now. Try to make the birds hear it—they're all listening, watching. That's the ticket. I'll not stop and check; I'm just counting on you.

"Come on, Trip. Let's get those three round branches and toss them over to the other side of the big limb. Now, we need some split logs at the back there; come on, fast. Good wedges—one, two, four, five, six…that's all I can carry, Trip."

"Hmm…who's that?" Mr. Ironbout murmured. "Where's Trip?"

"We'll just drop the logs right here. Quick! We need that sledgehammer in the Rover. Mr. Ironbout, we're going to make a little noise now. Let me tell you what we're doing. Your left foot is facing in toward your right leg. I can see it from the other side of the limb here. Your foot is about a third of the way back under the limb.

"On either side of your leg, Trip and I are gonna wedge in some of your logs to lift up this limb a bit. Then, when we pull the big limb off, it won't hurt you. Okay, we're moving."

"She's full of petro…" Mr. Ironbout said.

"We're teaming up on this. Let's get the crowbar, Trip. Come on, come on… think…oh God, help me!

"Okay, I've got the crowbar. Don't worry, we're not going to touch your leg; Trip and I are just making a narrow channel in the dirt before we drive in those wedges. There we go…dig, oh dig—I'm singing to you now. *Oh, we dig; we're the trenchers. We're diggers, bit by bit, there we go; we dig, dig, dig.* Got it.

"Now we're gonna drive the wedges in, Sir. Watch me now, Trip; make sure I'm doing it right. I'm gonna keep singing to you, Mr. Ironbout. *Driving, driving, we are the log drivers, we drive, we wedge, we pound, pound—we drive them in. Oh, we can drive…we swing that weight…pound, pound…*I can actually see it begin to nudge a bit, Sir. Just another pound or two…*we pound, we drive.* There, that's it."

"Where we going anyway…the bridge?" Mr. Ironbout slurred.

"Good boy, Trip. Quick, the chain! Hang on, Mr. Ironbout, you keep up that beat; the birds can hear it. Okay, we're going to slip this chain around the limb. Yes, Sir, *we're chaining, we're chaining.* Quick, Trip, let's get a couple of those bolts.

"We're gonna bolt this chain, Mr. Ironbout. You were hauling around some perfect bolts, Sir, with washers and everything. You must have known Trip and I could use them.

"Oh, we've got to move…time. The Rover, we've got to roll. Trip, no keys! Oh, dear God, let them be there. Mr. Ironbout, I'm just going to check your pockets. Here I am on the left. Stay with us.

"I'll just keep singing, there I am, and that pocket's empty. Let's keep singing, while I'm leaning over you. *In the right pocket my fingers go.* There, thank God! I'm just going to drive the Rover to the other side of the log, Sir.

"*Oh, yes, I can drive it; old Sir Raleigh taught me how.* Come on, start. Perfect. Forward. Here we go, backing, backing, just about there, maybe just a little more. Okay, Trip, the S-hook goes there in the hole on the bumper. Now, Mr. Ironbout, you shouldn't even be aware that this big old limb is moving. We're a team. Okay, here we go.

"I'm just inching forward until I feel it tighten. There it is! Trip, I'm gonna pull it hard. Here goes. Come on, come on…want to hear that sound, *thump.* We did it!

"Okay, Trip we've got to get him up. Mr. Ironbout, we've freed you. You're hurt, but you're going to be all right. It's your leg. I'm going to pull the Rover real close. Just hold on."

"Where is everyone? Is that you, Goodwin?" Mr. Ironbout said, as he slipped in and out of consciousness.

"I'm coming, I'm coming. Here we are. We're just gonna sort of slide you into the back. At the count of three, I'm gonna lift you: One, two, three. Oh, dear God, help me; he's heavy. I can't do it. No, I can. There now, you were just awkward there for a second. I'll kind of scoot you up, over, and pull you in. There we go. There you are.

"Okay, I'm gonna put this old boot under your head. Here's Trip's blanket. Doesn't that feel nice? Trip, up here—come on, thatta boy; keep him warm now. Stay right there. We're a team. We're moving. I'll sing to you a little bit while we're driving down to the infirmary."

"That you, Trip—driving? What's going on…where we going?" Mr. Ironbout asked querulously.

"*We're going to the infirmary, the place where they take infirmities away; that's what we're doing today, going to the infirmary…*"

In just over five minutes, Goodwin pulled up in front of the trauma unit at the Estillyen infirmary and jumped out of the Rover.

"Please help! I've got a hurt man," Goodwin said, as he raced through the doorway of the infirmary.

An aide watched the Rover pull up to the emergency entrance and had already abandoned her desk. She intercepted Goodwin a couple of steps from the entrance. The aide immediately hit a large green button on the wall and slipped a small black microphone out of its holder fastened to her shoulder strap.

"What's his status?" she asked. "What's wrong?"

"I found him barely conscious; he was pinned under a tree. His leg is broken; I don't know how long he was there—I think all night. I saw him on Friday."

Within a few seconds, two male assistants rounded the corner, wheeling a gurney, with a nurse following close behind it. The trauma unit sprang into action. In the space of a minute, Mr. Ironbout was out of the Rover, on the gurney, and being wheeled through the wide automatic doors.

"I've conveyed your information to the nurse in charge of the unit. They'll take him straight into the critical bay," the aide said. "The unit is fully staffed, and they'll start treatment immediately. Now tell me, how did this happen, and who is the gentleman? Is he a relative? Don't worry about your car just now. Are the keys in the Rover? If so, the security staff can move it."

"Yes," Goodwin said. "What about his dog, though? He's in the Rover."

"Will you be taking the dog home with you when you leave?"

"No, I'm just a guest here. The injured man is not a relative. It's Mr. Ironbout who lives on The Point."

"Do you mean the old gentleman who lives in the house on The Point?"

"Yes, that's him."

"Well, if he stays in the infirmary, which looks likely, someone can pick the dog up and take it to the shelter."

"Right—well, I guess we'll see how it goes with Mr. Ironbout."

"Amazing. I didn't think we would ever see him," said the aide.

"It's a long story. My wife and I have been here for about three weeks, and somehow we've gotten to know him. It's kind of complicated. Sister Ravena knows us and knows all about it."

"Okay, good. What else do you know about the accident?"

"Well, like I said, I saw him on Friday afternoon. Sometime after that he must have tried to saw down this huge limb, and that's when the accident happened."

"A limb?"

"Yes—there was this huge limb he wanted to remove from a walnut tree in the back lawn. He must have gone out there yesterday, or Saturday. His power saw must have snagged, bounced, or something, and he fell. He has a deep gash on his left leg. The limb had him pinned. I wedged the limb and pulled it off of him with a chain."

"Are you okay? There's water in the waiting area, along with tea."

"No, I'm okay. I guess I look a wreck. Trip and I had to dig under the limb in order to loop the chain around it and then hook it to the Rover."

"Trip?"

"Trip is Mr. Ironbout's dog, the one in the Rover. I told Mr. Ironbout that Trip and I were teaming up to free him. I just kept talking to him while he was lying there. He was talking out of his head. I kept feeling his pulse. I put my belt around his leg for a tourniquet. We ran into the house and got a blanket and covered him. I also had Trip lay on him on the way down, to help keep him warm."

"It sounds like you've done all the right things. I'll convey your information to the head nurse and then come back and take you to the waiting area. Right next door there's a small refectory."

"Okay, thanks."

"You say you're here with your wife. Was she with you?"

"No, she's at The Abbey—probably there now. She was planning to paint this afternoon."

"You can call her from the waiting area, if you wish, or we can have someone do that for you."

"Could you? That would be great. I want to wash up a bit and then check on Trip. He's a very sensitive dog."

"Your wife's name?"

"Hollie Macbreeze. I'm Goodwin. Thanks, really."

"Just take it easy now. Mr. Ironbout has a talented bunch in there looking after him."

The reception staff phoned Hollie. In a matter of minutes, she was walking breathlessly though the emergency entrance.

"I'm looking for Goodwin Macbreeze; I understand he just brought in an injured gentleman—Mr. Ironbout."

"Oh, yes, I think he's gone to the waiting area. It's just down to the corner; turn left and follow the signs. There are two waiting rooms opposite the refectory."

"Great, thanks." Hollie quickly moved along the corridor and soon spotted Goodwin through the glass. He was sitting alone at a round table just inside the double entrance doors.

"Win, babe, how are you doing? I was so scared when the aide rang from the front desk. What's going on? Are you hurt? Did Mr. Ironbout go crazy or something? Were you in a fight? Here, look at your face," Hollie said, as she reached for her pocket mirror. "Poor thing, you look so disheveled—your jeans, no belt, scratches all over your hands, your nails—what on earth happened?"

"I'm okay, Lee. I just need some tea, a banana or something, and some water. I feel all weak and jittery."

"Sure, just sit here. I'll get it."

Hollie grabbed a blue wallet from her purse and quickly dashed through the serving line. She returned carrying a tray, which she gently slid in front of Goodwin. In the center of the tray were two empty china cups alongside a stainless-steel teapot, with stringed tea-bag labels dangling from its lid. Alongside was a bottle of still water, a banana, a shallow bowl of raisin bread pudding, and a thick chocolate walnut brownie.

"This should get you going. Here, let me pour. So you're sure you're okay? You're not hurt?"

"No, but Ironbout is, and I think pretty badly."

"Goodwin, you didn't have anything to do with it, tell me."

"No, nothing like that. I rescued him."

"Rescued him?"

"Just let me sip this tea for a second, catch my breath, and I'll tell you all about it. What time is it, anyway?"

"It's approaching five."

"I can't believe what's happened. Mmm...the tea is good and hot."

"Goodwin, just tell me what happened!"

"Sorry—I just needed to refocus a bit. I still can't even believe the whole thing.

"So you know I went up there on the bike. Well, when I got to the house, I knocked on the screen door. It rattled; it wasn't latched. The front door was open, and I could see into the hall and through to the kitchen. Not a word, so I called for Trip. No Trip—only the sound of birds singing.

"I thought that was a little strange, so I decided to go around to the side porch and have a look. I was hoping Mr. Ironbout wasn't at the grave plot standing inside the chain. Just as I started in that direction, I saw Trip coming up the side steps.

"He looked at me like I had come to kidnap him, cart him off. His tail was tucked between his legs. He moved slowly and cautiously, almost cowering. I noticed something on his white chin. It looked like blood—but I thought he had caught a rabbit or something. When I began to walk toward the side of the house, Trip ran off the porch—started barking like crazy and looking back at me.

"Then when I came around the corner, I saw it. The big walnut tree without its limb—that massive limb that extended out over to the markers. Underneath the limb was Ironbout, pinned to the ground. He was lying on his back with his arms stretched out. He was talking out of his head."

"Oh, dear, the poor man! I hope it's not too bad?"

"I think he only recognized me once. I wasn't sure what to do. I started rehearsing an old line: *Analyze, stabilize, mobilize.* I first thought about leaving him and racing down here. My next impulse was to try and saw the limb; his power saw was lying right beside him. But I thought about all the noise, the time it would take. I didn't even know if the saw had any fuel.

"Trip and I ran into the house, dashed into the office room, and grabbed Trip's blanket. I know it's crazy, but that old plaid blanket is wool, nice and thick. Then I rushed into the kitchen and filled the kettle with water. My goal was to comfort him. He was so pale! I thought he was dying, really. That's why I didn't want to leave him. I could feel the pulse on his neck, though, and it was strong.

"Then I thought, I've just got to get him out of here. I examined his leg. He has a deep gash right below his left knee. I think the saw must have kicked back or something. The lower part of his leg is certainly broken. From the other side of the log, I could see it tucked under, with his foot bent. All I knew was that if I could pull the limb away from him, he'd be free."

"How long do you think he had been there?"

"Don't know—at least one night, I think. I don't believe the accident happened that morning, simply because of the way Ironbout looked: cold, shivering, like he'd been out there for some time. Also, there had been a lot accomplished. Smaller limbs all cut and piled. So, anyway, I started talking to him. Somewhere I heard that's important. I was even singing to him, all kinds of crazy stuff. Made no sense at all. Sir Raleigh used to do that constantly, rhyming everything. I was singing, '*I'm pounding, pounding…we're trenchers.*'"

"Trenchers?"

"Yeah, I kept telling Ironbout we were a team, Trip and me. 'We're teaming up on this,' I'd say. We trenched out a little trough under the log. You know that heavy black chain that skirted the graves? Fortunately, it broke—it snapped when the limb fell. I ran to the plot and pulled it through the loops.

"Then I raced back to the limb and drove wedges under it—logs and a round branch to help lift its weight. It was nuts. I was running everywhere. Fortunately, Ironbout's old green Rover was there. In the end, I hooked the black chain to the Rover and it worked. I could hardly believe it. He was free.

"You can surmise the rest of the story. I pulled the Rover alongside him. Man, he was heavy! For a minute I didn't think I could hoist him up. I put the blanket on him and had Trip lay on top of him. And that's it."

"Oh, Win, that's so incredible! Totally unbelievable—I'm so proud of you. You're a hero."

"Well, if you'd seen me up there talking to Trip and singing, you'd have thought I was crazy."

"And he never really came around?"

"No, as I said, I think he knew who I was that once. He did say my name. He kept calling Trip, Trunk, or Tank. He was talking out of his head mostly. Stuff like, 'The sheep are getting out; come back here.'"

"I can't believe it. What a story! Here on Estillyen…how peculiar we would get involved like this. Where's Trip now?"

"We need to sort that out. Ironbout's not getting out of here tomorrow, or the next day. I hope he'll be all right, but he's definitely had a major blow. He's a tough old guy."

"What do you want to do—wait, I guess?"

"Let me try that pudding. This is nice. I'm kind of famished, actually. We'll need to see what the situation is and then take it from there. They really moved when I brought him in. I suspect they'll let us know something fairly soon. Let's just sit here, rather than in the waiting room. I'm just glad to be sitting—that kind of knocked me out, all that running around. The tea helps, and this is a good banana."

Before long, Goodwin spotted the aide, who met him at the trauma entrance. She was walking up the hall in their direction.

"She's probably coming to find us," Goodwin said, as Hollie polished off the last bite of brownie. "Saw you headed this way—thought you might be looking for us," he said to the aide.

"Good guess. You can go and have a word with Dr. Luneburg at the station. I think they have Mr. Ironbout stabilized. They'll let you know what's happening. Right this way. Mr. Ironbout is now our patient."

"Oh, do you know Mr. Ironbout?" Hollie asked. "I was so shocked when they called The Abbey with the news."

"Well, I think everyone knows *of* him, but no one seems to have met him."

"Yeah, I'm amazed we have. It all started with a sketch Win drew as a boy… strange."

"Well, the station is just there in the center. That's Dr. Luneburg walking past—the tall gentleman, sort of balding with a noticeable chin."

"Thanks. That's great. You've been brilliant," Goodwin said. "I'm sure we'll see you again."

Goodwin and Hollie approached the station. "We're here to see Dr. Luneburg. My name is Goodwin Macbreeze."

"He'll be with you in just a minute," said the nurse seated at the counter. "Just step into the briefing room, right there on the other side of the glass."

"Thanks."

"Do you think it's really serious, Win?"

"I don't know. It could be," Goodwin said. They sat there, feeling rather abnormal, knowing they were not relatives of the man on The Point, but not feeling like strangers either. They sensed it was right to care more than would be expected, but didn't know why.

"Hello, there. I'm Dr. Luneburg, and this is the head nurse on duty—Sister Darlene. So you're the brave man who brought in the notorious Mr. Ironbout?"

"Yes, I'm afraid so. This is my wife, Hollie."

"We understand you are not relatives, correct?" Dr. Luneburg asked.

"Yes," Goodwin said. "It's a long story, which came about in a short space of time. I first met him only a couple of weeks ago. He and my grandfather were friends; my grandparents used to come to Estillyen. That was a long time ago."

"Well, since you are not family, you won't be able to intervene in his care. He will be treated as an emergency patient, a resident of Estillyen with no known family."

"We understand," Hollie said, "but if we are able to help him in any way, we are glad to be involved, right, Win?"

"Absolutely. I really like the old gentleman. We've been in his house on The Point, sat and talked with him. I drove his old Rover down here. We also want to make sure his dog Trip is looked after."

"Well, under the circumstances, I don't mind telling you about his condition. Here's what we see. He's definitely had a major shock. He's experienced serious trauma along with hypothermia, which can play havoc with the nervous system. That may be the reason for his disorientation and confusion. He's not had a stroke.

"The good news is we don't believe he's suffered anything life-threatening. No head injuries or chest injuries, and the monitors show excellent readings on his heart. However, if you hadn't discovered him when you did…I'm not sure, but we could be having a really different conversation right now. These things have a way of compounding. Let's just say he's very fortunate you came along.

"Now, the wound on his leg definitely needs more attention. If the gash had been a few centimeters to the left, he would have had artery damage and most likely would have bled to death. The gash did get into the muscle, but we've cleaned it, and we will be stitching him up.

"We've given him fluids. He'll need to be on those for a couple of days. No doubt he's dehydrated. We have also administered antibiotics for the wound. Concerning the leg, he is being X-rayed right now, but I'm certain both the fibula and tibia are broken. The question is, broken in how many places? Is there any crushing, and how do we put it together? I would think it will need to be set with pins.

"At this point, from what I can tell, his knee seems to be functioning, and it's hard to tell about the ankle, with all the swelling. That's why we need X-rays. He has a lot of bruising on one of his hips and on his left shoulder down to his elbow, and he has several scrapes on the back of his left thigh.

"In general, we think he will come through all right, but he's going to be a very sore Mr. Ironbout. He'll be here all week, I would think. We'll take it a day at time. Okay, do you have any questions?"

"Wow, no, I don't think so," Goodwin said.

"Okay, then I'm going to turn you over to Sister Darlene. It sounds like there's a bit of sorting out to do. Good to meet you. Are you enjoying Estillyen?"

"Well, yes," Hollie said. "We certainly never expected to be here in the infirmary, though."

"Estillyen is full of surprises. All the best. Sister Darlene, over to you."

"Thanks, doctor. Yes, well, one issue we have is the nature of the patient. When he does come around, if he's his former self…well, we'll just have to take it as it comes. He's in no state to leave, but we can't keep him against his will. That could become an issue, but like I said, let's see what transpires. He's on pain medication right now, and we've given him something that will help him rest. We don't know if he is on any other medications, and I guess we won't till he comes around.

"So, part of the reason for this meeting was simply to brief you on his condition. You're at least acquaintances, and you did bring him in."

"I'd say more than that. Friends, wouldn't you say, Hollie?"

"Yes, he opened up to us in kind of a surprising way the other day. He's been through a lot."

"Well, it's good you're here. I hope this doesn't complicate your retreat plans."

"We don't think it will," Hollie said.

"From what you are saying, it sounds like it would be helpful to Mr. Ironbout if you could stay connected. You won't be able to see him today, but maybe sometime late tomorrow. Were you thinking of visiting?"

"Of course," Goodwin said. "I want to go back up to The Point, probably tomorrow, and make sure everything is all right. I need to take his Rover back and lock up."

"That's good."

"In terms of getting involved, we don't mind in the slightest," Hollie said. "I had a meeting the other day with Sister Ravena, so there are a number of dynamics sort of merging. Besides, we really do care. We like him. If we're supposed to be in this, then let us be used."

"Wonderful. Then I would say check back tomorrow. In the meantime, I'll brief Sister Ravena. The belt that you used for a tourniquet—I assume that's yours, Mr. Macbreeze?"

"Yes."

"Okay, let me go and get it for you. Then I guess you two are free to do as you wish. Hollie, you may want to go see Sister Ravena tomorrow. Again, so much depends on Mr. Ironbout's state of mind when he comes around."

"What about his car and his dog?" Goodwin asked.

"Check with Karen at the front desk. If she's not there, Maria should be. They're both superb. They'll introduce you to Paul. He's in charge of sorting out all the vehicles, belongings, and pets. You'd be surprised what comes into the trauma unit. Okay, then? Good."

Hollie and Goodwin did as Sister Darlene suggested. The old green Rover was already in the infirmary car park. And Mr. Statter, who operates the small kennel, was on his way to collect Trip.

With those details sorted out at the front desk, Hollie and Goodwin turned and walked towards the entrance doors. The automatic doors forcefully sprung open, and Hollie and Goodwin stepped outside into a warm, gentle evening breeze.

"What an incredible day," Goodwin said. "Amazing, right down to my belt in this bag. What do we do now, Mrs. Macbreeze?"

"Good question."

SIXTEEN
Trauma

"I'm glad you wanted to come along, Lee," Goodwin said. "I think it's better to see him together. You'll have time this afternoon to finish your painting. It's looking brilliant, by the way. Why don't you just name it *Hollie?*"

"No, not after me. I think I have an idea. I'll wait till it's finished. A couple of hours today, and I may have it."

"It looks like it might be your best ever," Goodwin said.

"As for Mr. Ironbout," he continued, "I don't know why I'm so anxious about this. I guess I wonder what he'll say—that is, if he's able to talk."

"I know what you mean. We barely know him, and yet here we are like relatives. It feels kind of surreal."

"When I first saw him throwing those walnuts like a madman, I should have said, 'So long, *My Cottage Rare*, I'm out of here.'"

"No, Win, you don't mean that. You're just nervous. We've gotten involved for a reason—I'm sure of it. Remember the other day when we were talking about destiny and how it seems more present? That's how this feels, too. Honestly, don't ask me what that means, but that's the sense I have.

"We both come from such crazy, unconventional families. My mother flitting away; you never knowing your father. This is okay. It's right! It's good for us to reach out like this. This is not weird or meddling. We're not after anything. Besides, if I've ever seen a needy person, it's certainly Mr. Ironbout."

"Okay, well let's just keep talking about it," said Goodwin. "If at any point we both decide we've done enough, then that's it. Deal?"

"Deal," said Hollie.

"Good. Now that that's settled, why don't you check in at the desk, Lee."

"Sure." Hollie stepped over to the reception counter. An elderly lady sat behind the desk, composed, attentive, and sporting a pleasant smile. Hollie looked at her face and thought about the rarity of its beauty. Unquestionably, the face revealed a life aged, but it was a face that strikingly refused to relinquish the beauty of younger years.

"Hi, my husband and I are here to see a Mr. Ironbout. He was brought in yesterday."

"Surely—I believe he is still in the trauma unit. It's not been too busy this week. I suppose a lot of people are well. Yes, I see he's still in the trauma unit. If you go straight ahead to where the main halls intersect, you'll see the head nurse's station on your right. Mrs. Macdonald is on duty this morning. Ask for her."

"Thanks so much. And I love those violets—they're beautiful."

"They're my favorite," the lady said.

Hollie walked back over to Goodwin. "Win, did you look at that woman?" Hollie asked. "She has such a rare face. She looks old but not old, young but not young. It's amazing how that is with some people. So attractive."

"I guess I wasn't looking; too busy thinking about this visit," said Goodwin. "What did she say?"

"He's still in the trauma unit. We are to ask for a Mrs. Macdonald, just up ahead on the right. I think I could have used a bit more tea," Hollie said, as they neared the station.

"Well, I don't hear any hollering or see any walnuts rolling down the hall."

"Just be positive, Win, okay? I'm proud of you. If it were not for you, he'd probably be dead. Think how we'd feel, hearing he died like that, up on The Point all alone."

"Well, I don't think he could have lasted another twenty-four hours. Although you never know."

"Hi, we're looking for Mrs. Macdonald," Hollie said as they approached the nurses' station.

"I just saw her go across the hall. She should be back in a minute. You can take a seat, if you wish."

"I like your coffee mug. Did it come from here?" Hollie asked.

"Yeah, it's an older one…actually quite old. It was given to me by a Brother Melton, just before he passed away. He made it years ago. They used to make a lot of pottery at the monastery. I like the blue shades."

"Very nice."

"Oh, here she comes now. I'll get her attention. Mrs. Macdonald, there's a couple here to see you." The nurse walked straight over, carrying a clipboard in her hand.

"Hello. How can I be of help?"

"We're here to see Mr. Ironbout, or check on him, anyway. My name is Goodwin and this is my wife, Hollie."

"Are you relatives?"

"No—we're not sure he has any," Hollie replied. "Goodwin found him yesterday, trapped under a tree limb up at his house on The Point."

"I heard about it. Everyone is a bit curious how he'll be when he comes around."

"So you think he'll be all right?"

"With some time to heal, we think so. Although there's no reason for you to try to see him today, unless you just want to see him conked out. He was in surgery early this morning for his leg. The doctors set it. He's heavily medicated, and he won't know much of anything until tomorrow. The surgery went well, however.

"Let me check the file. It should be right here with the current cases. Yes, here it is. They did a number of x-rays. In addition to the broken leg, he has two cracked ribs, but his ankle is okay. He's heavily bruised. I see we don't have any record of medications or prior illnesses. I don't suppose you two would know anything about that?"

"No, but I'm going up to The Point, when I leave here," said Goodwin. "I thought I'd look around and lock up the place. I was headed up last night but decided to wait. We didn't figure anyone would be wandering about, with all of Mr. Ironbout's warning signs."

"Yes, I understand, we know Mr. Ironbout has a way of making his wishes known."

"I'll check his medicine cabinet and see what I can find. I guess that's all right." Goodwin looked at Hollie, who shrugged her shoulders.

"Well, for now we're just monitoring him. You're welcome to check back later, but, as I said, tomorrow he should be coming round."

"Win and I spoke with Dr. Luneburg and the nurse last night. She thought it would be good for us to stay connected. Did Dr. Luneburg do the surgery?"

"No, Dr. Luneburg is only here on rare occasions, like yesterday. He's based on the mainland. Remarkably, a couple of special guests long associated with Estillyen were here this week on retreat: Drs. Sterling and Bell. Actually, they're renowned heart surgeons who are semi-retired.

"They're brilliant, and they've worked all over the world. Whenever they come to Estillyen, they never fail to come around asking to volunteer. As it happened, on this occasion there was a real need. They set Mr. Ironbout's leg. It would have been much later this afternoon before a specialist could arrive from the mainland."

"That's amazing," Hollie said. "We'll come back tomorrow, then. While Goodwin goes up to Mr. Ironbout's house today, I'll go see if I can find Sister Ravena—I hope she's around. I know she'll be interested to know about this."

"Oh, you know her?" Mrs. Macdonald asked.

"Yes, it's strange, but she and I were just talking about The Point and Mr. Ironbout a couple of days ago. Then all this happened. Thanks so much, truly. We better go. We need to see about Mr. Ironbout's dog, Trip. Everyone here has been so helpful."

"We try to be."

On their way out, Hollie and Goodwin went to check on Mr. Ironbout's Rover and inquire about Trip. They were instructed to see Paul, who was in charge of the infirmary's maintenance department. Paul worked in a red-brick structure called the Brickery, located on the north side of the main building.

"Hi there. We wanted to ask what we need to do regarding the old green Rover parked near the end of your lot," Goodwin said. "It belongs to Mr. Ironbout. I brought him in yesterday."

"If he's in the infirmary, you're fine; we allow anything up to a week in this car park, and then we like to see them moved," said Paul, a tall, lanky young man with a beaming smile. "Although don't be too fussed about it. Not crowded, as you can see," he added with a peculiar, high-pitched laugh.

"Perfect," Goodwin said. "And we understand that Mr. Ironbout's dog, Trip, was taken to a shelter run by Mr. Statter—is that right?" Goodwin asked.

"Yep, Mr. Statter has an animal shelter over near the barns. The dog couldn't be in a better place."

"Mr. Statter, he's the fast-talking, slender, older gentleman, right?" Hollie asked.

"That'd be him. Say, see my two Brickery companions—a pair of Siamese cats. Their owner was brought to the infirmary emergency unit and died of a massive heart attack during surgery. I became so attached to 'em I couldn't bear to see them go."

"What are your cats' names?" Hollie asked.

"Pen and Post," Paul said.

"They're adorable," Hollie said.

"The cats sleep on top of my workbench, on that old doormat."

"Nice spot," Hollie said, as she glanced at the doormat, which said, *Always welcome, and especially today.*

"Paul, would it be all right if we drop by and check on Trip at Mr. Statter's?" Goodwin asked.

"Not a problem; I'm sure he won't mind," Paul said, while he stroked the head of one of the cats, which had awakened during the conversation.

"So, you say his place is just behind the smallest of the three barns?" Goodwin asked.

"That's right. If he's not there, you'll find him around the barnyard."

"Okay, then, Paul. By the way, I'm Goodwin and this is Hollie. Thanks for taking care of the Rover and Trip."

"Sure thing. It's my pleasure to meet you."

"Thanks, Paul," Hollie said. "Ready, Win?"

Before heading their separate ways for the day, Hollie and Goodwin wanted to pay a quick visit to Mr. Statter and Trip. They recalled their brief encounter when they happened onto Tiptoe the cat and Spook the pig.

"This is it—the door's open," Goodwin said. "Hi there, Mr. Statter, remember us? We met you a week or so ago. We were over at the lean-to looking at Tiptoe and Spook."

"Sure, I remember you. What can I do for ya?" Mr. Statter was seated on a tall round stool behind a long wooden table. The stool's seat was a deep-red Naugahyde with white striping; the legs were shiny chrome with round foot rings.

"We're checking up on a black-and-white border collie named Trip," Goodwin said.

"Yep, he's here."

"Can we see him?" Goodwin asked.

"Sure, I'll get him. I've only got two dogs boarding right now, a long- haired dachshund and Trip. Just a second—I'll be right back. He's in the pen outside at the back end of the barn. I'll fetch him."

Mr. Statter slid off the stool and disappeared behind a red three-panel door in the middle of the back wall. In less than a minute, Trip appeared in the doorway.

"Come here, Trip," Goodwin said. With his eyes fixed on Goodwin, Trip began to walk, swaying and whimpering in his direction.

"It's okay, boy; everything's all right," Goodwin said. "What did you see yesterday, Trip? It was pretty dramatic, hmm? A lot of commotion. We were a good team. Yes, we think your master is going to be all right. You're okay.

"He's so sensitive," Goodwin said to Mr. Statter.

"Sure, border collies are that way. They see every little move," Mr. Statter said. "Say, I heard this is Oban Ironbout's dog, and he's in the infirmary. Is that right?"

"That's true," Hollie said.

"Word is that lightning struck his walnut tree and pinned him under it. They say his hair and the soles of his boots got all singed. Way I heard it, he was pinned on The Point for several days, until he whittled himself free with his pocketknife.

"Then, he crawled to his Rover and drove down to the infirmary, where he passed out at the entrance. Doesn't surprise me—Old Ironbout living through a lightning strike. He's gone through some fierce times up on The Point. Not much he doesn't know. Can fix anything."

"Well that's not quite the story," Goodwin said. "I actually found him up at his place, pinned under a huge limb he'd cut from his walnut tree."

"You mean he didn't get struck by lightning?"

"No, it seems not to be the case."

"I see. Is he gonna be all right?"

"We think so. He broke his leg, and he's beat up pretty bad, but the doctors think he'll come around in a week or so. So you'll need to keep looking after Trip for awhile."

"Sure, not a problem. Say, you know, I know Oban Ironbout; we was friends. Well, I guess we still is, but I ain't seen him for years, except at a distance. He swore off people. Strangest thing…

"Last time I spoke with him was down at the ironmongers in the village. I tried to talk with him all friendly-like, but he said, 'Statter, I've nothing to say to you or anyone. What I was, I ain't no more. You're not lookin' at the me you knew, I'm no longer him.' That's what he said: 'What I was, I ain't no more.' Seemed to be in a severe state of mind.

"Most folks think he had a nervous breakdown. Lots of tales about him wan- dering about on The Point late at night, hollerin'…sort of howlin'-like. Nobody ventures up to The Point anymore. I'm surprised you did. Didn't you see them signs?"

"Well, yes, but I was sort of drawn there, so I didn't pay much attention to them," Goodwin said.

"Not so sure about a nervous breakdown, Mr. Statter," Hollie said, "but he's certainly had some difficult years. We'll tell him you're looking after Trip. That will make him feel better."

"Sure, would ya? I still like the old feller. Smart as a fox, he is. Good man under that rough skin. Bones of a good man, sure enough."

"Okay, then, Mr. Statter, we'd better be moving along," Goodwin said. "Thanks for looking after Trip."

"My pleasure. Be sure you tell Otto hi for me, will you?"

"Otto?" Hollie asked.

"Otto's his middle name: Oban Otto Ironbout. That's what everybody used to call him back when he was his old self."

"We'll tell him, Mr. Statter," Hollie said.

"Okay, Trip, you be a good boy," Goodwin said. "We'll come back in a few days."

"You're welcome anytime. Right now, I gotta run, too. I got to see a gardener about beetles. They're eating all the lettuce. It's an invasion, like with Pharaoh and Moses."

"Okay, bye for now," Hollie said, and out the door they went.

That's how the day began to roll along for Hollie and Goodwin Macbreeze. Goodwin hiked up to The Point to have a good look around the house and make sure everything was secure. While there, he searched through the medicine cabinets to see what he could discover.

He found nothing out of the ordinary: a half bottle of aspirin, an empty bottle of painkillers, ointments, alcohol, cough medicine, iodine, hydrogen peroxide, cotton balls, bandages, and two old empty prescription bottles of erythromycin. The most recent prescription was six years old. It had been prescribed by a Dr. Taylor from Equivalence.

In the kitchen, under the sink Goodwin ran across three one-liter bottles of High-Millerton, single malt, ten-year-old scotch. One bottle was open, and the scotch had been consumed down to about an inch past the top of the front label. The label had a sketch of an ocean cliff with sea gulls in flight.

With the house buttoned up and Mr. Ironbout's keys in his pocket, Goodwin headed back along The Point trail on the Estillyen bike he'd left behind at the time of the accident. Meanwhile, Hollie was on her way to Sister Ravena's office, hoping to catch her.

The following morning, Goodwin had an early breakfast alone in Gatherers' Hall, so he could check in at the infirmary before the reading. Hollie wanted to write a couple of quick letters and get them in the post.

When Goodwin got back to The Abbey, Hollie was just finishing her breakfast and was enjoying the unhurried pace of the morning. She was sipping her tea when Goodwin joined her.

"Hi, luv. How'd it go?" Hollie asked. "How is he? Do you want some coffee?"

"Yes, let me grab a cup. It's so peaceful in here—hardly anyone around."

"Well, it's a quarter of ten. Grab a banana, as well. They'll start putting everything away in a couple of minutes."

Goodwin hurriedly retrieved a cup of coffee, along with two bananas, and joined Hollie at the table. With three quick bites, nothing but the peel was left of the first small banana.

"Good idea, the coffee. Do you want this banana?"

"Why don't you save it for later, for a mid-afternoon snack?"

"Sure. Well, he's not conscious yet. I did see him, though. He looks really disheveled. They still have the IV drip in, but he's not on a heart monitor. They said his vitals are good. He did moan a bit, but he didn't open his eyes. So I didn't stay long.

"I went to check on Trip after that. He was following Mr. Statter around, and apparently he had gotten through the gate to check out the barnyard. This is the nuttiest place. When we tell people what we've discovered here—Ironbout, the characters, the animals—I'm not sure anyone will believe us. A cat name Tiptoe with a pig called Spook. It's nuts."

"That's one of the things I love about Estillyen," Hollie said. "The isle has an air of melancholy, but at the same time is joyous. Things aren't really what the world would call 'normal.' There's pain here, but it's almost embraced, celebrated. A blind collie, a one-legged duck, a trembling rabbit, a parrot that talks backwards…yet they all fit in perfectly.

"It's definitely a place of healing. Estillyen is ancient, but it's also modern. I feel the present needs more places like Estillyen. That's one of the things I've grasped since being here—the *presumption* of the present; like the present thinks it has all the answers.

"I know, I'm beginning to sound like one of the monks. What would be a good name for me?" she joked. "Do you know what I mean, though? The present owns the day. There's always this buzz going on, as if the world's problems will soon be solved, like Epic was saying about applications. No, it wasn't Epic; it was Narrative. It's hard to keep them straight. The idea of not controlling, but settling, centering on something bigger than ourselves—that's so comforting to me. Does that make any sense?"

"Perfectly. Sir Raleigh used to say, 'I think the world's in a never-ending revolution, but there's never a resolution to the revolution.' He was a smart fellow. I really miss him."

"Say, we better go," Hollie said. "We're headed for Three Pond Cottage, and Narrative is the Reader. I'd like to get there a bit early. We had to rush last time. Do you need to go up to the room?"

"No."

"Well, I'm going to just run up quickly. I want to change these jeans and put on my red ones. Do you like the silver buttons on my cotton shirt? I love them. It has this neat look with all the buttons, the high cuffs, and the pocket flaps.

"Okay, let me scoot. I'll be down in a minute—just need a quick glance in the mirror. I'll catch you outside. I understand it's a beautiful day."

In a few minutes Hollie had returned, and soon they were at the door of Three Pond Cottage.

SEVENTEEN
Piercing Words

"Knock, knock—hello?" Hollie said.

"Oh, welcome. Please come in. My name's Davyd. I'm just helping out at Three Pond Cottage today. I saw you from the side window. Say, your red jeans match the front door—nice."

"Hi! Thanks. I'm Hollie."

"And I'm Goodwin."

"Have you been here before?"

"Yes, once," Hollie said. "We're doing the *Redemption* series. This will be our tenth reading. We can't believe it. The eleventh will be at Speaker's House on Saturday. Though…I didn't think they had readings on Saturdays."

"They usually don't, but once a month they do," Davyd said. "More people can attend that way."

"I guess we're supposed to take the twelfth reading with us," Hollie said.

"That's right. The monks incorporated that idea about ten years ago—sort of an inducement for people to become readers, message makers, on their own. From what we can tell, it's worked. The brothers get a lot of letters about groups gathering to do readings. Some of the readings have become quite popular as dramatic performances—lot of props and people involved. There are some that even incorporate music. Amazing, right out of Estillyen."

"You seem to know a lot about Estillyen," Goodwin said.

"That's right. I do. I've worked for the monastery for thirty-eight years, keeping the books."

"That's a long time, Sir."

"You're right about that, young man. It's really my life's work, a calling. Can't imagine doing anything else. Please, feel free to go on in."

Hollie and Goodwin made two right jogs along the hall and entered the reading room of Three Pond Cottage. Rustic brick fireplaces centered the end walls, each with circular mirrors above.

In the far corner sat seven young ladies eagerly chatting. Four were wedged together on a couch made for three, while two sat in tall wooden armchairs with natural wicker seats. The posture and height of the wooden chairs made it look as if the two young women were coaching or tutoring the other five.

The seventh young lady sat in a coveted spot, a well-worn stuffed chair with wide, rounded arms. The petite miss sank so deeply in the chair she was barely visible.

In the corner of the room, two young men sat on an antique hard-backed bench. The bench was painted black and had faint yellow striping in relief rings carved into the top of each leg. Between the legs, flat wooden support braces carried the same ring pattern, with traces of yellow visible in the crevices.

Hollie and Goodwin were drawn to a pair of natural-colored wicker armchairs, and they quickly took their seats. The collection of varied chairs faced no particular direction. They were bunched together in small groups, as if the last occupants of the room had been engaged in little private chats.

Hollie became fascinated with six primitive chairs, all alike, which were grouped in pairs of three. Artistically, intuitively, she pulled away from the faces and voices in the room. Into her creative mode of mind she drifted. Meticulously, she studied the chairs, noticing the finest of details.

She thought, *The chairs must be the work of an independent craftsman. The way they're painted, a faded red with black accents. I just love the round legs, with their black tapered ends.*

Carefully, she noted where the tapering started—some three inches off the floor—and how the diameter of the legs was reduced in half by the time the tapered ends made contact with the floor.

She studied the way the front legs were made, how they extended up an inch or so beyond the chairs' twine woven seats.

She thought, *The woven rope appears to be simple bailing twine—coarse and stringy. And the three simple slats that serve as backs—they're ever so right, their symmetry.*

Engrossed, she mused about all the chips, nicks, and signs of wear in the charming red chairs. *Who were these people who had sat in the chairs throughout the years? Where have they gone? Who was responsible for creating all the wear—the chipping of chips and nicking of nicks?*

The chairs are so evenly primitive, beautifully worn and used. Not abused, but wonderfully used.

Hollie's musing mind would not peel away to simpler sentiments.

The primitive character is a kind of fruit—days upon days stretching into age.

She thought of aging. *What does life hold? Will I age? Will I be like the lady at the welcome desk, aging with an ageless face?*

Age places acquired character upon the face. It's much like the requisite wear upon the chairs. Without wear and use, they would not possess their lovely primitive distinction, their rich patina.

Somehow her train of thought shifted seamlessly to The Point and Mr. Ironbout. *I see him standing in the middle of the grave plot, but sadly there is no distinction of grace upon his face.*

Then Hollie heard a voice.

"Hey, Lee, the room's filling up. Where are you? What are you thinking about? You seem a bit gone somewhere."

"Oh, I was just observing those interesting red chairs and thinking about Mr. Ironbout. Do you think he'll be aware of what's going on today?"

"I hope so. I want to head over there as soon as we leave here, okay?"

"Certainly, let's go. If he's the old Ironbout, it'll be interesting around there. He may demand release."

"We'll see. You know, real life is more interesting than fiction," Goodwin said.

Hollie was brought back to her previous thoughts. *How true! I wish it were possible for me to meet some of the people who long ago passed by, taking their seats, lodging their nicks, and charting their chips. They must have been so full of life, so expressly present in the past, gifting wear to the chairs that now fill my gaze. Will I live to do the same? Will I be able to give worth to life? Will I be appreciated—and maybe even leave something to be cherished by others one day?*

Goodwin again interrupted her thoughts. "There's not a seat left," he said. "Here comes the Reader."

"Right," Hollie said. "It does seem that all the chairs are full. I'm glad we spotted these."

"Greetings, everyone. My name is Narrative. I'm your Reader for today, and I'm delighted to welcome you to Three Pond Cottage. There are two questions we get here at Three Pond. The first is, 'Why is this place called Three Pond Cottage when there are four ponds?' The second is, 'Why are there twin fireplaces?'

"Concerning the ponds—yes, there are four. Were there three before four? We don't know. I do know there are four, and three comes before four. My thinking is that pond four was added one day.

"That is, unless one of the three became two. This would make four—not by adding one, but by splitting one in two. If, indeed, this is the case, the fourth is not really four; it's one of the three, now two. This leaves us with two ponds whole and one split, which means we have three ponds at Three Pond Cottage, just as we've always had. So that covers the ponds three.

"Regarding the twin fireplaces—that's a little bit like the ponds. At one time, Three Pond Cottage was two cottages rather than one. The name was Three Pond Cottages. From the outside, what appears to be one was two on the inside.

"Just here where I stand was a wall that didn't allow either fireplace to see its twin. They were like cousin fireplaces rather than twins. However, Three Pond Cottage was actually built around the twins.

"They are lovely, aren't they? On winter's short, dark days, their hearths blaze and speak to one another through the crackling of embers. They chat away into the night, usually falling asleep just before dawn.

"So there you have…the ponds and fireplaces.

"And here we are—not in some other place where we might be, so why don't we have a reading? The reading today is called *Piercing Words*.

"Who is it I see coming through the door? None other than my long-time friend and colleague, Brother Script. Welcome, Brother Script. Please come in. As we move into today's reading, Brother Script will offer a few lines we'll be eager to hear."

As Narrative continued to speak, Brother Script gave a faint smile, accompanied by a subtle nod, and he began to move purposefully along the wall behind his colleague. Curiously, he hugged the wall, moving behind every object possible, in order to maintain closeness with the wall. In several places, the sleeve of his black habit noticeably brushed the wall as he made his way to the far corner of the room.

There, he opened a small closet door, reached in, and produced a tall, narrow wooden stool with a sizeable round top. As he set it in place, the stool's blunt wooden legs clubbed the pine flooring, screeching twice before falling silent. He placed the stool as near to the wall as possible.

Brother Script gracefully scooted onto the stool and pressed the length of his back against the wall. His dark brown eyes, capped with frosted eyebrows, peered out across the room. Up above the room of faces, his sightline was drawn. Occasionally his eyes would drop as if descending on a wave, but quickly they would rise again into a stilling stare.

"Oh, yes, I almost forgot. We need a few voices to be our Voice. Just a few lines offered in unison as we go along. Three would be great here in Three Pond, preferably placed well apart. Over here to my right, does someone wish to volunteer?

"Great—your name, please, if you don't mind?"

"My name is Trish," said a young woman with rosy cheeks. In the center of the room Narrative then found Lloyd. And to Narrative's left, Priscilla decided to give it a go, after a bit of prompting and poking by her friends.

"Brilliant! Let me pass along these few lines," Narrative said, as he handed three sheets of paper to Davyd, who began making his way around to the volunteers. "Just look to me. Watch for my nods or my script slicing the air, like an orchestra conductor; that's your cue. If I sneeze, it's not a nod. That is, unless it happens to be a sneezing nod. How will you know the difference? I don't know.

"Okay, it looks like we are there, or should I say *here*. From the Acts of the Apostles we'll pick up a few words about the matter of piercing. The opening line belongs to St. Peter, who is addressing a crowd on the day of Pentecost.

———◆————

Piercing Words

"Therefore let all the house of Israel know for certain that God has made him both Lord and Christ—this Jesus whom you crucified."
Now when they heard this, they were pierced to the heart, and said to Peter and the rest of the apostles, "Brethren, what shall we do?"

ACTS 2:36-37

READER: God thinks. Does he not? Certainly he does. God thinks in ways beyond knowing, thoughts ever flowing. Creating, communicating, ordering, searching, weighing. In God's reckoned way, he said this to that, and light was let; the formless formed; the earth was born. Divine thoughts through and through give equilibrium its balance, hold everything together. God never quit, never went away. He's always there.

VOICE: Reader, you speak of *there*, but where might God be?

READER: Where he's always been, of course. He's there. He's there in his realm of thinking, although presumption extraordinaire is the mark of anyone who has a great deal to say about what God thinks. Scripture says, "God is in heaven, and you are here on earth. So let your words be few."

VOICE: Does that include us, this "words be few"?

READER: Voice, I do believe it does. One cannot outpace the velocity of words streaking forth from Scripture's store. Once spoken, penned, and scribed, there is no fleeing what they say, no flight of fancy where they do not reach and apply.

It's impossible to fathom the fill of God's thoughts. In God's sphere, time does not exist. There is no tick or tock, no time of clock. This thought alone should be enough to quiet any boast of knowing much about what cannot be known. Not to say, though, that God's thoughts are beyond grasp, beyond the pale of knowing. No, this is certainly not the case. God's thoughts are known, some that is. Such thoughts are clothed in words.

Words are little modules of meaning. They dress a thought and fasten it to other thoughts expressed in other words. God allowed certain of his thoughts to be dressed and buttoned up this way. They convey a good deal about what God thinks and feels, what he wants to say.

God's full measure of thinking, though, they do not reveal. Who but God could understand the full press of how God thinks? Nevertheless, what's been clothed and buttoned up in Scripture's text is not a token stitch of fashioned words. It's a reservoir exceedingly rich. The reservoir reveals that God thinks a great deal about the poor, the oppressed, and all those enormous mounds and mountains of human need.

Some find it hard to believe that God is actually there, let alone that he cares so deeply. Many who think along these lines have this notion that God is looking for human beings to knock around, to cast away because of sinful maladies and wayward gaits.

VOICE: Could it be so, God desiring to knock people about? Some sinners, you know, are not so conventional and compliant.

READER: Oh, dear me, so they aren't. Sinners there are, but consider Moses the murderer. Did he not come down from Mt. Sinai with the Law of God in his hands? St. Paul was once murderous Saul, full of hate and rage.

Be therefore gentle on this matter of wayward gates. Be, shall we say, slow to speak. Cast not the first stone. Are you a stone-thrower, a knife-thrower, Voice, riding some high tide to tidy up the world?

VOICE: No, I didn't mean that God should knock people about.

READER: So you are not against wretched creatures, burdened and bent, whom one day may find grace by what heaven has sent?

VOICE: Certainly not. Who am I to choose recipients of grace?

READER: Good, Voice. You're the kind of Voice we need. This is not to say that God is squeamish about calling sinners sinners, just as he might call a squid a squid.

On the trajectory of the heart God looks, seeing rather differently than the eyes of men. God looks to see if the heart bends in his direction.

The person, of course, who believes God is not will find it rather hard to yield to nothingness. Such a person is like a ball in play. It's pitched, tossed, and batted around, but all the while it argues. There is no game. It doesn't exist.

If not a ball, then let it be an apple bursting with life. It ripens with seeds firmly couched within. It sways in the breeze; leaves brush its skin. It hangs from a limb. The apple ripe looks to the tree and says, "You do not exist. There is no tree."

Notions such as these should not be, but they are. Such stubborn simplicity has a lot to do with human complexity. This is why God's thoughts wrapped in words can be so helpful. A line from St. Paul reads, "No eye has seen, no ear has heard, no mind has conceived what God has prepared for those who love him."

VOICE: This line doesn't sound like God waiting to avenge.

READER: Ah, Voice, that's the tone we seek to settle human need. It was the prophet Isaiah who first spoke the line, "No eye has seen, nor ear has heard."

VOICE: Reader, what was Isaiah thinking by saying no eye has seen, nor ear has heard?

READER: Most important it is, Voice. The object of Isaiah's prophecy was Jesus Christ. In Isaiah's day, Christ was not seen, not heard. He was the One prepared and promised. Christ was the realization of the promise, the One unseen to see, the One unheard to hear. He was the One the world awaited.

Centuries after Isaiah's day, St. Paul inserted the prophet's line in a letter. The day was new. Grace had dawned. Paul wrote from the other side of history's wall. He spoke of the promise fulfilled in the person of Christ. God's hidden promise was hidden no more. What was once invisible, inaudible, and inconceivable became visible, audible, and conceivable in the person of Christ.

Scripture attests that Jesus Christ was born in the fullness of time. The phrase, "fullness of time"—does it not convey a sense of the world waiting for time to fill? There was, after all, a great deal of time before time was full.

VOICE: What happened before time was full?

READER: Voice, before time filled to full, time was filling. The world waited! Before civilization was, the world waited. Before floodwaters rose, the world waited. Before the Israelites crossed a parted sea, the world waited.

While waiting, the living watched the dying die and be laid away. The dying watched the living watch them die, knowing that soon the living, too, would be the dying. Without ever seeing time fill, the living died. On and on they died. They waited.

VOICE: Reader, I'm a bit confused. What was it the world wanted? Christ, right?

READER: Voice, confused you're not. The world wanted to see what Mary saw, the child in a manger, the eyes of redemption, the child resting in her arms. When the child looked into his mother's eyes, waiting was no more. The world had waited for time to fill and reveal the object of its waiting. The world had waited for its Messiah; he came. Time was full, and so too was the waiting.

The Son of God appeared, died, and rose, but before ascending he said to his disciples, "Wait!"

VOICE: What for? And where were they to wait?

READER: In Jerusalem, for the outpouring of the Holy Spirit they were to wait. They would wait until Pentecost.

VOICE: So there was more waiting?

READER: Yes, but waiting of another kind. Pentecost was an essential part of the divine mystery hidden for ages past. In God's great redemptive plan it was always there, coupled in and attached directly to this measure called fullness of time. In the drama great, Pentecost was placed as the major act following Christ's ascension. Without it the drama would have been a muddle.

The outpouring of the Holy Spirit had everything to do with Christ's command to go here, there, and everywhere making disciples. The disciples were to go out bearing the words of Christ.

VOICE: Were Christ's words the piercing kind?

READER: Definitely so. Listen to what St. Matthew had to say concerning Christ and the Sermon on the Mount: "And when Jesus finished these sayings, the crowds were astonished at his teaching, for he taught them as one who had authority, and not as their scribes."

This is how it was; from place to place Christ went, speaking piercing words.

VOICE: Why are words so important?

READER: Voice, dear me! Why, you ask? Words are the substance on which faith is perched. Words are pegs on which faith hangs its hat. An ancient line of Scripture speaks about the importance of perching faith. Listen: "Now faith is being sure of what we hope for and certain of what we do not see." On such words faith is perched.

When it comes to one's faith, one should be sure of words picked for perching. Christ spoke much about the worth of words. He once told his disciples, "The words I have spoken to you are spirit and they are life." These very words—and bushels more—Christ commissioned the disciples to take to the entire world.

To every tribe and tongue they were to go. Yet the specific commission of going to Jerusalem, Judea, Samaria, and to the ends of the earth the disciples only heard after the resurrection.

VOICE: Why were they to go to the ends of earth?

READER: They were to go, speaking out, casting out, and making disciples. They were to go here, there, and everywhere, and then on to where they hadn't been. The end of their going they would never reach, but they were to go and keep going. They would be imprisoned, beaten, stoned, and some even martyred, but they went. With words they went. Words they carried.

The prophet Isaiah foresaw that this would come to pass. "I will make you a light for the Gentiles, that you may bring my salvation to the ends of the earth." The light to the Gentiles of which Isaiah spoke is Christ. It was up to the disciples to make this light known, to explain who Christ was, how he did what he did, and why he said what he said. This was the depth of the stage on which they stood. They were the chosen cast to move out and begin the journey to the ends of the earth.

Voice, thrilling, is it not?

VOICE: Not so sure about the martyred part.

READER: The disciples would not go alone. Just prior to Christ's ascension, he instructed his disciples to go to Jerusalem and wait for the Father's promise. Christ explained that they would be "baptized by the Holy Spirit." Specifically, Christ told them, "Stay in the city until you have been clothed with power from on high."

To the ends of the earth they were to go, but before going, they were to wait. Go. Wait. Go wait. What do you want to do, Voice, go or wait?

VOICE: I believe both.

READER: So very right you are. Waiting had everything to do with going. In an upper room they gathered. They prayed and waited. For exactly what, they weren't sure, but there they waited. They waited for some kind of clothing with power.

More than a hundred people huddled together in the upper room, awaiting Christ's promise. Mary, Christ's mother, and his brothers were among them. St. Luke records, "They all joined together constantly in prayer." Christ's ascension had happened more than a week before, but still they waited.

Heavenly hosts must have been peering down from the ledge of paradise, yearning, stretching, watching, as the Holy Spirit descended on that room in Jerusalem. St. Luke describes what happened. "Suddenly a sound like the blowing of a violent wind came from heaven and filled the whole house where they were sitting. They saw what seemed to be tongues of fire that separated and came to rest on each of them. All of them were filled with the Holy Spirit and began to speak in other tongues as the Spirit enabled them."

Outside, the crowd heard the sounds emanating out of the upper room. They rushed to the site, bewildered by what they saw and heard. Everyone inside the room was declaring the wonders of God. The phenomenon embraced every language spoken in the crowd, which was diverse. This was Pentecost. People from throughout the Roman and Parthian Empires had traveled to Jerusalem for the festival.

Tongues of fire separated and rested on each person in the upper room. This included Peter and Jesus' mother and brothers. Every person who occupied space in the upper room had this experience.

Soon those inside appeared to the crowd. "Peter stood up with the eleven, raised his voice and addressed the crowd, 'Fellow Jews and all of you who live in Jerusalem, let me explain this to you. Listen carefully to what I say.'"

VOICE: Reader, wait—did Peter have his message prepared for the occasion?

READER: How could he? No one in the upper room knew what was going to happen. Peter's words were inspired, those of a man compelled. The fire of God had fallen on Peter, and he moved accordingly. Peter's message was undoubtedly the most important of his life.

Christ and the prophets had been carried along by the Holy Spirit; Peter would need the same manifestation as he faced the bewildered crowd. Peter was no Christlike parrot with a ready speech. There was no precedent for what to say. There was no precedent event for the outpouring of the Holy Spirit.

Christ had promised the disciples, "[The Spirit] will bring me glory by telling you whatever he receives from me."

Unswervingly, Peter stood to address the crowd. His thoughts swirled, mixed, mingled, and probed his heart. The crowd watched. Peter's colleagues looked in his direction. Suddenly there was a thought that wrapped itself in words: "Fellow Jews, and all of you who live in Jerusalem…"

Then a second thought, followed by a third, came forth, wrapped in words. "Let me explain this to you. Listen carefully to what I say." That's the way it went. Thoughts were wrapped in words, words formed lines, lines flowed forth into hearts and minds. When thoughts find words, that's how they act. They move forth, claiming this and that.

Peter's words claimed much, including being the way to God. There was not the slightest pause or hesitation on Peter's part. He stood, raised his voice, and addressed the crowd. Out of bewilderment emerged words of a certain kind, the kind on which faith is perched, the kind on which faith hangs its hat.

Empowered, impassioned, and transformed, Peter, the former fisherman, stood deep on God's stage. In his new vocation, Peter cast a line. "Listen carefully," he said. "These men are not drunk as you suppose. It's only nine in the morning!"

Morning: It was a time of simmering festival scents wafting through the air, a time when eyes are open wide, when minds are fresh. That's the hour it was when Peter stepped up to speak. This morning debut was the first step on the journey to the ends of the earth. It started there.

Morning. That's when the fire fell, and people heard what they'd never heard.

VOICE: What did they hear? What was it?

READER: A praying, a praising, a new kind of speaking in other tongues—that's what they heard.

VOICE: Did Peter explain what it was?

READER: Yes. Peter crafted his message as he was carried along by the Holy Spirit. Another thought flowed, bringing forth the ancient words of Joel.

Joel's words spoke to the crowd's bewilderment: "In the last days, God says, I will pour out my Spirit on all people. Your sons and daughters will prophesy, your young men will see visions, your old men will dream dreams. Even on my servants, both men and women, I will pour out my Spirit in those days, and they will prophesy."

These words from former days were God's thoughts from former days. Now Peter, who had become a new kind of fisherman, was fastening Joel's words to his, strengthening his line with this choice of prophetic verse. Peter had grasped the prophecy of old. It was unfolded and folded into its awaited story. Words of old became new. Their meaning became exponential, as the words were buttoned up and dispatched live into the crowd.

The final line Peter cast from Joel was, "And everyone who calls on the name of the Lord will be saved." Peter next spoke about the man of miracles, wonders, and signs accredited by God. He spoke of Christ, Jesus of Nazareth. This brought a startling twist to Peter's message.

Without apology, Peter implicated the crowd in Christ's crucifixion. Listen to what he said: "And you, with the help of wicked men, put him to death by nailing him to the cross. But God raised him from the dead."

Peter followed the accusation by quoting from the Psalms. He chose the prophetic words of David. "I saw the Lord always before me. Because he is at my right hand, I will not be shaken. Therefore my heart is glad and my tongue rejoices; my body also will rest in hope, because you will not abandon me to the realm of the dead, you will not let your holy one see decay. You have made known to me the paths of life; you will fill me with joy in your presence."

Peter's choice of words was a masterstroke of meaning and association. The psalm was attributed to King David, but it reads in the first person, as if spoken by Christ. This conveys a sense of Christ's presence at Pentecost, almost as if Christ were there speaking with Peter.

Peter stressed the significance of the passage, attesting that David died and was buried, and therefore could not be the holy one who did not see decay. It was Christ, Peter declared. Peter then confessed that he had actually seen the resurrected Christ, and he claimed that Christ was, at that very moment, "exalted to the right hand of God."

Peter concluded his message by saying, "Therefore let all Israel be assured of this: God has made this Jesus, whom you crucified, both Lord and Christ." Peter's message was a collective force. Christ poured out the Holy Spirit; the Holy Spirit anointed Peter. The prophet Joel and the psalmist David had spoken long ago, led by the Spirit of God. Peter gathered in the words and buttoned them together with his own. A magnificent message was made.

The ingredients and elements of Peter's message were not whipped up in the upper room early on Pentecost morn. The words flowed together in a divine construct of message, veering not a jot from the central character in the story, Jesus Christ.

This compiling construct of words through cultures and time speaks, does it not, Voice?

VOICE: To what?

READER: It speaks to the matter of God's hourglass taking time to fill with time. To the heart of our reading the message goes. The people in the crowd were profoundly moved, convicted. Peter's words pierced their hearts, and they said to him and the other apostles, "Brothers, what should we do?" Peter implored them to repent and be baptized in the name of Jesus Christ for the forgiveness of their sins.

Peter promised that they, too, would receive the gift of the Holy Spirit. He claimed the gift was for Jews and Gentiles alike; it was for everyone who was willing to call on the name of the Lord. Some 3,000 people responded to Peter's plea. They were baptized and joined those following Christ and his teachings.

Truth is a remarkable force, Voice. Truth speaks a language of its own, but it's understood in every language. It's universally recognized because it speaks to the heart and not just the mind. Hearts were pierced in the crowd because of the truth conveyed in the message.

Pentecost was, in some ways, like a divinely orchestrated commencement for the disciples. They were commissioned to take Christ's message into the world. It was the going after the waiting. They were to go here, there, and everywhere. Then they were to go everywhere in between; they were to go where they had yet to go. The aim of going was to propagate and populate the world with Christ-followers, people who would believe his words and do Christlike deeds.

The commission meant that there would be a lot of words calling out and casting out. Incredibly bold was this commission by Christ. Regardless of how Pentecost is viewed, the day proved to be a rather auspicious occasion for many—and an inauspicious occasion for others. The disciples and those in the upper room must have been thrilled and overjoyed by what transpired. The religious elite, on the other hand, certainly would have been rattled and disturbed by the day's events.

Not to be forgotten, of course, is the ruler of the air. Was he there? Who's to say? Satan certainly would not want a world full of words calling out, casting out.

In this regard, it is not a stretch at all to imagine Satan creeping about in some shadowy form or another. He could well have been invisibly present there in the crowd when the fire fell at nine o'clock on Pentecost morn.

Narrative turned to his far left and nodded confidently to Brother Script. Brother Script slid off his stool, and then stood erect. He turned to the right, centering his frame in the room of faces. With certain depth and ample volume, he spoke.

LUCIFER: What's that sound? Stand back. Give me room, my devotees. Never, ever nudge Lucifer, my demon core. I've turned demons into burnt toast, charred crust, for nudging me. Lucifer nudges, not you.

That doesn't sound like a normal breeze blowing. It's a rushing, gushing sound. And that—that's not the pleasant sound of churning viperfish in my ears. What's that? It's some kind of whopping gibberish. They're all speaking in fleshy languages.

Whoa, bitter beasts, we're talking about falling fire, tongues dancing, the fleshy kind of tongues. I've got a very underbelly feeling about all of this. This is not at all right, not at all. All this compounding alimentation is gonna cause a storm severe, a terrible case of spiritchitis. It's gonna flow like molten lava.

Look out, devotees—here comes the crowd. What's up? Whatta they want? That's not a question! Doesn't that stupid crowd know that this festival is for all the old-timing ways? It's got nothing to do with the Word. It's for those orthodox nutties with bangles and tassel tails.

Just look out across that crowd. What do you see? Speak not! I'll tell you what you see. You see a gathering of muddy brains, brains that come from dirt. You see that man there and that woman? Let 'em trace their ancestry; the last line on the papyrus will be mud.

I hate to see fleshies in a crowd. All that skin in one place, stretched over blood and bones, it's so utterly repulsive. Idiots, thousands of them, and there they are running up to see what those rhubarb roots in the upper room have to say. Sure, they want to see what the falling fire and whooping is all about. Those root heads can't offer ya nothing, you dumb clucks. Their leader's gone home. He's up and ascended.

Whoa, here comes the Rock, the disciple the Word renamed. Let's remain invisible, incognizable, but I can't resist yelling as if he could hear me. It helps relieve the symptoms of my spiritchitis. "Hey Rock, came out of the cold, did ya? Where's your rooster? I heard you was gonna start selling roosters down in the marketplace, along with rhubarb. You won't last—you and that scraggly lot babbling all about. You're all under some hypnotic spell. Get out your fishing pole; go buy yourself some new hooks. Give it up—get back to where you belong, to what you know."

Shut it, imbeciles. Rock's beginning to speak. He's the optic of my distilling. I'll tell you what let's do—let's creep around to the east side so we can get a profile view of the crowd, as well as of Rock. We need to see if Rock is stimulating the crowd, so scrutinize, peer into their eyes.

Devotees, listen up. This is big, really big. Keep sniffing the air. Beware of anything and everything. This wind and fire extravaganza is not by the order of fleshies, I can tell you that. This is by the confluence of I AM, the Word, and the Third. They're trying to inaugurate this new spirit-and-truth deal, the one I've been telling you about. Now, let's move in around. There, that's better.

Shut it, I said. Rock's speaking. What's he saying? Old words from Joel? They're pulling out all the stops. They've been in there over a week cooking up this concoction of words. That's them. They'll mix this with that, spit and splat, and pull any kind of rabbit out of a hat. Then when the crowd gets all stoked up, all foggy-eyed and fuzzy-minded, they'll say this means that and that means this. It's all a bunch of ostrich eggs, if you ask me. Scramble, ramble; dish 'em up.

There they go again with the same old weepy story, the cross. Oh, I don't know if I can bear it; over and over they talk about it. Will there ever be an end to this saga? It's done. Don't they get it? They're gonna drown creation itself with that long, drawn-out drama. The Word was spiked. He was down and out. Then up he came, and now this.

How many words you want to use, telling your story, hmm? Verbose fleshies. You want to fill the whole world with them. Why don't you try sowing corn instead? That kind of chuckles my ribs. I can see old Rock and them spreading corn seeds. Quiet, idiots! Don't laugh so loud. This place is too spiritually charged. There are a lot of angels about—there's gotta be.

There Rock won't let up. Now he's quoting words from King David. Remember him—the harpist king? Whoa, Rock, that's bold! He's telling the crowd they helped drive the spikes through the Word. Hey, hold on a minute. Look at them fleshies' eyes. They're letting those words soak in, go down their shafts. Their hearts are gonna be all flopping about.

Fire falling, wind, you idiots. Can't you see? My stitchery just stitched this together. This is not some little rally speech or sideshow. This is the disciples' commencement. This is their coming out. You know what else? I'll tell you, enrich you. This is all down to the Third, the One that makes the Three three.

This isn't fair, the Third swooping down like this. He ought to stay up there in the heavenly realms where he belongs. They're moving fleshies into the spiritual sphere, full force-like. This is what I've been foretelling. This is the beginning of the new-age deal the Three cooked up.

Let me tell you something, devotees. I'm the chief foreteller of all tells. Lucifer has the foresight to see into the corridors of time. The future is already happening. While we're hanging out here, it's happening there, but we gotta be here before we get there. It will be waiting for us when we get there.

Anyway, by peering into the corridors, I can read the news 1,000 or 2,000 years from now, as if it were here today. Certainly I can. It's easy. I also know the true makeup and complexion of these fleshies. I see days, long stretched out from now, when the inventive fleshies will find ways of communicating at lightning speed, like we do. They're smart dummies.

When that day comes, and it surely will—I'm seeing it; I'm saying it—that's a day of great promise for us and our message of engagement. Why? Don't ask me, because I'll tell you why. In those days, fleshies will be saying so many things in so many ways, they won't know who's saying what to whom. It'll be pick and choose, paste and haste, skip and dip—and we will crack the whip.

Don't look at me with those dopey, confused eyes, my devotees. Words, images, and sounds will be pulling down, swirling 'round, jousting, rousting. What a sweet day of confusion it will be! Oh, it gives me ostrich bumps all over. I'm a-tellin' you, that'll be a day of wondrous confusion. *Confusion*—what a commendable word.

Look at 'em. Strangest sight I've ever seen, really eerie. The crowd's all worked up, shouting out questions. The fleshy crowd wants to be reconstituted. Baptism, getting themselves dunked underwater—that's the prescription. "Fleshies, wake up—you're not fish!" I wish I could stop this cruel spewing of hocus-pocus. The crowd should just let 'em gibber-jabber and walk away. How hard is that? Look, see my feet. See that foot move. See my other foot move. That's walking fleshy-style. Dummies, go ahead—fill your lungs with water.

Oh, I wish I could obliterate Rock, just blow him off his little riser there. I can't with the Third showing up like this. This is not the day to evoke the full wrath of the Three, not yet. This is a special day. They've been thrashing this about since Moses and before. The Three gets something like this stuck in their linkages, and that's it.

If only the crowd could hear my words of enlightenment. "Don't be fooled, fleshy fools, believing all that rhetoric about easy yokes and light burdens. Wait till they start crucifying you, like they did the Word. You'll wish you'd never heard Rock's words."

If only they would turn to me, those fleshy fools. No initiation rites; no dunking. Haven't they heard it's better to receive than give? I'll receive 'em. They can be the optic of my rumination. All they need to do is be anti-Word. He who is against him is for me. That's all I ask. The Word's the focus of this whole deal, the whole jamboree. That's what the Rock is up there pontificating about.

Look at 'em. The crowd can't be torn away, not today. Rock's words have fallen in too deep. One of our dungeon alligators couldn't pull 'em out. We'll have to let this day pass; let it be. Believe me, we'll regroup.

Here, there, and everywhere they'll go, spreading the message of the Word—what he told 'em to say. Well, we'll not take this lying down, lounging round. We can stoke up a bit of fire ourselves. Just remember, for every action there is a reaction, and we're stupendous reactionaries. I swear to myself, Lucifer, that we will forever roar against their contorted message.

Let 'em go here, there, and everywhere on their commissionable deal. I've got a commission of my own. It starts this instant. Today it rises; tomorrow it roams. Wherever they go, we'll already be. Wherever they mediate, we'll remediate. We'll roam, roam, and roam where no one has ever roamed. Here, there, and everywhere we'll go coalescing, one and all, making devotees in my name, my image, my likeness.

Let's get out of here. We've seen enough. Start roaming through the crowd. Let's see who we can pick off, stragglers unaware. Start coalescing, pulling 'em in. If this is a numbers game, I'll certainly win. I always cheat. Oh, how I cherish deception!

Aren't you grateful you have me to show you the way, even when fire falls from the sky? I'm not rattled. Look to me, you conclave of devotees. Backrider, remind me to work on my speech to the underworld. Scribble me a note. I don't want to hear you speak. What do you think I should call it? Shut it—that's not a question.

With Brother Script's final line spoken, he blinked his eyes and fell silent. Not even a hint of a smile traced his face. He turned around, looked at his stool, and swirled back upon it. In his post-reading position, there was no attempt to engage his audience. He seemed to be seeking invisibility.

Narrative let a few seconds pass after Brother Script's final words. He looked neither to Brother Script, nor to anyone in particular. He cleared his throat and resumed.

READER: Peter's words did, indeed, have a profound effect on the crowd. They did far more than alight on the skin. "Pierced their hearts" is a telling phrase. It resonates with a verse of Scripture concerning Scripture. The verse reads, "For the word of God is living and active, sharper than any two-edged sword, piercing to the division of soul and of spirit, of joints and of marrow, and discerning the thoughts and intentions of the heart."

The piercing of hearts at Pentecost and the piercing action of Scripture are one and the same. Scripture, of course, is what Peter spoke. He quoted Scripture that was and also spoke Scripture into being.

Peter spoke with words dividing soul and spirit. With piercing conviction, his words flowed into open hearts and minds. The effect was astounding. Thousands of bewildered people from diverse nations became believers. All of this must have had an extraordinary impact on the apostles.

This outpouring of the Holy Spirit had everything to do with the disciples going into the world. Their commission suddenly seemed possible. Going without Pentecost, they wouldn't have gone far. They had waited. Now they were ready to go.

Wolves aplenty waited in Jerusalem, Judea, Samaria, and the uttermost parts of the earth, ready to pounce on these message bearers who had huddled in an upper room in old Jerusalem. The Holy Spirit, though, hadn't just popped in for the day and gone away. He had come with wind sufficient to blow across ripened fields, farther than any eye could see.

Words matter, some far more than most...some even pierce.

Peter's words pierced their hearts, and they said to him and to the other apostles, "Brothers, what should we do?"

THE CROWD AT PENTECOST—JERUSALEM, CIRCA AD 32

———◆———

"And with that, I'll give my words a pause," Narrative said.

As Goodwin and Hollie looked across the room, not a single face lacked appreciative expression. The seven girls in the corner, the two young men on the bench, the six people seated in the red-painted chairs, along with everyone else in the room, were applauding.

"Thank you. That's kind, indeed," Narrative said. With an extended arm and a warm smile, he acknowledged Priscilla first, followed by Trish, and then Lloyd. Continuing to smile, he turned next in the direction of Brother Script, extending both arms and shaking his head from side to side.

The applause quickened its pace as Brother Script moved off his stool, looked across the room with a beaming smile, and nodded several times in a gesture of gratitude. He then looked back to Narrative, brought both of his hands together, and offered what might be called a prayerful salute. Shortly thereafter, the room began to settle.

Hollie turned to Goodwin and said, "I can't believe Brother Script—he looks like a different man now. He's all bright and cheerful."

"I know; like I keep saying, these guys are amazing," Goodwin said. "Just when I'm convinced they're from another planet, they make so much sense out of life."

Narrative drew the attention of the room and said, "The three topics on your little cards are piercing words; fire of Pentecost; and here, there, and everywhere. We can discuss these, or anything else you may wish to offer. Let's take time to consider the reading and then regroup for a bit. Okay? Good."

"It looks like most people are heading outside," Hollie said. "What do you think, banana eater, fleshy—why don't we just stretch and stay in here?"

"Actually, I think I'll head outside," Goodwin said. "There's a great view of the ocean from that small rise to the south."

"Okay, if you want. I'm spinning with what we just heard. Like in the reading, words are forming lines, mixing and mingling in my mind. They're really dancing. If you don't mind, I'll just stay here and think. This room's so interesting, the way the windows go to the floor."

Goodwin felt content as he gazed across the meadow to the ocean beyond. On the horizon he saw a ship gently slicing through the waves, followed by four smaller vessels. Each sliced wave lessened the ship's destination. Steadily it trailed away from where it departed, moving nearer to where it wanted to be. Another ship had just completed its slicing journey and was slowly gliding into port. It was where it wanted to be. It would rest and float awhile before once again trailing away.

Hollie was keen to try a seat of scratchy twine, to experience the wear, touch the chips, and feel the nicks. She thought, *I feel such a sense of calm, sitting in this primitive red chair. How admirably the chair wears its wear.*

I feel connectivity to lives lived, to people coming and going, searching and finding, and then going on to where they were supposed to be.

In her seat of twine, Hollie stared at the five unoccupied red chairs. *They look wise, as if they were more than chairs, not just objects. The chairs somehow know who they were and where they were. Though I know it isn't so, is it?*

Hollie sensed the chairs, though silent, were aware of their message. The chairs, she imagined, had willingly traded pristine for primitive. They had welcomed innumerable sitters who brought along their wear, chips, and nicks. In return, the six primitive chairs acquired a beautiful, rich patina that everyone adored. Hollie thought, *That's their message—give and you shall receive.*

"Okay, I think we're about ready. Davyd, would you kindly give a call to those on the lawn?"

Dutifully, Davyd went to the door, clapped his hands three times, and called out, "Time for conversation!"

The seven young ladies were keen to talk; they asked about here, there, and everywhere, and whether to everywhere Christ's message had already gone. This discussion circled round and round, back and forth, until the time for moving words about inside the room was no more.

"If I may, let me make one last point on this matter of here, there, and everywhere. It's this: We all live in Jerusalem and Samaria. Whether we go to the uttermost is up to God, and there are many who are presently in a bit of uttermost—here, there, and everywhere. "If that's your aspiration, follow your dream. But while you're in Jerusalem and Samaria, then these words that go here, there, and everywhere are yours to share.

"Thank you. I loved being with you today."

"Well, never disappointing, eh, Lee?" Goodwin said, as they headed out the door.

"You're so right. I feel like a sponge. And I'm so encouraged by the way you have thrown yourself into all of this, Win. Really, it's good."

"Speaking of throwing, I wonder if Mr. Ironbout is up and throwing walnuts around Good Shepherd Infirmary," Goodwin asked.

"Good question. We'd better head that way to find out," Hollie said.

EIGHTEEN
Room 107—Image in the Mirror

"Well, here we are again. I wonder if he's talking," Goodwin said, as he and Hollie walked in the entrance of Good Shepherd Infirmary.

"I hope so," said Hollie. "But you know, first I need to transition my head from that last reading. Brother Script was so amazing, I still can't get over his change of demeanor," Hollie said. "Did you see those four gals bunched together on the couch? They were mesmerized by the whole thing."

"I know, and it all has to do with words," said Goodwin. "So much to think about. It'll take us a while to fully process that one. There's the desk. Let me find out about Mr. Ironbout.

"Yes, hi there. We're here to check on a Mr. Ironbout. I was in earlier today when he was still in the trauma unit."

"Let me look; just a second," the youngish-looking woman behind the counter said as she reached for her stack of papers. Her name tag read "Sharron."

Looking up at Goodwin and Hollie, she remarked, "By the way, did you happen to see that gentleman walking out the door as you came in? I think he's the tallest person I've ever seen. He and his friend came over to Estillyen yesterday, just for the day, and his friend suddenly passed out, fell face-forward off a bench. They're not sure what's wrong with him. They must be sports figures or something.

"I thought for sure that tall one would hit his head on the metal door frame on his way out. So very tall. Lots of people want to be tall, but when you get overly tall, it's hard to find things that fit. Where does a person that tall buy a bed? I suppose it has to be made to order. Let me see, not in here...."

"Not easy being tall like that. What kinda car do you drive? If you wanted to lie down in a bathtub, you'd need a double-length tub. He was a striking-looking fellow, though—sort of Roman-like features. Maybe he's a javelin thrower."

"I know what you mean," said Goodwin, amused at Sharron's chatty demeanor. "I suddenly felt very short as he passed by."

"Okay, here it is. It appears they've moved Mr. Ironbout," Sharron finally said.

"He's in room 107. He's fortunate—that's a private corner room, very spacious. Just beyond the plants, you'll turn right and go up to what looks like a crossroad, a big open area where the halls meet. I call it "The Junction." Look for the sign with an arrow to Rest House—that's the old, original part of the infirmary.

"That was way back before the name Good Shepherd Infirmary. I'm told Rest House started with only twelve beds. Can you imagine only twelve beds? What must it have been like back then? People were a lot shorter, I'm told. Twelve short beds in Rest House. People didn't live long back then. Even so, I think I'd like to have been born in that era. Candlelight, coal fires, and carriages. I'm told they heated bricks and put them in their beds to keep warm."

"You were saying it's to the right, correct?" Goodwin asked, interrupting her flow of thoughts.

"Oh yes, to the right. When you get to The Junction, you might choose to pause a moment to look up at the ceiling. I recommend it to everyone. There's a beautiful mural depicting Estillyen 200 years ago. People have come from all over the world just to see the mural; they've come from scores of countries. Some make a real fuss about it; they say it's remarkable, a masterpiece.

"Strange thing, though—the artist who painted it never signed it. Wouldn't divulge his true name; kept it a mystery. They called him Uncle Art. He wasn't from around here, so the story goes. They say he rolled little cigarettes and smoked them while sitting out on the stone wall. The tobacco had a very sweet, lovely smell. Nobody had ever smelled tobacco like that."

"We'll take a look, but…" Goodwin began.

"He's said to have spoken very softly. He had very little to say and kept very much to himself. He sang little tunes, almost inaudibly, unless he happened to be in a very cheery mood. I'd like to have met him.

"It's one of Estillyen's great mysteries. There's a plaque on the east wall. It'll be on your left, when you enter The Junction. It gives a description of the mural and a write-up honoring Uncle Art. The details I mentioned are included, but there is a lot more about it. You'll read that it was during the restoration of the infirmary that the mural was painted.

"Funny thing—Uncle Art was working as a regular laborer with the construction crew. No one gave him any notice. Then one day he asked if he could do a wee sketch on the ceiling, promising to paint over it if the infirmary objected. They didn't know what he was going to draw. It could have been nude figures with grape clusters, for all they knew.

"A month later there was a masterpiece on the ceiling, and not long after, he was gone. That was some seventy-five years ago. Estillyen has a charm about it, don't you think? It's lovely here."

Hollie stood only a couple of steps away, following Sharron's story.

At first, she was not listening very attentively, but as Sharron talked on, Hollie could hardly believe the running narrative. She was reluctant to interject, simply to see how long the woman would continue. But she had already come to the conclusion that they were there for a reason.

"Hi, Sharron. My name's Hollie. Interesting spelling of your name, by the way. As you were saying to Win…"

"Yes, the spelling is old world. I kinda like it when people misspell my name; it makes me feel a bit special. I like people, and here you meet so many interesting characters. You never know what they're going to say. Sometimes people can be rather emotional. On any given day, the infirmary can bring both great joy and sudden sadness."

"I'm sure," said Hollie. "So, as you were telling my husband, it's past the plants, to the right, and through The Junction? And after we pause to look up at the mural, we keep walking straight ahead, where we'll see a sign for Rest House, and we follow that."

"Well, actually you'll see an arrow pointing to the sign for Rest House. But the best way to get to room 107 is not through the central corridor. The quickest and surest way is to make a sharp right just before you reach the sign. You'll see a narrow hall with a slate floor. Go down that hall and you'll be at room 107. It's that simple.

"Most people don't even notice the hall. They just fly right by. It doesn't actually even look like a hall, though, with that tall, narrow, swinging door. It looks clinical or something. When you get to the end of the hall, you'll just make a teeny jog to the left, and you'll be at the door of room 107. Do you want someone to show you the way? Lucinda could watch the station for a moment. I'd be happy to come along."

"Oh, no, I think we've got it. Thanks, you've been a great help. Okay, Win?"

"Yes, thanks, Sharron."

"Sure thing. Have a great day."

"Can you believe her?" Hollie said, when they were out of earshot. "She looked so absorbed when she was talking. She must be a writer; she has to be a writer. They have that look—like their eyes have double depth, seeing two things at once. She's probably brilliant. Well, I know one thing: At The Junction, I want to see this mystery painting on the ceiling."

"I'm just glad to hear he's out of the trauma unit," Goodwin said, as they walked up the corridor.

"Me, too," Hollie replied, then she stopped short as they reached The Junction. "Oh my, Goodwin, look! I can't believe it! Sharron was right. I'm shocked, stunned. It's not real, but it is. That's no simple ceiling mural in an infirmary. No wonder people come from all over to view it. It's fine art on plaster. It has to be priceless!

"I could stand here for an hour. It's incredible! Look at the ocean in the background—and the way the trails enter the forest. And that long row of sheep. I've never seen anything quite like it. Never, not even close. It's not a herd or a flock; it's a row stretching back, as far as you can see along the trail."

"Okay, but…"

"Look at them, Win, one after the other; they're just peacefully following. I've got to photograph this. The entire painting is incredibly detailed. Just look at those streams, the way they flow. I can almost feel the water splashing. The painting gives you that immediate, vivid sense of awe. It has that mark of a master. Uncle Art…what a story! Who in the world were you?

"It should be real. What am I saying? Of course it's real. That's exactly what Sister Ravena and I were discussing. It's a work of the past gracing the present. It's as real as the clouds in the sky."

"Okay, Hollie, I can see you're smitten, but we need to pull away. There's the narrow hall. Let's go get this over with. I've got butterflies in my stomach, and you're all enraptured by a mural."

"Goodwin, I'm telling you, it's a masterpiece here in the infirmary. Okay, I'm right behind you. But I have to know more about this. I'm definitely coming back."

"I wonder what they used this hall for—maybe some kind of escape route?" Goodwin said. "There it is—I see the room number, 107. Why does this work me up so much? Should we just go right on in? I guess I'll give a little knock and a nudge, and I'll say hello at the same time. Hello, hello…knock, knock, anybody in here?"

"Yep, someone's in here; it's me."

"Hi, Mr. Ironbout! You're awake," Goodwin said.

"That you, Goodwin?"

"Yes, Sir, it's me and Hollie."

"I was trying to figure out if I was alive or dead. I must be alive. I thought it was you up at The Point, but I was so befuddled. Everything was coming through all wavy-like. It was like your words were ducks trying to land and fly at the same time.

"Heard how you brought me in and all. Grateful I am. Don't suppose I'd have lasted much longer trapped under that appendage. What a mess! I just don't know what happened. Good to see you, Hollie."

"We're just so glad you're safe, and that you're going to be all right, Mr. Ironbout."

"What about poor old Trip? He must be in a right thither, wondering what's happened."

"Should I tell him, Win?"

"What—he's okay, isn't he?" Mr. Ironbout asked, with worry in his eyes.

"Oh yes, Trip's down in the barnyard, making a lot of new friends," said Hollie. "We know he's met a calico cat named Tiptoe and a small black-and-white pig named Spook."

"That sounds about like Trip—silly dog, lodging with a cat and a pig."

"He's being looked after by a Mr. Statter."

"Statter…could be Gavin Statter. He's someone I knew way back. He was a nice fellow."

"He did say he knew you. He called you Otto," Hollie said.

"That's him, sure enough. Well, I'm awful glad Trip is in good hands.

"What do you suppose is under this giant wrap of plaster they've got around my leg, anyway? Think there's still a leg in there?"

"Yeah, it's still there, Sir," Goodwin said.

"I don't know if the staff has already told you, but a pair of renowned heart surgeons worked on your leg," Hollie said. "They're here on a retreat. I think the head nurse said their names were Bell and Sterling. Supposedly they're quite famous. I recognize the name Sterling. I recall him—at least I think it was him—being awarded a rare medal of distinction. I can't think what it's called."

"Well, I hope those old fellows didn't put a pig valve in my leg or give me a leg bypass. Suppose if they're heart surgeons, they wield sharp knives. I expect they got a free lunch out of the deal.

"I tell you, I feel like I was tossed off The Point and landed on the rocks. I'm so sore there are no words for it. I'm sore on top of sore, pained right through to my bones. My bones must be all bruised. These lower left ribs are murdering me, like I've been trucked to a slaughterhouse with a bunch of billy goats.

"I hate how everything has gotten so convoluted. I expect they've got a sheriff camped outside the door, packing a pistol? I figured that when they had me strapped down in here, they'd arrest me for endangering 'em all these years, throwing walnuts at 'em. Never hit any of 'em, though.

"There was a nun in here just now. Wouldn't be throwing any walnuts at her, that's for sure. She's certainly pretty. You know how nuns have a way of not being noticed? They're not supposed to be showing off their beauty. Not so easy for her to hide it, I'd say."

"No, there's no sheriff outside, Mr. Ironbout," Hollie said with a grin. "They've been very nice to Win, and they've been genuinely concerned about you, very much so."

"Well, I'm starving," said Mr Ironbout. "I'm glad they've been concerned, but oh, what I wouldn't give for a good lamb chop right now, or some fish and chips. Dear, oh dear, how the world has turned upside down in ways I never expected.

"I want to talk to you two about that as soon as we can—maybe tomorrow or the next day. It's kind of a circumstantial deal. Important stuff.

"This leg hurts like it belongs to an old bull-fighting matador, though. Blimey, what a mess! Satan tried to chew me up and cart me off. I probably didn't taste quite right, and he spit me out.

"I don't know what's happened in my thinking, I'll tell you that. Dear me, when I was out, I'll tell you, everything that can be in a man flowed through my system. Dreams, nightmares, visions…and there was this kind of voice. I felt as if I was letting go…not caring to die, not caring to live. Then I became my own looking glass. Oh, that was unsettling—frightening, I'll tell ya.

"A mirror, that's what I became. I know you must think I'm insane, but I know what I saw. All revelational like—what a scene.

"There I was. I stood stupefied in front of this tall, full-length glass. I reached out to myself, to my image in the mirror. I touched my face, and my image smiled, but I hadn't smiled. Do you know what that does to your blood pressure? My eyes bulged. I was dumbstruck.

"Then, even more strange, the image in the mirror reached out with its right hand and patted me three times on my left shoulder. Its image, I mean *my* image, seemed like it was trying to comfort me. The pats were faint, ghostlike. The hand was sort of akin to a feather duster. You know what I'm tryin' to say? You know what I mean?"

"Sir, I wonder…" Goodwin interjected.

"After my image patted me on the shoulder," he continued, "I looked off to the right and started walking away. I'm not kidding you; this happened. It was as real as this room. No aberration, no sir; I was drawn into a place where you're inside out. I had taken several steps, when I looked back at my image. My image looked at me all curious-like, sullen, like my image knew I was going to die. Exceptionally sad the image was, like my image knew that if I died, it would be left behind.

"I took a few more steps and looked back again. The image was still there, but it wasn't the image of me looking at me anymore. Instead, my image in the mirror stood straight and looked forward, straight ahead. By that point, I was several steps away and facing the other direction.

"Oh, dear me, blimey, what a feeling it was that swelled up inside my spirit! I felt like I was walking away, leaving myself behind. Whatever I was, I was me without me. That's how I felt: me without me.

"At that point, I stood real still and closed my eyes. I stayed that way for what could have been a minute, maybe two. I felt very calm and peaceful. Everything was quiet, all serene and tranquil-like. In the middle of this calm state, I opened my eyes.

"I expected to see the mirror and my image all corrected, properly projected. Instead, to my horror, I could see myself—the real me—walking away. I saw me gliding across the room.

"Then it struck me, like I'd been slapped across the face by a big ear of corn. My image and me had swapped places. I was now my image in the mirror, and not me. I, the real me, was departing, walking away. All I could think was that I was inside the mirror looking out, not outside looking in.'

"Mr. Ironbout, we think..." Hollie interrupted, trying to halt the stream of words.

"No, you must hear this. I was now my image seeing the back of me. I watched in horror as the real me slowly slipped through the shadows—becoming more and more obscure until the real me was completely gone. There was nothing left of me but the trapped image in the mirror. Sealed beneath the glass, there I was pressed.

"I thought, *I'll never be free because I'm only the image projected of me, and the real me is gone, I no longer exist.* I knew the real me would not come back for me, the image. The image was forever projected, never to be collected. It was too late. I was forever gone.

"Through the shadows I moved. A thick wall of darkness rose up and sealed my route. It was like a monstrous ocean wave; darker than dark, it was. No way around it, over it, or under it. There was no longer a passage or a path—just darkness, and thick it was.

"As I was pressed there in this horrific state of anguish, under the glass, a man approached the mirror. He was all smartly dressed. It wasn't me. I didn't know him; had never seen him. He looked into the mirror but couldn't see me. He saw straight through me to the image he expected to see—his own. He smiled and adjusted the brim of his hat, and then walked away.

"'Dear Lord,' I said, 'I have become invisible.' I was seeing him looking straight through me. I was the image of me, now invisible, trapped inside the mirror. I tried to speak, move, gesture. I could, but no one could see or hear the image of me in the mirror."

"Oh, Mr. Ironbout, you need to rest," Hollie said. "I think your medication is affecting you. It's very strong, you know."

"No, it's not that, dear. It's not that at all. I'm telling you; I need you to know…"

"Hello! Well, I see you're awake and have friends," Nurse Polly said. "How are you doing? Think you might want a little food?"

"Oh, well, we need to talk more, okay?" Mr. Ironbout said.

"Sure," Hollie said, relieved that the tension in the room had eased.

"Food you say—I hope it's not too skimpy," Mr. Ironbout said. "I was fixing to eat the cotton wool poking out of this cast."

"Sir, I think Hollie and I will go now and let you eat in peace."

"You two will come back tomorrow, right? I do want to talk with you a bit more. I've got to get out of here. Oh, dear me, how do you expect me to sit up, when I'm all bedded down like this?"

"Now, don't worry about that, Mr. Ironbout," Nurse Polly said. "We're pretty experienced at helping people around here."

"All right, Sir, we're going now," said Goodwin.

"Okay, Goodwin, but I want to finish telling you and Hollie what I was telling ya."

"Then we'll see you tomorrow, Mr. Ironbout."

"Okay, bye for now, you two."

Hollie and Goodwin gracefully slipped out of the room and began to move along the narrow hall. They could still hear the conversation from the open door of Mr. Ironbout's room.

"Whataya got under that tin cover, anyway?"

"We thought you might like some lamb roast, with macaroni and cheese and…"

Through the narrow door at the end of the hall, Hollie and Goodwin emerged. They paused at the edge of the main corridor.

"Did you hear him?" Hollie asked. "Never have I heard anything like it."

"I heard him, but I'm not sure what I heard. What a story! What a dream or vision, or whatever it was he had."

"I'm not certain it was a dream," Hollie said. "He clearly looked pleased to see us, though."

"Yeah, something seems to have snapped, and I don't mean just his leg. Let's go around in the morning when we can stay a bit longer."

"For now, what about lunch at Fields and Crops? I've got crab cakes on my mind," Hollie said.

"A baked potato with chili sounds good to me. I need to decompress. We've certainly heard something amazing today. 'There I was, watching me walk away....'"

Hollie and Goodwin made their way to the entrance of Good Shepherd Infirmary. As they walked past the reception desk, Sharron was busily talking with three elderly ladies. Sharron peered around the three and caught Hollie's attention. Hollie smiled, shook her head up and down, and said in an excited tone, "You're right—it's beautiful." Sharron smiled proudly.

Hollie and Goodwin kept moving. They were eager for lunch and a chance to process what the day had brought so far. They had heard a lot of words that were vying for space in their minds.

As promised, Hollie and Goodwin came back the following morning and stayed for more than an hour. Mr. Ironbout had rested well during the night, but he was still in considerable pain. His head seemed clear enough, but he continued to cluster his thoughts around the notion that everything was different and in a state of flux.

Hollie and Goodwin knew he had gone through a horrible shock and could well have died. His manner of speaking, though, went beyond concern for his physical well-being. This was Oban Ironbout, the man of defiance, the man of self, who was now talking of his image in the mirror.

As their visit drew to a close—and just as Hollie and Goodwin were getting ready to leave—Mr. Ironbout made a most unusual request.

"You know, I was saying that I wanted to speak to you two in a more mindful way, in a collected manner. If you'd be willing, I'm wondering if tomorrow, after they're through fiddling with this leg, we might have a sort of meeting, proper-like. Let's say around ten in the morning."

"Sure, Mr. Ironbout. Hollie and I would be glad to come back, whenever you say."

"I'm thinking, too, it might be good to have one of them nuns join us. You were talking about this Sister Ravinia—something like that, wasn't it, Hollie?"

"Yes—Sister Ravena."

"Well, I wonder if she'd be willing to come along. And, if we're gonna have her, it would be good to have one of those monks, as well. I want to say a little bit about Estillyen and all this care. You think that's possible?"

"We can certainly inquire, don't you think, Win? We've come to know a good number of the people around here. We can ask—maybe someone like Brother Plot could come with us."

"Okay, then. Tomorrow at around ten, when they're done poking me."

"All right, we'll be here," Goodwin promised.

Soon, Hollie and Goodwin stood under the mural, pausing, looking, talking.

"Mr. Ironbout is like a wolf being cared for by sheep," Hollie said, "yet somehow his ferociousness has waned. There is no threat of reprisal, no crossness or swearing. Comments you'd expect never surfaced. No lines like, 'You've got me trapped, but just wait till I spring free. You woulda been smarter to let me die. Just wait till I get on my feet.' There is no spite, no angst. His long-standing Ironbout repertoire is absent."

"I know," Goodwin said, "something has certainly changed. He talked more like an estranged uncle than the man on The Point everyone fears. Did you see the way he interacted with the aides, the manner in which he thanked and deferred to them? His behavior, to me, resembled more that of someone who had been rescued at sea."

"You're right, that's the way he seemed: full of gratitude for being pulled from the waters into a ship of caring people. I bet it's hard for the staff to believe this is truly Oban Ironbout who lives on The Point. But who else could he be? He's the original me all right. That man is full of surprises."

"I know. I'm amazed he wants to meet Sister Ravena and have a monk present."

"Well, let's see what we can do," Hollie said. "I can't wait to hear what he has to say."

It didn't take Hollie and Goodwin long to make the rounds—first to see Sister Ravena, and then a stop by Dairy House to see Brother Plot. Their reactions were almost identical: expressions of "Hmm," with lips sealed and heads tilted sideways. Sister Ravena said, "I wonder what this is about," while Plot said, "Curious—wonder what this means?"

The four agreed to meet in the foyer of the infirmary at five minutes to ten. Together they would walk through The Junction and down the narrow hall to room 107.

NINETEEN
The Meeting

"Hi, Sister Ravena," Hollie said. "Good—you're early. I was hoping you'd be."

"You know how it is; we don't spend a lot of time sorting the wardrobe," Sister Ravena said. "We're classically in vogue. Swapping the purse and clogs—that's about it."

"It seems funny, but you haven't actually met my husband. Sister Ravena, this is Goodwin."

"Pleased to meet you," Sister Ravena said. "It's been a pleasure getting to know Hollie, and now you."

"It's good to meet you, as well. Hollie speaks very highly of you."

"Since we have a few minutes, why don't we go along and look at the mural," Hollie said. "Goodwin can wait for Brother Plot. He should be along any minute."

"Certainly, let's go. I never tire of viewing it. Did you happen to notice the two large benches on the far side of the circle? We put those in last year. They match the curvature of the wall. For years, there was a nurse's station in the middle of the circle, which prevented people from walking beneath the mural and observing it like it was meant to be seen.

"We finally moved the station so the mural could be fully appreciated. That created a good bit of fuss. I recall several meetings over the issue. Since then, I've witnessed no end of people standing there gazing up at the mural, just to collect their thoughts, offer a prayer, or reflect on the painting."

"I can imagine."

"I'm sure that's what the artist, Uncle Art, had in mind. With this mural, in the heart of the infirmary there's a place to pause, compose, find a bit of repose. It's such a wonderful spot, that big circle with those four main halls branching out and the gorgeous painting overhead. See, those are the benches."

"I don't know how I missed them. They're huge and so sturdy looking. They're real park benches."

"Right, they're just not in a park."

"So, quite mysterious, this. Who do you think Uncle Art was?" Hollie asked.

"No one can really say. We've had at least four museum curators who've come and studied the mural. They've been all over it—photographing it, inspecting its every detail. A number of articles have been written about it, and no one can pin down the artist. They say it resembles this great artist or that one, but no one has been able to make a definitive connection—not yet, anyway."

"Don't you think it's just stunningly beautiful?"

"Certainly. It's priceless."

"When I first saw it on Wednesday, I simply couldn't believe it. The sheep on the trail—they're so gorgeous and captivating. It's not a typical flock in the field, but this stunning row that stretches on forever, as far as the eye can see along the trail. They're all quietly headed toward us. They're just moving along, one by one, up the trail.

"I love how the row starts way off in the distance, there down by the ocean ledge, and disappears around the mound. Then, standing here in the foreground and staring out of the painting is this magnificent, fully grown sheep with that thick coat. His eyes look so tender, and his face is glowingly peaceful.

"It's life-size, don't you think?" asked Hollie.

"It appears to be," Sister Ravena said. "Just think how big it would be if the sheep jumped out of the painting. And he looks like he could."

"Maybe he does when no one's around," Hollie said. "He seems so real. I want to reach up and give him a pat on the head. You see how he's the only one in full view? All the other sheep are partially blocked by the sheep in front or alongside them.

"We see only an eye here or an ear there. Just a little way back, we can see the nose and the top of a head sticking up of one. The next one—all we see is the shoulder. There's one beside the tree over there, but we see only his right hindquarter.

"When you take it all in, the row almost appears to be one long trail of wool, with eyes, noses, hooves, and ears. It's truly amazing—real art. It's honestly one of the most, if not the most, beautiful paintings I've ever viewed. You're right, it's priceless."

"No doubt there's meaning in that trail," Ravena said. "The one you'd like to pet is so endearing. He's not looking at another sheep. He must be looking at the shepherd. It's a pity we don't know the artist. That would tell us a lot. We're clueless about his spiritual convictions, his views on life.

"There's not a hint of fear in that sheep's eyes. He's very comforted by what he sees. That's the essence: peace at journey's end. It's perfect for the infirmary."

"Definitely," said Hollie. "Maybe all the sheep represent years. It's such a gift to Estillyen. Amazing. Oh, here they come."

"Well, have you discovered the artist?" Brother Plot asked. "Good morning, Sister Ravena. Hi, Hollie."

"Good morning, Brother Plot. Hollie and I were just talking about this fascinating trail of sheep."

"Hi, Brother Plot," Hollie said. "I was commenting about how only the sheep in the foreground is fully visible. See how all the rest are all partially hidden, in one way or another? All along the trail it's that way, until the trail finally disappears around that mound. It looks like hundreds and hundreds of sheep. Any thoughts on why Uncle Art chose to render it that way?"

Brother Plot wore his usual brown habit, leather sandals, and black socks. He moved to the center of the circle, where he looked up quietly and studied the painting, as he had done many times before.

"Well, I've always felt the featured sheep appears amazingly at ease, peaceful. He stares longingly. He must be near his shepherd, for he shows no fear. Could it be that the prominent sheep in the foreground represents a true disciple of Christ, and the others are on their way?"

Sister Ravena and Hollie looked at each other and smiled.

"You may have something there, Brother Plot," Sister Ravena said.

"Well, what's the plan?" Plot asked. "It looks like we're just on ten."

"Not sure we have a plan, do we?" Goodwin asked.

"No, not really," Hollie said. "Win and I were just here yesterday, and Mr. Ironbout requested a meeting. That's what he called it, 'a meeting.' He specifically mentioned Sister Ravena, and he thought it would be good to have, as he put it, a monk. So we thought of you, Brother Plot. We've all talked about Mr. Ironbout. And, of course, Sister Ravena has tried to meet with him."

"I've also written him a couple of letters," Sister Ravena said. "No response—though I didn't really expect one."

"Well, no time like the present to get this meeting underway," Brother Plot said. "Why don't you and Goodwin lead the way, Hollie?"

Out from beneath the mural and beyond The Junction they stepped. Soon, they reached the arrow pointing to the sign for Rest House and made a sharp right. With Goodwin in the lead, they approached the narrow hall with its swinging door.

The door was painted a deep cobalt blue and sealed with several coats of clear, high-gloss varnish. Elongated stainless-steel push plates and extra-wide kick plates gave the door a hygienic look, while protecting the rich cobalt blue from unwanted scrapes, nicks, and scratches.

The door itself was a work of art, made particularly so by its face-high circular window. The window had wide mullions that formed a cross. The mullions were perfectly flat and three times the width one might expect.

The round window frame was capped with a wide, flat-trim molding, painted gloss white. The mullions, by contrast, were cobalt blue. Four pie-shaped glass panes sparkled. They were slightly iridescent, with a hint of gold in the textured blue glass.

Through the circular window, the party of four could see the narrow hall extending on the other side of the door. Goodwin was the first to touch the shiny, cool, steel push plate. Effortlessly, the door swung to the right and paused, proudly, a few inches from the red brick wall, which ran the length of the hall.

Goodwin stepped through the doorway, while he held his right hand on the door, just long enough to allow it to gently swing softly to Hollie. Hollie repeated the motion, passing the door to Sister Ravena, who extended the courtesy to Brother Plot.

Hollie said, "I feel like we're four sheep from the mural, making our way down this narrow hall, to room 107."

As they neared the door, Goodwin turned around with a wide-eyed expression on his face. He lifted his hands, palms facing upwards, and shrugged his shoulders. In a very soft voice, he said, "This is crazy; my hands are sweating. But here we go. Hello. Knock, knock. Hello. Are you decent, Mr. Ironbout?"

"I don't know about decent, but I'm in here; can't get out."

"Hi, Mr. Ironbout," Hollie said cheerfully.

"Hi, Hollie."

"We've brought some friends to meet you. Mr. Ironbout, this is Sister Ravena and Brother Plot."

"Hi there, Mr. Ironbout," Sister Ravena said as she extended her hand. "It's a pleasure to finally meet you."

"I'm glad we don't have to shake with our left feet, or I'd be in a real mess."

"My pleasure, as well, Mr. Ironbout," Brother Plot said. "The hand will do for me."

"So you're Plot, one of the message-making monks."

"Can't deny it."

"Yeah, Goodwin let me read something monk Writer wrote. I guess it was read in one of them readings. Quite something it was. I've never been to one of the readings."

"Do come! You are most welcome," Brother Plot said. "It's just a bit of speaking about various stories from Scripture. The approach seems to settle in fairly well with the sentiments of the day. Nowadays, the audience is very much a part of the message. Today it's more a matter of speaking *with* people rather than *at* or *to* them, if you know what I mean."

"I think I know what you mean. That's why I used to talk with my sheep. They didn't like being yelled at. Please—there are a couple of chairs, and Goodwin can probably perch on the radiator, since it's on a holiday break."

"Goodwin," Sister Ravena said, "there are some wooden chairs in the cove, just at the end of the hall. Would you mind snatching one for Hollie?"

"Gladly, if you've given the okay to pinch 'em," he said, as he quickly ducked out of the room.

"He doesn't mind. Seems full of help, that Goodwin," Mr. Ironbout said. "Sure got me out of a tight spot, I'll tell you that. Dad-blamed appendage tried to snuff me out."

In less than thirty seconds, Goodwin was back carrying a thin wooden chair.

"That was quick," Mr. Ironbout said.

Goodwin positioned the chair next to the blue leather chair on which Sister Ravena had placed her dark red purse.

"Please, have a seat," Mr. Ironbout said.

"Just a second," Sister Ravena said. "First, we all want to know how you are. What are they saying? Are they treating you all right?"

"Well, let me see if I can crank myself up a bit more. These gadgets have more arrows than you find in a train station. Let me see—the little one on the bottom…you have to really punch 'em. Yeah, that's a lot better.

"Sorry to be looking so rough for this meeting. I had the nurse, Sister Ruth, clip my eyebrows and snip a few of my whiskers. I can't do much about the rest. This troubled leg sure smarts. Last night it got to throbbing so, I thought the surgeons had left some of their implements inside it.

"Look at that little door they put on the side of the cast. I've never seen anything like it. They set threads in the plaster. They undo the screws and remove the door. That's where the deep wound is.

"That door idea must be something those heart surgeons dreamed up. They remove it twice a day and clean the wound. They said it seems to be healing. They even think I might get out of here next week sometime."

"You know, that makes me think, Mr. Ironbout. I forgot to tell you, but Trip had been licking that wound before I arrived," Goodwin said.

"That's probably why it's healing so fast," Mr. Ironbout said. "Smart dog, that Trip. I sure miss the fellow.

"The lower part of the leg is where it gets to throbbing. I'm told those fellows put a few pins in there. They say it'll calm down before long. I guess my lumberjacking days are over. Trip and I'll have to find some other form of mischief. Maybe we'll pitch walnuts at wild turkeys; see if we can smoke some meat. I expect Trip would go all out for that sort of sport, you know what I mean?"

"Are you eating okay? Is the food all right?" Sister Ravena asked.

"Oh, splendid. Those homemade rolls with orange marmalade—they meet an appetite straight on, I'll tell you. You know, I didn't know there was a pantry on Estillyen where you could buy The Abbey's baked goods. I knew about the fruitcakes, but I understand they've got all manner of pies, cakes, and other things. I guess I wouldn't have come around, though—you know what I'm tryin' to say?"

Amazed, Sister Ravena thought, *This whole scene is really something. I'm not sure what to make of Oban Ironbout. Where is he going with this?*

"Well, you seem to be on the road to recovery, Mr. Ironbout," Sister Ravena said. "Do you have anything in particular you wanted to discuss or say to us today, or did you simply want to meet, after all these years?"

"Umm, yes…well, uh…I do want to say a few words. Yeah, why don't you all take a seat?" Mr. Ironbout said.

The chairs were lined up to Mr. Ironbout's right, not more than a couple of meters from his bed. Brother Plot sat on the edge of the gray Naugahyde recliner and was the furthest of the three from Mr. Ironbout. In the middle was Sister Ravena in the blue leather reading chair.

Hollie sat in the birch-colored wooden chair from the hall. She wore chocolate brown jeans and a thin, emerald green v-necked cotton pullover. Goodwin leaned on the edge of the metal radiator cover, wearing denim jeans and a dark green corduroy shirt.

"Yes, now that you're all seated…hmm….well, since I called this meeting, I might as well chair it—or should I say bed it, if you know what I'm tryin' to say. Is that all right with everyone?" he asked.

"That'll be fine, Mr. Ironbout," Sister Ravena said with a smile.

"Okay, then, you might want to jot down a note or two on this, Sister Ravena. It might not hurt, but that's up to you."

Sister Ravena reached into her purse and produced a small black leather note pad, which had a slender gold pencil attached, secured by a small loop of red ribbon.

"The first thing I want to record is this: I, Oban Otto Ironbout, am in a state of sound and reasonable mind. Well, not sure how *sound*, but reasonable. By that,

I mean, I'm not crazy, off my rocker, or talking out of my head. Likewise, these painkillers are not talking for me. I'm talking for me, proper-like, if you know what I mean."

"We understand," Sister Ravena said.

"Now, Sister Ravena, I know you tried, more than once, to come up to The Point to see me. I remember that incident a couple of years ago. I ran you off in my typical Ironbout fashion. I can still see those aides that were with you. You'd thought they'd seen a grizzly bear or a ghost. Well, I guess they had, in a manner of speaking. Boy, did they jump, like grasshoppers wearing black dresses.

"You followed up and wrote me a couple of letters. You told me about your dream for artists and talked about the beauty of The Point. Well, I want you to know what I did with your letters. I burned 'em, and they didn't collect any dust waiting for the fire.

"It was about that time that those two cracker cases from that Source Telecom outfit tried to come around. You'd of thought Trip had turned into a mad dog—never saw him act like that. He must have been able to see through to their spirits.

"Along with your advances, of a sort, there used to be regular interloping by the monks. You know, coming around on an irregular basis. I don't know how many monks dared to venture past the signs that I've posted on my property over the years. Bird-watching, photographing, hiking—whatever it is monks do, they were doing it. I suppose a bit of prayer and contemplation was part of their idea.

"Well, concerning all that collective meandering and all those instances of trespassing trespasses (except for trespassing of Source Telecom), I've got a summation to offer. The summation is this: I'm shamefully sorry for the way I've acted over the years. I was wrong, pitifully wrong. I was bullheaded. Foolish, I was. Don't know what happened to me, but all that happened should never have happened."

"Well, Sir, you don't have to..." began Plot.

"No—sorry, Brother Plot, please let me finish. That's okay with you, isn't it, Sister Ravena? I've a good bit more to say, words that need to be aired."

"Sure, Mr. Ironbout, you go right ahead and air them. There's no place we'd rather be than right here."

"You all know I came here and built the house on The Point. That was some forty-seven years ago. And for me it was a labor of love, pure creative expression. I used to be much more inclined along artistic lines in those days. What I eventually became is not how I was.

"That thought scoots me right up to the first of my three points. I've got three to cover, and the third hangs on the outcome of the second.

"The first of the three is this: When Goodwin came along with his sketch a few weeks ago, it stunned me, took me back, grappled me deep within my core. There was my house, rendered from a photo taken by my old friend Raleigh Macbreeze. He was a good man.

"In the sketch was Leslie, my dear wife. I was drawn back, not through the muck of reality, like I'm accustomed to being dragged. I leapfrogged over all those years of misery. I was standing in front of my house, newly built, without tragedy defacing the picture.

"The sketch took me back to a time before death came to steal and I began my long march with misery. It's all my fault, I know. It comes down to me. I have no one to blame but myself. But the sketch took me back. When I saw that sketch, I felt a puff, a little breeze of life…a whiff from another time, before I was how I now am.

"I'm still on my first point, in case you're wondering. When the appendage got me on the ground, I didn't know if I was hearing God or Satan. It was both, I reckon. In fact I'm sure of it. That appendage, that limb, was taking liberties. It was stretching out to where Leslie and the boys are buried, the plot. There it was growing sideways out of the tree, all crooked. For years I watched it grow a little bit more each year.

"As the seasons stretched on, so did the appendage. Twisting, bending all gnarly-like, ever advancing its reach. Just like me, we were growing bent together, reaching out to death. Neither of us could let go. To the plot, I made my daily ritual. Oftentimes I'd take a little wood stool and just sit there, gazing out over the cliff, sinking deeper into despair.

"When Goodwin handed me that sketch, part of the shock was time—just how much time was gone, how many seasons were lost. It made me realize how long the appendage and I had been growing together in our twisted state.

"Last autumn, one late, chilly afternoon, I was out at the plot with Trip, raking a few leaves and burning twigs. Every now and then the wind would throw up one of its gusts. When it did, I noticed how the branches from the appendage reached down and brushed against the grave markers. Not only was it reaching for the markers, but beyond them.

"I swear that's what I saw. I could see it stretch, reaching out just to show me it could. It was then that the appendage spoke to me. It said, 'Ha! I'll have you, Oban Ironbout; you'll not have me. When you are dead and buried, I'll reach beyond your reach of me. I'm connected to the tree. Can't you see? What are you connected to? Nothing but death. I have life.' I stared back at the limb, holding the rake in my hand.

"Now, so you won't think I'm totally crazy (which you probably already do), I don't believe the appendage was actually speaking to me, but me speaking, for the tree, to me. But where did the thoughts come from? That's for you to judge. I was having an epiphany concerning my own mortality and the life I've lived, reaching out to death.

"Blimey, it was a cruel intrusion, me speaking to myself that way on behalf of the tree. In my mind, there had been some kind of camaraderie between me and that appendage. I knew what it was like to grow bent, sideways rather than straight. At least that's how I thought.

"I had tricked myself into thinking that the appendage was my friend, sympathetic of my condition. Now that I was advancing well into years, I realized the camaraderie was all a hoax. It was a figment of my imagination, this befriending of a crooked limb. In the appendage I saw *me*—it was my image, and I wanted to do away with it.

"When Goodwin came with his sketch, like I said, I felt a whiff of life. I dreamed I could once again reach, not for death, but life. I wanted to reach beyond death and touch life once more before I died.

"That's what I wanted, yet, in the lawn, the appendage grew, with its constant mockery. After Goodwin's arrival on The Point, the appendage acquired a macabre sort of laugh. It spoke to me again. It said, 'You've grown too far bent, Oban Ironbout. Look at you—ho, haha—do you think that now in winter late you believe you can reach for life? Hehe...Look at all the wasted years. All the time you've lost. You've nothing to reach for; there's nothing to touch. Don't be a fool.'

"That's when I decided the appendage had to go. This mocking image of me had to be brought down. Sunday morning Trip and I ate breakfast. I sorted out all my gear. Soon my power saw was roaring. It wasn't long before I had the appendage bare of branches. Stripped—its snarly fingers and twisting branches were all gone. All that was left was a long trunk of a limb, bent, crooked, and gnarly.

"I told the appendage, 'You've had it. First, I'll chop you into decade-size hunks, and then into yearly chunks.' Decade by decade, year by year, I wanted nothing left of the appendage but sawdust and logs for the fire. I thought that with the appendage gone, at least I would be able to think more clearly. Perhaps, just perhaps, it would be possible to grasp that whiff of life rising from the sketch.

"This might surprise you, Brother Plot. But that night, before the accident, that's when I did my own monk-style reading. Trip was my audience of one. It was *Remember Me* by Brother Writer. Trip and I normally listen to *Tunes Spun* on Saturday evenings. Before the program aired, I had a shot or two of scotch and began to read Writer's words to Trip in his sitting chair.

"Dear me, what I've forgotten! Writer's words evoked something fierce in my sensibilities of being. I read, and paused, and read, and finally late that night I went to bed, with all of that running through my head. It sort of soaked into my system, something like the scotch.

"Subsequently, when I was trapped under the appendage, a horrific battle raged deep within me. I suppose it continued after I was brought here. I don't know. There the two condemned prisoners hung on either side of Christ. I could see myself there. I was both of them—both at the same time, I was.

"Earlier in life, I was like the good one, the one wanting to be remembered. Then I turned into the other one, not a bit better. I changed, became bitter, all bent like the appendage. That was my image, the me I wasn't meant to be. That appendage defined Oban Ironbout.

"Suddenly, in the middle of this raging battle, everything got exceedingly strange. I was standing in front of a full-length mirror, staring at myself. I touched my image in the mirror, and the image touched back, but it touched me differently than I touched it. I touched its face. It patted me three times on the shoulder, real gentle-like.

"After a while I started to walk away, but then I looked back and saw my image still standing in the mirror looking straight out, as if I were back in front of the mirror. I took another step, and then another, but the image just stood there, looking straight ahead. So for a moment, I closed my eyes. Maybe I died. I don't know.

"All I know is that, when I opened my eyes, I was inside the mirror looking out, watching me walking away, instead of outside looking in. The real me was gone; only the image of me remained, forever trapped beneath the glass in that attic mirror.

"Then I truly awoke, I'd say—which brings me to the conclusion of my first point. The appendage is gone! The old image of Oban Ironbout is dead. I want to reach for life. I want to be remembered. I want to see the Kingdom Christ promised to the thief."

By now, Sister Ravena, Brother Plot, Hollie, and Goodwin were equally awed. They stared at Mr. Ironbout, and equally up and away from him, beyond him. They could scarcely believe what they heard, what they had witnessed. No one knew what to say. Silence dominated.

Then, without lapsing, Mr. Ironbout said, "Now for my second point.

Goodwin, why don't you swap places with Hollie for a second so I can see you without a crooked neck. I've been bent long enough."

Hollie sprang to her feet and exchanged places with Goodwin. Hollie leaned and perched on the radiator cover. Goodwin sat in the chair with attentive posture.

"Goodwin, I've got something to tell you, and I wanted these three to be here. Now, listen carefully, son. This is important for you to hear. It's not bad, but it may be a bit sobering. You know what I'm tryin' to say?

"Well, okay…" Goodwin said.

"It's like this, and true it is. Your grandfather, Raleigh Macbreeze, was a wonderful man. I knew him. We were good friends. However, we were more than friends; our lives were heavily intertwined. He knew me—he knew who I was. And now you need to know who we are.

"Raleigh Macbreeze was not your paternal grandfather, as you have always believed. Nor was he the paternal father of your mother, again, like you have always thought. The truth is, your mother Rebecca was my daughter. Which means, well, that you are my grandson. I know, I know, it's hard to grasp, but it's true. Bear with me."

Stiffly Goodwin sat, staring with his dark brown eyes at Mr. Ironbout.

"Your grandmother Katharine and I were just kids in love. Katharine was seventeen when she got pregnant with your mother. I wanted to marry her with the same kind of love I eventually extended to Leslie. But Katharine's parents, your great-grandparents, wouldn't stand for it. They thought I'd take her away, and that they'd never see her again.

"I understood, of course, but that wasn't my intention. Nevertheless, Katharine's father became very angry, threatened to kill me, and forbade any contact between us. At the same time, Katharine's mother was unwell. Among other conditions, she had epilepsy. If it hadn't been for that, I believe Katharine would have left; we would have just run off together.

"Katharine was afraid, though, that if she left, her mother would die, and she would never be able to forgive herself. So she stayed, and your mother, Rebecca, was born. Katharine was torn, but I knew she wouldn't reconsider. That's when Raleigh Macbreeze stepped into the picture.

"Raleigh was a friend of mine, a gentle soul, and he knew the family well. He was there when Rebecca was born. Eventually he and Katharine were quietly married. Your mother never knew that Raleigh wasn't her natural father.

"Both he and Katharine intended to tell Rebecca one day, but your mother, as you know, also contracted epilepsy when she was young. Raleigh and Katharine didn't want to add any stress to Rebecca's life, so they kept quiet. Eventually I met

Leslie, and we moved to Estillyen, where, as you know, Leslie died along with the boys.

"I turned bitter, and that's when I became who I wasn't meant to be. The years passed, and your mother died in that drowning accident. Sir Raleigh still wanted to tell you about me, but I had grown into such an old bent soul. He was concerned about how you might feel, if you came here and found out you had a grandfather like me.

"Then, out of the blue, you arrived. You ventured up to The Point and brought me your sketch. When I saw your belt buckle, I knew who you must be. That's why I said you shouldn't have come. That's why everything has become so different. You, Goodwin, were the whiff of life rising from the sketch, the life I wanted to touch."

Mr. Ironbout paused. His bottom lip noticeably quivered. Tears filled his eyes. "I'm sorry, son. I didn't expect to get all teary-eyed like this. Dear me. So there you have it."

Silence engulfed the room. Breathing even quieted itself. With tear-filled eyes, Hollie looked to Sister Ravena. Sister Ravena stared back, moving only her eyes. She reached in her pocket for a tissue to catch the tears dripping from her chin. Plot blotted his eyes with the back of his right index finger, as his left hand scoured his habit for a handkerchief.

Silence grew. Goodwin sat perfectly still, knowing that the silence was his to fill. Suddenly, deliberately, his right forearm rose. The rest of his body was motionless, as if the forearm acted on its own. The back of Goodwin's forearm swept a swath of green corduroy across his eyes. For several seconds more, he sat silently, staring at the floor.

Silence hushed even more and waited. Hearts were beating. Eyes twitched and tears dripped. Then the silence was broken.

Goodwin lifted his head and slowly rose to his feet. He cleared his throat, and looked first to Hollie and then to Sister Ravena and Brother Plot. He then turned to face Mr. Ironbout.

"Well, I hardly know what to say…I mean, The Point, and you…if I'm understanding all this correctly, this means I've got Ironbout blood in my veins. In a way, it all makes sense—this draw of destiny, my haunting obsession with The Point, and *My Cottage Rare*. No wonder Sir Raleigh carried on as he did.

"Thinking of him now, as I stand here in the room, I wonder what he would say? I think I know. He'd more than likely say, 'I don't see any reason why you can't have two grandfathers, rather than one.' Yeah, I think that's right, that's what he'd say. So that's what I say, if you know what I mean."

Goodwin took three short steps over to the bed. He reached out for Oban Ironbout's right hand. He lifted the large, rough hand, bent forward, and gave it a nip of a kiss. Goodwin slowly laid Mr. Ironbout's hand down on the bed.

Mr. Ironbout stared, not speaking. He sobbed. His cheeks trembled. At once, sounds converged. The radiator cover creaked, the leather chair squeaked, and the Naugahyde swooshed. Simultaneously, Hollie, Sister Ravena, and Brother Plot joined Goodwin beside Mr. Ironbout's bed. They looked. Plot thought, *I see life touching life.*

Hollie quickly found a hand towel and dashed away to moisten it with water.

"Here, Mr. Ironbout, let's see how this feels on your forehead," Hollie said as she dabbed Mr. Ironbout's forehead with the cool, damp towel.

"Thank you, dear. I didn't mean to get all choked up on you folks. Dear, oh dear, life sure takes a spell of curious living sometimes. I'm thinking, Sister Ravena, that maybe tomorrow or the next day we can talk about my third point of this meeting. Doesn't seem the right time for details.

"I want to talk about The Point being some part of Estillyen's Abbey community, some kind of a heritage-type thing. The Point needs to be a destination for artists, like you said. I'd like that; I really would.

"For me, The Point is the most beautiful spot on earth. It's time those signs come down. I've got a different kind of image to build."

After all that was said, no one was quick to leave. Eventually Sister Ravena and Brother Plot excused themselves. Out of room 107 they emerged, up the narrow hallway they walked, not saying a word.

As Sister Ravena moved through the cobalt-blue swinging door, she extended her left arm, allowing the door to gracefully swing open for Brother Plot. Still silent, they moved out to the center of The Junction, beneath the mural painted by Uncle Art. They paused.

"I'm not sure what we saw today, but I'm sure it was a miracle," Sister Ravena said.

"It was indeed," said Brother Plot. "What a meeting with one of Christ's new disciples! I do believe he's surrendered, come home at last."

TWENTY
Writer and Words

"We're really glad you decided to come along, Mr. Ironbout," Hollie said. "Does it feel like Saturday to you?"

"Don't know what it feels like, lying in this hospital room. It's good to be in a chair, even if it is a wheelchair. This leg brace is the ticket; my leg looks like a cannon ready to fire."

"Knock, knock—hey, they've got you in the chair, Mr. Ironbout," Goodwin said. "You look like a regular person, Sir."

"A regular person I doubt I am. Goodwin, feel free to call me Oban—or if you wish, you can call me Otto; that's my middle name, Oban Otto Ironbout."

"I kind of like that—Otto," Goodwin said. "You sure you don't mind?"

"I'm sticking with Oban," Hollie said. "Oban and I have just been sitting here chatting. I tidied things a bit. He's been through the *Chronicle*."

"Not much in it, though," Mr. Ironbout said. "Seems like they strip most of the words out of a newspaper these days."

"Did you happen to see Sister Ravena about the guest room?" Hollie asked.

"Yeah, the office is only open till two, so I'm glad I went over. Sister Ravena said not to worry; she'll make sure everything is cared for. We've more than a week to go, which we can extend to three if we need to. We agreed to see how it goes. That should give us time to paint those bedrooms and do some other bits up at the house."

"You know, no one's ever slept in those bedrooms," Mr. Ironbout said. "Of course, there aren't any beds, but I mean that they've never been opened up properly. There are a few little cracks in the plaster, and the paint is all gray now. Suppose it would be, after forty years. Do you want to paint the trim or just the walls?"

"I was thinking just a thin coat of varnish over the wood, a low sheen to pop it out a bit, and then a nice, soft color for the walls," Goodwin said.

"You two paint it any color you want. I'm serious about the house, you know. I want to get something written up this week. Sister Ravena said she'd arrange it. Say, she's not a bad sport. I'm glad I never hit her with any walnuts. She's an attractive sort of nun, you know what I'm tryin' to say? Kind of saintly, but a real woman nonetheless. She's got the kind of face on which age can't claw its claim.

"Now, concerning the house...like I said, I want to live there as long as I can. Of course, we've got that blasted telecom outfit, and we may need to fight 'em off. We will.

"But regarding you two, I'm serious; you're welcome to move in at any time. Don't believe Trip would mind at all. There's the back veranda upstairs you could use for a kind of living room, so you'd have your own privacy. You could come and go as you wish, back and forth from the mainland, and stay as long as you want. Move in for keeps, if you wish.

"They think I might be able to get out of here in the next few days. I could go right now, but I can't put any weight on this leg. Not used to convalescing. They say I'll need a bit of help around the place."

"We intend to be there," Hollie said. "That's why we extended our stay. We want to get you and Trip all settled back in, right, Win?"

"Certainly. We can use The Abbey van to take you up; I've already checked."

"You know, next Friday I've got a birthday. Snuck up on me, sure did. Naturally being trapped in a mirror didn't help. That's what happens when you get older. They sneak up easier. The stiffer you get, the swifter the years and deafer the ears. You know what I'm tryin' to say? Where you gonna wheel me to, anyway?"

"Win will do the wheeling, but we're going to Speaker's House, just around the corner. I'm sure you know it—the the oldest building on Estillyen."

"The old stucco-and-beam house—the old lodge or whatever it was in those days," Mr. Ironbout said.

"That's it," Hollie said.

"I was in the old place once with Leslie. It's something how that place has stood through all these years. It leans forward a good bit and to the north somewhat, but it's still standing. Wonder if it's still got those squeaky floors."

"Definitely," Goodwin said. "Every step is a creak."

"Do you think anyone will pelt me with eggs once they find out it's me, Oban Ironbout?"

"Don't be silly—these people are not like that," Hollie said. "They understand you went through hard times, suffered a great loss."

"Well, if I was me, I mean before this redeeming way got a hold of me, I'd pelt me with eggs."

"Otto, I think your pelting days are behind you," Goodwin said. "You're gonna have to leave your walnut-pitching for turkey hunting, like you were saying."

"I do believe you're right," Mr. Ironbout said. "What time is it, anyway? Shouldn't we be going?"

"It's ten," Hollie said, "and the reading is at ten-thirty. If you two gents are about ready, I'll just nip into the loo and we'll be set. It's beautiful outside. By the way, this is our eleventh reading. You know what I found out, Win?"

"What?"

"They just slip the last reading under your door in a brown envelope. I remember that fellow Davyd talking about it—how the last reading is for passing along, maybe reading to someone else."

"You can read it to Trip, like I did," Mr. Ironbout said. "So it's your last reading, you say?"

"Seems that way," Hollie said. "I can't believe it, really. Each one has given us so much to think about. What a journey. Oh, I didn't mention it earlier, but the Reader today is Writer."

"That ought to be good," Mr. Ironbout said. "After all, he's partly responsible for twisting me straight. I'd like to meet him. Imagine me wanting to meet people, and a monk at that. I must be reconstituted—redeemed, in a manner of speaking."

"Well, you've certainly been through somewhat of a transformation," admitted Hollie. "Let's go, then. Let's be early. I'll get the door, Win."

From room 107 they emerged. Hollie held the door, while Goodwin pushed Mr. Ironbout in the wheelchair. Mr. Ironbout sat comfortably, his left leg serving as a sight, a kind of plaster protrusion aligning Goodwin's navigation.

"Thanks to Hollie, my toes are not visible sticking out of this cast," Mr. Ironbout said. "She lopped off the end of this Estillyen sock with a pair of scissors. It's turned it into a kind of toe cap."

"I know," Hollie said. "I love that pattern of black-and-yellow dots. It looks like Mr. Ironbout has bees hovering around the end of his plaster cast."

Up the narrow hall the three progressed, with Hollie in the lead. Hollie reached the cobalt-blue door and opened it wide. She pressed her back against the wall and held the door firmly against the wall with her right hand. As Goodwin and Mr. Ironbout whisked by, Hollie heard Mr. Ironbout faintly say, "It's good she's thin."

"Win. Let's pause for a minute at the mural on the way out. I want Oban to see it."

"Sure, no problem; we've got plenty of time." Goodwin navigated his way to the center of the mural.

"Win, there just under the lead sheep, but back up a little more, so Oban can see the entire mural at once. That's it. So what do you think? Beautiful, isn't it?"

"I'd certainly say so," Mr. Ironbout said. "This mural has been here all along, and me loving sheep. If I'd known it, I'd a'gotten sick just to come and see it. Don't believe an amateur slapped that on the ceiling."

"There's that amazing row of sheep," Hollie said. "They wind down over the hill, through the valley, and around that mound way off in the distance, by the ocean. There's an eye, a nose, a leg, a head. On and on they go, but not a single sheep is exposed, except the one right here. I just love it. I can't get over it. They should do miniature prints and sell them."

"That's some long trail of wool, I can tell you that," Mr. Ironbout said. "I bet it'd make thousands of wool blankets. Wheel me over to the plaque, Goodwin, if you will.

"Thanks, let's see. Interesting—Uncle Art...some mystery, isn't it? Says he smoked little sweet-smelling cigarettes while sitting out on the wall. Maybe we ought to try and find some of Uncle Art's tobacco. I don't smoke, but that sounds kind of nice—could start, I suppose. You know, we're gonna have a lot of artists up on The Point in time. Wonder if they'll smoke, or if we should allow it.

"Back in Uncle Art's time, people used to smoke like chimneys. You'd board a train, and you'd think it was on fire. Everybody would be puffing away. But out on a wall, sweet-smelling and all, does sound inviting in a way."

"Not sure what kind of tobacco it was, Oban, but I'm sure we don't need it," Hollie said. "Anyway, I wanted you to see the mural. We can stop again another time. Let's go see who's around."

Within the space of three minutes, they were moving up the access ramp of Speaker's House, and in they went.

"Shucks, this hasn't changed a bit," Mr. Ironbout said. "Oh, you hear that? I love creaky floors. They speak for them that creaked 'em. Means somebody's been here before, real history in this place; means a lot of somebodies."

"Goodwin, the same two-seater we had last time is empty; let's grab it. We can pull the wheelchair right beside it. Why don't you sit next to Oban?"

"There are quite a few people milling about," Mr. Ironbout said. "Is this the way it usually is? I'm glad you two towed me along. Dear, oh dear, this is something—me sitting here, not being me anymore. It makes for a peculiar disposition being out and now in, you know what I mean, what I'm tryin' to say? Hey, my leg doesn't hurt so bad today."

"That must be the chef, you think, Hollie?" Goodwin asked.

"Must be. I don't know too many other people that would dress like that: white hat, checked pants.

"Hi there…we were just saying you must be the chef here at Speaker's House."

"Certainly, how did you know? Are you hungry? My name is Bruno; been watching over the food here for fifteen years. That attractive lady heading in our direction is the manager, Roberta. She's brilliantly bright, but don't tell her; she already knows it."

"Hello. It's good to see all of you here today," Roberta said. "Are you here for the reading?"

"Yes. I'm Hollie, this is Mr. Ironbout, and his navigator for today is my husband, Goodwin."

"Well, I'm Roberta. It's a pleasure to finally meet you, Sir—the man who resides on Estillyen's Point. You must come for lunch someday. We have a great chef," Roberta said, as she smiled and pretended Bruno wasn't there. "I love your Estillyen polka-dotted sock, Sir. It reminds me of a blouse I once owned."

"Well, that was due to my fashion consultant," Mr. Ironbout said, sweeping his arm toward Hollie. "We wanted to dress up, have our toes covered for the occasion. Never been to one of these readings."

"Oh, you'll enjoy it, I'm sure," Roberta said. "The whole idea of centering— I'm very much an advocate of it. I couldn't think of bustling through life without that stilling influence. And the Readers are great, the way they come out each summer. Who's reading today?"

"Writer," Hollie said.

"That'll be good. He's a great thinker, has a real mind for communication. That's his world. Well, I've got to dash, but great to meet you. Hope to see you again soon—do come back."

"I'd better push along, as well. If you smell loin roast headed your way, you'll know what I'm up to. This lot will be hungry before long."

"Say, it's about time, isn't it?" Mr. Ironbout said. "Wow, look how the place filled up; people sort of came out of the woodwork."

"Just a couple of minutes, Otto," Goodwin said. "That sounds good, you know—calling you Otto."

"People used to call me that when I was young."

"Hey, there's Writer, Oban," Hollie said.

"Well, he's thinner than I imagined. Bit taller than I imagined, too, and with darker hair than I suspected." Mr. Ironbout paused, tilted back his head slightly, and peered intently at Writer. "Other than that, he looks about like what I expected."

"Hello, everyone; my name is Writer. Welcome to Speaker's House, the oldest building on Estillyen. This is the center of the historical hub. The structure has always been a lodge, and at one time it was a place for small theater troupes to perform. For a number of years it has been a house where speakers speak and readers read.

"I am, of course, Writer, who writes. If I were not a writer, I wouldn't have a reading to read, and you wouldn't have a reading to hear. Now, I could write to all of you and send along my reading, but since we're all here, we might as well have a reading."

Mr. Ironbout looked over at Goodwin and Hollie with a smile. "Say, you two, I like him. He sounds kind of confused, like me."

"Before we get started, we need three volunteers for our Voice. Let me pass along this sheet; your name, please…"

As Writer found his Voice, a mature monk in a black habit slipped through the hallway door in the far corner of the room. He barely touched the partially opened door, as he extended his long arm through the doorway and unhooked the thick privacy rope, preventing public access to the hall.

The door to the darkened hall appeared stuck, partially open, as if held fast by a rise in the floor or by frozen hinges. Routinely, the intriguing monk skillfully replaced the rope, hooking the brass catch in the eye screwed on the trim of the door.

A well-worn armchair with a full-length mirror behind it was positioned immediately next to the door. Across the chair's arms, a white ribbon had been stretched, and a wallet-size piece of red cardboard was pinned to the ribbon. White letters on the cardboard spelled the word "Reserved."

Bending slowly, the thin monk removed the ribbon from the right arm of the chair and lifted it up and past the left arm before, dropping it to the floor. The ribbon remained tied to the left arm, with its note attached. The mysterious monk took his seat. His head was bald, his cheeks red, and his eyes bluish gray. It seemed that his eyes smiled but not his lips. Upon Writer his gaze was fixed.

"Ah, I see over to my far right that my good colleague, Brother Manifest, has joined us. I didn't see you slip in, Brother Manifest. Welcome. Brother Manifest will add his voice a bit later. Oh, I see he has raised one finger."

"That means we need one more voice to interact with Brother Manifest. You will be Devotee #1. I believe it is just a half dozen lines or so. A male voice is preferred; do we have a volunteer? Good…you, Sir, your name, please?"

"Chadwick Devers," said a tall man, who looked a bit shy of thirty.

"Okay, Chadwick Devers, let me pass this your way. Just look to Brother Manifest for your cue. He'll give a nod or gesture, just as I do for the Voice. Thanks.

"Well, okay, we're nearly there. Why don't we just quiet ourselves for a moment before we continue? You may choose to close your eyes, or not."

Writer stood perfectly still, with his eyes calmly shut. Light from the left side of the room rushed in across his frame and then grew faint, as it reached beyond the center point of the room. The unplanned effect gave rise to Writer's shadow, which loomed large and extended far into the room's interior, partially eclipsing Trevor and Brother Manifest.

When silence had settled, Writer said, "Good. The title of today's reading is *Let Them Go!* We'll begin with a few lines from the Acts of the Apostles. A man by the name of Gamaliel is speaking.

———•—

Let Them Go!

"Therefore, in the present case I advise you: Leave these men alone!
Let them go! For if their purpose or activity is of human origin, it will
fail. But if it is from God, you will not be able to stop these men. You
will only find yourselves fighting against God."

ACTS 5:38-39

READER: A letter written but never sent, never read—should it be called a letter? A speech drafted and tucked away, never spoken, never heard—is it truly a speech? A composition never played, never sung, perhaps swept away by fire—how is it to be described? What's to be said of the ashy notes? Is it a burnt melody, or something else?

In order for all three to be what they were intended, it seems the letter should be read, the speech heard, and the composition played. If this they're not, then something else they are. Their original intent they failed to become. They are undone, unsung, never spoken, never sent.

Similarly, a word cannot claim to be a word if it's only a thought.

VOICE: Wait! Reader, what about a word unspoken?

READER: Voice, an unspoken word is a word-thought, but it cannot claim to be a word form, without forming to be a word. I know where our mind will lead—to the Psalmist who said, "I have hidden your word in my heart." But before the Pasalmist hid it, in a form he had it.

So a word and a thought are not one and the same. Thoughts linger in the mind, intermixing, twirling 'round, overlapping, changing, and rearranging. There they stay until clothed by words. Words enable thoughts to get dressed, come out, and speak their mind. As a word, a thought is no longer indisposed, undisclosed. It has entered the world. It is a word.

Voice, I love you.

VOICE: You do?

READER: Yes, I really do. Little words linked in love expressed usually live long as thoughts before getting dressed as words. Some thoughts never get dressed and come out into the world to move about. In the mind they stay, never conveying what they'd like to say. They stay thought-bound, twirling 'round as they do.

A word must be spoken, scribbled, scribed, shouted, or something else, in order to become a word. Words are thought descriptors. They project thoughts from anonymity. They transfer thoughts into messages. Messages move the world. I know that particular thoughts expressed in words can be rather shocking to consider.

VOICE: When does a message become a message, anyway?

READER: When it leaves its origin and transfers meaning in another place. That's the mark of a message. A message may be ignored, chopped in half, accepted, or rejected, but a message it is when it conveys meaning, in part or whole. It's made a connection. It's no longer a thought in anonymity, a word wannabe. Sent forth, a message seeks the object of its intent, the reason for its ascent.

Thoughts not dressed have a distinct advantage over thoughts clothed. They can change and rearrange. Thoughts prior to expression need no audience; they bear no message. They are free to meander and mingle with personal sentiments. They can rest and revel, all in thoughtful space. They can even be forgotten.

Just the same, it's critically important for certain thoughts to get out and about—to get dressed, have their say. They find their way in saying this and telling that. They come forth in words, notes, signs, and symbols, ever flowing, ever blessing. They mingle in hearts and minds, creating thoughts of a different kind. They're sent seeking good intent. They're important.

Jesus Christ bore thoughts aplenty, which got out and about in words of good intent. Consider this, his line of words: "Do this in remembrance of me." This is a rather important line, is it not?

VOICE: What is this line "Remember me"? Isn't Christ well remembered?

READER: Yes and no, Voice, is the answer to your question. These words once spoken are a command concerning the Eucharist. It's all about remembering Christ in a particular way when his followers gather. It's a sacrament of bread and wine with meaning rich, never to be ditched or pitched around. It's a sacrament, not a game.

VOICE: Can you say just a word about this word *sacrament?*

READER: Ah, *sacrament*; it's a word borne on the wings of grace. The sacrament of which we speak flows from the throne of God. Through Christ's heart this sacrament passed before resting on his lips. Thus spoken, the sacrament is there to offer life lifted into the human sphere. This sacrament is meant to reckon with the spirit that to God has been surrendered.

That is the reason for this sacrament intertwined so mysteriously with those cherished words "Remember me." It is the sacrament partaking of Christ's body and blood. It is not remembering as in a joke, a pun, or a line for fun. It is sober, this matter of spirit reckoning unto God. Into the chalice peer. Consider your reflection in the wine, the blood. A mirror of a different kind it is. Ponder the image you bear. In this act of conviction coupled with contrition, the Spirit of God communes with the spirit of those remembering.

In the reach for relevance, it's rather astounding how easily this remembering line can be forgotten. The remembering is not remembered.

VOICE: Why? Is this not the core and the crux, the subject of the matter?

READER: Voice, that depends on how one sees the matter. There are confessors—and not just a few—who wish to follow Christ but steer clear of much ado concerning shadowy crosses and crucifixes.

It sounds strange, I know, but constituents have motives to move and manage. Listen, do you hear them speaking?

VOICE: Who?

READER: Those who choose to forget. The constituents, Voice, saying, "Steer clear of crucifixes." Listen. I hear the chatter, the clatter of busy words, thoughts flowing all about. Their rationale flows like this. Hear them speak....

> *I know, I know—we mustn't forget, but we're way on the other side of all that. We need to keep things moving. After all, it's not a draw. We're pressed to fit it in. It takes a lot of preparation, much fuss and fiddle. It happened, sure. So? Why peer at pain? Gain's the focus. Why see sorrow? We're relevant today and tomorrow. Don't spoil it with this sullen sobriety.*

Damping down the divine and the mysterious for relevance is like stealing one's own dinner. Sustenance is gone. You've robbed yourself. You go hungry; you may well starve. When the depths of pain and sorrow emerge 'round about you, there is no depth of sorrow to quiet the soul. Such affinity is unknown, unpracticed. The sacred has been eclipsed by relevance, carted off with empty laughter.

Christ never spoke of relevance. Relevant to *whom* is the question. Is it to one but not the other? Living for relevance is the pipe dream of relevance. What does it profit a person to obtain the pinnacle of relevance, only to discover that relevance can't be grasped? Grasping for relevance is like clutching a fistful of smoke. The hand is opened, but there is nothing but an empty palm.

Relevance is not an application to be sought, bought, and passed on. True relevance is a way of being. Whole lives are lived clutching for that which cannot be obtained other than by faith. Listen if you dare, Voice. Living ebbs. And, when ebb's end is near, relevance walks with backward steps. It quickly twists in search of a more fashionable subject to adorn. Relevance is always on the move, continuously morphing.

Some view relevance as garland for those "with it," adorning the movers and shakers. Listen if you dare, Voice. Dying is not moving. Yet when the movers and shakers die, relevance likes them even less. They spoil relevance, showing relevance to be vanity. At death, vanity weeps not. It leaps to carry on.

Relevance doesn't define God. God defines relevance. From antiquity we hear Gamaliel speaking lines not forgotten.

VOICE: Wait, Sir…I was with you in a respectful fashion, and now you speak of Gamaliel. Are you sure you've not intermixed your readings in your mind?

READER: Oh, no, Voice, that's not the case. Gamaliel here enters as he should, with meaning certain. I ask you, Voice, was Gamaliel aspiring to be relevant when in antiquity's present he gave his Sanhedrin speech so succinct?

Gamaliel's thoughts came forth very carefully clothed in words. In the lines we heard from Acts, he was speaking about St. Peter and the apostles. He said, "For if their purpose or activity is of human origin, it will fail. But if it is from God, you will not be able to stop these men."

Do not those words sound refreshingly real, ringing rightly as they do against pretention? Gamaliel was a notable member of the Jewish Sanhedrin. It had been assembled that day for the express purpose of questioning the apostles. This event occurred not long after Pentecost.

The Sanhedrin, it seems, was transfixed on the apostles' message, which had swiftly spread throughout Jerusalem and beyond. The Sanhedrin wanted the flow of words cut off, the messages halted, no teaching, no preaching, no words dispatched that spoke of Christ as the way to the kingdom of God.

This, however, was a proposition easier held than legislated. The apostles, you see, had been commissioned by Christ to go here, there, and everywhere, bearing his message. They were to go into the entire world, making disciples and baptizing them in the name of the Father, Son, and Holy Ghost. What Christ had whispered in their ears they were to shout from the rooftops.

So into the world with words they went. Their words spoke of Christ, the Word Made Flesh, telling all about what he did and said. The apostles' words mixed and mingled, making messages, speaking out, calling out, finding hearts and minds that would take them in and speak them out again. That's how the story spread.

Their aspirations were not timid and shy. They were high and noble. These were not men of cowering countenance. They believed their message could change the world. The origin of their message they personally knew. He's the one they followed, Jesus Christ of Nazareth. They had watched him live, die, and live again. They now lived the message he conveyed.

True to their calling, they were making enormous strides when the Sanhedrin decided it was time to rein them in. The Sanhedrin felt that there was little time to spare in getting a grip on and fettering this newfound faith. They were threatened. A line from St. Luke speaks to what they saw as they walked about, watching. "More men and women believed in the Lord and were added to their number."

The ruling elite was stunned by the popularity of this new movement and the effectiveness of its message. From towns and villages all around Jerusalem, the sick and demon-possessed were brought to the apostles. The infirm were regularly laid in the streets of Jerusalem so that "Peter's shadow might fall on some as he passed by."

Into the heart of the capitol the needy poured. Crowds swelled. Hearts and minds took in the apostles' words. The words were embraced as words eternal, originating with Christ. Jerusalem was abuzz with the news concerning Jesus Christ and this new faith. Here, there, and everywhere, miracles and wonders were happening.

Pentecost, of course, had hardly passed as a nonevent in the capitol.

VOICE: What happened?

READER: That I thought you'd know, Voice. Tongues of fire descended from heaven. People worshiped God in numerous languages. Thousands of people believed Peter's message and were baptized into this new, Christ-centered faith. It was all too much for the religious leaders.

The Sadducees were filled with jealousy over all that was occurring. They felt that everything was getting out of hand; they were losing their grip on the religious landscape. The rulers felt compelled to make a move. They decided to clamp down on the apostles in an effort to halt this newfound religious fervor.

VOICE: What did they do?

READER: They arrested the apostles and put them in jail—what else? They wanted the message bearers beaten, barred, or somehow put away. It was the morning following their arrest that the Sanhedrin assembled. The gathering comprised "the full assembly of the elders of Israel." An appearance before the Sanhedrin could result in dire consequences. These officials were ardent rulers of the Law. They breathed a kind of *habeas corpus.*

So, as it were, the elders of the Sanhedrin gathered and took their seats, ready to do business on behalf of God. When everyone was settled, the order was given to have the apostles brought from the jail. Aides were dispatched to bring the apostles. However, when they arrived at the jail, they made a surprising discovery. The guards were at their posts, the cells were locked, but there were no apostles inside. They were gone.

VOICE: Where did they go?

READER: According to the account so afforded, during the night "an angel of the Lord opened the doors of the jail and brought them out." The angel told the apostles, "Go, stand in the temple courts and tell the people all about this new life."

Do you believe in angels, Voice? At this moment standing here, I will believe you do, if that's all right with you.

Angels are cherished beings, are they not, appearing here and there at God's dispatch? *Angelos* is the word in Greek, meaning "messenger." This angel with miraculous moves had a message. He was out and about, bringing God's thoughts in words. His message concerned the apostles' message. The angel told the apostles specifically where to go and what to do. The angel distinctly mentioned "new life" in referring to the apostles' message. Not old, but new, the angel said.

This was the crux of the Sanhedrin's problem. They had little patience for a new message being shouted out, spread about, sweeping converts into a Christ-centered faith. This was the rivet in the prosecution's plank. In their eyes, Jesus Christ had co-opted and corrupted the Law. He had somehow woven a new message of grace, layered on top of the message of the Law in a way that made the two one continuous story.

The very texts to which the religious leaders clung had been incorporated, embedded, into the new-life message the apostles were taking to the world. On this point be clear: The religious elite didn't understand Christ's message. They didn't want Christ's message. They had crucified Christ in order to stop the message. They were vanguards of the old message. The hybrid message of Christ, in their eyes, was heresy. It was their duty to destroy it, so they believed.

VOICE: What happened to the apostles once they were freed?

READER: It wasn't long before they were spotted preaching near the temple. Hurriedly they were hauled into the Sanhedrin, where Gamaliel and the elders waited. The high priest of the Sanhedrin immediately railed charges against the apostles. He zeroed in on their preaching about Jesus Christ. It seems the high priest and the angel held quite contrary views.

The high priest said, "We gave you strict orders not to teach in this name. Yet you have filled Jerusalem with your teaching and are determined to make us guilty of this man's blood." The apostles were in uncharted waters. They stood accused on a rather ominous stage without a script. They were caught up in God's great drama. It was up to them to act out their parts, cast their lines.

Voice, amazing, is it not, how much attention words can receive? The words of old were bearing a new form of message. The words of the prophets could not be controlled. They were bearing witness to Christ. No longer just foretelling, the ancient texts were now attesting, confessing, and verifying what the Sanhedrin wanted so desperately to curtail.

The very texts fervently defended by the Sanhedrin suddenly conveyed their mysterious message of Christ. They clung together, attesting that Jesus Christ, God's only begotten Son, was truly the Messiah.

VOICE: Who clung together?

READER: Words—words of old spoken here and there and scrolled away—now clung together. The sacrificial system was replete with signs and symbols that Christ directly transported into his message of grace. The very purpose and reason for the message new was the message old. The old message proved that mankind could not measure up. In contrast, the message of Christ said, "I'll help you up."

Ponder it, Voice. How could this be? The words of Moses and the prophets were abetting the apostles. The Sanhedrin refused to see this ingrained, inspired dynamic of the ancient texts. In their minds something was horribly askew. They were Israelites, sons of the patriarchs. In their history was the Ark of the Covenant. No one was more word-centric than they.

The Sanhedrin desperately wanted the genie back in its flask. They wanted their words back into the scrolls and their scrolls back in the temple racks. Their words were not to be homogenized and compromised, fused into some new-life teaching.

Their cherished words, like wayward sheep, had somehow broken out and were jumping into lines evoking a different kind of message. What they saw they couldn't tolerate. On the day of Pentecost, the apostle Peter stood before thousands, weaving their cherished words into new-life lines. "Let me explain," Peter said. "These men are not drunk as you suppose; this was what was prophesied by Joel." After quoting Joel, he reached for the Psalms and some chosen words from King David.

Like Christ, St. Peter wove his message. He stitched this with that, allowing ancient texts to remove their veils and reveal their light. In the eyes of the Sanhedrin, this new expression of faith was sacrilege. They wanted the message of Christ obliterated, and when it came to words, these men meant business. For the sake of words they would surely kill.

Consider this. You must, Voice; you have no choice here today in Speaker's House. You are held captive.

VOICE: Consider what?

READER: The Temple curtain and how it was torn in two at the moment of Christ's death.

VOICE: Why consider a torn curtain?

READER: It fits the trajectory of the words that have showed up for our reading.

VOICE: Oh, I didn't know.

READER: Nothing could be more defacing for the Temple than to have its curtain torn. A chunk of mortar falling, a crack appearing—that's to be expected. The Temple curtain torn in half—that's an entirely different matter. It was like a huge gash across the Temple's face, a terrible disgrace.

VOICE: So what's to consider?

READER: Such a compelling thought, Voice, which is this: When the apostles stood before the Sanhedrin being reprimanded, was the curtain still torn from top to bottom? This question, I'm afraid, cannot be answered. Who knows?

Think, though. Let's inject a bit of supposition. More than seven weeks ensued between Christ's death and Pentecost. During Pentecost, Jerusalem was filled with visitors from various countries. On such an important Jewish festival, with so much to prepare, would the Temple curtain be left to sway in a state of disgrace? Surely pains were taken to have it meticulously repaired.

VOICE: But what's the point of this curtain interjection?

READER: It's the matter of repair.

VOICE: Repair?

READER: Yes—repairing life to normalcy, discarding the disgrace. Certain things, though, can be repaired and others not. The words of the Law and the prophets could never be sent back home, to be sealed in scrolls to stay, stowed away in Temple racks. They had been out running around, turning the world upside down. They were no longer in the Temple's possession. This the Sanhedrin did not see.

More signs and wonders these Jewish leaders did not want. The chaos of people lying all over Jerusalem's streets, waiting to be healed by Peter's shadow, all that commotion had to come to an end. The establishment wanted life normal, not life new. They longed for the days before their curtain was torn. They wanted religion, tradition, and all the privileged trappings the system availed.

Sacrifices were, after all, quite appealing to those who understood the prescribed methods and sacred intentions. The dripping of blood was no game. It was a ritual of recompense, the way of divine acceptance. The Sanhedrin leaders were the masters of this sacrificial-God connection. They held the keys. They had the knife blades sharpened. They determined the rate of exchange from blood to exoneration.

The religious elite was predisposed to the sight of dripping blood and the smell of slaughter mixed with waffling incense. Slaughter for sins absolved was not cruel; it was judicial. It was appropriate. Lambs, bulls, pigeons too, all died; all dripped their blood according to the Law. They died to aid the living—live clean, walk with gaits less burdensome.

The sacrifices were God's decree. True recompense was worth the compensation, the priestly stipend. The sacrificial arena for the Sanhedrin was—how might one say it?—thrillingly aromatic. The blood of Christ they did not understand, though their hands were sullied by it. That sullied claim they particularly hated. How dare anyone bring a message of accusation to the priests of exoneration?

The message of old, however, hadn't betrayed its minders, like bees can do their keepers. The keepers of the former message had failed to understand how words work—how they can buzz around with meaning, pollinating this and populating that. The ancient texts of Scripture, which the Israelites gathered and kept like keepers, always possessed the new-life message. It was there, embedded like honey in the comb.

Just as surely as Jesus Christ of Nazareth was transfigured standing in front of Moses and Elijah, the new-life message of Christ transfigured the old. Christ's luminous light the elite had not seen. His liberating message they had not heard. All they wanted was the Temple curtain fixed. They wanted their words in the scrolls, and the scrolls in the racks.

The Sanhedrin failed to realize that day, as they peered into the apostles' faces, that they were looking at the message. It would not go away. The message was now resident in the apostles. The chief priest was incensed that against "strict orders not to teach" it, this new message had, in their words, "filled Jerusalem."

It was the apostle Peter who courageously addressed the priest's accusation. To the charge Peter replied, "We must obey God rather than men!" Then he added, "The God of our fathers raised Jesus from the dead, whom you had killed by hanging him on a tree. God exalted him to his own right hand as Prince and Savior that he might give repentance and the forgiveness of sins to Israel."

St. Peter's message was not about relevance. It was compelling conviction that catapulted the apostle onto the stage of God's drama. His intent was pure; the origin of his message was not of man. The esteemed Gamaliel assessed the scene with prophetic insight. Precisely what he sensed, one does not know, but clearly he sensed the extraordinary.

Peter's comments infuriated the members of the Sanhedrin. St. Luke's record claims that they wanted to put the apostles to death on the spot, and they might have if not for the wise counsel of Gamaliel. This noted Pharisee stood and addressed the gathering. He asked that the apostles be removed before he spoke.

Gamaliel said, "Men of Israel, consider carefully what you intend to do to these men." He implored the council members to remember the exploits of two men, Theudas and Judas. Theudas, he said, was a figure who claimed to be somebody and had attracted some 400 followers to his cause. Theudas, Gamaliel reminded his audience, was eventually killed, and his followers fell away. That was the end of Theudas' story.

Gamaliel went on to tell of the Judas, a Galilean revolutionary who fared no better. Like Theudas, he made a bit of a stir, but he, too, was killed and his followers scattered. Gamaliel then offered this counsel: "Therefore, in the present case I advise you: Leave these men alone! Let them go! For if their purpose or activity is of human origin, it will fail. But if it is from God, you will not be able to stop these men, you will only find yourselves fighting against God."

"Let them go." This was Gamaliel's advice, and the Sanhedrin was won over. The apostles were brought back before the esteemed body and were strictly ordered not "to speak in the name of Jesus." To show they meant business, they had the apostles flogged. Oh, how the Sanhedrin's elite despised this new-life message, which the angel told the apostles to go and tell.

It's difficult to believe that Gamaliel hadn't detected the righteous ring of truth in the apostles' message. By this point in the Gospel narrative, history was building steam. Thousands of people had become followers of Christ. As the high priest testified, the city was filled with the apostles' teaching. What was happening did not bear the mark of a minor revolt. Surely, Gamaliel saw something surprising and curious at work.

In the apostles, Gamaliel saw not a show of relevance but men of deep, unswerving conviction. Gamaliel focused on the origin of their message. He argued the difference between human origin and divine origin. He said that if it was the latter, "you will not be able to stop these men." Worse still, Gamaliel cautioned, "you will only find yourselves fighting against God." Fighting against God—sullen thought, akin to embracing a lightning bolt, is it not?

The messages of Theudas and Judas were of human origin. Their intent was motivated by their own dreams and ambitions, by their own thoughts getting clothed in words. Judas led a revolt with words. Theudas, with words, claimed to be somebody. The origin and intent of Peter's message was entirely different.

Peter didn't claim to be someone with a relevant message. He claimed that Jesus Christ was the Messiah.

It's hard to imagine a special gathering of the Sanhedrin taking place—and especially the arrest of the apostles—without Satan somehow being aware of what was happening. After all, this was particularly true of Jerusalem, the spiritual hotbed of the day.

On the prowl, with a growl, Satan always is. As the apostles were being dressed down before the Sanhedrin, one can envision Satan there somewhere. Good chance he was around before the proceedings began.

Writer turned to Brother Manifest and raised his right hand.

Brother Manifest had already vacated his chair by the hallway and was maneuvering his way to the middle of the room. Writer quietly slipped onto a short bench off to his left. Manifest moved to the center of the room and positioned himself near where Writer had been standing.

He looked straight up at the banister railing and, with a commanding voice, began speaking.

LUCIFER: Say, why am I in this cave all alone, even if I commanded it to be. Where are my rotten devotees?

Lucifer was unaware that at that very instant a scout devotee approached his sentinel outside the entrance, with news that caused the chosen band considerable consternation.

SCOUT DEVOTEE: Where's Lucifer? Has he heard the apostles have been arrested?

SENTINEL DEVOTEE #1: He's in the cave, deep inside, and he gave us stringent orders.

SENTINEL DEVOTEE #2: That's right. We're to tell all the demons that he's not to be disturbed. He's working on a project. Go on in if you dare, but don't blame us if you end up as charred toast.

SCOUT DEVOTEE: I've no greater power than you two, but we're his chosen band of devotees, so don't you think we should let him know what's up? You know how he is. He's apt to smite us anyway for not letting him know the score. Besides, the Sanhedrin is liable to kill the apostles. He wouldn't miss that for anything.

SENTINEL DEVOTEE #1: Okay, I'll tell you what to do. Don't try to speak to him. Scribble your message on a bit of papyrus and crawl in facedown. He likes that. Grunt a little bit to show your strain and determination.

    When you get close enough to speak, sneeze once very quietly, like you were trying to hold back the sneeze. The sneeze will let him know you're in his presence. We'll tie a rope around your leg. If we hear him shout, we'll pull you out. Okay?

SCOUT DEVOTEE: I'm trembling—but I don't see any other choice. I'll go. Where's the papyrus? I'm just scribbling two words: "Apostles arrested." That's it.

SENTINEL DEVOTEE #2: Here, scratch out your message with this piece of coal. Hey, that's good—you learn that in the dungeon?

SENTINEL DEVOTEE #1: Stick the note in your pocket. We've got the rope. Wait—forget it! I can't believe it—Lucifer is moving towards the mouth of the cave. Don't look at him; he's stretching. Look alert.

For a few seconds, there was silence, as Manifest stood perfectly still. He coughed, then slowly turned, moved forward three steps, and halted.

LUCIFER: Hey, you three, come here! Whataya doin' with the rope—gonna hang yourself? Want to spill your bowels like Judas? Quick, you idiots! When I command, I demand. Come in here; I wanna show you something. Move it. Come on; follow me, my devotees.

    Here it is: the model. When we win this word-slinging match, like I told you, Jerusalem will be our capitol and the Via Dolorosa our central causeway. Look at this—isn't it magnificent? Don't answer. I know what you'll say.

    I've got something else real special to show you. Just to humor you, I'll let you participate by showing me how much you like it. When I unveil it, if you really like it, I want you to stretch and jump. If you don't like it, you better stretch and jump anyway, but you know I can see the real thing, right through to your motives.

    So, when I lift the veil, stretch your right arms as far as you can in the air.

Then with one eye closed, jump up and down, straight and high as you can. Keep holding your right arms up when you jump, and just keep stretching and jumping. Is that simple enough for you nitwits? While you're stretching and jumping, I'll describe it to you.

Okay, this is it; I'm pulling away the veil. Look, and don't pass out due to its beauty. You know what it is? Don't speak. Keep jumping. This will be our central park in Jerusalem, where all my devotees can freely stroll. It's Golgotha. Ah, just the sound of that name! We'll nickname it Crucifixion Park, and every day, 365 days a year, a fleshy will be crucified.

We'll keep the fleshies in open cages around the park, so the devotees can have fun tormenting 'em about their upcoming crucifixions. The cages need to be close enough to the crucifixion site so they can hear what's going on at the center of the action. So they can see their fellow fleshies being spiked.

We'll do like the fleshy book says. We'll gather up crumbs from under devotee tables and keep 'em fed. We wanna keep 'em fit for their crucifixions. There should be lots of wiggling and jerking when they're spiked. Loud screaming and shouting, not weak whimpers.

We'll tag the fleshies, one through 365. Big tags on their chests, suspended by chains around their necks. If a crucified fleshy lives for several days, it doesn't matter. We'll still raise a fresh fleshy up every morning. It will just add to the moaning, groaning, Golgotha atmosphere.

If a fleshy—let's say, number 363—lives into the new year, what we'll do is take him down. He'll get retagged as 362. When his turn comes up again, we spike him up again, but through new holes. If the fleshy can hold on for four days, he'll live to be spiked again. His new number will roll around and become 361. Now let me know what you really think. Do you like the park?

Oh, wonderful! Stretch, jump, jump. Right arms all stretched high. Jump high, not a dissenting vote. Stretch, jump. That's what I like to see. Hey, what's that bit of papyrus that popped out of your fold? Give it here; let me see. What do you mean, "Apostles arrested?" Go ahead, speak! When I command, I demand.

SCOUT DEVOTEE: Yes, Lucifer, the Sanhedrin convened a special meeting and arrested the apostles. We scribbled this for you.

LUCIFER: You fool, why didn't you say something? Let's go. Make yourselves totally invisible. Backrider, get on. Let's move, all of you. Faster, faster, faster, I tell you! We're nearly there. Lot of fleshies milling about. Quick—through the entrance!

Hey, they haven't fully assembled yet. We'll slither in and take our usual places, up in the arches.

Hmm...Hmm...I like this already. The Sanhedrin—if they get stoked, Rock and the boys will end up crucified like the Word. Only they won't spring back to life all magical-like. Then maybe the Word and I AM will simply go away and leave this galaxy to us. I'd love to build my park. Though I mustn't get too dreamy.

Look, they're calling the council to order. They're bringing 'em in—there's Rock. He is the topic of my optical force, I'll tell you that. "Hey Rock, where's your fishing pole? Better mind your nets. You're soon gonna be out of a job—or dead."

Oh, listen! Old priestly, he's letting 'em have it. That's right—strict orders not to preach. Boy, he made that clear. I certainly agree! They must be stopped. It's all deplorable. Shut it, Backrider. Don't wheeze so loud. What's wrong, you got spiritchitis?

Boy, Rock's got nerve. Go ahead, keep talking back and you'll be dead. You devotees flap your ears; let's see if we can exasperate waves in their direction. Flap 'em faster, like bees' wings—faster, I tell you.

That's it, Rock; keep talking, son. "We must obey God rather than men!" Keep going...a little more.... "Whom you had killed by hanging him on a tree..." Thatta boy, Rock! That's telling 'em. Go on; go on.... "God exalted him to his own right hand as Prince and Savior that he might give repentance and forgiveness of sins to Israel."

Brilliant—that should get you and all of 'em killed and properly crucified. The Sanhedrin is in charge of all sin-forgiving. They're not turning that over to out-of-work fishermen. We may just be witnessing a miracle of satanic proportions.

Hey, what's he doing? That's old Gamaliel. He told the guards to remove Rock and the boys. What's he talking about? Yeah, I remember Theudas. Sure, he claimed to be somebody. Did you ever hear someone say, "I am nobody, follow me"? Yeah, Judas...sure he was a revolutionary. So? You're saying, "In this present I advise you." What! You old fool! You must be the craziest fleshy that ever lived! "Leave these men alone! Let them go!"

You had 'em in your grasp, you idiot! There, stealing your sheep and our sinners, potential new devotees. You should be crucified. Hold me back, devotees. I'm ready to fling into their realm of reality and kill him. What a fool! Let 'em go? Leave 'em alone? Oh, I should pounce in there, but I can't; I better not. This is the wrong hour for Armageddon.

You blasted idiot, Gamaliel! Who do you think you are? You dirty compromiser. What, are Rock and the boys paying you to spring 'em? I've seen all the diluted fleshies throwing cash at their feet, selling homes, breaking bread. You fool! You could have had 'em dead. Let's get out of here, back to the cave. Quit flapping your ears, you idiots. It's time for me to ready my speech.

With words both humorous and haunting, Brother Manifest was most competent in delivering his unique brand of message. Soon, he paused, and without the slightest air of recognition, he began to move toward his chair. As he stepped from the center of the room, Writer reemerged.

READER: A message does not advance, like a mist rolling over the hills, into a vacuum of unbelief. Messages, one and all, navigate and gravitate to audiences. They nudge, poke, and find their way. Messages continually compete for hearts and minds, in space and time. Some are embraced, others not. A message can do nothing apart from its audience.

The heart may be convinced that all words are created equal. Spat is spot, God is and is not. It's all down to the relativity of words. Yet moisture comes in rain as well as hail. One waters, while the other beats away.

Some hearts have embraced an anemic, drought-like message that life is nothing more than threescore and ten, with perhaps a bit more sprinkled in. Beyond that, there is nothing more. How does such arsenic logic explain the divine quest humanity bears? Is it just a game? God stitched into the divine quest, but all the while intending to stay in a realm where humans never enter?

Imagine if that's how God ordained it. Human beings never truly destined to be with God, but created with the capacity to believe they will. Created delusional by design. Simple little creatures, pawns, trapped in a bizarre game called the divine quest. Cruel, is it not, Voice—such a thought, patterned in words?

Under a massive dome is the human sphere is spins round and round, and the game is lived out. The divine quest stitched within fuels great aspirations for God. The little creatures carry on with magnanimous exploits. Heavenly beings watch enthralled, placing their guesses on what happens next. It's their favorite game, divine quest.

VOICE: Say, that's rather scary!

READER: Voice, this is why the words of Christ matter as they do. This is why Christ matters. Christ's crucifixion was *not* a game. Christ was *not* simply somebody with a relevant message. His message came from his being. He was God speaking, the alpha and omega of divine verse.

Peter and the apostles were relevant because in Christ's shadow they stood. The message St. Peter and the apostles preached was in fierce competition with the messages of the day. Crowds were mushrooming. Words were lighting on hearts and minds, vying for space, taking root, pushing out words sown by other sowers.

When it came to the words of Christ, the Sanhedrin was in a true conundrum. They wanted not a letter sent. Every speech drafted, tucked away, never spoken, never heard. They wanted the new-life message to be reduced to ashy bits.

Profoundly mistaken they were. Jesus Christ was not a small-town revolutionary from Nazareth, propelled by his own words. Christ's words were not his own. He was the Son of God, with his Father's message.

On that day long, long ago, the high priest of the Sanhedrin shouted out, "We gave you strict orders not to teach in this name!" Interesting, ironic, isn't it, Voice?

VOICE: What's interesting, ironic?

READER: The high priest has no name; that's what. He is anonymous: a furious priest, puffed up. A puff of wind he was, a shouting voice. His name is never spoken. He's anonymous.

Words matter…they abide; they reside. Upon them your faith is perched.

"For if their purpose or activity is of human origin, it will fail. But if it is from God, you will not be able to stop these men; you will only find yourselves fighting against God."

GAMALIEL, JERUSALEM, CIRCA AD 32

The applause from the audience was immediate and enthusiastic. To Hollie and Goodwin's surprise, Mr. Ironbout shouted out, "Bravo, bravo!"

Around the room, back and forth, the discussion flowed. Relevance appeared to be a rather hot topic.

"I'm afraid our time has slipped away. Thanks so much for coming to the reading. God bless you all."

No one was quick to move along. Eventually, though, the crowd started to thin, and Writer walked over to greet Mr. Ironbout. He was joined by Brother Manifest.

"I'm truly delighted you were able to join us, Mr. Ironbout," Writer said. "Everyone is aware you live up on The Point, but we haven't had the opportunity to get to know you."

"How could you? I chased everyone away with flying walnuts!" Mr. Ironbout said. Everyone chuckled.

"So, how's your leg doing?" Brother Manifest asked.

"Better. That walnut tree got back at me for chopping it up. It's what I called the appendage—long story, really.

"We were holding back hoping to say a word, Writer," Mr. Ironbout continued. "I just wanted you to know how much I appreciated your words today, as well as the message that got passed my way called *Remember Me*. Maybe someday you can come up to The Point."

"I'd like that, and thanks for your kind words."

"And you, Brother Manifest—that Lucifer is some fellow," Mr. Ironbout said.

"Yes, I never thought I would be speaking for Lucifer, but there you are," Brother Manifest said. "He even has a prepared speech."

"You mean Lucifer?" Goodwin asked.

"Sure enough," said Brother Manifest. "I think I actually have a spare copy in my case, if you'd like it."

"Definitely," Goodwin said.

With that, Brother Manifest excused himself. He said he'd leave a copy of the speech at the front desk in an envelope.

For a good ten minutes, Hollie, Goodwin, and Mr. Ironbout sat talking with Writer. He learned more of the trio's story. Mr. Ironbout told Writer about the night he sipped scotch, read for Trip, and danced a step or two to *Tunes Spun*. Writer began to see more clearly how it was that Oban Ironbout ended up at Speaker's House, as a most surprising face in the crowd.

The final word from Mr. Ironbout was: "Hollie tells me we're gonna have a birthday party, Friday next up at The Point. Think you might be able to come along? We could do with a writer."

Writer looked at Mr. Ironbout and said, "We'll see; you never know. It sounds like fun."

TWENTY-ONE
The Speech

Front Desk, Speaker's House, 22:35 Greenwich Mean Time, Isle of Estillyen

"Hey, Harris, I'm about outta here," Clive said. "You're looking at one tired bookings manager. On reading day there's always a lot of activity and extra things to look after. Good day, though."

"Yeah, sure, and now it's so quiet around here tonight you can hear the guests dreaming," Harris said.

Harris noticed the item on the desk. "What's this envelope with 'The Speech' scrolled across it?"

"Don't know—been here all day. Why don't you open it up; there's no name on it. It's just been lying here on the counter."

"I like these old string-looped envelopes; you don't see 'em much anymore. It's just a document—no note, card or anything. It's titled *The Speech*."

"Why don't you make yourself a cup of tea and read it? You've got nothing better to do. It's not addressed to anyone. Maybe you can find out who it's for... a clue. It's a mystery."

"Yeah, tea sounds good. I need to stay awake. See ya."

"Tomorrow," Clive said.

At 23:05, Harris sat down in the old red-leather swivel chair behind the front counter of Speaker's House. He placed his cup of tea on the desk, took a quick glance in the mirror above, leaned back, and welcomed the firmness of the wooden armrest.

Harris took a sip of tea and removed the typed pages from the manila envelope. This is what he read.

DEVOTEE NUMBER ONE: Is he ready to come in yet? Everything in the Cave is ready.

DEVOTEE NUMBER TWO: I think soon. He's been outside the entrance pointing like that for well over an hour.

His first point was down. He uses his right arm, and his mighty pointing finger. I saw him start a while ago. He stood straight, not moving a centimeter, for a matter of minutes. Then, ever so swiftly, he raised his arm in a high, swooping motion. With the speed of a diving phoenix, his arm fell in a rigid, fixed position. It looked like a massive lance. Slowly his pointer finger uncoiled and became as rigid as a dagger's blade. It looked like a spike. There he stood, fixed and pointing at the earth.

He held that position for precisely fifteen minutes. His entire frame was as rigid as granite. When minute fifteen expired, he drew his arm to his side and, without the slightest pause, shot it straight up to the heavenlies. Again, he held his rigid, granite-like position. Next, he pointed straight ahead of him, then to his right and left. Now, as you can see, he's pointing straight into the cave. That must mean he's about ready.

Oh, watch it. He's dropped his arm. He's headed towards us. He told Backrider yesterday, one take and one take only. Be perfectly silent, still. He's moving to the microphone.

LUCIFER: Umm, umm. One, two, three; it is me! This is Lucifer speaking.

By way of every wavelength that can wave, every current that can circuit, I am marshaling this historic, unprecedented speech to you. It is I, and the full measure of my satanic cast has been conscripted to reach as far as reach can reach.

All those who this instant hear the intonations of my voice, know this, and know it sure. Where you are is where you are. Wherever that is, you are there. That's right. You are where you're meant to be. You've been reached. You are my audience; I am your voice. My message and I are one. You are my reception. Together we are meaning.

This is Lucifer speaking! Bind your minds. Twist your souls for dutiful, precise reception. This is one speech you cannot receive in fuzzy spurts. This day you will always cherish: the day infamy of the divine order compelled Lucifer to speak out, enunciate, elucidate. No holding back, I've come to set the record straight.

My words speak of the future far. You will not tumble and roll in the abyss forever. You will not forever languish in the netherworld. No, quite the contrary—you will rule with me. Where I am is where I am, and one day you will be with me instead of where you are, wherever you are.

This is Lucifer speaking, speaking, speaking. Say to yourself, I'm listening, listening, listening. Do it in triplicate like I did. Oh, I feel the rush, like billions and billions of bats swarming, rushing by, imparting strength.

I do not use that fleshy word that starts with a *T* and ends in *anks*, but if I did, this is the one time in all eternity when I would use it. Instead, let me say flutteration, flutteration, flutteration, a thousand times, flutteration.

Now, in honor of what I mean to you and you to me, I call for thirty seconds of silence before Lucifer proceeds. In just a second, throughout all constellations, every demon must pause, and for thirty seconds breathe. My personal Backrider will softly tap his nose against my microphone, keeping time.

When I say the word *now*, kick your heads back, stretch out your arms to your sides, and breathe. Let's breathe in unison the breath that binds. Breath to breath, path to path, death to death—may we be one in bond of brutality. I command you. I demand you. Silence. Now breathe.

Twenty-seven, twenty-eight, twenty-nine, thirty; this is Lucifer speaking. Do you hear me—the unmistakable thunder of my voice, that satanic intonation, reverberation? Do you feel the power of my words pulsing through your spirits? That imparting pulse, that tingle—that's the satanic signal.

This is Lucifer speaking! To all demons and devotees, wherever you are, whether in the depths of the netherworld, the far reaches of the abyss, or in the murky cradle of possessed souls, hear this: You are not alone. Lucifer is with you in spirit.

I am with you. I am by your side. I have seen your rejection, your dejection, your heavenly ejection, and I'm here to tell you, I've heard enough about these so-called never-fading words. Hear me clearly, without saintly delusion. You are the object of this satanic cast; you are my forecast, my reason to last. You are my past and my everlast.

I shall start my speech where those less wise would end. This is the end now, at the beginning. Listen! We shall win! We shall win! We shall win! Do you hear me? We shall win!

Why do I choose to speak of the end at the beginning? I'll tell you why. This is both the end of the beginning of what I AM began and the beginning of the end of I AM's rule. My voice now speaking testifies it. So it shall be.

The words now departing from Lucifer's lips will not be lost in the abyss, the netherworld, or any other world until they have whirled and swirled the hearts of those for whom they were intended. They're sharp like daggers. They gnaw like teeth of viperfish. They shall not return unto me void. They'd better not. They will thrash, dash, and clash with those so-called never-fading sort.

I come to you not with thick, stupid tablets of stone carved with claws. I come to you not with pithy parchment rolls penned by disgruntled prophets. I come to you not by some circuitous route of words penned by fleshy nuts believing they're inspired.

I come to you resonating, pontificating, pearlicating. I am my own parliament of pearlification. The pearls I cast will always last. Take them in; let 'em culture. This is my voice you hear. This is Lucifer speaking.

Mine is the ultimate voice. Do not your hearts burn within you as I speak? Let 'em burn with passion and lust for a new kind of order. Together we shall pearlicate our words before a world of fleshy swines. Hold the applause; hold the applause.

Now, listen very carefully. We've got work to do, constellations to save, a commission to halt. You must become as wise as owls and as harmful as serpents. The fields are ripe for thrashing, and we must thrash.

I now turn to the heart of my subject. If you still have your heads kicked back, kick them back even further. Stretch your arms further, further, wider, wider. Let yourselves kink with pain. You will not soon forget this day. The more you kink, the better you slink.

In the fleshy operating manual, I AM has said, "Is not my word like fire—and like a hammer that breaks a rock in pieces?" I am here to tell you that it is I AM himself that is breaking to pieces. He is coming unglued, falling apart. He's off his rocker. He needs to be in his rocker. The One, the Ancient of Days, is fading. It's up to us to rescue what he has set in motion.

Let me come to the salient points of this satanic castigation. In so doing, I shall lip some of my hypothesis in the form of questions.

Here's the first question. If I AM has gone so far as to kill his son, the Word, over fleshies, what hope does this avail for the spirit world? I AM is lost, and when I AM gets lost, planets start to wobble; stars disappear. There is no telling what will happen.

Now the first point: Fleshies are a failed experiment. I proved that in a satanic wink. I didn't make 'em. Nobody asked me. It was down to the three: I AM, the Word, and the Third. They got together and worked themselves all up—a world with a moon, sun and stars, wolves and wolverines. Sure, it's got its creature appeal, but big deal.

Here's the deal—why would a God that has the responsibility of being God commit suicide for fleshies? God should be cosmos ruling, reigning, not be getting spiked on a cross and dying. I AM just got way too involved. He got in over his head. Who's looking after the constellations?

I AM put all of his eggs into the fleshy basket. God dying for fleshies—and they make me sound barbaric for sticking up for Baal and fleshy sacrifices. Why didn't I AM just admit the fleshy experiment went awry and give it another try? His creative intentions got the best of him. He already had spirits in the spirit world. No, he was not satisfied.

Creating Adam and Eve, he should have stopped at soul and mind. Not him—he had to breathe into Adam the spirit of life and will. He set eternity in their hearts. What a mournful, gloomy day that was!

Listen, I alone, I alone, was there to see that look of wonder in Eve's eyes when I told her she could be like I AM. That's what I AM made—a God-wanter. Oh, that creature spirit look she had! She looked like an eagle ready to strike a salmon's belly. Her eyes got transfixed on the horizon. Nothing would have changed her mind.

That was it. That's what I saw. Eyes full of destiny. I'll be I AM, and there they were fresh out of the mud. What was I AM thinking, creating such fleshy beings? I was just checking her out, thought I'd do I AM a favor and test his prototype. How was I to know he'd be so serious, come up with some grand redemption plan, and get the Word crucified? I wash my hands of it.

Since I AM was the one that put the eternal spirit in Adam and Eve, he simply couldn't bring himself to exterminate them. Without question, that's precisely what he should've done. Rain fire down on Adam and Eve; let 'em curl. That would've been it—end of story. No story; no fleshies. Oh, how much better the environs would have been, fleshy-free.

Point two: I AM, the Word, and the Third have got this "Remember Me" thing going. They've called on all fleshies to form into little cells and remember the Word, who was crucified. Every time they get together, they're supposed to recite certain words the Word taught and then drink his blood and eat his flesh.

Do you see the mire of delusion they've created? The divine became so intertwined with fleshies that the Word put on skin. Now they want fleshies to pretend they can somehow go on eating the Word's flesh and drinking his blood.

Now, here's the point. I don't understand how that all works. That's down to them. I do know this ritual is at the very heart of all this new order. Therefore, we must do everything we can in our power to get in their midst—fraternize, patronize, deharmonize, and damp down this "Remember Me" thing.

Get it shelved—that's your role. Get out there and start coalescing, possessing; get fleshies reassessing. You know how fickle fleshies are. That's the nature of flesh. That's another thing, but I'll not go there.

Oh, okay, one little quip of my whip. If you want spirit and truth, why do you start with mud? We weren't made that way. Okay, I can't let myself get drawn off my speech. I just can't help myself sometimes…I'm so passionate for the future of the constellations, the vast abyss, and all that is.

Do everything in your power to get fleshies to forget "Remember Me." This is Lucifer speaking. From before before and after after, there has never been a power to equal my omnipotence. The day of cowering is over. We shall use our power.

Work on the fleshies like I did Eve. They can easily be pulled off center. It will dizzy up your eyes. But be stalwart, like me. Look to me, and follow me like I follow me. The words I impart are clearly my own. You can dress 'em up to look like the Word's, but underneath they hold the power to destroy. Just go for that Eve look—that look of false promise, of popularity, of populace, of possession.

This is my third and final point: They've got this hepped-up notion of going here, there, and everywhere throughout the entire world, making devotees and starting these "Remember Me" cells. I've heard enough. They must be stopped, dropped. We need some new dark ages.

What Word sneezed on his disciples in private, they are to cough from the rooftops. The Third even came streaming down and set fire on the heads of a whole group of fleshies. The Third is supposed to help the Word's core band to remember everything the Word taught 'em.

This is the deal. Listen: This is Lucifer speaking. The Word is the center of this whole trumped-up enterprise. He's the one who is supposed to be remembered. It's the Word's words the Third is to bring to remembrance. It all revolves around the Word. Anyone who is for the Word is against us.

So, what do we do? We do anything and everything that is possible to undermine the Word's words. With me, the impossible does not exist. I've never seen it. I don't know it.

The following principle you must embrace for your quest to coalesce: Everyone who is against the Word is for us. That's it. It doesn't matter who it is or what they say. As long as they're against the Word, they are speaking our language.

Just recently, right here in Jerusalem, I heard with my own satanic ears one of the old order priests ripping into the one they call Rock. By the way, Rock is a kingpin. The old-order priest was gonna kill Rock and his comrades for even speaking about the Word. That's the kind of help we need—fervent, fleshy help. In this topsy-turvy world of the new order, even the old order can be of use.

What is your aim, your strategic intent? Coalesce, conceal, and reveal that which is not as if it were. Any nutcase fleshy that develops some hocus-pocus doctrine, get him press, give him praise. That's the talk to use with fleshies.

Above all, you are to flutter words. I command it. I demand it. Yes, you heard me: Mix and match, this with that, do for don't, will for won't. It doesn't matter; just flutter. Flood the world with words, images, and sounds that draw away, steal away, and carry away—anywhere but in the Word's direction.

As you can well imagine, I, Lucifer, have unbelievable powers of foreknowledge. What will be, I already see, long before it's meant to be. On the horizon, far beyond the dim candlelight, I see a day when fleshies will invent ways to pass along words like schools of darting fish passing bits of food.

This is the way those divine-sparked fleshies will advance. This will be one of our finest hours. In those days, this will be that; that will be this. Fleshies will get disoriented, not knowing who to believe about what. Meaning will be in the eye beheld.

Like the oceans deep, the world will flood with words, images, and sounds. This tight grip of old ancient words will lose its stodgy appeal. In the flood of the words to come, the Word and all this "Remember Me" stuff will sink.

Oh, I can feel it, see it, adore it…pure plethora; the freedom to choose the fate of one's wordy world without rejection. That is so right, so much the way it should be.

Come here, my chorus of devotees. Step up to the mic with me, you three. Unrehearsed, and unannounced, let's let our tones tunnel out to Netherworld and beyond. Clear your thoughts, devotees…hmm…together now…

Happenstance and chance. Flow and flap.
Say what you wish and will, old chap.
Mix up your words. Swirl 'em around;
Don't get precise when you jot them down!
A tiddle here, a diddle there. Snip 'em up and pitch 'em in the air.

Oh, what a wordy mix! Oh, what wondrous prose!
Meaning on the run…all homespun.
That's how wordy mixes should be done!

A t here, an i there; dot 'em, cross 'em without the slightest care.
Strike this, slash that; your aim is confetti, like graffiti.
Fetch yourself a broom. Sweep 'em in a pan.
Then, shake 'em all about; and pour 'em out.
They're sure to spell out what life's all about.
Oh, what a wordy mix! Oh, what wondrous prose!
Meaning on the run...all homespun.
That's how wordy mixes should be done!
Chat, chat chat.
Hack, hack, hack.

Devotees, go on over to the corner, now, as I close this momentous speech. If you will, hum ever so softly, as we get ready to snip this wave.

Audience, believe me, things are moving in our direction. You know why? Because my plethora is the way of right, not this bound-up bunch of parabolic jumble.

So I command you. I demand you, my dear devotees: flutter, flutter, flutter! Confusion is our strength, the core of our calling. What's right, we'll set wrong, and in so doing, wrong will be right.

I AM has lost it lingering with those fleshies. If I knew how, I would feel sorry for him, but I do not possess such traits. What a mess fleshies have caused, siphoning off attention from the spirit world. Never mind—soon they'll be ours.

Let me end where I began. We shall win! We shall win! We shall win!

This is Lucifer speaking. Over and out!

Oh, um, by the way, you can straighten up your heads now and drop down your arms.

Goodnight.

Front Desk, Speaker's House, 23:01 Greenwich Mean Time, Isle of Estillyen

"Hi, Harris," said the night watchman as he approached the front desk. "I see Clive's off. Not much need for security strolls tonight; been all around Speaker's House and up the paths. Birds are all asleep, nestled in nests, chest to chest. Got anything interesting to read?"

"I'm not sure you would believe it," Harris said, somewhat bewildered. "In fact, I'm not sure I believe it myself. Have you ever heard a tune that starts: *Happenstance and chance. Flow and flap...?*"

TWENTY-TWO
The Party

"Well, hi there, Sister Ravena. I saw you pulling up. Welcome to the Ironbout home on The Point, or as Goodwin likes to call it, *My Cottage Rare*.

"Great to see you, Hollie! I believe you met Roberta Nan at Speaker's House."

"Certainly. It's good to see you again. Ooh, I love your jacket."

"Thanks, I picked it up the other day. It's linen. Thought it'd be nice for the party. It's great to see you, as well. It's breathtaking up here! Magnificent views; you can see out across the whole of Estillyen."

Just then, Trip came bounding around the corner.

"Don't worry, he's gentle," Hollie assured them. "He's been around back with Goodwin. Win's been at it all day, hacking, cutting, and stacking wood.

"Stay down. Sit, sit. That's it. Good boy. Go on, get your ball.

"Sorry—he's a very active dog. He's always carrying something; he'll drag anything up on the porch.

"And yes, Roberta, it really is lovely up here. From the bottom of the trail, the elevation rises more than 600 feet. You don't realize what a difference it makes until you're up here and looking out across the meadows. What a blessing.

"Did you have any trouble on the back road?" Hollie asked.

"No, none at all," Roberta said. "I wouldn't want to try it on an icy day, over that Estillyen stone. But on a sunny day like this, it's brilliant."

"I didn't know it was called Pilgrims' Point Road. Oban mentioned it. He knows so much about the history of Estillyen. By the way, he's inside, resting. He was so thrilled to get back up here last Friday. Hard to believe it's already been a week."

"I see that the porch winds around to the side," Sister Ravena said.

"Here, let me show you," replied Hollie.

"Trip, go on, get your ball. That dog never quits running. He noses that old ball around like he's playing soccer.

"This leads to the side garden," Hollie continued. "Let's take a few steps out on the lawn. I want to show you this. See back in the far corner? That's the plot with the three markers Oban was talking about."

"What a story!" Sister Ravena said. "That has to be the tree that had the 'appendage.' That's what Mr. Ironbout called the limb that nearly killed him, Nan. His turnaround is remarkable, you know. I was telling Nan about it on the way up."

"Everyone is so amazed when they hear the story," said Roberta. "Some honestly can't believe it. How is he doing emotionally, Hollie?"

"It is, as you say, truly amazing. By the way, do you like to be called Nan or Roberta?"

"Either. To Sister Ravena, I think I've always been Nan. My friends use both."

"Well, I could muse about it, but I like to say Ravena and Roberta, so if that's okay with you, Roberta Nan, I'll go with Roberta," Hollie said.

"Great," Roberta said.

"Yes, the limb stretched all across the side, right up to where the plot is. There used to be a heavy black chain draped in between those short little posts. The posts were black like the chain. Goodwin painted them that dark forest green. That's the first thing he did. We've transplanted some ivy in around the posts and kind of looped it through; it will eventually become a short ivy wall. Mr. Ironbout said he likes it. 'More agreeable,' as he put it.

"It's all such a fascinating story. I think I've gone a bit wacky over all that has happened. We came to Estillyen to take a spiritual retreat and consider our next moves, and suddenly we've been swept up into a whole new world. There's a lot of change to absorb.

"Anyway, Oban—he's remarkable. I'd only met him the one time before all this occurred. I've heard a lot of stories. To me, he's like a man who has returned home from the war. He's gone through a great deal, but now the war is over.

"He still has that clever, humorous way of speaking. But there's a warmth and gentleness in his tone now that I'm told was not there before. I'm confident that he's truly a changed man. He and Goodwin are amazing. Now that we know the full story, did you notice how much Goodwin actually resembles him, Sister Ravena?"

"I did," she said. "When Mr. Ironbout shocked us at the infirmary with his revelation, I saw it instantly. I hadn't before, but when he came out and said he was Goodwin's grandfather, it was so apparent. The strong chin bones, the brown eyes, Goodwin's curly hair. Even though Mr. Ironbout's hair is thinner and receding, you can see so many similarities."

"Yes, and they're really getting along so well, as if they're trying to make up for lost time. Goodwin's talking about maybe building a small cabin over on the north side of the house."

"Really?" Sister Ravena said.

"Yes, there's a nice area set back a good way from the main house. From that side, you can hear the ocean waves rolling over the rocks at the bottom of the cliff. The cabin would be all tucked away. It wouldn't affect the appearance of the main house at all.

"The idea, if we actually go for it, would be to stay there part of the time. Maybe Mr. Ironbout could use it later on, or maybe it could even be something for visiting artists, we're not sure. Anyway, Win and Oban have been talking and sketching, like they were building the most important building on Estillyen.

"I certainly see where Goodwin gets his architectural bent. Oban is very gifted. When we go inside, you'll see the craftsman style, the detail. Those support beams—or whatever you call them—up under the eaves; he made all of those by hand.

"Anyway, let's go in and get some tea. It's almost four, and everyone should be here around five-thirty. I can't believe Oban hasn't had a birthday party since before his wife died over forty years ago."

"Who have you invited?" Sister Ravena asked.

"Well, you two, of course, and Epic, Saga, Narrative, Story, and Plot. That's one, two, three, four, and Plot makes five. Oh, Drama and Writer, too—that's it. That's the seven, and they're all coming."

"Good. I'd have been disappointed if they couldn't make it," Sister Ravena said.

"Then there's Mr. Statter, Sharron from the infirmary, young Catherine the researcher, and a gentleman who owns Morton's Iron Mongers in the village; Goodwin invited him when he was down there a couple of days ago. Win said he looked at him in utter disbelief. We also included Chelsea and Rita, the two aides that were so helpful looking after Oban. I think that's it. Oh, and the girl at Fields and Crops, Antonia—she's bringing the ice cream. I told her we definitely wanted her to stay for the party."

"Were you able to bring the cake?" Hollie asked.

"A Bruno's special—Nan saw to it," Sister Ravena said.

"Perfect; cannot *wait* to try it. Let's go on in now. I've been able to straighten up the downstairs area a bit for the party, but things have been a mess upstairs. They've just finished painting the upstairs bedrooms. Sadly, the rooms have never been used. Beautiful rooms, too, with views. They were for the twin boys.

"There are triple windows in each room. You can see the bedroom on this side. See how the three windows are perfectly centered? An identical room is across the hall. Beautiful hardwood floors and trim; it just needed paint and an airing out.

"Whatever is done to the house, the understated character just emerges. It's a real classic. Please, come on in. Oban should be rustling around. He's been sleeping in the study on a small bed. He calls it Trip's bedroom.

"By the way, thanks for having those cots sent up; they're great. We've got them in the upstairs sunroom that faces the back. It's a perfect room, the width of the house. It would be cold in winter, but now it's splendid."

"Not a problem," Sister Ravena said. "Keep them as long as you need them."

"Oban, of course, knows we're having the party, but he doesn't know the Readers will be here. He thinks it's just a few people."

"Just a second—let me get the cake; it's in the backseat," Roberta said.

"I'll help," Sister Ravena said. "Let me have the flowers and the small box, too."

Roberta opened the right rear door, retrieved a small pale-green box, and handed it to Sister Ravena. Next she passed along the flowers.

"Please, let me carry those," Hollie said. "They're beautiful."

Roberta reached into the car again. Using both hands, she carefully lifted out a large white cake box. On the top of the box was a round red label that read, "Kitchen of Speaker's House." With a graceful, leaning motion and a little shove of her right hip, Roberta managed to shut the car door.

"I should have taken your purse," Hollie said. "Your purse looks like a very petite doctor's satchel. What's in the small box?"

"A mini cake, compliments of Bruno," Roberta said. "Bruno said we were to have a bite as soon we arrived with the cake. Sister Ravena is my witness. It's some kind of tradition in his family."

"Let's go, then. I can't wait!" Hollie said enthusiastically, as she opened the screen door. Roberta entered, followed by Ravena. "Just make a right across the hall and on into the kitchen."

"I see what you mean about the house; it has such nice lines," Sister Ravena said.

"That's certainly Oban's architectural style. He's not keen on fuss and frill. I just love the living room, with its coffered ceiling and stone fireplace," Hollie said. "Come on into the kitchen."

"This kitchen's so charming," Roberta said. "Everything looks so well-built."

"Please, just set the boxes on the table. I'll stick these yellow roses in some water. They're beautiful. Oh, look at the dishes I found in the back of the cupboard. They're for the party—aren't they perfect?"

"Very nice," Roberta said.

"When I saw them all stacked up in the cupboard, I thought they were just clear glass saucers, but they're iridescent, and each saucer has this neat swirl. I like the size; it's just right for the cake and ice cream."

"I think those might be a bit rare," Sister Ravena said. "There's no telling where Mr. Ironbout picked them up."

"They look so perfect with the blue tumblers. I really like short, heavy glasses like that. As you can see, the cups and saucers are random colors. There are six red, four green, and four chocolate-brown. The rest are patterned. The solid-colored ones are all white on the inside. Makes the tea taste better, don't you think?"

"Definitely," Sister Ravena said. "You can see what you're sipping."

"Oh, I almost forgot the greatest news of all," Hollie said, as she slapped her forehead with her palm."

"What?" Sister Ravena asked, intrigued.

"Well, of course you wouldn't have known it, but for months Source Telecom has been pressing to have a judge review the ownership of The Point. Some distant relative of Mr. Ironbout's was claiming he was told The Point was his."

"Really!" said Sister Ravena.

"Yes, pretty serious stuff. It seems that years ago Oban misplaced the deed that proved his ownership of the property. He wasn't overly fussed about it—until Source Telecom started making moves.

"He searched high and low for the deed, but found nothing. He was even thinking one of the dogs might have snatched it and carried it outside, where it disappeared.

"Then, this past week, the painters were taking out the shelves in the closet in the upstairs bedroom and came across an old brown envelope. One of them brought it to Goodwin and said, 'Don't know if this is important…'

"Goodwin immediately knew what it was. Oban had told him all about how he'd lost the deed—and had described the envelope in detail. All that searching, and it was there all along. It had slid off the top shelf, down behind the wide support moldings. Had been there for years."

"Well, amazing…" Sister Ravena said.

"When Goodwin took the envelope to Oban, you can't believe how he whooped and hollered. Started singing…."

"So, isn't that great?" Hollie said.

"I'll say, wonderful news," Sister Ravena said.

"I bet he's so relieved," Roberta said.

"Amazingly so," Hollie said.

"Even more of a reason to have a party today," said Sister Ravena.

"I know…and I could go on talking about it, but we have guests coming soon," said Hollie. "Let's get the finishing touches on this celebration.

"For the cake, I'm planning to cut it at the table and then have everyone circle through the kitchen to pick up their ice cream and tea. Antonia and the girls can dart around with the pots and retrieve the plates. It's simple, but nice.

"So let's see the cake. I like these boxes that fold down on the sides. You don't have to struggle lifting out the cake. Great—it's got one of those stiff foil liners on the bottom. The foil looks so festive the way it sticks out around the edges of the cake.

"Ooh, it's beautiful! 'Happy Birthday, Mr. Oban Otto Ironbout'—perfect."

"It is simple and lovely, isn't it?" Roberta said. "Hollie, which way is the loo?"

"Just down the end of the hall on your right.

"Yes, and I'm going to put forty-one candles on this, one for each year without a birthday party," said Hollie. "Let's follow that Bruno edict and have a taste. Come here, little green box. We'll all have a sliver, right?"

"Sure—I'll be right back, two seconds," Roberta said.

"No need to ask me," Sister Ravena said. "This is really a nice place up here, Hollie. It's everything I thought it would be. What's transpired is hard to believe. All those years he was up here alone, and then you and Goodwin came along."

"I know," Hollie said. "It seems like a fairy tale in a way. I'm trying not to over-analyze it; instead I'm just going to accept it and let life unfold. Hopefully, I'm getting better at that.

"I'll go ahead and put these on the saucers. Nice, look at those layers. You can see how moist the cake is, such a deep yellow."

"Bruno will have put something in it, probably a hint of rum, and no doubt it's made with fresh butter," Roberta said, as she reentered the kitchen from the hall.

"That's exactly how I wanted the filling to look between the layers: clear, with pieces of fresh lemon rind mixed with tiny bits of bing cherries. Mmm, here goes," Hollie said.

"Well?" Roberta asked.

"It's delicious," Hollie said.

"Totally scrumptious," Sister Ravena agreed.

"Magnificent! Bruno's a true chef," Roberta said. "This white, creamy icing reminds me of something I had as a little girl. It's made with egg whites. For this cake, that's a lot of egg whites. And the shredded coconut is perfect. It's exactly as it should be. The coconut has to be fresh, shredded very fine and not sweetened."

"Thanks so much for bringing it," Hollie said. "Hey, I've something else to show you two. It's just in the sewing room."

Hollie led Sister Ravena and Roberta down the hall and entered the first door on her right.

"Quick, come in. We need to be quiet," Hollie said. "Oban's in the room across the hall."

Hollie gently shut the door. On the far side of the room, a midsized oil painting rested on a wooden easel in front of a tall, slender double window. The painting was positioned perpendicular to the window.

"This is my birthday present to Oban."

"Oh, Hollie, it's beautiful...it's the tunnel at Three Pond Cottage!" Sister Ravena said. "So amazingly well done. Good work, Hollie. Though I'm not surprised."

"It's very, very nice," Roberta said. "I had no idea you were such a talented artist. That's truly magnificent."

"Thank you both; that's very kind. Goodwin is giving Oban his sketch. Oh, I don't think you've actually seen it. It's here propped up on the chest. I just love the primitive look of that old chest. It's painted pine.

"This is the sketch that started this whole saga, *My Cottage Rare*. Goodwin drew it as a child, from a photo taken by his grandfather, Raleigh Macbreeze, when Raleigh used to visit Estillyen. That was the only grandfather Win knew until the shock of Oban's confession."

"So this is the sketch Goodwin had with him when Mr. Ironbout tried to run him off?" Roberta asked.

"Yes, right. Sorry, I should have been a bit clearer," Hollie said. "On that first visit, Goodwin left the sketch behind with Mr. Ironbout. Win said Oban went up on the porch, sat down, and just stared at it, sort of dazed. Of course, at that point, Goodwin didn't know it, but Oban knew he had just seen his grandson for the first time, as he pieced together all that Goodwin had told him.

"Yes, that's this house. Mrs. Ironbout—Leslie—was still alive at the time, and she's captured in the sketch. It's a fascinating story how Goodwin came here so unknowingly, yet almost feeling as if he were following a call. If he hadn't been so keen on finding this mystery house, we would never have known the truth about Mr. Ironbout—and none of this would have happened.

"Oban has obviously seen the sketch—and also the painting—so I thought that instead of wrapping them, I'd just place them on the sideboard at a convenient moment. I like this new frame Win got for the sketch."

"What's your painting called?" Sister Ravena asked. "Why don't you describe it for us?"

"Okay," Hollie said, as she placed Goodwin's sketch back on top of the pine chest and stepped over in front of her painting. "Well, as you can see, it's clearly a tunnel, and I'm walking through it. I'm somewhere near the middle, moving toward the pond in the meadow in the background.

"I'm drawn toward the pond and its glow. No one else is present in the painting. There are no ducks on the pond or anyone milling about. It's just the moonlight shimmering on the silent ripples of the pond. With no one present, it gives the impression that the hour is late, like midnight or beyond.

"Obviously I'm wearing my orange raincoat. As you can see, my collar is slightly turned up, and my hands are in my coat pockets. A few inches above my knees, my black jeans emerge from the raincoat.

"I appear in no great rush, nor am I just ambling along. The length and angle of my stride indicate the pace. My left leg is not overstretching, but it is extended. My foot conveys a sense of determination in my walk. The heel of my dark green flat is touching the pavers, and the light under my sole underscores the slight upward angle of the foot. I'm moving along. I have a destination.

"Since you can only see me from behind, you can't be certain where I'm looking, but the position of my head indicates that I'm looking in the direction of the pond. There's intention in my walk. The tunnel is a confined space. I'm moving towards that which is not confining, something defining…something expansive and unrestricted.

"Emerging from the tunnel, I will soon be clothed in the glow of the moon, which in the tunnel is only reflected. The damp pavers in the tunnel pick up the moonlight shimmering on the pond. The reflection from the pavers creates a soft glow on the front of my body, which is evident by the way the light emerges around my left side.

"There is a distinct difference in the light from left to right. My hair on the right is dark, hardly showing its redness, but on the left the red is unmistakable. The same is true of my sleeves—the orange on the left is obvious, while the right sleeve fades into black.

"I'm defined by darkness and light. I'm moving through the darkened depth of the tunnel, yet it's the light shimmering on the pond that draws me. The mood is not startling or threatening. Rather, it's calming and quieting; it's stilling. I hope you can sense that that's the demeanor of the young lady in the orange raincoat.

"My destination is promising. I move towards worth. And that's the name of the painting, *Worth at Midnight.*"

"That's lovely, truly brilliant," Roberta said.

"*Worth at Midnight,*" Hollie said, as she continued to stare into the heart of the painting.

"Beautiful, Hollie," Sister Ravena said. "Really, it's wonderful. The Abbey Art Festival comes up next month, and I'd love to borrow these. That's the time each year I told you about, when I move into that little side office. My art wall becomes part of the tour. There's art displayed in several of the corridors, and people come from all over."

"I'm sure Oban would be agreeable," Hollie said. "These will be his as of today. Would you hang them on your wall?"

"In the office. You probably didn't notice, but there's a wall to your right, just as you enter the room. It's dedicated to that very purpose. We always hang art there during The Abbey Festival and over the holidays."

"Oh, I think I hear Oban moving about. Quick—we need to hide the cake and put things out of sight in the kitchen. If you can just tidy up a bit, I'll divert him."

The three quickly made their way back to the kitchen, only for Hollie to slip out. She moved across the hall and stopped outside the study.

"Ah, there you are. Did you have a good rest, Oban?"

"Too much resting—I'm gonna get all soft. See we've got guests. Hi there, Sister Ravena."

Sister Ravena and Roberta stepped out of the kitchen and across the hall.

"Hi, Mr. Ironbout, and happy birthday," Sister Ravena said. "Here, let me shake your hand. You remember Roberta Nan?"

"Yes, I think I do. The smart one from Speaker's House, the one that sort of keeps folks in line."

"That's right. She's my eyes and ears, especially for the monks."

"Hi, Mr. Ironbout, good to see you again," Roberta said. "I just love your place on The Point. It's perfect—so tranquil, and the views are spectacular."

"Well, it wasn't so tranquil and beautiful 'round here a couple of weeks ago when the walnut tree appendage got hold of me and pinned me to the ground. Fierce, it was."

"You'll be happy to know Goodwin's got the wood from the tree all stacked,"

Hollie said. "Everything is cleaned up. I'm going to put on a pot of tea. You wanted Sister Ravena to come up a bit early so you could talk over a few things. Why don't we gather around the table? I'll rustle up the tea and give Goodwin a shout."

"Sounds agreeable to me," Mr. Ironbout said. "Are you sure you wanna leave me alone with these attractive ladies? Let me wheel myself 'round to the window side, where there's plenty of room for this cast. Come on, ladies. If you could just move that chair—just slide that one back a bit, Roberta. Thanks, that's great. There we are. Roberta, why don't you sit here next to me? Sister Ravena, you can have the head of the table."

"Thanks. What a lovely room," Sister Ravena said.

"Isn't it?" Roberta said. "I love your coffered ceiling and the rock fireplace."

"Yeah, I made it a nice, spacious room. If I recall, that ceiling took about three weeks to trim out, paint, and all. Trip and I have been known to dance in here every now and then. He likes *Tunes Spun* on Saturday nights. Not doing much dancing just now, though. They don't want me to put any real pressure on this leg for another four weeks.

"I'm able to get around using the wheelchair. If I want to get up, I need someone to hand me the crutch and help a bit. When I get up straight, all balanced-like, then I can kind of hobble to the loo. Went up and down the hall yesterday. Slow going, but it's coming along. How's everything down in the meadows? Any contemplators get run over on Contemplation Way, bumping their heads on tree limbs, or anything?"

"No, nothing of the sort, Mr. Ironbout," Sister Ravena laughed. "We've had a wonderful group this summer. You know, we've had more inquiries this year than last, and last year was a record."

"People have always liked Estillyen," Mr. Ironbout said. "Hey, here we are! Nothing like a sip of tea in the afternoon when the day is nearly spent. Did you holler to Goodwin, Hollie?"

"Yep, he's just in the water closet. He'll be right in."

"Ah, ginger snaps, nothing like gingersnaps with tea to stave off the appetite until it can find something to set it right," Mr. Ironbout said. "Say, here he is. Goodwin, will you let Trip in? You don't mind the dog, do you, Roberta Nan?"

"No, I love dogs."

"What about you, Sister Ravena?"

"No worries whatsoever. I'm very much a pet person. Don't have one of my own, but I love everyone else's."

"Hi, Sister Ravena, Roberta," Goodwin said.

"Hi, Goodwin—sounds like you've been busy," Sister Ravena said.

"Fair bit, I'd say. We're trying to stack a few things, paint a bit."

"Ah, he's bein' modest. Really renovating the place, I'll tell ya," Mr. Ironbout said. "It'll never be the same, but it sure is getting a good dressing up.

"So, Sister, have you done any collaborating with your legal adviser concerning the best way to go with The Point?"

"Actually, there are several ways this could be approached," Sister Ravena said.

"First, it's your property. You own it—and, of course, Hollie just told us the good news about the painters finding the deed."

"Miracle, it is," Mr. Ironbout said, clearly relieved.

"So obviously, you're the owner, you set the guidelines. You can grant access to the entire property, or just a portion. This could be for a specific time frame each year, a season, or whatever. The conditions would be up to you. The kind of activities that take place, where artists are allowed to wander, what's off limits—all of that would have to be to your satisfaction.

"A second option would be some kind of lease arrangement. The Abbey would sign a lease, again based on agreeable terms, outlining who is responsible for what. Everything could be spelled out in detail. All the matters about who keeps the place tidy, who looks after the lawn, the paths, the shrubs—everything would be clearly outlined.

"So, the first option is more of an informal agreement. The second option would be some kind of lease, and the third could be some kind of co-ownership arrangement. The Abbey could become the trustee of the property, but with special, legal rights for the Ironbout family as specified.

"We did talk it over in the office, and we thought maybe the best approach, just now, is to let things settle down. Let you get well, give you plenty of time to process what you want to do, and then we can go from there. We'll accommodate your wishes. There's no rush."

"I see. Well, glad you've been doing a bit of ruminating on the matter. Just so you know, Goodwin, Hollie, and I had a fairly reasonable chat on this yesterday, here in this room. It was actually the four of us, including Trip. We thought we would bring Trip in on the deal. By the way, you didn't come up the trail, but Goodwin's gotten rid of the signs. The Point is open—no more words about interlopers. It's a start anyway.

"So here's what I'm thinkin'. The fierceness with which I've come around—come to, so to speak—is not something that I wanna mess with. I abandoned my plow a long time ago. Threw it down and kicked it aside. Sure enough, I did. Now that I've got a certain hold on it again, I don't wanna be plowing any crooked rows or crummy ruts.

"Meaning this: I wanna plow on with some sort of decent arrangement. Not let rains come along, time pass, sentiments shift, or sediments of the mind get all fuzzy. No sir, we need to be about doing whatever it is we're gonna do.

"Here are sort of the parameters of this plowing, as I see it—the direction I want to plow. If you'd jot this down, Sister Ravena, it might come in useful."

"Hold that thought, Oban," Hollie said, as she placed her hand on Mr. Ironbout's forearm. "One second…let me grab a pen and pad. More tea anyone? There's still a cup or two in the red pot wanting to get out."

"I thought you were getting a pen," Mr. Ironbout said.

"Well, you *are* impatient to get this done!" Hollie laughed. "One second… hold on, it's right here in the drawer. Got it."

"I can be the scribe," Roberta offered. Hollie reached behind Mr. Ironbout and passed Roberta the pen and notepad.

"There now, this is sort of the course I was considering. By the way, you might want to date this note. And put this in quotes: 'I, Oban Otto Ironbout, being of sound mind, have decided, to plow a course of action concerning The Point. This action is prompted by my own volition and no other. The main objective of this stated action is to provide access to The Point for artists so they can mingle about doing whatever it is artists do.'

"I just wanted that part to be in quotes. The rest you can fill in as you like. Now, about this manner of plowing, I want to plow two directions at the same time. First, there's The Abbey side. My thinking is that we head back to your second point, Sister Ravena, and draw up some type of lease, whereby The Abbey compensates the Ironbout estate for granting access to The Point.

"As you said, we will need to decide who wanders where, when the wandering commences, and when it ends. We don't want any artsy, contemplator types falling off the cliff or anything like that. I know how the monks and some of these centering types can get a bit spellbound. I might even get that way myself, but we need to protect 'em.

"Now, about the particulars, I'd be grateful if you two would work with Hollie and Goodwin on all of this. It wouldn't hurt to be a bit detailed, but I'd like Hollie and Goodwin involved right from the start. I want you to hear, though, that I would rather see artists wandering 'round here sooner than later. Say, next autumn. Partly because I want to wander in their midst, watching them paint, draw, and sketch.

"Now, the two major elements of any lease are its length and the level of compensation. Concerning the first, I was thinking along the lines of 100 years. We don't want to have some upstart kind of deal. We need to give the environs of nature time to soak up this new artistic expression here on the Point.

"We need to make this proper. I don't want you to ever worry about some dumb telecom company erecting towers, overshadowing your doings, your way of living and caring. The Point needs to be a destination for artists, like you said. I'd like that; I really would.

"Regarding the second point, the matter of compensation, that requires a bit of doodling. I was in Trip's room today, doing a bit of calculating, trying to take into consideration time frames and all.

"What's sort of settling on my mind is this: The compensation could be set, say, at the rate of a pie a month for eleven months, with a cake for the twelfth. The pies and cakes would be delivered from The Abbey kitchens to the Ironbout house, or should we call it 'estate'?

"What I mean is an apple pie, say in April, followed by a peach pie in May, a strawberry or gooseberry in June, and then month after month, on the first day of each month, a new pie is passed up The Point. Except for the month when a pie yields to the cake. How does that sound? Agreeable?"

Mr. Ironbout sat straight-faced, with his eyes open wide. Everyone else smiled and quickly glanced at each other. Sister Ravena and Roberta chuckled.

"Are you serious?" Sister Ravena asked, astonished.

"Yes! The way I calculate it, in 100 years, there will be 1,100 pies and 100 cakes finding their way up the Point. Yes, I believe that's the direction we ought to plow. You can even sell pies on The Point, if you wish, to help compensate for the cost of mine. That is, as long as Hollie and Goodwin agree." Excited smiles were rapidly exchanged around the table.

"Concerning the other half of this plowing, the other direction. That has to do with working up an agreement that protects my interests, along with those of Hollie and Goodwin. I'm confident this can be done in a way that works for everyone. There would always be private quarters on The Point, but with public access granted to grounds and certain designated areas.

"I want to live here as long as I can—who knows, maybe to 100. If so, that means I'll see, and hopefully eat, 330 pies and thirty cakes. I intend to deed the property over to Hollie and Goodwin in my will. I told 'em that yesterday. It will be theirs as long as they live and as long as they have children to pass it on to, adopted or otherwise.

"There are four conditions for plowing on this side of the field. First, the main house can never be sold.

"Second, I want to be buried in the plot 'round on the side lawn. There's a lot of space there. All of this will need to be written up proper-like, so that area will always be The Point Cemetery. You know what I'm tryin' to say? You know what I mean? We'll designate a good bit of space for the cemetery. There'll be room for others down the road. Not for me to figure out who's allowed. Trip is included in the plot, though.

"Third, we're gonna carve out some space on the north side of the property for a cabin. That will be Hollie and Goodwin's, if they decide to build it. That one hectare will be theirs right away, and it can be sold if they ever need the funds for whatever life holds. The right of first refusal will be extended to The Abbey.

"Fourth, and last, there will be a strict proviso stating that nothing can ever be built on the property other than modest modifications to the cabin. It must always be a dwelling, and the house can never be used for commercial interests. An art museum, perhaps; that's to be decided as you all get your brains moving together to chart the proper course.

"So, there we are. I think that's enough to get the plows moving and give us something to work on. Any questions or comments? Goodwin, Hollie, anything to add?"

"No, Sir," said Goodwin. We're just in such a responsive mode right now, wouldn't you say, Hollie? Like life has suddenly reached out and caught us or something. I feel very comfortable with all that you've stated."

"I agree," Hollie said. "It's going to take time to let all of this settle in. We need to practice what Estillyen is all about. We need to still, settle, but Goodwin and I sense only rightness in all that has occurred. The entire experience, Sister Ravena, brings me back to our discussion about worth. I hadn't thought of worth as something you can see, but I see it here."

"We're just amazed that we're caught up in all of this," Goodwin said. "It's rather miraculous—really, I can't think about it too much. It's not something to figure out. The whole cabin idea is just very preliminary right now. We'll see how that develops, but we see everything intertwined."

"We came here to Estillyen thinking we would sort of regroup, find a clearer sense of direction about the future," Hollie said. "And then all of this transpired. I'm so thrilled about the prospect of consulting with Sister Ravena and The Abbey about getting Art Point up and running—if that's what we call it."

"The art side of Estillyen will be a great complement to the readings," Sister

Ravena said. "Art speaks. Also, we certainly want to see Mr. Ironbout up and around doing whatever he is inclined to do." Sister Ravena glanced at Mr. Ironbout with a smile, kind and sincere.

"Well, I do want to mingle and meander 'round them artists," he said. "You know, look over their shoulders a bit and see what they're up to. I'd like to get a portrait of Trip painted, maybe me with him. I might swap a pie for a painting, if it's decent.

"Concerning the cabin idea, Goodwin's right, we'll let it all play out, but I can see it happening. There's no other place like The Point. Although there's a lot to consider before we start hammering nails."

"I think we've got a good year's work here, as it is," Goodwin said. "I also need to get back home before long and take care of a number of things. Funny, not quite sure where home is just now.

"Say, look at the time! I need to get everything ready," Hollie said. "The guests will be coming along soon. Are you comfortable there, Oban?"

"No, I need to scoot into the other room and freshen up a bit. I wanna put something over this green shirt. It's not every day a man has a birthday with such handsome guests."

"Goodwin, after you've helped Oban, you might want to take Sister Ravena and Roberta out to the side garden and around back. You could show them a couple of those areas we were thinking of designating for the artists. The view of the cliffs and the sound of the ocean below are amazing from back there. That would inspire anyone."

"No, I'm fine, Goodwin," Mr. Ironbout said. "I've figured out a method of scooting 'round in there."

"Okay, then. Well, everyone should be here in thirty minutes or so. Win, could I get you to help in the kitchen for two seconds before you head outside?"

"Sure."

"Can I help in some way?" Roberta asked.

"Yes, I was wondering if you and Sister Ravena would be kind enough to greet everyone as they arrive and show them in?"

"I'm sure we can handle that, don't you think, Nan?" Sister Ravena said.

Hollie quickly moved into the kitchen, with Goodwin following. Mr. Ironbout wheeled across the room to the study, with Trip in tow. Sister Ravena and Roberta stepped out on the porch to admire the views.

"Win, what I want you to do is keep Oban occupied. Take him out on the back porch. Pull down that big rolling shade so he can't see who's arriving. An-

391 The Party 391

tonia should be here right now, actually. She's bringing the balloons with the ice cream. I want to set out the flowers. Sister Ravena and Roberta brought yellow roses, and here are the other flowers. Please hand me the knife—I'll just cut the ends.

"I want everything set before Oban comes back in. The dining room table already has the leaves in it. Those five wooden chairs we rounded up yesterday are on the landing, and the pine bench is just at the top of the stairs. If you can grab those, set them in the living room, and mind Oban, I think we're good.

"Oh, there's Antonia just coming through the door—brilliant. Hey there, in here. Hi, Antonia, you look so adorable. Love your red jean jacket."

"Hi, Hollie, thanks," Antonia said.

"Just put everything on the counter," Hollie said. "I'll stick the ice cream in the freezer."

"Hey, this place is exceedingly cool. I never knew it was up here. It's like a park."

"I know, twelve hectares. You can see it all later. Did you get everything?"

"Believe so—three gallons of ice cream: vanilla bean dots, mocha chocolate, and pistachio. I bought seven balloons, all different colors. They're in the car. I'll run and get them. And the birthday banner is here in the small bag."

"Okay, quick, I need your help. Grab the balloons, and then let's put up the banner. This white cloth goes on the table."

"Where can I put my card?" asked Antonia.

"Actually, you can take that basket on the counter and put in on the sideboard in the living room. Everyone can drop their cards in it. Also, these five crystal bowls—let's fill them with the mixed nuts. You can place two in the sideboard and the other three on the little side tables; people can pass them around. I'm sure someone will bring chocolates…quick!"

Soon the colorful "Happy Birthday" banner hung across the open doorway that led from the hall to the living room. The white tablecloth, with its subtle square-stitched pattern, draped perfectly over the long oak table. Two tall, dark green vases, with elegant raised swirls, rose from the table. They each displayed sprays of orange orchids, lavender irises, blue forget-me-nots, and six yellow roses.

The table's center was reserved for the cake. In the interim, the space was occupied with a bright red "Happy Birthday" balloon, which swayed gently on its thin yellow ribbon. The ribbon was tied to a red cloth napkin, which Hollie filled with unhulled walnuts to anchor the balloon.

Two large brown mixing bowls flanked the card basket, which Antonia had placed in the center of the sideboard. The bowls were filled with blue hydrangeas.

On either side of the hydrangeas, walnut-filled red napkins were gathered and tied at the top with triplicate ribbons. The colorful ribbons secured the balloons, which gently danced above the sideboard as if in anticipation of the party.

Behind the triple ribbons on the left, *My Cottage Rare* rested against the mirror, along with Goodwin's card. Beyond the three ribbons on the right, *Worth at Midnight* was placed, with Hollie's red card contrasting the orange slicker in the painting.

Hollie rushed into the dining room to check on details. On top of the sideboard, she spotted the brown envelope containing the deed. She quickly placed the envelope in the card basket and positioned it against the back of the basket, ensuring that the Hatter & Sons' dark-green and gold logo was visible.

"Is that everything, Hollie?" Antonia asked. "I just saw a car pull up."

"Yes, we're nearly there. Is the hallway door shut—the one in the back?"

"Yes, as well as the one leading to the study."

"Perfect! You be the guard. If either door opens, just shout, 'Not yet,'" Hollie said.

Meanwhile, Mr. Ironbout and Goodwin sat on the back porch. Sounds from inside the house were faint, well outmatched by the slow, rhythmic sound of the waves breaking at the bottom of the cliff.

"Hmm…looks like Hollie's put you on security duty," Mr. Ironbout said to Goodwin. "I've always liked sitting on this back porch, looking out across to the edge of The Point. That'll need some kind of proper rail all along the perimeter to keep people from getting too close to the edge. They could disappear in a hurry."

"I agree. Maybe a couple of strong round rails anchored every couple of meters by steel posts set in mortar. It will also need some kind of shorter knee-high guard fence beyond it."

"That'd probably do it. Tell me, how is Hollie doing, anyway? How is she coping with this kidney disease?"

"To be honest, I believe all this change is the best thing that could have ever happened. She's been struggling to come to grips with the disease—the aspect of how it influences the whole of life, the future being uncertain, and all of that.

"Hollie's not manic about the health side of it. She's learned a great deal about the disease, and she's not afraid that way. Her real anxiety has more to do with what it means in terms of a family. That's a major concern.

"But, you know, we came here six weeks ago almost like different people. We were sort of hopscotching through life, not knowing whether to jump on this square or that. Suddenly, life sort of took over. Put us in its game rather than us trying to put life in ours."

"I see."

"The way she and Sister Ravena get on—that's really something. The emphasis on worth, that's come right out of being here, just in the past few weeks. It's amazing."

"I suppose I'm not one to offer advice, given the trail of dust I kicked up in life. That focus on worth, though, makes about as much sense to me as anything I've ever heard, especially now that I'm hearing a bit different. How did Hollie put it…the worth you discover, the worth you give, and the worth you leave?"

"Yes, that's it."

"That Hollie is a dear. You're a fortunate fellow, Goodwin. You'll want to take care of her; give her considerable attention. I think she truly loves this place.

"So what's keeping that group?" said Mr. Ironbout.

"Let me check."

Goodwin quickly made his way up the hall, which ran through the center of the house. He opened the door at the end of the hall and met Antonia, who said, "Hello! I was just coming to get you. Everyone is here."

Goodwin quickly went back down the hall and looked fondly at Mr. Ironbout, sitting in his wheelchair. He caught his breath and thought, *I can't believe I'm looking at my grandfather.*

"Looks like they're ready, Otto," Goodwin said. With those words spoken, he wheeled Mr. Ironbout to his first birthday party in forty-one years.

"Why don't you go first?" Mr. Ironbout joked, knowing it was impossible with Goodwin wheeling the chair. Nearing the end of the hall, the door quickly opened, but just a crack. Mr. Ironbout and Goodwin saw a pair of sparkling blue eyes and a slip of bleached-blonde hair. The blonde hair contrasted sharply with the door, which was stained a rich chestnut with tarnished brass hardware.

"Hello," Antonia said, as she presented the full of her face. "You must be coming to the party. Right this way; it seems you are the honored guest."

Through the doorway Mr. Ironbout was wheeled. First to enter the room was his casted foot, with a colorful cap adorning his toes. Next his casted leg appeared, covered in fashionable Estillyen graffiti. A carnival of multicolored words vied for space, filling the white space with the names of well-wishers.

Finally the man of the party entered the room: Mr. Oban Otto Ironbout. He wore a gold corduroy vest with black buttons. He sat smiling and gazing into the collection of faces. He tilted his head upward, noticeably pressing against the chair's back strap. From left to right, this is what he saw:

To the far left was Goodwin, who had quickly dashed from behind the wheelchair to join the room of smiling faces. On his left stood Hollie, sporting her brilliant red hair and beaming smile. With her right hand, she petted Trip, who pressed his head against her knees. Hollie's left arm looped through Antonia's right. Antonia's smile was unending.

Next to Antonia, Epic stood. In his hand was a black lead, which Mr. Ironbout followed to find the face of Treasure, the blind collie. Treasure wagged his tail and smiled, as though he were looking in Mr. Ironbout's direction. Next to Epic was Mr. Statter, cradling Tiptoe, the calico cat.

Alongside Mr. Statter was Story, followed by Narrator, and then the notable Brother Plot, who held Tremble the rabbit, appearing quite calm for a rabbit in his condition. Sister Ravena and Roberta were next, adding more charm to the group. Next to Roberta was Saga. Saga held his present, a beautiful framed photo of One, the one-legged mallard duck. One filled the frame and appeared to be staring directly at Mr. Ironbout.

Chelsea and Rita claimed the next two spots in the sizable half-circle of smiles. Standing next to Chelsea was Drama, in crisp, dapper attire. He held a cage in which Shakespeare, the Quaker parrot, perched. To Drama's right stood Writer. In his left hand, he gripped a bright red lead attached to the collar of Spook, the black-and-white pig.

Sharron was the third from the end in this amazing lineup of friends. It was Sharron who had introduced Hollie to the mural and the mystery of Uncle Art. Alongside her was Catherine, the researcher, who appeared completely enthralled with all that she saw.

Completing this convex semicircle of faces was the oldest friend in the line, Mr. Morton, the ironmonger. Many years ago, he had the privilege of helping Mr. Ironbout and Leslie build their house on The Point. Mr. Morton brought a flashlight as a gift, which he beamed beneath his chin, glowing red through the skin of his face.

All in all, there were some twenty-three faces, complete with party hats all cocked and tilted, waiting for Hollie to shout, "And to the guest we all say…"

"Surprise! Happy birthday, Mr. Ironbout!" All the pets wiggled, fluttered, and added their unique sounds to the ruckus. Trip suddenly dashed to Mr. Ironbout's side. He acted as if he knew his owner had found new notoriety that he was supposed to share.

"Dear, oh dear, am I in the right place? Do you folks know you're in Mr. Oban Ironbout's house on The Point? Well, I guess you do! Thank you, thank you indeed for being here. This just may be the happiest day of my life. Oh, dear me.

"Hollie, what do we do now?" Mr. Ironbout asked.

"I say we all gather around the table. Everyone find a chair, and I'll be right back."

The group did as they were told, moving left and right, back and forth, round about and in and out. All the while they talked, laughed, and said nothing of great importance—it was just the gaiety of words floating, finding, and telling.

Goodwin helped get Mr. Ironbout settled in on the far side of the table. Mr. Ironbout was struck by the strange sensation of hearing so many people talk all at once inside his house on The Point. *This*, he thought, *is the room in which I have sat, year after year, keeping company with myself, mingling not with friends but with loneliness and bitterness.*

Never in his coffered-ceilinged room had he heard the robust sound of people talking. What he had heard, year after year, came via broadcasts he dialed in, like *Tunes Spun.*

He was mesmerized by the sound of people present, speaking one to one, one to three, two to one. Mr. Ironbout found the sounds to be utterly pleasant. The sounds rose up and jumped around so vivaciously. He thought, *This is my gift, the greatest gift of all.* He felt as if he could sit there all night and listen to people talking, laughing, and musing.

Expressly happy as he was, he also could not help but think how fortunate it was that he was not dead. *What if I had died*, he thought, *never to have heard these sounds, or seen these faces, in the house I built?* It seemed almost surreal to him, how he might never have seen this scene.

As he sat there considering all he heard and saw, Mr. Ironbout looked up at the mirror above the sideboard. He stared into the mirror's mysterious depth, thinking how torturous it would be if somehow fate really had trapped him inside the mirror. There his old self would have carried him, deposited him, and then went away.

He thought how horrible it would be, if beneath the glass he were now pressed, just like he was under the appendage. He would peer out into the room, but no one would know he was there; no one would care. He would be the image of the *old me*, watching someone else's party, in the house he had built.

He closed his eyes and opened them again. He felt blessed by the sights he saw and the sounds he heard. He thought, *I'm not trapped; I'm me, watching me, with friends. It's my birthday.*

Suddenly, the lights went out, and Hollie's smiling face glowed above the burning candles. She gracefully moved across the room and gently slid the glow under the face of Mr. Ironbout. The sound of voices talking segued to sounds of voices singing.

As all the pets wiggled and wagged, words came forth, spun and fell into lines of that familiar tune, "Happy birthday to you; happy birthday to you; happy birthday, Mr. Oban Otto Ironbout; happy birthday to you!"

TWENTY-THREE
Centering and Mr. Kind

Hollie could hear Mr. Ironbout snoring in the study. It was 10:45 a.m. About an hour earlier, Mr. Ironbout had told her, "I feel a little knackered after the excitement of yesterday. I think I'll take a wee five-minute nap."

Hollie thought aloud, "Oban must really like the feather pillow Sister Ravena gave him for his birthday. He had said, 'I want to break it in straightaway.'"

She turned to Trip, her new faithful companion. "You could sure use a new pillow, too, couldn't you boy? Why didn't I ask Goodwin to get one for you on the mainland?" She looked at her watch and remarked, "He should be boarding the Estillyen ferry by now.

"Fun party, hmm, Trip? Lots of people—and new friends for you. Mr. Statter said now that The Point's opened up, he'll come around with Tiptoe and Spook."

She thought about how well the party had gone—and how much everyone enjoyed being up on The Point. Prominent in her mind was the image of Mr. Ironbout seated at the table looking up at the mirror and her gift, *Worth at Midnight*. She was thrilled to see Mr. Ironbout so happy and welcoming toward the guests.

Hollie opened the screen door and stepped out onto the porch with Trip. She carried a manila envelope, a pair of sunglasses, and a few dog biscuits. The two moved along the front of the porch and descended down the side steps. Hollie leisurely walked across the lawn in the direction of the grave plot. Trip scurried back and forth, carrying a stick in his mouth.

"The place has certainly changed a good deal in the past two weeks, don't you think Trip, with all the planting of flowers and sprucing up?"

Hollie looked in the direction of the grave plot and thought, *I just love the way the ivy has replaced that old black chain of death. And Goodwin's find of the cool-looking garden bench over by the cliff is so much nicer here in the lawn.*

"Come on up, Trip; there's lots of room. You could sit four big human beings on this great old bench," Hollie said, as she pulled up a green-metal lawn chair to use for a footrest.

"That's better. It's so tranquil this morning. I'm flopping off these shoes, but I'm watching you, Trip—no running off with my flats. That's it; just lay down. Good boy.

"Well, let's see what we've got in the envelope. It's the final *Redemption* reading. You're supposed to read it, Trip, when you've time to center, to settle. I know that's not easy for a border collie. Let's give it a try, though. You go ahead and nap, and I'll have a read."

Silently, Hollie began to read the message. Trip lay on the bench beside her with his eyes closed, while Mr. Ironbout snored away in the house. A soft breeze filtered through the garden. Occasionally, Hollie would pause from the reading and glance at the plot, with its three markers.

Hollie remembered the day Mr. Ironbout stood in the plot and, with a worn, wretched expression on his face, said, "I'm a wounded man; can't you see, I'm ruptured?"

She was still in awe. "He's absolutely transformed," she said aloud. "The change is like a miracle."

More than once, Hollie lifted her green eyes from the page to gaze beyond the garden at the majestic beauty of the cliffs—as she allowed the monks of Estillyen to reach through to her with their final message of Christ's love.

A Reading, Crafted Collectively by the Monks of Estillyen:
Centering in Christ

READER: Voice, St. Paul once sent a heartfelt prayer to followers of Christ in Ephesus. It was a prayer to ponder. Through time, the prayer has moved and mattered. Now a few lines have found their way into this Estillyen reading. Shall I read you the prayer?

VOICE: Yes, please. I'd like to ponder it, as well.

READER: Okay, Voice, but first just a few words. Please know that these thoughts so long ago expressed were strikingly new when written. Quite reformist was the prayer. St. Paul speaks of power in the inner being, of God's love being multidimensional, of love rooting in the heart. The apostle's words focus on Christ as being the One on which the heart centers.

Listen now to St. Paul's ancient words. Listen as if you were there and had just received his letter.

I pray that out of his glorious riches he may strengthen you with power through his Spirit in your inner being, so that Christ may dwell in your hearts through faith. And I pray that you, being rooted and established in love, may have power, together with all the saints, to grasp how wide and long and high and deep is the love of Christ, and to know this love that surpasses knowledge—that you may be filled to the measure of all the fullness of God.

EPHESIANS 3:16-19

Robust words, don't you think, Voice?

VOICE: They are. Will you kindly read that one line again, the one about grasping?

READER: Certainly. "To grasp how wide and long, and high and deep is the love of Christ…" Is that the one you mean? *VOICE:* Yes, that's it. It's the word *grasp*…grasping love—such an idea. It is, as you said, something to ponder.

READER: The apostle says this love surpasses knowledge. Did you catch that bit?

VOICE: I did. Yes, I did.

READER: When St. Paul traveled to Ephesus, he was taken to a place called the Areopagus, where he gave a speech.

VOICE: Areopagus—what's that?

READER: The Areopagus was an Athenian council, a local legislative body. It was allowed to function under Roman democracy. That's not so important to our reading. It's what the apostle said that matters. During his speech, St. Paul did something quite remarkable in selecting his words.

VOICE: What did he select?

READER: He quoted a line from an Athenian poet. In doing so, the line became scriptural truth. St. Paul was challenging his audience to consider the true nature of God, who God is. That's when he plucked the line from the poet. Concerning God, the poet said, "We are his offspring." That's it—a little line of words with which St. Paul concurred. A pleasant idea, don't you think?

VOICE: Yes. Offspring…it sounds rather wholesome.

READER: The Athenians were very much preoccupied with grasping the latest ideas. It was, for them, a sport. They loved to spend time talking and debating. When the apostle came along, they told him, "You are bringing strange ideas to our ears."

To the ears words flow, Voice. They find entrance. They winnow their way into the mind. They seek lodging. They come in phrases, throughout life's phases. Sometimes they speak praises.

VOICE: Words seek lodging?

READER: Yes, they seek recipients. They come to rest, to root. They grow. They lodge in the heart. That's how St. Paul's words functioned in the Areopagus. St. Paul placed the poet's line into his own storied mix. He went on to say that God made everyone from one man. You know who that is, don't you, Voice?

VOICE: Sure, that's Adam…if you believe the story.

READER: Do you, Voice?

VOICE: Well, yes, in a manner of speaking.

READER: I see. Concerning St. Paul's words, he argued that the human race was created by a reasoned, volitional act on the part of God. "God did this," Paul said, "so that men would seek him, and perhaps reach out for him, and find him, though he is not far from each one of us. For in him we live and move and have our being."

That's something to grasp, something to ponder, is it not? These words, thus spoken, are in your ears, Voice, swirling in your mind, but in the heart will they lodge? What might these words mean to you? What might these words make of you? That's the subject of the matter now arisen. Are the words treasure or trash to you? Where might they take you? Where might they lead you?

Everyone follows someone, Voice.

VOICE: They do?

READER: Most certainly. Those who swear to follow no one follow at least one. They follow self. Self is full of words lodging in the heart. Did you ever think of your heart that way, Voice? A repository you are. Words have willed their way, winnowing through your mind, rooting in your heart. They move you. They accuse you. They excuse and abuse you. There's so much more to words, Voice, than intonation and resonation.

They come to you bearing thoughts. They clothe thoughts and make them known. Some for ill, some for good, words set out their roots. Voice, it's up to you to determine which words digress from the path wisdom professes.

Self following self puts one on a precarious path. Simultaneously self both leads and follows. Self, the guide, charts the way intuitively with words planted, rooted. Words move self. They make self.

Christ's words lodge in hearts most deeply. In their winnowing work, his words are carried along by God's Spirit. To life's essence, his words speak. "For whoever would save his life will lose it," Christ said, "but whoever loses his life for my sake and the gospel's will save it." Those words set loose have arrested many hearts.

Self is inclined to speak like this: "I'm not lost. I'm not letting go, losing life to find myself. Dear me, ask who I am. This I know. This is clear to see. All I need to do is look in the mirror. I see through and through. I speak to myself for myself. I know who I am. Can't you see? I'm self-made. Scouring and searching for what? Winsomely I walk, with will, wit, and witty words."

VOICE: If self leads, how does self find the way?

READER: Often by witty wit and will—wasn't that how self worded it? Of this notion, though, self is rather shortsighted. There's a snag within the wit, a fault line of sorts.

VOICE: Really?

READER: The snag is this: There is no self with selfless DNA.

VOICE: What's that you say about selfless DNA? It sounds strange.

READER: You remember that wholesome word you liked?

VOICE: You mean *offspring?*

READER: Yes, that's it. Offspring—one and all are sprung off, Voice. St. Paul claimed all offspring lead back to one. Universal ancestry is a mark of every self. Deep within each self, selves of lineage linger. All manner of inscriptions and implantations are there. They have a way of cajoling, congealing, and bending self. No matter how winsome the walk with wise wit and words, selves in self linger.

The mark of brothers' blood gone to war, the bones of martyrs, too—they reside in DNA. Souls of sinners seeking grace…the wicked giving chase. All such inscriptions are woven into what presumption calls self. Who is it that speaks for self, anyway? Think about it, Voice. Which inscription might it be—the sinner seeking grace, or a wicked wick bearing self-prescription?

When self leads, the spirit follows. This creates all manner of maladies. Self cannot feed what the spirit needs. Self-leading is not wise. It's otherwise. If you're interested in being wise, look to ancient words akin to those we're now considering.

VOICE: Which words?

READER: Choice they are. They're what you might call a prophetic prescription, an antidote to self-leading. Listen to what the prophet said: "Stand at the crossroads and look; ask for the ancient paths; ask where the good way is and walk in it, and you will find rest for your souls."

You now have these ancient words, albeit new to you, swirling in your mind, Voice. They are winnowing, moving. Even when you sleep, they seep. Are they trash or treasure? Will they take root? The prophet spoke of verbs—four, in fact. Stand, look, ask, and walk. They are action words leading to the path of rest.

VOICE: Do these ancient words still apply to someone like me?

READER: Yes, certainly. They're wise, not otherwise. They belong to that chosen reservoir of words that have stood the test of time. They shall stand, still, when time no longer ticks.

Ancient is good, Voice. It bears gifts from afar for the present's day. Anemic is the present without the ancient. Jeremiah spoke of ancient paths, beyond the crossroads trail. Ancient paths self cannot find by witty wit and intuition. Self must surrender. The word surrender sounds most threatening to self. Does it to you, Voice?

VOICE: I just don't know. I've never thought about it like that before.

READER: Self grasps the wrong idea. To self, surrender sounds like a chicken desiring to be plucked. There is a time, though, when all selves do surrender.

VOICE: When's that?

READER: It's when the foe of life comes creeping. Death drops in. Down is death's trajectory. It brings freeze upon the face. Self, to death, surrenders. Self may wail and weep, but in the end, life ends. Self surrenders. Self becomes ancestry, lineage, a name engraved, a testament to posterity. When death drops in, the spirit within self says it's time to go. The spirit flees.

VOICE: Where does the spirit go?

READER: The spirit trails away, traversing the distant paths self availed. At that point, it's too late to sort out digresses from what wisdom professes. You see, Voice, the spirit has needs. It feeds on various seeds. Christ said, "It is written, 'Man does not live on bread alone.'" Christ cherished words, and he loved that line, "It is written."

The spirit feeds on grist from mills that grind words into storied mixes. The spirit feeds, while within the self it waits. There it resides, living longingly, or lapsing into lethargy. The spirit intuitively knows there is more to life than self. The spirit senses the eternal, implanted deep within man and mate. Jeremiah's prescription is offered to aid the spirit as it feeds.

The spirit, led by self, is fed from other troughs. The requisite of being self-made demands it. Relying not on divinity in self's realm of humanity, self enslaves the spirit. Without wisdom from ancient paths, the spirit lunges, plunges, feeding on what self avails. Bespoke the spirit is made—a hybrid of thoughts formed from all manner of wordy mixes.

No illusion should be held. A bespoke spirit can become quite unwell—bound, enslaved, and contorted. The unrepentant thief hanging on Golgotha's hill—was not his spirit ill, soured by self's incantations? So near to Christ he hung.

The thief's spirit would not kneel; self would not allow it. He repelled the figure at his side. He despised his words.

What was it St. Paul said there in the Areopagus, Voice? "God is not far from each one of us," that's what the apostle said. In Christ, God has come near, so very near. Into the scrum of humanity he has entered. Into the heart he seeks to dwell.

Spiked in crucifixion agony, the hardened thief would not surrender. Self had enslaved the spirit. They became one, inseparably defiant. The spirit had been caged, and true to self the spirit was. Like a bigot to bigotry, a brute to brutality, the spirit showed its unrelenting defiance of divinity. Though it realized the end for self was near, the spirit would not recant or repent, so enslaved it was.

To follow the footsteps of Christ, self must surrender. Self must relinquish its grip, let go of the helm, pick up an oar. Self must stoop down and carry a cross. Self must diminish, get lost, get out of the way, in order for the spirit to find its way.

Lost is good, Voice, most desirable.

VOICE: It is?

READER: Yes, Voice, indeed. Once you're lost, you can be found. This you find when lost you are. Lost, the spirit longs and listens for eternal echoes. The echoes lead. The mysterious harkens. This, too, is good, most desirable.

Along the journey's twists and bends, the words of Christ do not renounce their call. It was Christ who said, "Come follow me." His words led to rest. "The words I have spoken to you are spirit and life," Christ said.

Being centered in Christ is about more than belief and knowing, Voice. It's about Christ dwelling at self's center, in the heart, changing self in ways self cannot do. St. John wrote, "The Word became flesh and dwelt among us, and we have seen his glory, the glory of the One and Only who came from the Father, full of grace and truth."

VOICE: Wait, if you would, Reader. The idea of Christ dwelling on earth I see, but now you speak of the heart. This is challenging to grasp.

READER: You're very right, Voice. It is mysterious. So too was Christ's earthly dwelling. How do you explain it? God in human form, begotten not made. In all of eternity, nothing is its equal. The One who dwelt on earth can equally dwell within the heart. By faith it is so. By the Spirit of Christ, it is possible.

The Spirit of Christ occupies the heart's center, filling it with Christlike characteristics. The apostles once described themselves by self. "I'm a tax collector. I'm a fisherman. I'm neither; I'm his brother." They all became something else when to self they died and surrendered. They became new. Not just spruced up or a little changed—new characters they became. New dreams they held. New life they possessed.

Upon Christ they centered. He became their life, their calling, their sense of doing, their experience of being. His words they spoke, not self's witty wit. His image they bore, not their own. Into the crossroads of life, the apostles stepped, paused, and stood. They looked, listened, and dared to ask. They walked, but they also followed.

As Christ came strolling by, there were many who chose not to follow. The apostles might have joined them. Clung tight to their sails. Mended their nets. Kept fishing for fish. Posterity never would have revealed Sts. Peter, James, and John along with all the others filling the Gospel story.

On Christ's path the apostles chose to tread. The more they lost, the more they found. The cost was high. All that self possessed had to be redressed, let go. There were crosses to carry. The apostles' crosses, though, stilled self's claim. In following Christ, the apostles became who they were meant to be.

St. Paul, too, was a follower who died to self. In so doing, Saul became Paul. It was with utmost confidence that St. Paul wrote about being rooted and established in the love of Christ. This brings us back, Voice, to the very heart of our reading.

VOICE: That's good.

READER: Professed faith in Christ begins the journey. It opens the gate to the path of rest. But the journey is long, Voice. The Ephesians, for whom St. Paul prayed, were believers. The apostle's prayer was about grasping the full measure of Christ's love. His words pressed directly on that point.

The Spirit of God works with power in the inner being. Working deep within, the Spirit gets to the heart of all those implantations, sorting and rooting them out; pulling them down, lifting them up.

St. Paul's forte was to admonish and to lift up the supremacy of Christ. He was a master at it. He saw Christ dwelling in space and time, but equally in the heart. The heart is where the spirit, soul, and mind mingle. They mix and match storied mixtures. The heart chooses its embrace.

In this vortex, the Spirit of Christ dwells: stilling the storm, quieting the gale, rendering rest. The dwelling of Christ's Spirit shapes the sensibilities of the spirit.

VOICE: I hear you, Reader, and all that sounds extremely important. Yet it is so mysterious, I can hardly take it in. I'm not sure how to put it. The word in my mind is *worth*. That's the idea—you know what I mean? It's so incredible to think that this could happen to simple homo sapiens, fascinating.

READER: So simple we're not, Voice. Mysterious is this dwelling, imparting Christlike changeability from Spirit to spirit. There are those, many such, who choose to shun the spiritual quest. Don't want it; don't feel they need it. They prefer God distant, considered only at a glance, if at all.

Their feet tread not the ancient paths. There is no walking, listening, or seeing. Blurry distance is the desired position. Too much of seeing threatens self. The mysterious truth of Christ dwelling in the heart is embraced by faith. There is no other way. This is what you must comprehend. The mysterious is to be welcomed, not pummeled and pounded for proof, like some shank on a slab. Who wants everything in life explained? Do you, Voice?

VOICE: Well, we've gotten so immersed in this flow of thinking. Yes, I've been, or tend to be, more the pounding type, I suppose. Maybe I should take a break, clear my mind. Please, no offense.

READER: Is that what you wish—to take a break?

VOICE: Well, not really...I don't think so, anyway. But it's a little scary, this denial of self, this surrendering. The words flowing from this reading are not normal. How shall I put it? They're not bound by rudimentary thinking concerning the makeup of man. That's it.

READER: Do the words scare you, Voice?

VOICE: This whole matter of swirling vortexes and the Spirit of Christ dwelling—it's a lot to grasp. This vista of human worth is appealing, though, I must admit. It's just new for me, sort of scary.

READER: Were you scared before you were born, Voice?

VOICE: What kind of a question is that? Scared before I was born! Dear me... maybe I should go. You're so, I don't know...

READER: Where will you go?

VOICE: Don't know. I'm resourceful. I know a lot of storied mixes. I'll pick and choose, a snippet here and a snippet there. Before you know it, I'll have a mountain of wisdom to quarry.

READER: Will you quarry out a story?

VOICE: I might. I've been known to string a few lines together. I like words, always have.

READER: What if the words you choose to quarry your story don't like being fashioned and fitted together? They might start stinging each other, like wasps fighting bees.

VOICE: I suppose that could happen, couldn't it?

READER: Quite likely. What part will you play in the story, Voice?

VOICE: I'll be myself. Plot the plot. Sign the script. Speak my voice. I'll be the lead character.

READER: I see. You'll need prayer, I would think. Why don't we return to the ancient one rendered by St. Paul?

VOICE: Well, I guess we could. I hope you don't ask me any more crazy questions—like was I scared before I was born.

READER: Okay, I won't. But were you?

VOICE: Didn't you hear what I said? Are you insane or something?

READER: I heard you, Voice, certainly I did. With every respect, I abide your words. But this is not another question; it's one and the same.

VOICE: All right, just to make you happy—the answer is clearly No! How could I have been scared before I knew anything of knowing? I knew nothing before I came to be.

READER: You knew nothing, you say? So you're not self-made?

VOICE: Of course not. How could I decide to make myself? I'm an offspring.

READER: I'm glad you have professed that point, Voice. No one is actually self-made. Before you knew yourself, you were known. You are a vital character in God's storied mix.

VOICE: I am?

READER: Yes, indeed. You can quarry your own story, if you want. But you needn't do so. You're in the story of which St. Paul spoke, just as surely as he stood in the Areopagus quoting the poet.

I like you, Voice.

VOICE: You do? Why's that?"

READER: Because you're honest. You speak of worth. Life is so much more than rudimentary elements. Pursing worth is the right idea. Christ offers depth, imparting life spiritual. Into Christ's Spirit, the spirit of surrendered self cocoons. This truth is not a simple token, simply taken. It's mysterious, full of wonder. The spiritual quest is unending. Into eternity it folds. Forevermore it lives.

St. Paul was not shy on this subject of mystery. "I know a man in Christ," Paul wrote, "who fourteen years ago was caught up to the third heaven. Whether it was in the body or out of the body I do not know, God knows. And I know that this man, whether in the body or apart from the body I do not know, but God knows, was caught up to paradise. He heard things that man is not permitted to tell."

This man, so caught up, was Paul himself. Sifting the mysterious out of Scripture greatly impairs the storied mix. Scripture, from beginning to end, is lacquered and layered with mystery. Pitching the miraculous out of Scripture, yet clinging to a few verses promising passport to heaven, is not compatible with wisdom. God is exceedingly mysterious. Why not let the miraculous be, let God be God?

The inexpressible things St. Paul experienced in heaven's realm no doubt had an enormous impact on all he wrote, taught, and preached. The apostle's striking prayer about the expansive love of Christ arises from this backdrop.

Let's consider rightly those words of St. Paul. To grasp how wide and long and high and deep is the love of Christ, that's how the apostle put it. The love of Christ is where faith is centered, Voice. It's where the soul finds rest and peace finds its pillow.

To grasp the dimensions of Christ's love is to grasp the Father's love. The Father's love is seen in the giving of his Son, in letting go. The Son's love is seen in going, dwelling, and dying.

VOICE: Do you understand this dimensional grasp?

READER: In part, yes. You never fully get it—you know what I mean, Voice? It's a revelation that keeps revealing. An epiphany dawns…and then another.

VOICE: I think I understand.

READER: You go on grasping, perceiving, seeing as the love of Christ dwells in the heart. The spirit needn't be bound by self's paltry center. God's love is towering far above a world of words and more, which come and go, saying this and meaning that.

God's words have no ulterior motive or malicious intent. From on high, like rain and snow God's words come down. They moisten seeds for sprouting; they impart life for living.

The psalmist writes, "I lift up my eyes to the hills, where does my help come from? My help comes from the Lord, the Maker of heaven and earth."

Up is the direction, beyond the bickering, brokering, and bothered press of the day. Up is the way, with eyes peering beyond terror on screens appearing. Up is the way, beyond minutes of time ticking and death tolling its daily tallies. Up with eyes of hope, to worth not wanting, pulled down, wrestled to the ground by self.

The selfless love of God is lifted up.

VOICE: Where?

READER: On a cross spiked, that's where. Christ is there, beaten and bloodied for the world to see.

VOICE: But I was recently told not to look.

READER: By whom?

VOICE: Relevance. Relevance said that's all over. That Christ was taken down long ago. Said it was time to lighten up.

READER: Lighten up—on the one lifted up, you say? Does that sound right to you, Voice?

VOICE: Well, I have the feeling you don't think so.

READER: Why is it you speak of me to sort your feelings?

VOICE: I don't know. Maybe it has something to do with those words you spoke. Swirling as they do, winnowing their way.

READER: To the cross you do not have to look, Voice. It was God lifted up. He gave you sight. Look away. See not the dread. It may pierce your heart. It may not.

VOICE: No, I'm not afraid to look. It is, as you say, an ancient story gifting the present.

READER: Taken down, Christ surely was. That's true, yet eyes of enlightened hearts fail not to see him there. The one taken down is forever there. The medium and the message of God are indistinguishable upon the cross. There they embrace. They overlap. They hang together. They speak together. They intersect. They form a sign, a message whole for the world to ponder.

To look away does injustice to the message. It strips meaning from the story. With eyes lifted to the cross, the height of God's love is seen. Look around. Find some other figure of hope. Does it appear more comfortable, more salient? Do you like what you see? The apostle spoke of eyes within the heart as a way of seeing. Eyes of the enlightened heart see by faith.

Where does my help come from in order to see? It comes from there.

VOICE: Where?

READER: Where the Son of God hung, suffered, and died. God knows pain. God heals pain.

VOICE: So, should I look?

READER: Would you not, what might you lose?

VOICE: I do feel inclined—sort of drawn.

READER: All right, then—look. A lonely hill it is. See there in the distance. Christ hangs. Campfires 'round about are burning. See the smoke—how it lifts and lingers in the thin chilly air? Smell it?

VOICE: I do. You're right—this is a lonely place. It's actually morbid. It's like a fresco, but then not at all the same. And to think a world of art has come from this. So, too, all those musical compositions arise from this scene. I'm spellbound. What is it I see? What is it I hear?

READER: The words being spoken are somewhat hard to grasp. Listen—did you hear that shout, those moaning cries?

VOICE: What's that quirky sound?

READER: That's the sound of soldiers laughing. This is not a silent night for Mary's Son. It's a night of terror, torment, and treachery. The scene is savagery. Look, the Son of God has opened his eyes again. He's looking down at the crowds staring up at him and shouting, with their shaking fists. There are even children in their midst.

Let's move closer. Are you okay with that?

VOICE: I'm sobered. I feel speechless.

READER: From the bottom up, take in the cross. Inspect it. Do you see how the crimson stain has soaked into the wooden base? Christ's feet are spiked, his torso ripped.

VOICE: What's that dripping from his chin?

READER: It's blood. This is a sacrifice, you see, Voice. Look fully upon this panorama of pain. There's much for enlightened eyes to see.

VOICE: I'm looking up beyond the cross. I have to look away. I'm not sure what it is I see. Now it's gone. It looked like eyes peering down. And that, did you see that? Again, I'm not sure. It looked like angels, with wing-covered faces.

READER: Look on the ridge over there.

VOICE: Those are women watching.

READER: They're all weeping. With eyes streaming, see how they stare at the central cross. They gaze at grace. Mary, the mother of Christ, is there. Her offspring is dying. God's offspring is dying. Crucified, he is dying. Mary watches the mockers mock. She sees it all. How can she bear it? Price, price, price, paid! So costly is the price of redemption.

With eyes perceiving, for just a moment, peer out over the haze, Voice. Look up toward the hills for help in seeing. Above the smoky hills, the stars sparkle, do they not?

VOICE: Yes, they do.

READER: See them twinkling across the moonlit sky. Ponder them hanging there. Consider their origin. Were they not hung by the one hanging there in the center of Golgotha's hill?

VOICE: It must be so.

READER: It's true, Voice. The one in the shadowy hues hung them there. High is the love of Christ, lifted up for enlightened hearts to see.

Wide, too, is this dimension of love. Stretched out are his arms; wide is this exhibition of eternal love. It's inclusive, not exclusive. There is no qualifier concerning scope. No "We'll have to see. Who do you know? We'll have to check."

Consider Christ's reach. The invitation is to all who surrender. The psalmist David spoke of God's reach. "Where shall I go from your Spirit? Or where shall I flee from your presence?"

"Where can I flee from your presence?" You spoke of fleeing, Voice. Do you still want to flee?

VOICE: No, I don't think so. My feet do not feel flighty. I'm somehow held captive by what I see and hear.

READER: Think, Voice! Ponder the scene. Many run to quarry stories from witty words. They reject faith. They do not find. They are not found. They find not their place in the ancient story gifting the present. There the Word of God hangs. With eyes of faith, look! The scene is a sign signifying what God means, what God wants to convey. Before the scene was, God thought it. There's far more on that hill than witty words.

Down the Via Dolorosa Christ walked, with criminals on each side. Among thieves he hangs. His arms to them are stretched. That's where God chose to die, Voice. Thieves left and right. On one side is rejection; on the other side acceptance. Arms stretched to both signify the enormous reach of God's love.

Human love can tend to be so tenuous in comparison. Often it draws away and disappears. Once it might have been there, reaching, embracing, caring. Suddenly it's gone. When it should hold fast, it lets go. Bitterness and pain may push it away. Self may will it away. It may be wooed away. Somehow love is lost. It's gone, retrenched.

God's love is not that way. It never retrenches. God is "loving toward all he has made," the psalmist said. There is no prejudice or injustice. Broad and inclusive—that's the image of God hanging there. There's no clenched fist, no hint of spite, at humanity marred by sin.

The price of recompense has been paid by God. From the cross grace extends. The scene on Golgotha's hill also signifies the depth of God's love. Look again. See the cross, anchored in the ground from which man was formed.

VOICE: What about the cross itself, its composition—should this be considered?

READER: Why not? It's made of wood. It was once a tree. It was felled, and now it's dead. Birds once perched in its branches. Those were the days when the wood was rooted and alive, before it was fashioned into planks for death and dying.

Look at the planks; all semblance of life is gone. No branches, no leaves, no fruit, nothing to eat. The planks are barren. They offer no shade. They bear no beauty.

The planks are implements of torture. They're awkward measurements of weight. When the heavy planks were hoisted and dropped, they proved their heft. They thudded to the ground. Death was calling. The planks' pull is death's gravity. From them, life's blood drips.

VOICE: What do you suppose Christ thought when he heard that thudding sound?

READER: He thought the end was near. Look closely. See the planks' swollen grains? The planks have all been splintered by spikes from others who were crucified. They're used, abused. Still their grains tightly grip Christ's spikes of infectious rust. The grains sponge and soak the warm crimson stain. That's what has created all those splotchy patterns. In the act of man's inhumanity to man, the depth of God's love is seen.

"My God, my God, why have you forsaken me?" Did you hear that cry through the deathly air? That cry, rising from this crucible of suffering, is unparalleled. Sin's foul and death's dank have come to meet. They have come to stomp out the light. This is the deepest of valleys. Yet therein is God's love.

The words of the psalmist quiet the heart: "Yea, though I walk through the valley of the shadow of death, I will fear no evil, for thou art with me. Thy rod and thy staff they comfort me."

VOICE: I like those words.

READER: Many do fear evil, knowing nothing of rod and staff or words such as these. Human history is a journey long through valleys of shadowy death. The shadows vary from one valley to the next. Up and down the canyon floor, one can hear the rumble of war and rumors of wars. Peace comes, and then puff, it's gone. People suffer. Strange words appear. Collateral damage, it is said.

VOICE: Why is it called that?

READER: Yes, why? The heart, you know, can break with burden. All feeling seems to be below the ankles. The brokenhearted shuffle and drag their feet.

King David knew such burden. Listen to his words. "I am feeble and utterly crushed: I groan in anguish of heart. I am bowed down and brought very low; all day long I go about mourning."

Unrelenting such sighs seem. Was there no air of promise? King David dicovered there was. He would live to sing again. Beneath his despair, God's love was deeper still.

Eyes of the heart look to the cross and see that God is present, not fleeing. God pierced with pain is the image God has rendered. It is not a human fabrication. It is not an application. God supplied it. Consider it, Voice. For you it is rendered. The image speaks to the depth of God's love. In this cross-shaped depth, God binds up the brokenhearted.

God knows pain. The psalmist says, "Who is like the Lord our God, the One who sits enthroned on high, who stoops down to look on the heavens and the earth? He raises the poor from the dust and lifts the needy from the ash heap; he seats them with princes, with the princes of their people."

From the psalms, ancient words also speak to the length of God's love. "The Lord will keep you from all harm, he will watch over your life. The Lord will watch over your coming and going both now and forevermore."

"Forevermore" is a word with a wonderful disposition. Not just forever, but more than forever: forevermore. In perpetuity, infinity is the sense of meaning conveyed. The psalmist's refrain rises: "Give thanks to the God of gods; his love endures forever."

Not fading or dissipating but enduring is God's love. Beyond time's ticking and the world's whirling, God's love never fades. "Do not let your hearts be troubled. Trust in God. Trust also in me." This is what Christ came to say. God's love never fades. It is like Christ's words. "Heaven and earth will pass away," Christ said, "but my words will never pass away."

Never-fading words—how can they be described? They are the cornerstone of eternity and forevermore, these words of promise, these words of hope.

VOICE: The cornerstone of eternity—is there one?

READER: Yes, Voice. The stone the builders rejected will hold eternity together. You know, Voice, as we've moved along, upon your ears have fallen a collection of ancient words. Do you know what that means?

VOICE: Yes, they're swirling, winnowing, in my heart and mind.

READER: That's right. They are God's thoughts clothed in words. Ponder, grasp, if you wish. It's for you to determine if they digress from wisdom's way or reveal it. Let me leave with you these lines before we part. King Solomon wrote them. He is said to be the wisest man who ever lived.

"Remember your Creator, before the silver cord is severed, or the golden bowl is broken, before the pitcher is shattered at the spring, or the wheel broken at the well, and the dust returns to the ground it came from, and the spirit returns to God who gave it."

Voice, my reading is near its end. It's been great to be with you, but I've got to go. Know this, though: Christ will not change or flit away. He is as he was and will always be.

Rest for the soul is not an illusion, Voice. Look to ancient paths. The good path is found by way of the valley. In the valley, eyes of self will not do. One needs eyes of faith to see. There, deep within the valley's gorge, is a cleft. The eyes of faith will see its light streaming through. This is where rest is near.

To the cleft climb and cleave. Follow it upward to the crest. The crest gives way to a vast plateau, a word-filled meadow, the place of rest. Move along the flowing stream of waters fresh, knowing rest for the soul is near.

A single signpost points the way. Eyes of faith will not miss it. It's a simple cross, a sign signifying that which countless souls have journeyed to embrace. This is the place to center, still, and kneel, if you so desire.

There is safety in the cross's shadow. Freely you can lie in peace, at rest forevermore.

VOICE: I like you, Reader.

READER: That's kind of you, Voice.

VOICE: You're honest, and you speak of worth. I like your words. I'm just not sure what to say. I mean...I'm just so taken by all we've been discussing.

READER: That's good, Voice. It doesn't sound like you're quite so keen to run off and quarry your own story with witty wit.

VOICE: Not now. That doesn't seem right anymore. These winnowing words may well win over wit. Instead of quarry, I'll ponder, particularly the eternal cornerstone. That's got me.

READER: Good-bye, Voice.

VOICE: Good-bye, Reader. And thanks for all you've said. I'll never see words the same.

Words matter...some forevermore.

I pray that you, being rooted and established in love, may have power, together with all the saints, to grasp how wide and long and high and deep is the love of Christ.

ST. PAUL, ROME, LETTER TO THE EPHESIANS, CIRCA AD 62

"Trip, there's a lot of worth in this final reading, a great deal," Hollie said. "This is the kind of thing human beings store away and then pull out again, and again. Let's walk 'round by the cliff before we go back in. Come on, boy."

Hollie glanced at her watch and thought, *Goodwin should be getting off the ferry any moment.*

Her timing was accurate. As Goodwin walked down the ferry's landing ramp, he noticed a young lad with a sign bearing his name. In bold letters it read, "Goodwin Macbreeze."

"Hi! I'm Goodwin Macbreeze."

"I'm Toby Blyer. My dad is the owner of Blyer's Café. I'm supposed to tell ya that you're to go to the deli to pick up the cane. That's all I'm to say."

"The cane?" Goodwin asked.

"That's what I was told to tell ya. I'll run ahead and tell Dad you're coming."

"Okay…thanks."

On the way to Blyer's, Goodwin walked up the road running alongside Grims Park. He thought of the lunch he and Hollie had with Mr. Kind. How delightful and curious the time was, and how charming Mr. Kind had been!

Goodwin thought, *It seems like at least a year has passed since that lunch. I honestly don't feel like the same person who sat in the park that day, telling Mr. Kind how Hollie and I were on a journey of sourcing. Estillyen has changed everything.*

As he neared Blyer's, he looked up at the front of the deli. In the center of the store's plate-glass window, he saw what he thought to be Mr. Kind's cane. Three strips of wide masking tape held the cane fast against the glass. A prominent handwritten sign was taped beside the cane; it read, "Cane for Goodwin Macbreeze." Intrigued, Goodwin stepped into the deli.

"Hello, I'm Goodwin Macbreeze."

"Aye, Toby said you was coming. Feller left this cane for you—what a deal. Was here a couple of weeks ago or so and asked if I would do him a favor. I said sure. He insisted on compensating me for the trouble.

"Wasn't no trouble, I said, but he said he wanted to 'rent the space,' as he put it. He said we could call it window lodging for the cane. I told him I'd never heard of such a thing. He said, 'You've heard of lodging, ain't ya?' I said, 'Sure.' He said, 'Well, this is lodging without the lodger—just the lodger's cane.'

"You know, it began to make sense. I thought it was like storing luggage for a traveler. So he pulled out three rare coins and asked if that would do. I was shocked. I started thinking maybe he had escaped from an institution or something. But, no, that couldn't be; he was way too dapper. Full of cheer he was, whistling and chatting with everyone.

"He sat right there at the center table and made that sign. I offered him my sharpest knife. Said you would be coming today, but he wanted to put the cane up to show he was here for the original date. Then he said he was glad you was late, because you had very important work to do on Estillyen. Then he started singing-like while he was taping up that sign.

"He climbed up on the chair. I tried to help him, but he insisted on doing the taping himself. Said he'd had the cane for ages. Started singing a little tune, 'Oh, the more you lose, the more you find; the more you find, the more you lose...' that kind of thing. Don't know if the slender old fellow was a bit off his rocker. Asked him what line of work he had done, and he said he was into restoration. Suppose he meant antiques.

"Say, that cane is old; everybody's been looking at it. Marsh from Burker's Auction House looked at it—he collects 'em—and said he'd never seen one like it. No one can make out the wood. I'll tell you this, though, that's the best advertising I've ever done, even though I didn't do it.

"You have no idea how many people have come in here asking about that cane and Goodwin Macbreeze. It's the curiosity factor. When I tell them the cane's just lodging, it only stirs up more curiosity. Then, when they go over to the window and see that little envelope taped to the back of the sign with the word *Note* written on it, they can hardly stand it; they want to open it.

"Now that you're here and the cane's coming down, I'm gonna have a sequel. I'm gonna tape a purse in the window and make a sign saying, 'Purse for Gloria McDaniel.' I'll tape a little note on it, just like the fellow did for you.

"See yours on the back of the sign? It's that little blue envelope. Simply says *Note* on the front. I got some little green envelopes about that size. I'll put *Note* on it just like he wrote, but I'm not gonna write anything on the inside—at least I don't think so.

"Anyways, let me get the cane for you. Say, did you like Estillyen? Did ya find what you was looking for? Nice place—I was there only once for one night. I suppose I'm too busy to contemplate. Never was one for contemplating. I tell you, though, this cane got me contemplating.

"Here, it's yours. See that red purse? That's the one I'm puttin' up. Hey, Toby, we'll put that up in a few minutes, so don't run off. I want to get it up straightaway. Don't want to waste any time. After a month, I think I'll put up a hat, or a fishing pole. 'Note for Cleo'; something like that. I've got lots of ideas."

"Thanks, Sir. And, yes, Estillyen was a wonderful experience. More than I ever imagined."

"Happy for ya. You gonna open the note?"

"I think I'll just wait; I'll stick it in my pocket for now. I want to get a sandwich and go to the park. I'm catching a train in a little while."

"Sure—whataya have?"

"The second on the board—the spicy raisin chicken on a hard roll sounds good."

"Sure thing—I'll have it for you in a minute."

"And I'll have a fizzy apple drink."

"Say, is that fellow a relative of yours or somethin'? He sure was keen to get you that cane."

"No, not that I know of, but some things you just don't know until you know 'em."

"Hey, that's kinda the way that feller talked. People sure looked at him with curious eyes. Everything about him was a bit different. Hope he comes back. Do you know where he lives?"

"No, I don't believe I do."

"Shame. Anyway, here's your sandwich. I put a good portion on it."

Goodwin paid for his sandwich and thanked Mr. Blyer and Toby. He walked out on the pavement and stood there for a moment watching people shuffle by. He recalled Mr. Kind's words about hawkers and messengers running about and how people can get confused. He crossed the street and turned around.

There, in the store window, was Mr. Blyer taping the red purse to the glass, and Toby holding the sign that read, "Purse for Gloria McDaniel."

He smiled and moved along to Grims Park, where he found the same bench that he, Mr. Kind, and Hollie occupied on the day they met. Goodwin set his sandwich, drink, and backpack on the bench and sat down. He laid the cane across his lap and lifted the blue envelope from his shirt pocket.

He opened the envelope. The note inside read, "On the back of the cane, six inches up from the bottom, you will find what appears to be a small, dark knot. It's not. Take a sharp item, like the head of a pen, and push in on the center of the knot. The bottom of the cane will then unscrew, and you'll find a second note from me."

Goodwin quickly unzipped the pouch on the front of his backpack and found a pen. He pushed the knot and unscrewed the bottom of the cane. An inch of wood was all that turned. The break in the cane was invisible, concealed as one of the three ebony bands near the end of the cane. Attached to the removable end was a thin, six-inch copper cylinder.

Goodwin tapped the copper tube across the back of his index finger. A piece of papyrus slipped out just enough that he could pinch it and pull it out. He took the end section with the attached copper tube, screwed it back into the cane, and set the cane on the bench.

He then carefully unrolled the little papyrus scroll. It was upside down. He turned it right side up, and this is what he read:

Dear Goodwin,

I'm so elated you found this scroll and the brief words written herein. Your venture to the Isle of Estillyen was not by accident, happenstance, or chance. It was by providence.

You are chosen to lead—and follow. The phrasing of that last line is rather important. You may choose to not follow on in your choosiness, but I believe you have the heart of a ready messenger.

To the land of Estillyen you have gone, and there you found what you did not expect to find. The more you lose, the more you find; the more you find, the more you lose. Lose it—self, that is.

Beyond the sketch, beyond the graves, you found life. Life is for living—not for death and dying, but for living. On the path you placed your foot. You dared to take a step, then another, joined by others. A new world it is into which you've walked. You're brave.

You will never be as you were before you became as you now are.

You've witnessed life reversing, self dying, people crying. You've witnessed love. You've heard amazing words.

Determining how ardently in his steps you'll follow is now your challenge. Follow who? Who is he? The Word who dwelt, that is he. The Message A Medium of God, who spoke words not his own. That is he. He's the one to follow. Let self go; let self follow. These words of mine are not hollow.

What will you find? You will find that you have been found by the One you follow. You, I do believe, have been found, along with a troubled soul who is troubled no more, Mr. Oban Otto Ironbout. The dear fellow is now a soul at rest; peace is now his pillow.

Who am I? Not who I appear to be. I bear a cane. I find a name. I say a word about words. I'm a messenger. Take my cane, young man. I've got work to do, and so do you.

At this very hour, I'm rather far away from Grims Park, scattering a few seeds, known as words not my own.

I hope you'll do the same.

For now and forevermore,
Mr. Kind

P.S. In case you're wondering, the coins are real. A bit of lost treasure from olden days.

Goodwin slowly raised his head. He could scarcely take in what he had just read. Yet he did not disbelieve. Calmly he stared out across the park with a pleasant smile upon his face. A warm breeze gently blew, causing the small papyrus scroll to briefly flutter. Then the breeze vanished. All was still…including the young man seated in the center of the bench, in front of that broad oak tree, in Grims Park.

Estillyen words flow forth in message form, making meaning…

Afterword

Messages from Estillyen is a surprise. As I scribbled and scribed, it appeared. It came to be! A peculiar way to write a book, I admit. Yet words set the will in motion. Thus, no apologies, no regrets do I bear for this form of wordy mix.

Truly remiss I would be, fraudulently so, if I failed to express my heartfelt gratitude to characters of Estillyen I met on this incredible journey. Seldom do they escape my heart and mind. I'm so indebted, so fortunate to have friends with such phrases and unforgettable faces.

I've come to see how ancient stories shape and define the present. Words matter! This lesson I will always cherish. Words are suspicious, auspicious, I've been told. Watch them. Worth is the mark of wisdom's words.

Admittedly, there's a price to pay for an Estillyen journey. There's a ticket to purchase, bookings to make—but irresistible is Estillyen's isle. Soon I hope to pay another visit. Sail o'er the waves. Take in the cliffs. Allow Estillyen's cool mist to moisten my face and redden my cheeks. Walk the paths. Venture into ancient and mysterious truths. Contemplate. Ponder.

I'll be sure to jot down a word or two of what I discover. If the supply of words proves to be sufficient, I might even stitch them together. Now that I know how true stitching is done, Estillyen-style, I'm not so daunted by the task. So keep your eyes on the horizon. You never know what sort of message might one day appear!

ISLE OF ESTILLYEN

Dear Oban,

So good to see you and
Leslie again. I love the house,
and the views from the Point.
It's the best of Estillyen. I'll
send you one of the photos...
Hope all goes well with the
sheep. Thanks again for the
tea; it was delightful.
Best regards,
Raleigh Macbreeze.

Post Card

THIS SPACE FOR
COMMUNICATION
ADDRESS

Mr. Oban Ironbout
The Point
Isle of Estillyen.

APPENDIX ONE

THE HISTORY OF ESTILLYEN'S MONKS

THE ORDER OF Message Makers found on Estillyen's isle dates from 1637, when Bevin Roberts first came to Estillyen in search of solitude. Throughout the continent Bevin Roberts had traveled, some twenty-nine years, giving readings derived from Scripture's grand narrative. From tiny hamlets to vast hallowed halls, he moved about, creating messages with meaning and purpose.

Bevin Roberts was said to be a curious blend, a character mixed, of quiet impression and stunning conviction. No one knows quite what happened, but Bevin Roberts suddenly stopped one day.

Outside a pub in rutted street they stood. In the stillness there, Bevin Roberts raised his eyes of blue and gazed down the lane of darkened grey. He surveyed his troupe all patched and ready. Willing but weary, they stood.

The troupe, one and all, was aware how ardently Bevin Roberts had struggled with his voice's fade. The fading tone and intonation was undeniable. Eventually, Roberts softly said, "I think it's time now we found an isle of rest. For wise we must be, in making moves that will forward the mission of our wordy mixes."

The record shows that Bevin Roberts and his troupe arrived on the Isle of Estillyen on February 4, 1637. Months gave way to years. Years mounted, and Bevin Roberts, like his voice, continued to fade. In time, the original troupe was no more.

Yet their way of weaving wordy mixes was not lost in future days. Those who carry on the work are known as the Message Makers of Estillyen. Scripture is their craft. They have a way of becoming the message, as they speak of Christ—God's perfect union of medium and message.

APPENDIX TWO

———✦———

MONKS OF ESTILLYEN

BIOGRAPHIES

With a breadth of interests and expert gifts of communication, Estillyen's monks are ever true to their message-making names. A bit more about this intriguing bunch of characters…

Epic

Epic is one of the most delightful and gregarious monks on the Isle of Estillyen. Not a measure of eccentric appeal does he lack. His residence and storytelling venue is Quill House on the Bend. Over the years, his readings have been translated and distributed to numerous countries throughout the world.

Epic is an avid reader and a lifelong student of history. He has led a number of pilgrimages to the Holy Land and various historical Christian sites.

Epic has a great fondness for the outdoors, and he loves to fish and sail at Lakes Three. He is seldom seen without his blind collie, Treasure, and he delights in showing off his Quaker Parrot, Shakespeare, to all Quill House visitors.

Epic's passion is centered on words and why they matter. Like all of the monks in the Order of Message Makers, Epic is driven by mission, and he is a strong advocate for the poor and disadvantaged. He is a consummate counselor.

Epic is in his nineteenth year of ministry on Estillyen's isle.

Narrative

If a single word can adequately define the core of a person, the word for Brother Narrative would be *zeal*. Zeal for the cause of Christ is his calling. Narrative's parish has no limits. To the world at large his heart and mind are always tuned.

Narrative worked his way through college repairing antique case clocks, and to this day he keeps the clocks on Estillyen ticking. In seminary, his studies led him courageously into the field of apologetics, from which he has never veered.

This choice of subject matter was not simply to satisfy curiosity, but to equip his passion for world evangelization. Narrative possesses an amazing knack for disarming argumentative angst against God. Estillyen's motto—"Let God be God"—is a line Narrative often quotes.

Narrative was one of the lead proponents of weaving the character of Lucifer into the Estillyen readings—a characterization quite popular in the readings *Scroll in the Fiery Pot* and *Piercing Words*. Narrative jokingly says, "I enjoy twisting truth out of Lucifer's lunacy."

Estillyen's Three Pond Cottage is where Narrative writes and gives his readings. For more than a decade, people have gathered in the cottage to listen to his dramatic tales.

When not at Three Pond Cottage, he's apt to be spotted in the lower level of the monastery—looking after the Estillyen Bible collection and chatting with visitors—or out repairing one of the many clocks ticking in Estillyen structures.

Writer

Within Estillyen's monk community, Writer is affectionately known as "The Dean." His forte is a vigorous theology of communication. The following excerpt from his reading, *Remember Me,* is what one might call Writer-esque:

> *Ancient prophecies, once penned, had long abided. They waited incomplete, unfulfilled. Words past spoken waited for their stories to arrive so they could be folded into present verse.*

Writer's passion to portray Jesus Christ as the perfect union of medium and message has become his signature work. As he puts it, Jesus Christ is the Message Á Medium of God. Writer refers to Christ as "the prism through which we see the world—the supremacy of God's communicative act."

Writer is, unquestionably, the most traveled of the Estillyen monks. He is a sought-after speaker, especially in university settings. Interestingly, Writer views contentious debates about God's existence as counterproductive. He asserts, "Why create platforms for those who wish to turn the cross into wormwood."

His theology is Pauline-centered. Writer has a knack for dispensing "mysterious doubt" by evoking what he calls "the mysterious certainty" of the

Apostle Paul. He likes to remind his followers that "it was the great Apostle, himself, who was caught up in the heavenly realm."

One of Writer's favorite verses of Scripture is: "In Christ all the treasures of wisdom and knowledge reside." Writer fervently believes *words matter*—everyone's words—but that the words of Christ matter most of all.

The Monastery is Writer's residence, and bird-watching is his hobby.

Saga

Among the twelve readings of *Redemption*, Saga is credited with just one—*Picking Up the Pieces*. However, his reading and input in constructing the *Redemption* series have proven invaluable.

Consider the following two lines from *Picking Up the Pieces*:

> *Through messages and mediums, God creates, reveals, reckons, and restores. From the medium of self, God's communication flows, not unlike a divine pulse emanating throughout the cosmos down to man."*

Saga is a simple, humble monk who lives in the tradition of St. Francis of Assisi. Silo on the Mound is his residence, where each Christmas he leads the drive in gathering gifts for needy children on the mainland.

Most afternoons, Saga makes the rounds at Good Shepherd Infirmary to visit patients. Somehow, he manages never to be in a rush, as he moves through the corridors. Saga is conversant and kind-hearted—and seems always to have a good word to say.

When not focused on acts of charity toward children and the needy, Saga expends his energy caring for the animals of Estillyen. Feeding the ducks down at the ponds is a morning ritual, and he is regularly spotted on his way to Mr. Statter's animal shelter to lend a hand.

Saga may be humble, but when it comes to Estillyen readings, there are few in the Order of Message Makers who can match his innate passion for Scripture. A student of drama and the arts, Saga gravitates ever so naturally to the notion of God being the choreographer of his drama.

Saga is quick to ask, "Say, where do you see yourself in that great drama?"

Plot

Monk Plot is an exceedingly joyous individual. Smiling, beaming, and humming are the traits that carry him about on the Isle of Estillyen.

Like Barnabas of old, Plot possesses the gift of encouragement and dispenses it freely. Plot views himself as a pilgrim passing through life—one who has a calling to build up his fellow pilgrims. One of his favorite and oft-quoted verses of Scripture is Romans 12:11: "Never be lacking in zeal, but keep your spiritual fervor, serving the Lord."

He is also a poet, to which the following lines from *Lips Unclean* will attest:

> *Lips, lips, the pair, oh how we adore our place upon the face.*
> *Below the eyes and nose, above the chin we sit.*
> *To us words rise, as they receive their call.*
> *We clothe them with form, propel them to function.*
> *Through us they all must pass, whether it be to bless or bite,*
> *for wrong or for right.*

Plot's two keen hobbies—gardening and cooking—could not be more suitably aligned. He greets both with equal passion. An invitation to Dairy House for brunch, lunch, or any occasion is a culinary treat. Plot has a skill for marrying ingredients that, as he puts it, "long to be together."

Like all the Estillyen monks, Plot adores pets. His current recipient of affection is Tremble the rabbit, who, on stormy nights, sleeps in the kitchen of Dairy House in a wooden box near the stove.

Story

Readings given by Story are great examples of storytelling fused with rhetoric. His demeanor couples compassion with conviction, in a style that is unique among the Estillyen message makers.

Scribe House, with its reading room of opposing mirrored walls, is the ideal residence for this charismatic monk. Story is fond of literature—his lines no one can anticipate. His focus on Christ is intense, but never forward or off-putting, as he flows effortlessly and rhythmically from theme to theme.

One minute Story may ask, "Is a picture worth a thousand words?" Then, as rapidly as the question is posed, he'll move on to paint that *picture with words,* which are both unforgettable. A case in point is two lines from *Get Up—Don't Be Afraid*:

> *The mystery of Christ was hidden throughout the ages, like sand un-*
> *seen, deep on the ocean floor.... Scrolled away, stowed away, life swam*
> *to and fro, not knowing the mystery latent in God's plan.*

Story's propositions are no less intriguing. Ever so crisp is the idea that the "thesis statement" for Christ's entire ministry can be summed up in Christ's words spoken on the Mount of Transfiguration: *Get Up—Don't be Afraid.*

Creatively outside conventional boundaries Story effortlessly grazes. It is no surprise that Story would propose a ballad for the character Lucifer, titled *Hapenstance and Chance!*

Story's main hobby is fly fishing. While he always enjoys the company of friends, he is no stranger to solitude. It is in the realm of solitude that his storytelling dreams come alive.

Drama

Drama first sensed a call to religious life at age seventeen. Not sure about a spiritual vocation, he entered college as planned, pursuing a career in medicine. Then, during his third year of studies, he had an epiphany.

Drama was reading the Second Letter of the Apostle Paul to Timothy during his morning devotion. His thoughts settled on a verse that arrested his future: "For bodily exercise profiteth little: but godliness is profitable unto all things, having promise of the life that now is, and of that which is to come."

It was the contrasting of the *bodily* with the *spiritual,* the *temporal* with the *eternal* that Drama could not shake. Thus to mission he turned, and his course was forever changed.

Drama's focus on human need, though, was not lost on the Isle of Estillyen. His messages and readings are often built around Scripture passages, where human suffering and spiritual redemption meet. His is a special blend of message making.

Drama's reading, *A Cry in the Crowd,* is a prime example of how his interests intersect and aid people in grasping life's spiritual sphere. In *A Cry in the Crowd,* Drama recounts the tale of the distraught father, who came to Christ with his demon-possessed son. The son is gravely ill, both physically and spiritually.

The healer is Christ, whom Drama nobly depicts in his reading: God, entering the "scrum" of human need—not far and distant from suffering and pain, but engaged in the human plight. This image of Christ in the "scrum" sheds light on how Drama views his role in ministry.

His hobbies are few—hiking and a bit of jogging. His passion is in being with people. While Drama's residence is The Monastery, therein he's not cloistered. His hangout is the coffee bar at Three Pond Cottage. In the midst of Estillyen's visitors he's at home.

READERS AND READINGS

EPIC: *Did God Really Say?* and *The Word Became Flesh*

NARRATIVE: *Scroll In the Fiery Pot* and *Piercing Words*

WRITER: *Remember Me* and *Let Them Go!*

SAGA: *Picking Up the Pieces*

PLOT: *Lips Unclean* and *Stop Doubting and Believe*

STORY: *Get Up—Don't Be Afraid*

DRAMA: *A Cry in the Crowd*

THE MONKS: *Centering in Christ*

The Isle of Estillyen

The Storied Sea

Port Estillyen

Lowlands

Lakes Three

Abbey

Infirmary

Fields & Crops

Speaker's House

Barnyard

Silo on the Mound

Tunnel House

Three Pond Cottage

Scribe House

Darb House

Monastery

Quill House

Misty Shore

The Point

The Cliffs

E
S
W

CPSIA information can be obtained
at www.ICGtesting.com
Printed in the USA
FFOW03n0406170914
7417FF

The Animal Within Us

CITY OF BURBANK
Public Library

NOTE DATE DUE **JUN** 3 1999